Atlantean Secrets

MW00534777

Volume 3

The Gods Are Wise

Samuel Sagan

Clairvision™

PO Box 33, Roseville NSW 2069, Australia
www.clairvision.org
info@clairvision.org

By the same author:

- **Atlantean Secrets, Volume 1 – Sleeper Awaken!**
- **Atlantean Secrets, Volume 2 – Forever Love, White Eagle**
- **Atlantean Secrets, Volume 4 – The Return of the Flying Dragon**
- **Bleeding Sun – Discover the Future of Virtual Reality**
- **Awakening the Third Eye**
- **Entities, Parasites of the Body of Energy (published in the US as Entity Possession)**
- **Regression, Past Life Therapy for Here and Now Freedom**
- **Planetary Forces, Alchemy and Healing**
- **Clairvision Astrology Manual**
- **Clairvision Knowledge Tracks, correspondence courses in meditation and esoteric knowledge including audio-cassettes, videos, printed material and electronic texts.**

Visit the Clairvision Website for book excerpts, free books, Atlantean Secrets music, and a full concordance of the *Atlantean Secrets* saga:

www.clairvision.org

Book cover by Michael Smith

Published in Sydney, Australia, by Clairvision
PO Box 33, Roseville NSW 2069, Australia
E-mail: info@clairvision.org
Website: www.clairvision.org

ISBN 0-9586700-9-9

Atlantean Secrets

The Tetralogy

Volume 1 – Sleeper Awaken!

1 – The Book of the Beginnings
2 – The Book of the Blissful Sleepers
3 – The Book of the Call of Destiny
4 – The Book of the Salmon Robe
5 – The Book of the Mysteries of Eisraim
6 – The Book of the Great Dragon of the Deep
7 – The Book of the Nephilim Spice

Volume 2 – Forever Love, White Eagle

8 – The Book of the White Eagle
9 – The Book of Elyani
10 – The Book of the Naga King
11 – The Book of the Princely Suite

Volume 3 – The Gods are Wise

12 – The Book of the Flying Dragons
13 – The Book of the Encounters with Evil
14 – The Book of the Ascension Ritual
15 – The Book of the World of the Gods

Volume 4 – The Return of the Flying Dragon

16 – The Book of the Nephilim Giants
17 – The Book of Paradoxes in Highness
18 – The Book of Death Terrible
19 – The Book of the Fields of Peace
20 – The Book of the Last Days
21 – The Book of the Valley of the Necromancer
22 – The Book of Virginia and Hiram

ACKNOWLEDGEMENTS

First and foremost to Lord Gana, whose flow of inspiration was the driving force to begin, carry on, and complete this epic novel.

Then to the people who edited, proofed and illustrated *Atlantean Secrets*: Avril Carruthers, Catherine Ross, Debianne Gosper, Eva Pascoe, Gilda Ogawa, Michael Smith, Oonagh Sherrard, Orna Lankry, Philip Joseph, Ros Watson, Rosa Droescher, Ruth Camden, Tobi Langmo and Wilhelmina von Buellen.

Last, but certainly not least, to Gervin extraordinaire, friend and master in Thunder. Without him, none of this would ever have happened. *All glory to the teacher!*

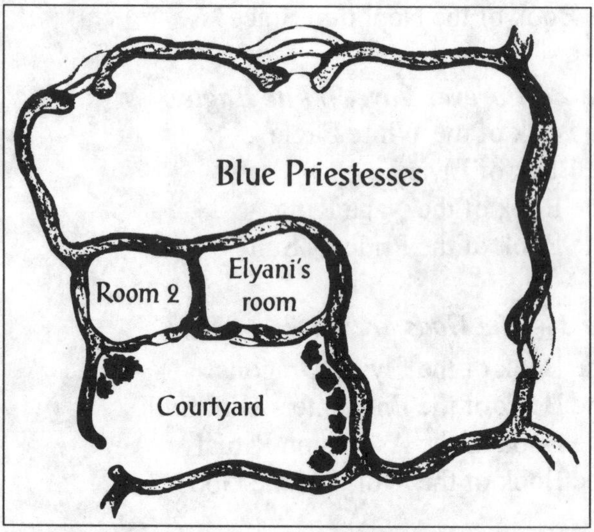

Elyani's Courtyard

Volume 3

Contents

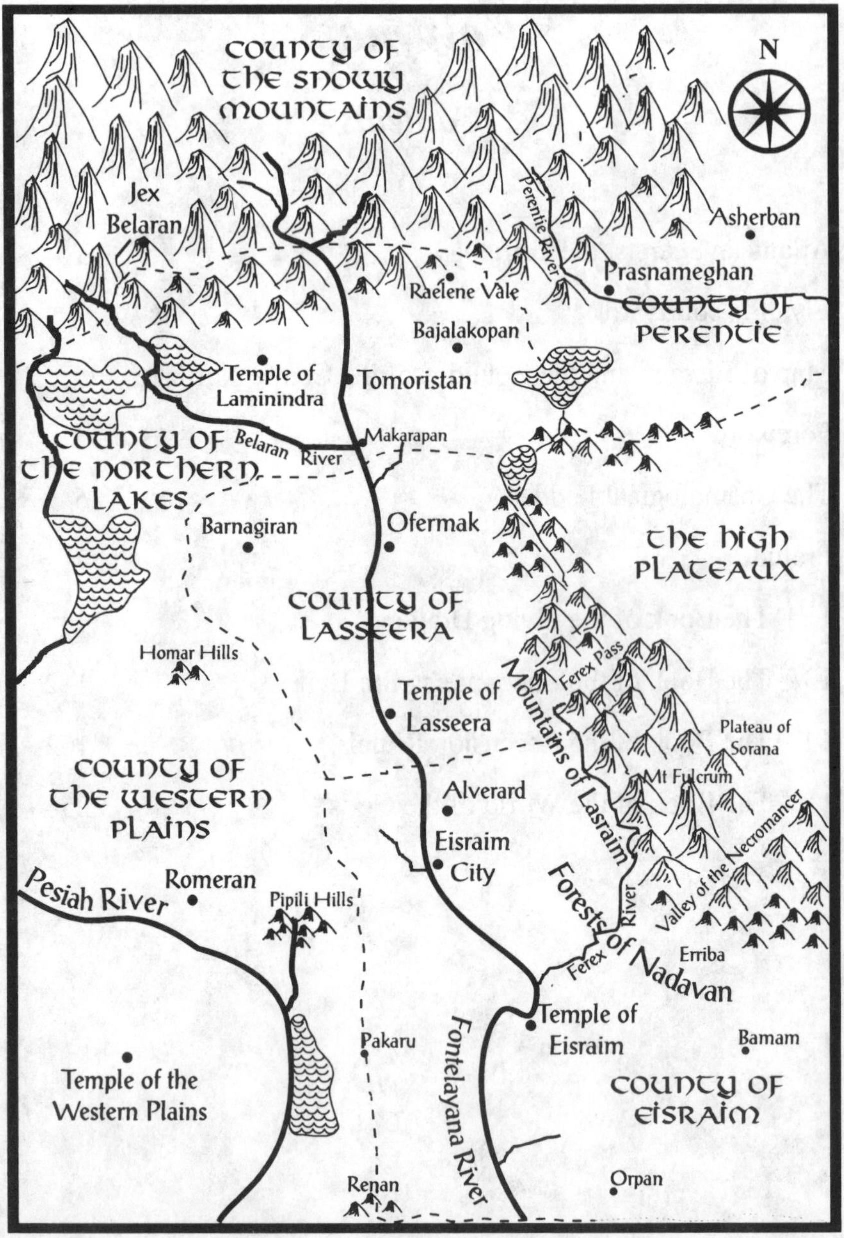

The Counties of the Centre North

Foreword

The twenty-two books which constitute the four volumes of *Atlantean Secrets* follow a carefully arranged sequence, designed to take you through a succession of spaces of consciousness and realisations. To enjoy the effects woven behind the lines, it is therefore essential to start from the beginning of Volume 1, *Sleeper Awaken!*

At the end of *Forever Love, White Eagle*, you will find a large map of the temple of Eisraim. For a map of the counties surrounding Eisraim, see p. 4. For a diagrammatic representation of the different worlds mentioned in *Atlantean Secrets*, see the cosmological ladder p. 6.

A glossary of the main names and terms used in *Atlantean Secrets* can be found at the end of *Sleeper Awaken!* For a more comprehensive study, see the saga's concordance, *From Eisraim to Philadelphia*, which can be obtained from the Clairvision School's Internet site.

Like Flying Dragons, the *Atlantean Secrets* epic is musical in essence. Characters, gods, angels and worlds each have their themes, and a number of scenes are accompanied by musical scores. This music, which forms an important part of the epic, can be heard in full at the Clairvision site:

www.clairvision.org

The prelude of *The Gods Are Wise* is set in the future. Virginia and Hiram have just died during a gigantic space battle – a story told in the novel *Bleeding Sun*. Arriving in the Fields of Peace they join Master Barkhan Seer, who shows them Archive records of the ancient continent, Atlantis. The whole saga of *Atlantean Secrets* unfolds in front of them.

Now, to the Archive halls, where Barkhan Seer's secrets are waiting.

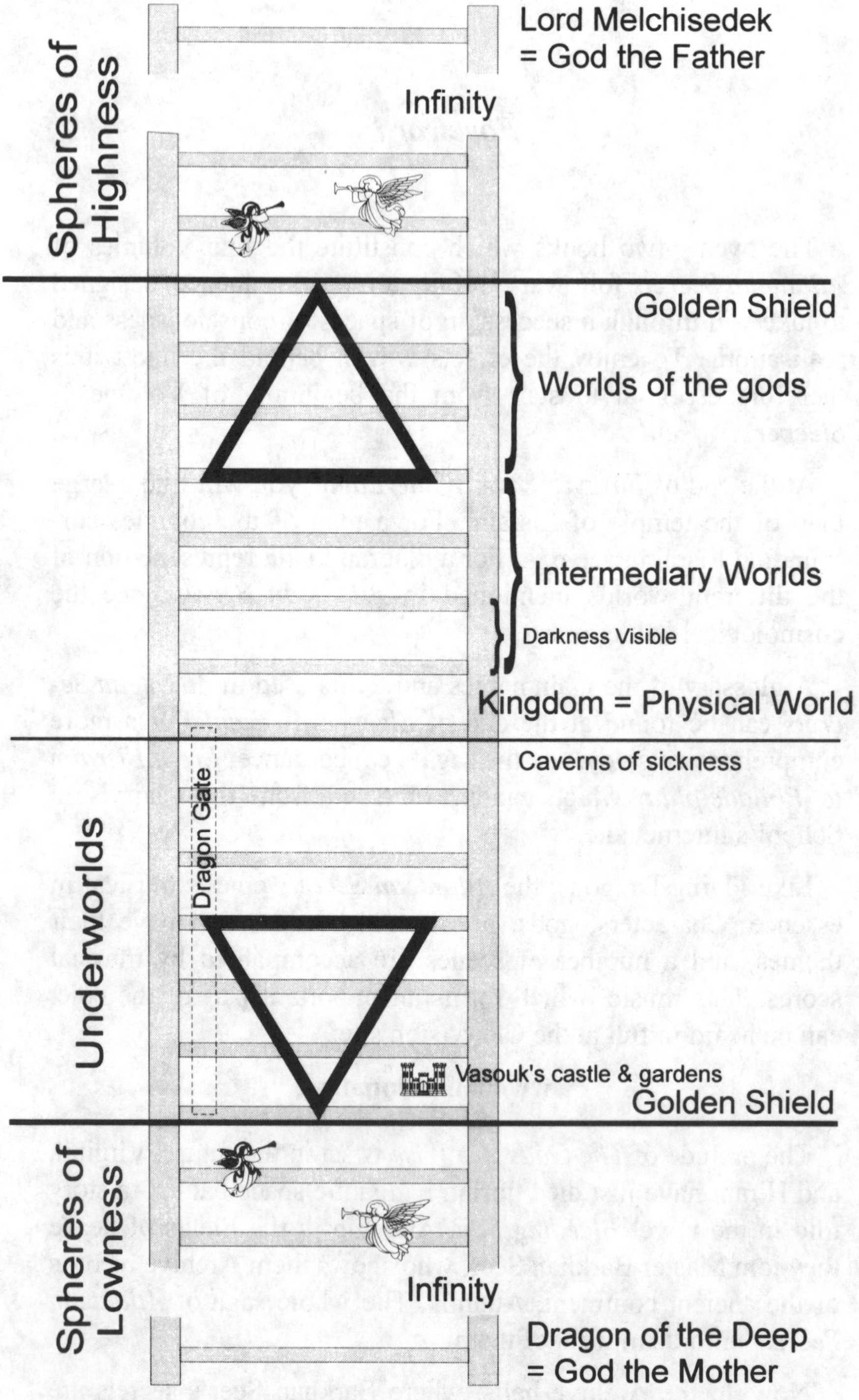

The Cosmological Ladder
Showing the Spheres of Melchisedek

Prelude

Archive Hall Five, Fields of Peace, Apocalyptic times

The crypt was lit only by the eerie greenish glow radiating from the egg-shaped soft stone on the central altar.

In the semi-darkness, a stunning young woman with long red hair walked to the altar, placed both hands a few centimetres above the stone and invoked, "I, Felicia, priestess of Verzazyel, call onto the power of the Watchers!" From the centres of energy above her head, she activated the soft stone, initiating a chain reaction.

An explosion took place. The Nephilim priestess fell on her knees, her hands glued to the stone.

She didn't even hear herself scream.

The crypt? Disappeared. Replaced by the immensity of space.

Gushing winds and gigantic whirling clouds of light.

Awesome presence of the Watchers.

Time turned insanely fast. Ten thousand thoughts rushing into her head at once, Felicia saw the birth of the kingdom and its end, another kingdom already finishing before she had even seen it begin, species and races being born and dying, exploding and involuting worlds, clusters of stars rushing after each other, intoxicating elixir of infinity flowing into her like a river into the sea.

And the music. Music? A hurricane made sound. The Watchers' mind is a tempest. Out of her mind, out of her depth, Felicia screamed.

"Strange screams. It doesn't sound human," Virginia commented.

"Completely mad!" Hiram shook his head slowly, shocked by the Point-violence that Felicia had unleashed onto herself.

The young priestess of Verzazyel kept screaming till her voice died out. She collapsed on the stone floor of the crypt, unconscious.

"Dreaming in the Watchers' mind," Barkhan Seer said, letting the Archive images die down.

"Did she really survive that?" Hiram asked.

"Barely," Barkhan Seer said. "Really, it wasn't just because Szar had left her that Felicia cried all the way back from the Red Lands to the Snowy

Mountains. Her encounter with the Watchers had left her completely burnt out. But she had powerful friends among the Hunters of Jex Belaran. They knew how to heal her."

In the next Archive scene, Felicia was lying in bed in the middle of a large room lavishly decorated with strange pieces of furniture rendered alive by fields, just like the princely suite of Tomoristan's palace.

Sitting by her side was an extremely tall blond man in his early thirties, his large hands caressingly running over her body.

He seemed perplexed. "But who did that to you? The Watcher?"

Pale, eyes half-closed, Felicia looked utterly exhausted. "What?"

"Your liver. It's completely healed."

"Szar."

"Szar! Szar!" the man sighed, half-amused, half-exasperated. "Do you ever talk about anyone else?"

She closed her eyes. "But you asked me!"

He kept sighing, "Did you really have to choose a Son of the Dragon? Couldn't you fall in love with someone else?"

Felicia was too sick and miserable to put her friend back in his place. "Didn't choose him," she just whispered. "He came to me. To kill me."

A wild spark in the man's eyes, "Had he attacked you, I swear on the Watchers I would have found him. Behind me there wouldn't have been *one* chapel left erect in his temple."

She turned on her side and started crying, "I miss him! I miss him so much."

The man took her in his arms, rocking her against him. In a soft near-Voice threshold, "I love you, Felicia. I'm with you."

"Perseps!" she cried, abandoning herself in his arms. "I'm so lucky I have you!"

"Oh yes!" Perseps answered clear and loud, and with such a tone of certitude that he managed to extract a smile from her.

Letting the Archive images fade, Barkhan Seer commented, "Unknown to Szar, Felicia was a childhood friend and former lover of Perseps, Grand Commander of the Nephilim Hunters. Had Szar killed her, it is quite likely the Hunters would have launched a massive expedition against Eisraim."

"But it just happened that instead of murdering her, Szar healed her." Hiram raised his arms, turning to Virginia. "Destiny!"

Virginia no longer looked grey and beaten, her sorrow washed away by the River of Remembrance and the light of the Eagle which Hiram constantly poured into her.

"Destiny?" she echoed. "But who decides these things? It wasn't by pure coincidence that Szar met Felicia, was it?"

Barkhan Seer made his voice thunderous, "Certainly not!"

Prelude

"So where did it come from?" Virginia questioned. "Was it Master Gervin's will?"[1]

"Destiny, destiny..." Barkhan Seer's molten gold passed through his voice, "destiny is the result of a great multiplicity of factors, not all under the control of the human will. Still, the desires and the aspiration of human beings are like flames. When strong enough, they reach through to high spheres and attract responses. For years, Felicia had prayed to be initiated into the fire of the Watchers. Without help, she didn't stand a chance. So Verzazyel the Watcher responded by pulling Szar into her time track. With the forces she received from Szar, she succeeded in the trial."

Hiram grinned, savouring the immense irony of this cosmic twist.

"And with Maryani, who decided?" Virginia asked, calling back Archive images they had watched the day before. After travelling for an entire night of the gods, a rainbow-feathered bird of paradise was landing on the branch of a gigantic fig tree. As it happened, two malevolent jealous gods came and discussed their plans under the tree. They were planning an attack against Vasoukidass, who was to be crowned King of the Nagas. Having overheard their conversation, the bird of paradise flew down into the Underworlds and warned the young Vasoukidass. Following which the Nagas annihilated the entire hierarchy of jealous gods in a three-day battle. As a result, thousands of years later, when Maryani reincarnated as an Atlantean priestess, she was given phenomenal powers by the Nagas. Following which she saved the Archive stones that were being prepared in the temples of Eisraim and Lasseera.

"It can't just be by chance if she chose that particular tree!" Virginia exclaimed.

"That was another level of causality," Barkhan Seer replied. "A resonance between two rungs of the ladder of the worlds. The Nagas are extraordinarily pure beings. Just as pure, the collective spirit of the birds of paradise resonated with the Nagas and sent them a grace."

"So pure! Things like this never happen to mere mortals, do they?" Virginia looked down, deeply dejected.

In her last life, destiny hadn't been particularly kind to her.

"Let's go back to Tomoristan. Let's watch the scenes with Jinia again. It doesn't matter if it hurts. Actually, let's start here!" Hiram brought back a scene in the temple of Eisraim. It was in the enclave of the jewels, so called because the plass of the building was mingled with the spirit of precious stones. Inside of the buildings, the *living walls* glowed like sublime Underworld caverns of gems. In the aquamarine chamber Gervin and Szar were sitting together in meditation. Szar was devastated, trying to come to terms with the daiva which the Eagle's oracle had revealed: a decree of the gods announcing he was about to lose Elyani. Gervin was tuning high in Thunder, searching for something to comfort him. "I see a present coming

---

[1] Pronounced Djervin.

for Elyani and you," he announced. "Tonight. Sent to you by high beings of compassion. It will not only bring you joy, but also new, precious friends."

Hiram interrupted the vision to point out, "Gervin said friends, *plural*! And yet..." He returned to the princely suite in Tomoristan, where jubilant Szar and Elyani had just landed: lawn-like carpet, works of art and field-gadgets in every corner, and a four-poster bed twice as large as a regular cabin in a Philadelphian space station.

"Really, it did them a lot of good to be in love!" Hiram digressed, moved by the strength of the attraction between Elyani and Szar, and the heart-warming space of their togetherness.

Affectionate and a touch mischievous, Virginia watched Hiram. She was amused at how her parents' story sparked his romantic nature, and at his devotion and fascination for Elyani.

Noticing her gaze, Hiram frowned, "Mm?"

"Nothing."

"Nothing what?"

"No, you're right," Virginia stifled a smile. "As soon as they fell in love with each other, they became much more awake. Striking."

Barkhan Seer remarked, "Falling in love wasn't such a common thing in Atlantis. People's personal structure was weak; so were their emotions. There was little or no passion. Only initiates fell in love like Elyani and Szar did. This is something you have to keep in mind while watching the rest of the story. From here on it mainly involves initiates – men and women who, because of the training they had received, were similar to modern people in many ways. But the immense majority of Atlantean people weren't like them. They were sleepers, much like Artold."

"Pioneering love! I find this immensely..." Hiram looked for words, "immensely..." He interrupted himself, "There! Look!"

In the vision, Elyani was jumping onto the bed and pulling Szar into her arms. "Did you say Gervin and Teyani both described this journey as a present from Highness?" she said.

"Totally safe!" Szar answered. "That's if I don't mess up the protocol, of course. And Gervin said I was to meet an important new friend, someone who held a thread to our future."

Hiram stopped the vision. He slammed his fist against his hand, "But how could that happen! Gervin had said friend*sss*."

Virginia rested in Barkhan Seer's momentous golden light, containing her tears. "Szar was so upset at the time. He can be forgiven for misunderstanding a word." But inside herself she thought, "A destiny missed, because a man missed a word. Shame it was *my* destiny!"

There followed the scenes with Hermina of the high caste of the Immaculate, her face hidden by a white veil, and her young assistant Jinia. Szar had come to the palace of Tomoristan to heal a little boy whom Hermina regarded as her own son. But it was too late, the child's soul was already on the Great Journey to another life.

Closing his eyes, Hiram realised, “This Hermina... I met her in the Philadelphias, didn’t I? She was the mysterious Ms X.”

“Correct!” Barkhan Seer sanctioned. “Her name was Keerah Kent.”

“Keerah Kent...” For Virginia, Hiram explained, “A friend of your mother. An old woman with incredible psychic powers, working for the Philadelphian army. I never knew exactly what she did. Top-level psychic warfare, extremely secret.”

“A number of spiritual masters have reincarnated in the Philadelphias, to serve the free world,” Barkhan Seer added. “One of the reasons why the Apocalypse is such a charged time: initiates and spiritual giants from all periods and horizons have converged on the Philadelphias, to take part in the final battles.”

“Ms Kent helped me enormously. But I hadn’t a clue how she was operating. Completely beyond my Point!” Hiram said.

“The full glory of Highness,” Barkhan Seer said, his deep Voice loaded with the power of Thunder. “As an Atlantean Immaculate, she was already a great saint, a force. Thirteen thousand years later, she has become one of Ahriman’s major causes of worry.”

They returned to Atlantis. In the palace of Tomoristan, Szar was walking into the room where the princely child was fast asleep. Sitting by the child’s side was the frail Jinia, a nineteen-year-old young woman with thin limbs, hollow cheeks, rings of exhaustion under her eyes. In the back of the room, Hermina the Immaculate had been standing for two days and three nights, calling on a grace to save the child.

Jinia took three white roses from a vase beside the bed and gave them to Szar. “Sir Szar, these are to thank you for what you have done for His Majesty yesterday, and also for the lesson in healing you gave me.”

In Archive Hall Five, Hiram turned to Barkhan Seer. “That wasn’t a coincidence, was it?” he said, referring to the fact that thirteen thousand years later the white rose was the emblem of the Philadelphias.

Tears in her eyes, Virginia was drinking the Archive images, “Hermina knew, she had foreseen the future.”

Barkhan Seer nodded, “Three white roses. Jinia, Hermina and Szar reunited in the Philadelphias.”

“But not for long,” Virginia took Hiram’s hand, tears rolling down her face.

Szar projected Lohrzen’s scream onto the child, with no result. He stood close to Hermina for a few minutes, then walked out.

“Szar often referred to this episode as the greatest mistake of his life,” Barkhan Seer said. “A crucial opening could have taken place for him, facilitated by Hermina. Something inside him was pulled towards Jinia but he didn’t listen to his heart because of his profound dislike for the caste of the Immaculate, and because he was afraid of revealing secrets about the Archive.”

Szar left the palace, hunting for soft stones, chased by the Nephilim Hunters. Meanwhile, Elyani was being recalled to Eisraim, where the daiva had finally been revealed. And Jinia was left with Hermina in the palace of Tomoristan. When she woke up, she burst into tears. She didn't understand why, she just felt an immense emptiness. She was inconsolable. In Hermina's arms she cried for a whole day and a whole night, then she let herself fall sick. In a matter of weeks she waned, losing the little flesh that covered her body. In Atlantean fashion she drifted away from her body and died.

Holding onto Hiram's hand, Virginia turned to Barkhan Seer, "I want to know! What would have happened if instead of ignoring me, Szar had connected me to my Flying Dragon nature?"

"He would have taken you back to Eisraim. Teyani and Gervin would have begun your training. Little Jinia would have become one of the White Eagles."

"Meaning I could have been part of the Archive people right from the start. Oh, father!" Virginia looked up to the dome of the hall, contemplating the starry sky, thinking of all the empty lives she had lived in the past thirteen thousand years. Mechanical existences with no higher purpose, out of touch with her Self, far from the White Eagle, ignorant of the Flying Dragons... the feeling was overwhelming. "Father, father... how could this be allowed to happen!"

Once more, she replayed the images. The palace of Tomoristan, the room with the young prince, Szar closing his Point to protect Gervin's secrets, then turning his back on Hermina and walking out.

Hermina called him, "Wait, Szar! Please, do not go now. Wait!"

Szar didn't stop. He left.

"Was it someone's will that it happened like this?" Virginia asked.

Barkhan Seer shook his head. "The randomness of the material world. Down there, not everything is the result of a higher impulse."

"It's called the second Law of thermodynamics," Hiram seconded. "In the physical world, the mess doesn't need anyone. It just happens."

Virginia went on, "I can't just accept that I have lost thirteen thousand years because of some random mishap! Oh I wish, I wish I could have been as lucky as Woolly!"

Hiram frowned, perplexed, "As lucky as Woolly?"

Virginia recalled images of the temple of Laminindra in the county of the Northern Lakes. Woolly, who at the time was still called Narbenzor, had just announced to his fiancee's father, the chief stone maker of Laminindra, that he had created "a blasting new stone with mind-blowing powers." That night a gang of Renegade Nephilim Hunters engineered a cataclysmic melt-wave in the warp of fields, with the chapel of the stone makers as its epicentre. As a result, the plass of the chapel's *living walls* liquefied in a matter of hours.

Amanzor the chief stone maker was running in all directions, powerlessly watching his chapel melt, yelling furiously, "Where is this madman? Bring him to me! I'm going to kill him!"

The melt-wave was taking huge proportions, with a dozen chapels reduced to nothing more than large heaps of amorphous whitish substance, and more than a hundred buildings loosing at least a wall or part of their ceiling.

Crying, screaming in despair, young Narbenzor was pulling his mass of whitish curly hair with both hands. He ran away, abandoning his fiancee, his parents, his caste, his honour.

Hiram scratched his head, "You call this being lucky?"

"Oh yes I call it being lucky," she said. "Blessed by the Mother of the Light! If it hadn't been for this grace, Woolly would have spent his entire life sleeping in Laminindra. He would never have met Gervin. He would never have met Maryani. What does it matter if it hurt at the time? Compared to how much it hurts to have been a sleeper for thirteen thousand years, it was nothing."

Lost in the mists, Woolly was out of his mind, running, yelling with pain, "But what have I done to the Goddess? What have I done to deserve this?"

Letting the image fade, Virginia turned skywards, contemplating the stars.

Barkhan Seer and Hiram held the silence with her.

Night sky in the Fields of Peace. Infinity made fields of stars.

All the secrets of the creation carved in luminous jewels.

"Can we resume the viewing?" Virginia asked after a while.

Barkhan Seer filled Archive Hall Five with a large, castle-like building at the top of a snowy mountain peak.

"Jex Belaran, the training centre of the Nephilim Hunters," he said.

"Magnificent!" Hiram gave a handclap. "These Nephilim people... they had taste! What are the buildings on the right?"

"The temple of Verzazyel, where Felicia had been trained. It was adjacent to Jex Belaran."

12

The Book of the Flying Dragons

12.1 Jex Belaran, the Nephilim Hunters' training centre in the county of the Snowy Mountains

When Ferippe returned to Jex Belaran, he went straight to Perseps. Despite the exceptional circumstances, he paused outside the unguarded thick wooden doors of the grand commander's office long enough to send the traditional Point-salute and recognition signal.

Perseps' Point-response came back instantly and Ferippe threw open the doors and rushed in, "Perseps, tell me! A boy or a girl?"

Perseps ran towards him, "A girl, Ferippe! A girl!"

Ferippe yelled with joy. The two gave each other a warm brotherly hug. "Kasia must be ecstatic!"

"And so am I!"

"Did you manage to get back in time for the birth?" Ferippe asked.

"Of course! What do you think? Kasia waited for me!" the very tall blond man exclaimed. "How could she give birth to her first child without waiting for her prian?"

Ferippe burst out laughing, "I see... being a father has made you smug as a Watcher's first-born."

"Of course it has! It's the most beautiful baby in the kingdom, Ferippe!"

"Of course it is! How did the birth go?"

"Magnificent! I held Kasia in my arms, heart and Point the whole time, and she felt almost no pain. I held the connection with the Angels of the Seed for her. The room was filled with their Light, I couldn't believe how beautiful it was."

"Do you mean the midwife allowed you to hold the connection with the Angels of the Seed during the labour? No wonder you are proud."

"Ferippe! If the Hunters' grand commander couldn't hold the angel connection for the birth of his own child, our order would have a problem."

"Phah! Midwives usually keep that privilege jealously for themselves. Which priestess acted as midwife, by the way?"

"Felicia."

"I see... did you bribe her with a jar of honey-pickled cucumbers?"

"Ferippe! The only time I ever did that was when we were both thirteen and I wanted her to let me into the holy underground crypts of Verzazyel's temple."

"When she vomited in the sacred crypt?"

"You should have seen how quickly she stuffed herself with those pickles!" Perseps shook his head, and the two men laughed loudly.

"Did she do well as a midwife?" Ferippe asked.

"Felicia always does well!"

"With Kayala-ha Perseps on one side and high priestess Felicia on the other, the Angels of the Seed had better behave themselves! How long did the labour last?"

"From sunset to sunrise. Kasia coped remarkably well. Felicia found it all went extremely quickly, but *I* didn't! It left me even more exhausted than Kasia."

Ferippe raised his right arm, palm forwards – the Hunters' traditional sign of appreciation for the feat of a prian. "Had you been at a birth before?"

"Of course!" Perseps said with perfect self-assurance.

Ferippe frowned. "Whose birth?"

"Mine!"

They went on laughing loudly, making Hunter jokes, talking of what it felt like to be a father. Perseps suddenly became serious, "Did you and your men end up making contact with Szar the Warrior?"

"No. He must have thought our intentions were hostile, so he threw the stolen stones on the deck of a passing boat. I had given Serval my word I would bring the stones back, so I decided to chase the stones rather than stop and talk to him."

Perseps grinned at the idea of Ferippe's men chasing the boat. "This Szar of the Brown Robe... has cunning."

"With what is about to fall on his head, he is going to need it," Ferippe said. "At least half the clans of Renegade Hunters are planning to ransack his temple, where it seems that fantastic hermaphroditic stones are being produced. And to make things worse, Progos the giant has sworn to kill him."

Perseps shrugged his enormous shoulders. "Have you heard what Felicia says? According to her, the Brown Robes are in reality the Masters of Thunder."

Sceptical, Ferippe scratched his head, "I know the man's Point-signature is completely out of the seven spheres, and I know he miraculously survived the Watchers' fire when he rescued Felicia in Verzazyel's holy crypt. But still, I find these Masters of Thunder stories difficult to swallow. We'll have to wait and see. If he survives Progos and Murdock's Black Hunters, and the Red Renegades, and Henrick's men, and the others, then I will believe in the Masters of Thunder."

"Ferippe," Perseps' direct gaze bore into him, "I have received alarming news about the Red Renegades. They have entered the county of the Snowy Mountains twice in the last month."

Ferippe was outraged. "How did they dare?"

"The Renegade scourge is getting out of control. They are training more Hunters every year. True, the Renegades' training is poor compared to *the regular twelve-year Point-pilgrimage as prescribed by the Hunters' Book of the Nephilim Law*. Still, they are not only growing in numbers, but also in strength. They're becoming a real peril."

"Perseps, I hate to imagine what would happen if one of the clans were to catch that Narbenzor stone maker and make him mass-produce hermaphroditic stones – or simply make him talk. The Renegades would become unstoppable. I think we'd better get rid of Narbenzor before it is too late."

"This is certainly an option. But there is worse. According to intelligence I received, the Citadel of the Nephilim giants has entered into negotiations with one of the Renegade clans to launch a joint attack against Jex Belaran."

"Which clan?"

"No one knows yet."

"Against the Point-field that shields Jex Belaran and Verzazyel's temple, even the giants do not stand a chance!" Ferippe was adamant.

"Ferippe, I have got other reports that are even more alarming. Grave disruptions of all fields in the northern counties are to be expected. Our experts consider that the Point-fields of our defence system could be among the first casualties."

"So the time is coming..." Ferippe twisted his hands in consternation. After a moment of silence, he asked his friend and grand commander, "You have a plan, haven't you?"

"Of course I have a plan," Perseps gave a grin. "Have you ever known me without a plan?"

12.2 Eisraim temple

The first thing I did when I landed at the temple was to Point-call Elyani.

There was no response.

I did not really expect an answer, Elyani had Point-sealed herself. Still, I had to try – again and again.

Again and again, the call remained unanswered.

I dragged myself to Gervin's quarters. Annihilated. I still could not believe what had happened. I had Point-communicated with several people in the temple. Their replies seemed unreal. My Dragon bluntly refused to believe them.

"Gervin," I begged the Master of Thunder, "I need to hear it from you."

Gervin was grave. He invited me to sit in front of him, keeping eye contact with me and sweeping the centres of energy above my head.

High above, the infinite softness of the Eagle. All the rest was nothing but a chaotic maelstrom. My gateways felt as if they had been shuffled. I was at pains to find familiar references.

Gervin spent a few minutes trying to restore some clarity in my mind. Then he began, "A few days ago, Holma the ascending goddess left her body. This is the first time ever an ascending goddess has died before completing her ascension ritual. Ascending goddesses are designated by oracles from the gods. Says the Law, *those who have been chosen by the gods always succeed.* Everyone in the temple saw Holma's failure as a sign that the gods had abandoned us. Despair sat heavily upon them.

But in the hours following Holma's death, the temple's main oracle received a new message from the gods. It revealed that Elyani of the White Eagle had been chosen to become the new ascending goddess. Elyani was immediately Point-contacted by the priestesses of the high caste of the Immaculate, who are to prepare her for the ascension ritual. They have instructed her to begin the practice of the strictest rule of the Immaculate."

Gervin's words hung in an atmosphere of unreality. I heard him as if from a distance. "What rule?" I asked, unsure which part of me was speaking.

"The Immaculate rule is one of high purity. It is extremely strict. Elyani is to keep her body covered in white veils, showing only her eyes and her hands. No one but the Immaculate priestesses is to see her or speak to her, and she is to speak to no one, not even the Immaculate. Nor must she use the voice channels of darkness visible, and her Point must remain totally sealed."

"Did you see her on her return from the county of the Northern Lakes?"

"No one saw her, not even Teyani. Elyani's instructions were to go straight to the high tower of Malchasek. She has taken residence with the two Immaculate priestesses who were taking care of Holma. And she has already started the preparations for the ascension ritual."

"How long will it take?"

"The duration prescribed by the Law can range from a few months to a few years."

"And then, what happens?"

"All the priests and priestesses of the temple gather in the central crypt. The ritual is conducted, and the ascending goddess leaves for the worlds of the gods, where she is to become a permanent denizen."

"Meaning, she dies."

Gervin spoke from Thunder. "Szar, she had no choice. The eleven hundred priests and priestesses of Eisraim saw Holma's death as a token of the temple's imminent downfall. *There was no way in the Law* Elyani could have refused to become the ascending goddess."

"I know. And what about the fact that the two Immaculate have let Holma die without allowing anyone to give her assistance? What tells us that Elyani's fate will be any different?"

"The first report Teyani received was good."

"Gervin, there must be something I can do! I can't just sit and wait while Elyani goes through the same ordeal as Holma."

"My son, here you have to be extremely careful," Gervin sent a dire warning. "If Elyani were to break her rule, the Immaculate would take it as a sure sign that the ascension ritual will fail. This could have disastrous consequences – not just for Elyani, but for the whole temple."

My wave of anger fell flat. Inside me, the black maelstrom remained, with one difference. Before hearing the news from Gervin, part of me had wanted to hope. Now, all that was left was a huge emptiness. There were no tears to cry, no anger to vent, no hope to express. Just desolation. I only wanted to run and hide. I needed to ask Gervin about my last meeting with Hermina, and the explosion of faraway voices. But I was too empty. I decided to keep the topic for later. There was only one thing that could not wait: the recent developments regarding the Archive.

"In Tomoristan I made some shocking discoveries. The situation was so out of control that I decided to keep everything secret until I saw you face to face, by fear of being spied on by a Point-field." I went on to tell Gervin about the Point-conversation I had overheard. It revealed that the Black Hunters knew not only about the Archive project, but also about the hermaphroditic stones that Maryani and Narbenzor, alias Woolly, had recently started producing.

Gervin responded with a long, loud whistle of consternation. He quizzed me at length about my encounter with the Renegade Hunters, while scanning my energy thoroughly. "What do you think?" he finally asked. "How could such a leakage take place?"

"Spying Point-fields in Eisraim or Lasseera?" I suggested.

"Impossible!" Gervin said categorically. "We would have found them."

I shrugged my shoulders. "Well, then, there must be a traitor in one of the teams, it's as simple as that! When spying on the Hunters' conversation I got the impression the leakage had been going on over a period of months, if not years. Which could well mean there is more than one traitor."

Gervin held silence, tuning high in Thunder.

"I think we should keep this information totally confidential for the moment," I said. "Do you wish me to mention it when I report to the Archive council?"

"Of course! The Archive council is composed of Masters of Thunder only. The traitor can't possibly be one of them." After a pause, he added, "I will inform Orest and Barkhan Seer immediately."

I didn't have the heart to discuss the Archive mission further. "Now, with your permission, Gervin, I will take leave."

Gervin had been holding my energy throughout the talk. Now he shook his head and smiled, "*No way, man of the Law!* I am not letting you go like this! Let's go for a walk together." And he took me through the alleys of the enclave of the jewels, telling me stories, pouring his high energy and love into me. We walked through the enclave of the High Priest, admiring the latest flowerbeds created by Pushpadiv of the Lawful Gardeners, and contemplating the statues of the gods. Finally we sat on a bench near the small lake that bordered the fourth hall of Melchisedek.

Gervin informed me that a new phase of my Point training was about to begin, and that startling discoveries were waiting for me. "The tradition of Eisraim is powerful in the Point," he said with his tranquil voice of Thunder. "That is one of the beauties of this temple: many visitors come to us and they enjoy the nice vibrations of our chapels. But they have no idea of the fantastic streams of Point-initiation which run under the surface. I sincerely hope your encounters with the Hunters will not fool you into believing that the power of the Point is just a weapon. Truly, the Point is not for war, even though of course some use it for this purpose. The Point opens to high awareness, Spirit, and glorious connections with angelic spheres. And it commands the supermind frequencies that activate the Point-fields, of course. In the coming weeks I would like you to explore the Point-marvels waiting to be discovered throughout our temple."

"I will start with the music halls."

"Uh oh!" Gervin smiled. "Have you discovered how much music is waiting for you in your time track?"

"A bit. Elyani often talked about it."

"Mm... By the way, in this new phase of your Point-training you are going to need an instructor. Who do you think we should give you to?"

"I leave this choice entirely up to you, Master Gervin."

"Mm... how about the retired grand master of the Blue Robe priestesses? A lovely person, she is. And she lives only one minute away from your courtyard. But would she be the ideal person to prepare you to fight against the Nephilim Hunters, I wonder?" Gervin twinged his beard. "That's it! I've caught you doing it!" he pointed his index at me.

"Doing what?"

"Smiling!" he winked at me. "Now, look! You are nearly doing it again! Anyway, for your instructor, I suggest... Master Gervin of the Brown Robe."

This would normally have made me jump with joy. Being taught about the Point by a master of Gervin's calibre was a rare privilege.

Deeply moved, I looked into his eyes. "Thank you!" But my voice choked, and I started crying.

Gervin did not say anything. He just stayed with me and opened.

After a while, he accompanied me along the straight path of the Law to the portal of the temple's female wing. There he left me to the good care of the corridors' guidance field.

I went straight to Elyani's courtyard.

When I arrived in the empty bedroom, I was hit by a huge wave of distress, like a giant's punch in the stomach. It took my breath away.

Elyani was not there. She was not coming back.

It was finished.

No more White Eagle opening her arms to me. Love was dead. Till our next life, perhaps. Or perhaps another life, much further away.

I wished I could have died. In the kingdom, simple folks could die when they wanted. If it had not been for Gervin's Archive, it would have been so easy... just let myself drift away from my body and farewell, kingdom!

I sat on her bed and became blank.

12.3 Alcibyadi the unstoppable

"Szar! Szar!"

I opened my eyes. It was night. Alcibyadi was standing in front me.

I looked at her silently.

At first, she did not speak. She came and knelt down by the bed. She took my hand and started massaging gateways on my palms. After a few minutes she pulled me by the hand and took me out into the courtyard, dimly lit by the diffuse silvery moonlight that peered through the mists. She made me sit right on the Dragon gate. She sat facing me and started talking to me softly.

I could feel the energy of her voice gently touching me, but the meaning of the words didn't reach as far as my mind.

"Szar," Alcibyadi abruptly raised her voice, "in the last days something went wrong for you. An awakening was to take place, and it failed. Some high forces could not find their way to your conscious mind."

Void, I looked through her. There seemed to be no one inside to respond.

"Szar!" Alcibyadi held my hands and my clear fountain. "Please, come back. The way you are drifting at the moment does not help anyone, and certainly not yourself."

I tried to follow the remote thread of her voice, but everything remained vague. I watched the scene, detached, hovering above the courtyard.

Out of nowhere, Alcibyadi dug her thumbnails into gateways on my wrists and screamed at me, projecting her high-pitched Voice, "Szar! Are you going to stop this? What you are doing at the moment is wrong!"

The acute electric pain forced me to rest on the Dragon.

Alcibyadi kept Voice-screaming, “Come back, speak to me! Now!”

“It hurts, Alcibyadi.”

“I know it hurts! There is nothing that hurts more than losing the people you love,” she shouted, pushing her nails deep into my skin, making the pain sharper by digging into the gateways.

“Stop this!” I protested, pulling my wrists.

She didn’t let go. “*You* stop this!” she kept Voice-screaming, slapping my aura with fierce sound waves, “Stop this! Come back! Face reality! She is gone!”

Her Voice-projection was turning into an attack. From the Deep Dragon, an impulse rose, and I freed my wrists by violently throwing her off.

Alcibyadi landed on the lawn twelve lawful feet away.

“*Oh Lord Melchisedek!* What have I done?” I went over to her.

On her knees, bent double, she was holding her stomach, gasping.

“I am sorry! I am so sorry!” I immediately put force on gateways in the heart area, ones the Warriors used when there was a shock from a bad blow.

It took a minute before she could sit up. While she was catching her breath, we kept eye contact.

“You’re back!” she said.

I didn’t want to be back.

When she could stand up, she took me by the hand and again made me sit on the Dragon gate.

“Listen,” this time she used her normal voice, “the situation is very serious. The Eagle told me something was supposed to happen for you while you were in that palace in Tomoristan. New forces of consciousness were to emerge inside you – forces that you are going to need desperately in the near future. But things went wrong.”

“The faraway voices... I know.”

“The faraway voices?” Alcibyadi asked.

“I first heard them long ago, during my initiation into astral travelling. I was about to have an accident. A strange voice came to me and whispered instructions, which I followed, and soon I was back on track.”

Alcibyadi took my left wrist and gently massaged the deep marks she had made with her nails. “I want to know more!”

“Gervin commented about the incident at the time. He said the voice was related to mysterious forces that held a key to my future. After this, the voices came back several times. When I was in the cave of Verzazyel the Watcher, their presence was with me the whole time. And in Tomoristan, there was a climax. It was in the middle of an amazing encounter with one of the Immaculate.”

“An Immaculate high priestess?” Alcibyadi was slightly disconcerted.

“Her name was Hermina. She was beautiful, Alcibyadi – one of the purest energies I have ever met. She was deeply attached to the little boy I was supposed to heal. When it finally became clear nothing could be done to save the child, she cried a flood of tears. It created an explosion of Light in the room."

Alcibyadi went on massaging the other wrist. Speaking from high in her clear fountain, "That is when the awakening was to take place."

I pulled a face. "The faraway voices were firing above my head. They instructed me to open to Hermina without reservation. But I did not want to drop the protective seal in my Point, for fear of revealing Gervin's Archive secrets. It looks like I made a major mistake."

We opened to the inspiration of the Eagle, breathing the silence of the night.

"Do you think Hermina was the key?" I asked Alcibyadi. "Was I supposed to awaken to the High forces behind her?"

"This I do not know. But the White Eagle told me that your awakening had been planned to coincide with the revelation of the daiva and your separation from Elyani. Your consciousness was to be projected so high... the pain of losing her could never have been as bad as it is now."

Alcibyadi placed my right hand back onto my lap.

"How is your ribcage?" I asked.

She was amused. "I can feel it really well! The right side, especially."

Her aura showed the early signs of major bruising. I placed my hand on the area, letting the concentrated life force of the Gate's breeze flow into her. "I am so sorry!"

Alcibyadi chuckled. "Don't! It was... interesting. Now, the Eagle told me something else. This awakening was not just designed to soothe your pain. It was to bring down forces into you – into your Point. You are going to need these forces, and soon! You *must* find a way to get in touch with them."

I tuned in, trying to recall the energy of the faraway voices. But as soon as my consciousness turned inside, I was struck with the overwhelming feeling of loss again.

I burst into tears, "Alcibyadi, what has happened to Elyani is also my fault. Only virgin women can be chosen as ascending goddesses. When I was in the county of the Red Lands, my friend Felicia told me to come straight back to Eisraim and marry Elyani. I wish I'd listened to her advice!"

"*Hush, man of the Law!* What is happening now was planned by the gods. This I know from the White Eagle of Highness."

"But why? Why did the gods have to separate us?" I whimpered.

"But Szar, where do you think you are at the moment? What do you think will be left of this temple in ten years? Or will it be five years, or even one year? We are *all* going to be separated. We are *all* going to lose everything – all of us!" she shouted.

I rested on the Dragon of the Deep. "All right! All right! Maybe the gods are doing her a wonderful favour."

"Maybe the gods are doing *you* a wonderful favour."

I held my breath.

Alcibyadi sat in front of me. She read my mind, "You are *so* angry at the gods, aren't you?"

Being angry at the gods was definitely not the right thing to do for a *man of the Law*. I shrugged. "I know it is not the gods' fault that our world is about to collapse. *Blame not the gods for the evils men have brought onto the kingdom.*"

"Still, you are angry at the gods."

"Yes, I am angry! Of course I am angry. She is being taken away from me, and I can't even fight to get her back."

Alcibyadi showed her teeth and roared like a lioness.

It made me laugh.

She grinned. "*When things are at their worst, the man of Thunder laughs*," she quoted the Law of the Brown Robes.

"Exactly."

"I wish I could be a giantess, so you could vent your anger by fighting against me," she said. "Can't you just scream at me? What did you learn at Mount Lohrzen?"

"Too dangerous. It's only good for killing."

"Show me! I want to see."

"No!" I shouted. "I don't want to hurt you. I don't want to hurt anyone."

"Nonsense!" she shouted back. "You want to kill!"

I remained very still, standing on the Dragon.

She looked straight into my eyes, "I want to see the black dance! I want you to black-dance for me."

She was not going to let go, I could see. I stood up. "Move back!" I yelled.

She went to stand with her back against the courtyard wall.

I started the first sequence of the black dance – slow, measured movements.

She stood straight like a pillar of heaven, holding the light from high in the fountain.

I started moving faster. And faster. Black-dancing the Underworld out of my Dragon.

Sensing that the Dragon was engaged, Alcibyadi shouted, "Now! Project the Voice."

Dragon anger – tremble! Tremble, man of the Law!

Dragon sound – pour the Word! Shriek vibrations of death.

Dragon depth – Voice from below the Earth. Endless pit.

When I finished the ritual murder of one of the Nephilim – forty lethal blows on forty gateways in less than five seconds – Alcibyadi screamed, "Do it again!"

Again, I rehearsed the deadly sequence.

Dragon rage – no limits! Total intensity.

Dragon ravage – stand in my way and meet your death!
Dragon wild – live and die.

At the last blow, she screamed, "Do it again! Engage the Voice!"

Dragon venom – vials of wrath and burning hells.
Dragon blast – break through me!
Dragon Deep. Endless void. Peace beyond all limits.

I fell on my knees, my forehead on the ground.

Alcibyadi knelt down close to me, placing her delicate hand on my shoulder, "Now! Look for the faraway voices."

High emptiness. Explosions. Faraway voidness.
Aeons of strangeness. The Abyss, far, far away.

"The crypt!" I whispered. "There is an answer waiting in the crypt!"

"Which crypt?" Alcibyadi asked.

"Where the Archive stones are kept."

"Let's go!" she pulled my arm.

"Do you mean right now?" I asked. It was unlawfully late.

She imitated Gervin's voice, "*Right now!*"

I laughed. "Alcibyadi, you are unstoppable!"

"Yes," she said, matter of fact. She pulled me by the hand, and we set off through the Point-guided corridors.

Eerie light. Who is at the top of the ladder?

The temple's lawful centre was empty.

Aeons of strangeness. The Abyss, far, far away.

Physsen was guarding the door of the Field Wizards' chapel.

"The voices! I can feel the presence of the voices!" I exclaimed.

Physsen looked at me as if I was strange. "*Praise the Lord Melchisedek, Commander!*"

Alcibyadi returned the lawful salute, and she and I went straight into the cellar that led to the crypt of the Archive stones. Late in the night, the chapel was empty. The cellars were bathed in the faint milkish glows from the *living walls*. Motley smells of white slime were wafting in the air. Arriving at the entrance of the crypt of the Archive stone, expectedly, all we found was an empty wall. The Flying Dragon device that controlled the doorway was sealed.

I placed my hands on the warm plass of the *living wall*. "Each time I come here, it's as if I was transported back to the cave of Verzazyel the Watcher. I can't understand why."

"What happened to you in that cave?"

"I dreamt. Superior dreaming, bigger than life. Fantastic visions, dancing in fields of stars. And then... I was led into a crypt where high-intensity energy was raging: the Point-fire of the Watchers – extraordinarily violent astrality that sets your body of life force ablaze and turns it into puree. It had nearly killed Felicia, she was agonising on the floor. But for some strange reason, it didn't do a thing to me."

"There is absolutely nothing here that resembles the energy of the Watchers," Alcibyadi declared categorically. Then her face lit up. "But then of course there is..."

She has understood.

I turned towards her. "What?"

She remained silent, smiling from high in the Eagle.

I Point-tuned into her. "You know what the voices are, don't you?"

The Eagle shone through her smile.

I became impatient. "Alcibyadi, why don't you save us a lot of time? I am totally fed up with this riddle."

"Open the device!" she ordered.

"Eh?"

"Open the doorway that leads to the crypt!"

"I have no idea how that thing works!"

"Yes you do!"

She was so adamant that I became perplexed.

"If Elyani was on the other side, what would you do?"

That hurt. "Why are you saying things like this, Alcibyadi?"

"Because it is the pure truth." Her prophetess' voice hammered into me, "If you cannot open this device, Elyani will die!"

The giantess' punch zeroed in on my stomach again.

Aeons of strangeness. The Abyss, far, far away.

"Open the device!" she shouted at me.

I faced the *living wall* and Point-tuned into it, but could not detect any Point-field.

"No! Not like that!" she said. "Go much higher up above your head! To the heights of your column of Spirit. Find the source of your fountain!"

The Mother of the Light shines at the bottom of the Abyss.

"Higher up! Higher up!" Alcibyadi insisted.

Nothing at all was happening, and I couldn't feel anything. "I am trying!"

"No you are not!" she used a near-Voice threshold.

Glorious infinity and spaces packed with stars.

She yelled at the top of her voice, "For Melchisedek's sake! Do it! Do it, now!"

I turned to her, "For Melchisedek's sake, stop screaming at me! It doesn't help!"

Behind me, a click.

I turned round. To my complete amazement, the doorway leading to the crypt was open.

"Do you understand?" Alcibyadi shouted. "Do you understand what this means?"

The Mother of the Light waiting for your visit.

Fly, Dragon! Fly! Cross the Great Abyss and fly high!

Alcibyadi came close to me. "Sit down, quick!"

I was too stunned to argue with her. I sat on the floor.

She stood behind me, her hands placed on the top of my head, and she poured force into me.

Instantly, the voices were back.

"Can we awaken him now? Is a time window open?"

"I see no time window in his sphere. He has missed the rendezvous. I cannot call upon awakening."

"Force a time window open!"

"We can't. The life-wave which occupies his sphere is too young. According to universal conventions, their time must be left to unfold linearly."

"Bring him here, then! Let us awaken him from here."

"I believe Thunder needs him where he is."

"What good will he be to Thunder in his unawakened state? I take the decision of initiating a transfer. Ready?"

"Ready for transfer! But the woman must move back, or she will be badly burnt."

"She is holding the connection for him. If she moves back, he will lose his thread to us. Begin!"

Instantly, Alcibyadi started screaming. It was unreally loud, eerie, completely out of the Law. Louder and louder. Incomprehensible. Screams like I had never heard before, nor even suspected could be voiced.

"The woman will not cope."

"If she stops now, we lose him."

"We need someone who has come to us before."

"Two of Thunder are within reach. Ignore the conventions. Send them a reversed-time message."

Gervin entered the room. "Move back, Alcibyadi!" he shouted.

Alcibyadi kept screaming, her hands sealed to the top of my head. She could not budge.

Gervin ran and violently pulled her back from me. She fell on the floor.

"Increase the intensity now."

"He is not receiving."

"Tell Thunder to force the connection into him."

I started screaming, even louder than Alcibyadi, and near-instantly lost touch with the room.

Aeons of strangeness. The Abyss, far, far away.

Peep into the Abyss, contemplate the glory.

The Mother of the Light is smiling.

Light beyond all limits.

Here to eternity.

Eternity.

Void.

...

"He is entering the communication matrix."

"Start spreading his Flying Dragon's nature through remoteness"

Fly Dragon! Fly high!

"He is responding to the impulse. Try to communicate with him."

"No answer. He is spreading through remoteness and he understands us, but he does not know how to reach us."

"Try universal language."

"15304 20666. 147365045 45345 7775406 345 346465?"

"15304 20666. 147365045 45345 7775406 345 346465?"

...

"15304 20666. 147365045 45345 7775406 345 346465?"

11 201 11 201 11 201

"Communication engaged!"

"Keep increasing the intensity."

"14395764502584930647349503495812430594834503094583240958209837459207610238461923847612349263487263054218732469182347620914210398732058395749211123345452099990024..."

"Space Matrix emergency signal!"

"Down there his column of Spirit is on the edge of breaking up."

"Keep on. Thunder will repair him."

"Full intensity. According to Space Matrix, he is not coping."

"We have no choice. Keep on!"

...

I was back in my senses. There was a man in front of me.

And smells. Beautiful smells.

The white slime of your Mother the Dragon. She loves you.

"Familiar, this man," I thought, third-eye-groping for the blurry shapes.

Thunder. Your friend.

Who?

I liked the smells. Immensely poetic.

The man burst out laughing.

Instantly, I was back in the cellar, sitting in front of Gervin.

"Ohhh, my head!"

One million million stars born from one of her smiles.

Alcibyadi was lying on the floor, her head on Lehrmon's lap. She caught my gaze and sat up. "Open it!" she said.

I turned towards the *living wall*. The doorway was sealed again.

"Open it!" Alcibyadi repeated, her voice soft.

High winds of space. Void towards eternity. Fly Dragon! Fly high!

Far above my head, something flicked, and the doorway reappeared.

Still laughing, Gervin clapped his hands.

Alcibyadi stood up and walked towards me. "Now, close it!" she said.

"But..." flabbergasted, I raised my hands in disbelief and started laughing with Gervin, "this woman... this woman never gives up!"

"Never!" Lehrmon's eyes were ablaze.

Alcibyadi began to laugh too, but the first contraction of laughter created such a stabbing pain in her chest that she stopped and gasped.

I jumped over to her. "Dragon of the Deep! I hope I haven't broken your ribs."

"I'm all right!" she was holding her right side – and her breath.

Gervin could not stop laughing.

Lehrmon came over and put a protective arm around her shoulders. "What happened?"

"I threw her from one side of the courtyard to the other," I explained.

Lehrmon's eyebrow rose in horror, "What?"

Alcibyadi was trying hard not to laugh, to avoid the pain in her ribs. With her head she pointed at the *living wall*.

Responding to her command, I turned to the doorway and activated the device's trigger from high up above my head.

The doorway disappeared. In its stead, only the *living wall* could be seen.

I clapped my hands slowly with satisfaction. Before Alcibyadi could say a word, I activated the device again and let the doorway reappear.

"Do you understand, now?" she asked.

Forever love, White Eagle of the gods.

"I think..." from high above the Point, something forcefully answered, "...I do!"

With all my heart, with all my mind. I am with you, even when I am far away.

"I am with you too," Alcibyadi held my hands, tears in her eyes.

High above. Infinity. Flying Dragon nature spreading through remoteness.

I closed my eyes.

Infinity.

When I reopened my eyes, Alcibyadi was in Lehrmon's arms. Gervin came close to me, "Would you prefer to talk now, or after the meeting with the Archive council?"

"For the moment, if you allow me, I think I need to go for a long walk in the corridors of the female wing."

Holding infinity above my head, I uttered a few unimportant lawful words to thank my friends, and left.

As I was walking out, Alcibyadi called, "Szar!"

I stopped and turned back.

She smiled mischievously, "You forgot to close the door!"

Gervin burst out laughing again.

For one second I found myself speechless. Then I pointed my index finger towards Lehrmon, "Brother," a mighty flow from remoteness pounded through my voice, "this woman will never give up!"

Shaken by the galactic momentum behind the words, Lehrmon raised *both* eyebrows.

I turned on my heel and walked out. At the same time, I triggered the Flying Dragon device and sealed the wall.

12.4 The first report to the Archive council

The first of my meetings with the Archive council was to take place at dawn. When the glows of morning appeared, I was still walking the corridors, to-and-froing the female wing, contemplating the infinite clarity of the Point-guidance field from the improbable standpoint of an elusive and much vaster infinity.

But where?

At the dawn of this cosmic cycle. When Space Matrix was reactivated.

How could such a lucidity and such a mess coincide in my head?

I had reached Elyani's courtyard. I sat on the lawn in meditation position and waited.

"I love you! I miss you! I miss you..."

Sky runner. Her dance has burnt out a cluster of galaxies.

The scenery started changing. I found myself in a large empty dark space.

Archive Hall One.

If it was a hall, it was enormous. No walls, no ceiling, just darkness. Liquid darkness of a strange kind, a superior peace, vibrant with joyful, fast-moving energies.

It brought some relief.

The Fields of Peace.

I began to discern shapes. A group of men dressed in brown robes, sitting at a long rectangular table. Gervin was presiding. Five Masters of Thunder were sitting on his left, Lehrmon and Esrevin among them, and five on his right. All were looking at me.

"Welcome to the Fields of Peace, Szar!" It was a solemn salute from Gervin.

A magnificent place. It breathes infinity. I don't belong here.

Gervin introduced me to the members of the Archive council: Alambar Seer and Firen Seer, two of Barkhan Seer's disciples, Matsyendranath, Ran Gereset, son of Orest and brother-disciple of Gervin, Olembinah, whom Gervin introduced as a dear friend of the Flying Dragons, Mairya, who looked the youngest, Efendir whose eyes were ablaze like torches, and Amitabhadass who shone the most of them all. The combined energy of these Masters of Thunder was awesome. I was contemplating a cluster of suns in a glorious field of stars.

"My brethren in Thunder," I found myself beginning to regurgitate the account I had carefully prepared for the meeting, "my first assessment of the background situation of the Archive transfer is grim, to say the least.

First, the temple of Eisraim is completely undefended, and indefensible. Our main security system rests on the fields. With the warp of fields in chaos, it is just a matter of time before our screening devices collapse. Strangers will be able to enter the temple as they please. Along the temple's perimeter I have identified more than thirty weak points that would be extremely difficult to barricade – the aqueducts, for example. Any enemy could make their way through in large numbers, and easily overrun the temple.

The Point-fields will be the first to collapse, resulting in a situation of utter chaos in the temple. Without the female wing's guidance system, nearly half our priestesses will be stranded in their rooms, or lost in the maze of corridors. How will they manage? What will they eat? With the termination of the controllers' fields, astral travellers who lose their way in the spheres during the night will no longer be rescued. They will die in their beds.

In a matter of weeks, the temple will be filled with rotting corpses. Mass pyres will have to be organised, and the proliferation of wandering souls in darkness visible is likely to attract diseases. Panic, if not mass hysteria, will spread. And in the ensuing pandemonium I cannot see how the security of the Archive stones could possibly be guaranteed. But even with the fields operating, it would be completely unrealistic to say that our defence system offers any real protection. Namron's security field could be infiltrated by any commando of Point-fighters. Nephilim Hunters, in particular, could break in without Namron's men noticing a thing. Namron's men, by the way, would not stand a chance against the Hunters or against any seriously trained combatants.

Which leads me to the worst part of this report. As Master Gervin must already have told you, the Black Hunters – and quite possibly other clans of Renegade Hunters – have been informed of our Archive project. As staggering as this may sound, the enemy has even been informed of our latest progress in the production of stones: the Hunters know that we can cook stones with Underworld fire instead of using the fields. And they know that we are producing hermaphroditic stones. The source of the leakage remains to be determined, but the consequences are obvious: presently, transferring the Archive would be impossible. The team transporting the super-charged Archive stones from the temples of Eisraim and Lasseera to the place of the transfer would be routed by Nephilim Hunters – redoubtable fighters for whom our present troops on the ground are no match."

"Has this leakage of information been confirmed?" Alambar Seer questioned.

"I myself have checked Szar's Point-memories. I carefully analysed the Point-communication that he overheard," Gervin replied. "The Black Hunters are definitely onto us."

"This leaves us completely exposed to attack, in particular in Lasseera," Lehrmon noted. "How many Black Hunters are there altogether?"

"According to my information, twenty-six," Gervin answered.

I shook my head, appalled, "From what I have learnt at Mount Lohrzen, I can tell you that twenty-six Nephilim Hunters represent a formidable fighting force. More than enough to annihilate entire battalions of the King's army."

As expected, the question of the traitor's identity created the most debate. Gervin, Esrevin and Lehrmon knew their teams well, both in Eisraim and in Lasseera. They found it difficult to imagine that a spy had infiltrated them.

"Are we so sure that no spying Point-fields have been laid in our temples?" I asked.

"We are absolutely sure," Ran Gereset said with tranquil assurance.

"When I was with the Hunters, I managed to spy on their communication Point-field without them noticing a thing."

"These were Black Hunters, Renegades who were taught by Renegades. Genuine Nephilim Hunters coming from Jex Belaran would have immediately detected you," Gervin was quick to point out.

"For hundreds of years, we have trained some of the most powerful Field Wizards in the kingdom," Ran Gereset explained. "Our Archive will be made of material transferred from the fields of the temples of Lasseera and Eisraim. This means that in both temples we regularly have to inspect all the fields: those we will use for the transfer, and those that will not be used but must be monitored to make sure they will not interfere at the time of the transfer. Apart from the outstanding work conducted by our teams of Field Wizards, we run constant checks from the Fields of Peace. There is about as much chance for a spying field to remain undetected as there would be for *a succubus licking the Holy Blue Flame in the middle of an annual celebration of the Law*."

12.5 Sweet Lord Melchisedek, what a night!

Recharging myself with the sweet breeze of the Dragon gate.

Go and pay Alcibyadi a quick visit!

Always ready to take a trip through the Point-guided corridors. The field took me to a large courtyard where I found the high priestess lying on the grass.

She didn't sit up. "*Praise the Lord Melchisedek, Szar of the Brown Robe!*" she said with a perky ceremonial voice. Her long black hair untied, she was shining, happier than I had ever seen her. She also looked very tired, unlawful purplish rings under her eyes.

I sat down beside her and returned a thoroughly lawful salute. "Lady Alcibyadi of the White Eagle, I have come to thank you for this extraordinary night."

She giggled.

The miracle.

"Strange!" I twinged that beard, "I've never heard Alcibyadi giggle."

I looked into her eyes suspiciously.

Pursing her lips, she gave a loaded nod, Gervin-style.

"Oh!" I opened my eyes wide, head tucked in my shoulders. "Really?"

The same nod.

I clapped my hands, "So you won!"

Sweet Lord Melchisedek, what a night it must have been for her!

"Yes! I won. But I must say, last night you helped me a lot!"

I burst out laughing, "I thought *you* had been helping me, Alcibyadi!"

With a mischievous smile playing around her lips, she elucidated, "Lehrmon finally changed his mind in that cellar when you pointed your finger at him and told him in your out-of-the-seven-spheres voice, 'Brother! This woman will never give up!'"

The near-Voice threshold imitation of my voice made me shiver.

"That made it for him," she whispered. "After this, all I had to do was to ask him to walk me back to my bedroom."

Now, go!

I took her hands, "Thank you for sharing your secret with me."

She did what the White Eagles were so good at doing: shining.

"And... thank you for yesterday." I stood up.

"Will you tell me more about what happened for you last night?"

"I need a bit of time to digest it, then I will come and give you a full report," I promised. "How are your ribs, by the way?"

"Oh, when I don't breathe, they're fine."

"I am so sorry, Alcibyadi!"

"I'm not! I told you it helped a lot!"

So she had won. She *was* more stubborn than Lehrmon.

As I was heading off to meet Gervin, my grief returned. Despite the constant explosion of forces and the strangely artistic movements of consciousness high above my head, despite the Flying Dragon's voices that flooded my head with noetic poetry, I felt completely overwhelmed.

Simple, plain sorrow.

"I miss you!" I sat in an empty stairway, holding my head in my hands, and cried. "I miss you! I miss you so much! I can't believe I won't see you again. I can't believe I will never make love to you."

I dreaded the days that were coming. I dreaded the nights even more. I dreaded a life spent missing her. But what I dreaded the most was time. What if time made me forget and drift back into a life without love?

I finally managed to pull my verticality together. Letting the guidance system Point-walk me again, a packed bunch of ideas unpacked itself into my mind. Had Lehrmon been making love to Alcibyadi while the meeting with the Archive council was taking place? If yes, then it meant Lehrmon was a 'parallel', living in both the Fields of Peace and the kingdom at the same time.

Conjectures were running fast. Once Elyani was received by the gods, would there be a chance that I too could become a parallel, one part of myself staying with her forever, the other serving Master Gervin in the Fields of Peace?

But who said Elyani would succeed in her ascension ritual? Why wouldn't she, like Holma, become sick and finally die. And all for nothing.

12.6 Flying Dragons, time windows and parallels

"*Praise the Lord Melchisedek, Szar!*"

Master Gervin of the Brown Robe never praised the Lord Melchisedek mindlessly. He always put intention and genuine praise in the greeting. I admired his consistency, and the love that he imparted through the words.

The Lord Melchisedek's Web of Love, shining afar in remoteness.

"*All glory to the Lord Melchisedek, Master Gervin! And all glory to the teacher!*"

He invited me to sit in front of him, "So, where shall we start? There is so much to discuss."

"Parallels?" I put forward tentatively.

Gervin became grave, tuning into me. But when he caught my drift he burst out laughing. "I see! You are wondering if, as a Master of Thunder, you could live in two places at the same time, one of them being the world of the gods, for instance."

Forever love, Flying Dragon.

"Yes."

Looking deep into me, through me, and beyond me, Gervin engaged his word of Thunder, "But, my young friend in eternity, you already *are* a parallel."

That left me cosmically speechless.

The strange blueness of remote Point-generated spaces.

"A parallel?" I managed to articulate. "Where?"

Gervin did not answer immediately. His eyes gradually changed, as he connected to distant spaces. The aquamarine chamber became charged with the humming eeriness of a strangely-familiar foreign presence.

For a split-second, I was back in Verzazyel's cave.

"The spheres of remoteness," Gervin finally announced.

Aeons of strangeness. The Abyss, far, far away.

"Do you mean to say a part of me lives in the spheres of remoteness?"

The master nodded, "With the Flying Dragons."

Forever love, White Eagle of the gods.

"Did I travel there?"

"No! You are one of them," Gervin said.

A Flying Dragon.

I had always known that.

Why didn't I know that I knew it?

You did!

I drink thy spirit of infinity. One thousand me's meeting in front of me.

Whose voice?

"Elyani had guessed, hadn't she?" I asked.

"Yes. Quite a while ago." Gervin was speaking from far.

I took my head in my hands. "Which Flying Dragons?"

"Those who live beyond the Abyss of the Deep and the Fault of Eternity."

Elyani in danger. Fly, Dragon! Fly high!

"They are the ones who sent an emissary, long ago: the Flying Dragon who planted his seed into our spheres. Is that him?" I asked.

Forever love. The legend.

"Correct! And this is why you are here. You were born from that seed."

The White Eagle watched your birth. So did the Spirit of the Great Ant.

"Gods!"

Yes, but the gods of which ladder?

"Gervin! How can it be that I remained completely unconscious of that part of myself for so long?"

"Gradual self-realisation. It is one of the beauties of the creation," Gervin opened a mysterious smile.

The smile of the Mother of the Light. Gervin contemplated it when he crossed the Fault of Eternity, on his return from the spheres of your father.

"Irony, irony... For years, I kept cursing the Flying Dragons! I hated them. I found them alien, incomprehensible. I blamed them for anything that was beyond my mind."

"I'm sure it gave the Mother of the Light a lot of fun," Gervin's smile illuminated the spheres.

Elyani in grave danger. Ask the Mother of the Light.

"Gervin, does this mean I am a stranger here?"

"*No way, man of the Law!* You are as human as I am. You were born to our spheres with a human Ego. You are here to stay, to take part in the evolution of the human life-wave. You missed the beginning of the story but don't worry, there is still a long way to go."

"But in the end, where am I to live? Here or with the Flying Dragons?"

"Everywhere!" Gervin's gesture embraced the space.

Spreading light in light. One in infinity.

"Nearly all the Masters of Thunder live in at least two places at the same time," he went on. "As you know, I live in the Fields of Peace as well as in the kingdom. In our tradition, being a parallel is a way of learning omnipresence, meaning living in *all* places at the same time."

He who flies beyond time knows no limits in space.

"Why do I get reminded of the cave of Verzazyel the Watcher each time the intensity of the Flying Dragon voices flares? Does this mean I have a connection with the Watchers?"

"Sweet Lord Melchisedek, no!" Gervin was prompt to correct me, "It just happened that the high astral fire in Verzazyel's cave made you resonate with your Flying Dragon nature. After this, the association remained: each time you resonated with the Flying Dragons, it made you remember the flavour of consciousness in Verzazyel's cave. But this will pass."

"So is this why I survived the Watcher's fire when I found Felicia agonising in the crypt? My Flying Dragon nature had no difficulty coping with the intensity?"

"Correct! Your Flying Dragon nature upholds powerful structures above your head, in the high end of your column of Spirit. In Felicia as in most human beings these structures were not yet developed, which is why she collapsed under the pressure of the Watcher's mind."

"How come she survived when she descended into the crypt for the second time? I didn't go with her."

"When you healed Felicia, you must have given her a Flying Dragon initiation without knowing it. You didn't just repair her column of Spirit, you awakened it. And so Felicia coped well, care of the Flying Dragons."

"All this sounds unreal!" I had to laugh with him. "I was convinced I had helped her by awakening her lower chakras – the Dragon of the Deep. So it was exactly the opposite! Flying Dragon forces high above her head."

"I must say the whole situation did not lack irony," Gervin curled his beard. "Szar-ka, great expert in the Dragon of the Deep and the Underworlds, a stranger to the magic of the Flying Dragons."

In the sphere of the Blue Lagoon, a Flying Dragon is waiting for your call. The white rose, he will receive.

"And so... was this one of the three influences Namron picked up in me on my return from Mount Lohrzen?"

"That's right. The Flying Dragon end of your column of Spirit had been set ablaze by your meeting with the Watcher."

"But how come I didn't feel anything?" I contemplated my left fist.

"These energies above your head are so much part of your nature that you don't even notice them! They have always been with you."

The sphere of the White Spider, so called because of its gigantic web of wisdom.

"And what about the first time I astral travelled, when I heard the voice in the field of stars?"

"You came in touch with Space Matrix, a very special guidance system which the Flying Dragons have established for themselves throughout the spaces of remoteness. As it is embedded in the very matrix of space, it operates in *all* spheres of remoteness, so the Flying Dragons can never lose their way. Whichever sphere they visit, the guidance system is available to them. It automatically assists them when they need it."

Fly, Dragon! Fly high!

"So, Gervin, you knew about my Flying Dragon nature right from the beginning, when you met me in the county of Sheringa, didn't you?"

"Of course, I knew!"

"Does this mean it was written? No matter what, I would have ended up in Eisraim, even if I hadn't helped you rescue the woman?"

"*No way, man of the Law!* If you hadn't connected with me that day, I would have tried twice more, then, finished!"

Jinia, how could I let you go?

"What about the others?" I persisted, catching a vertiginous glimpse of a thousand intertwined time lines. "In the kingdom there must be a number of souls born from the Flying Dragon's seed. If they haven't been as lucky as I have, it's likely they are completely ignorant of their origins."

"Correct."

"I think I met one of them in Tomoristan, at the time of my failed awakening," the certitude imposed itself on me. "Her name was Jinia. The attendant of an Immaculate."

Gervin kept silent, until I insisted, "By missing the rendezvous, I failed to help her awaken to her Flying Dragon nature, right?"

"You will find her," he said. "But that may take some time. Understand, you haven't yet fully awakened to your Flying Dragon nature. When you were in Tomoristan, a time window for full awakening was open."

Whirling stars and light dust. The Eagle knows.

"A time window?"

"Sitting at the top of a mountain, your energy is not the same as when sitting close to the ocean," the teacher began. "Meaning that location modifies your energy. So does time! Even when staying in one place, people's energy changes from day to day. This is only partly due to their moods. There are rhythms in time." Twinging his beard, he added, "I believe the concept of time window goes back to Barkayal the Watcher."

"What would we do without the Watchers!" I gave a teasing smile. "And so what do I do, now that the time window has been missed?"

"Wait for another one. Space Matrix will help."

12.7 The visitor from Jex Belaran

I came out of Gervin's apartment quite disoriented. A characteristic astral smell shocked me back to full vigilance.

"Oh no! How could I let this happen?"

I started running full speed, reached the door of the building, pushed a sleeper out of the way, climbed up a plass wall and hoisted myself up on the roof, not giving an Underworld pooh about the parrots of the Law who stared at me in disbelief.

I followed the smell, jumping from roof to roof.

Space Matrix access granted. Engage guidance procedure.

"Ugly Underworld!" I clenched my fists and yelled, realising that the smell was coming from the Field Wizards' chapel. "How could I be such a sleeper!"

Lady Teyani voice-channelled, "*Praise the Lord Melchisedek, Szar!* How come I haven't seen you yet? I believe you have been in the temple for more than a day."

No time for chatting. I sped over the rooftops, ignoring her.

Worried, the wise woman immediately launched a Point-call. *"Szar, what is happening?"*

"A Nephilim Hunter has erupted into the temple. I believe he is in the chapel of the Field Wizards. Call Namron and his men. Tell them to join me in the chapel as soon as they can."

Jumping down from the roofs of Baltham, I found myself outside the door of the Field Wizards.

The smell left no doubt – the Hunter was in the first room.

Without wasting a second I forced the door open and rushed inside, launching the Warriors' fierce Dragon scream and engaging the deadly energy of the black dance.

Oh, Ugly Underworld!

I stood still. Everything fell flat.

There was no fight going on in the chapel, only three men who interrupted their peaceful work to stare at me in utter astonishment.

One was Physsen. "*P... P... Praise the Lord Melchisedek, Co... Commander!*" he blurted out.

The second was Lehrmon, his right eyebrow raised even higher than the night before, when he had learnt how Alcibyadi had taken a beating.

The third man was standing by Lehrmon's side. Still like a beast of prey he was ready to strike, his piercing black eyes flashing with Point-ness.

"Fridrick," Lehrmon said, "let me introduce Szar, my brother in the Brown Robe, and the commander of the kingdom-side of the Archive project." Turning towards me, "Szar, this is Fridrick, who is visiting us from the temple of Lasseera, where he is part of the Archive team. And as you have already discovered, Fridrick was trained by the Hunters of Jex Belaran."

Fridrick was a tall man, his short whitish-grey hair contrasting with the fact he looked barely forty lawful years of age. The first impression wasn't particularly amicable. It came from his rock-solid Point, in which he was totally grounded. His energy immediately reminded me of another massive Point-fortress: Henrick the prian, the Renegade Hunter who had played up with me in Tomoristan.

Using only peripheral vision (eye contact left the door open for attack) Fridrick and I observed each other as if an engagement was imminent. Encounters between Nephilim Hunters and Mount Lohrzen's Warriors were rarely friendly. A large part of the Hunters' training consisted of mastering an arsenal of techniques specifically designed to eliminate Great Warriors. Marek, my teacher in the Dragon of the Deep, had hammered into me hundreds of times that, should a Hunter ever find me on his way, he would do *anything* in his power to kill me. And in Mount Lohrzen, for nearly eighteen months I had rehearsed the black dance and its ritual murder of the Nephilim, mentally preparing myself for my first combat with a Hunter.

Namron and two of his men appeared at the door, ready to detonate softstone weapons.

"False alarm, my friends in the Law!" Lehrmon went to reassure them. He then had to spend a few minutes voice-channelling Teyani and all the people she had called for help.

When he came back, Fridrick and I were still third-eyeing each other in frozen silence, Physsen trembling in the background.

"As you can see, Fridrick, we are well defended," Lehrmon told him with a friendly smile.

The thin, broad-shouldered man stayed silent. He didn't smile back.

"Fridrick has brought excellent news from Lasseera," Lehrmon turned to me, trying to engage a conversation. "Maryani and Woolly have done even better over there than here. Not only have they resolved all the problems caused by the noxious elemental slime, but the new generation of stones is already under way."

Was Fridrick the traitor? Who, better than he, could have passed information to the Hunters?

"Right!" The tension higher than the roof, Lehrmon remained perfectly composed. "Shall we go and inspect our stones, perhaps?" he proposed. Without waiting for an answer, he started walking towards the cellars.

Fridrick didn't budge. He was not ready to let me walk behind him.

I gave in and followed Lehrmon, totally ready to jump and turn the man's black forty into puree.

The Flying Dragon will return. The spheres will be set ablaze.

We went to meet Master Ferman, who was adjusting the field around a white slime preparation, assisted by Khej and Ashok, two younger members of the Field Wizards' team.

105754839676? 1232958396304786940928365723034958403045...

An explosion of Flying Dragon voices coming from all directions.

Likely it was triggered by the doorway device.

857620496581264059191919924305729929430572929203 05729...

My head overflowing, I preferred to stay out of the discussion.

From time to time, Fridrick glanced at me from the corner of his eye.

The Hunter senses Point-energies completely unknown to him.

No wonder.

12.8 Confused times

When I arrived at Teyani's door, I felt like a stranded wreck. I spent a minute contemplating the laurel trees, trying to gather my spirits, groping for clarity in the utter devastation of my inner landscape.

Virginia, Virginia... how I wish you were here!

"*Praise the Lord Melchisedek, Szar!*" The wise woman had come out to greet me.

Teyani, like Gervin, always put heartness in her words when she praised the Lord Melchisedek, turning the sempiternal greeting into a meaningful melody.

I did not reciprocate very well.

"So you met Fridrick the stone maker," the grand master gave her White Eagle's grin.

"How the Ugly Underworld can a Hunter be part of Master Esrevin's team?"

"Few people know soft stones better than the Nephilim, especially those of Verzazyel Temple and Jex Belaran. When Master Esrevin enrolled Fridrick, the Archive people celebrated."

"But I thought our people didn't like the Nephilim. There's not one of them in our temple."

"In Lasseera, it's different. Many Nephilim people live in the northern part of the county."

I should have known.

Sitting in her large, empty room, I heard myself ask what news she had received from Elyani.

Using one of her teaching tricks she closed her eyes, forcing my eyes closed by the same occasion, and she triggered a fresh ascending White breath that swept the energy centres above my head. "The Immaculate have reported good results. Elyani seems to be getting along with the rituals well," she said.

She didn't say more, and I opened my eyes. "Is that all?"

Teyani gave a quick nod, as if apologetically.

"Can't you ask for more details?"

"No, I can't. Speaking to the Immaculate is against the rule of their high caste. I must wait for them to contact me."

"Don't they have lawful attendants to whom one can speak?"

"The attendants won't speak. The ascension ritual is a highly secret practice, of which the Immaculate priestesses are jealous custodians."

"Did you meet these Immaculate priestesses? What kind of women are they?" I asked.

"They shine with the bright light of their caste. There is nothing wicked about them, they are just fixed on their strict principles. They refuse to hear about anything that goes beyond *the most ancient and holiest body of the Law*."

One day, God will ask you to destroy a city.

"Do you know how Elyani occupies her days?"

"She has rituals to perform from morning to night. Hundreds of them. And she is being instructed about the etiquette of the world of the gods."

A wave of anger rose from the Dragon. "Are these the rituals which offer the elementals of nature to the gods?"

"Some of them are."

I looked up to the ceiling. "These are the practices that killed Holma?"

Couldn't these damn Immaculate understand that nature was no longer made of lovely little elementals that could be joyfully taken in and surrendered to the gods? Hadn't they noticed the horrendous slime that kept being vomited from the sick warp of fields?

"It kills me to think of what Elyani must have to swallow at the moment," I clenched my teeth.

I realised Teyani was pinching her lips.

I smiled sadly, "You too, wise woman in the Law, biting your lip."

The closest to being distressed I had ever seen her, she raised her shoulders, "There is nothing we can do," she said, dropping them.

"What if Maryani and I established a drainage system under the tower of Malchasek? Same principle as in the Field Wizards' chapel: a sewage system for noxious elementals."

"I thought about this," Teyani replied. "But the Immaculate would immediately detect the device and demand its removal, as it is not prescribed by *the most ancient and holiest body of the Law*. Anyhow, even if the Immaculate allowed you to, I don't think a drainage system would help Elyani much. With the Archive stones, the situation is quite different. All we need is to control the elemental slime within Woolly's cellars. But for the ascension ritual, Elyani must offer the elementals of nature of the entire county of Eisraim."

Draining the elemental pollution out of an entire county was an impossible task, one on which the gods themselves had given up. The situation was getting worse by the week. Tens, if not hundreds of thousands of fields were pouring daily floods of elemental filth. And even if Eisraim could have been miraculously cleaned up, the sludge from other counties would still have been overflowing into our land. The cleansing of a county required nothing short of a restoration of the entire warp of fields. And this was precisely the nightmare that no one – humans or gods – knew how to tackle.

Teyani spoke soft words, asking questions about the journey to Tomoristan and the events of the last days. I answered mechanically, from far away, hardly noticing the room. She insisted, unfolding the heartness of the Eagle for me to land on. "I just can't think straight," I found myself saying. "When I am not overwhelmed with grief, weird visions of Flying Dragons and their worlds flash in my head. And this comes at a time when my plans for the Archive transfer have been shattered by the Black Hunters. How long before they ransack the temple? I haven't the faintest idea what my next move should be. To make things worse, my Point is still a jelly when it should be ready to match the power of the Hunters. And of course, the signs of the fields' imminent collapse are expected any day!" Hearing myself enumerate the list of my problems made me burst out laughing.

When things are at their worst...

Teyani took my hand. Closing her eyes, she directed her melliferous presence to the centres above my head. "There's a crack," she said after a few seconds. "A crack at the higher end of your column of Spirit."

Teyani's Light at the Edge of Highness. She knows.

I burst into tears, "I want to know what's happening inside Elyani at the moment."

"This you must not ask me, but the Eagle."

I looked down, disgruntled with the vagueness of the answer.

"No! Friend, you are not hearing me," she reprimanded. "Call the Eagle, and you will be surprised how much he will tell you about Elyani."

With all my mind, with all my heart...

12.9 The music of the Hunters

It rained.

Who cared?

Periphery of time. He travelled.

Standing in Elyani's courtyard,

Stretched beyond the Great Ant.

right on the Dragon gate,

He walks on the edge of two abysses.

I tried to call on the Eagle.

43290571056289378495901278615178394912875 4...

Too many Flying Dragon voices. Explosions above my head.

Bleeding sun.

Teyani was right: somewhere, something... something was cracked.

Lord Gana's mind impacting into my head. Too fast. It burns like fire.

Jinia, how could I let you go?

Universal Knowledge Banks Point-unfolding in front of me. Multidimensional cognitive fixture spherically revolving around an expanding focus. Incomprehensible.

Flying Dragons spreading... 91263784... through the matrix of space.

The future behind me. I saw. Multifarious futures, an infinity of time tracks racing after each other. Who is to follow them? Too fast.

Hissing sound. Too loud.

Elyani in danger. Ask the Mother of the Light.

Myriads of angelic hierarchies conversing with myriads of others. Talking all at once. Massive packed thoughts.

Crushed under their weight.

Jumping from world to world. Can't stop.

Philadelphia Six.

Try resting on the Dragon of the Deep. Doesn't work.

Fly, Dragon! Fly high!

For hours, it went on and on.

11 201 11 201 11 201 11 201 11 201 11 201...

From all directions, forces rushing into me.

11 201 11 201 11 201 11 201 11 201 11 201...

What if I lost control completely? For the first time in my life, I saw it.

I contemplated the edge. The insidious edge of insanity.

No time window for awakening in sight. Elyani will be badly damaged.

The limit is thin. Remain safely within the cage, and madness seems remote, impossible. Nothing more than a concept. But when you reach the edge...

To the Point, Brother Knight. Virginia, oh Virginia!

Capsize? How easy. Just capsize. Let the infamous chaos take me in its arms – and gone!

No limits. A herd of scaly beasts, ten times larger than elephantos.

Night had come.

Rush to Alcibyadi for help?

The woman is with the man, for the miracle of conception.

Alcibyadi! I can't possibly disturb you when Lehrmon is making love to you.

The boy will be powerful. In the land of Aegypton, he will be king.

The Eagle pouring his High Love into the two of them.

I Point-called Gervin. "Help! I am losing the Dragon."

"Go to the music hall!"

I stood and ran.

The corridors of the female wing, empty.

Face reality, it's finished! Nothing can save Philadelphia Six.

Running in the night.

If you don't destroy Philadelphia Six, the Rex will destroy us all.

At the portal of the female wing, a small priest. I bumped into him.

He fell over.

I didn't stop. Kept running through the park of lawful congregations.

No! Virginia, I love you! I don't want you to die!

It was still raining. Maniya was empty.

Virginia, I love you! No! No!

I reached the music hall. "Oh, no! Not again!"

The Hunter was there. Turn back? But the impulse to come was Gervin's. From outside the hall, I listened to the music in the astral space.

Exquisite harmonies carrying the clear light of high spheres.

The Hunter has Point-sensed your presence.

And so what?

I walked in.

The rows of the amphitheatre were empty. There was only one person. Fridrick the Hunter. Down there, in the semi-darkness of night-time plass glows. He was standing on the stage, operating the Point-field.

I sat way at the back and listened.

Liquid infinity flowing through the gateways of time.

There was no instrument, just a field. There were no physical sounds, the music resounding in the space of darkness visible.

Fascinating sounds, sometimes grand, sometimes subtle, always mathematically harmonious. The changes in rhythm triggered kaleidoscopic movements in my Point.

The effect was magic: a thread of clarity reappearing in my mind.

Szar healed by a Nephilim Hunter – Gervin's unfathomable sense of humour.

It lasted a while. Then Fridrick stopped and turned in my direction. "Were you looking for me, Commander?"

I stood up, walking down the amphitheatre steps. "I was just listening to your music, Fridrick. Magnificent."

"An interesting twist of destiny," he replied. "A Warrior of Mount Lohrzen complimenting a Hunter. On the music he learnt at Jex Belaran."

"I was told the Hunters have a great sense of humour."

"True. Sometimes venomous, though..."

I smiled at the pun, but caution prevailed. I stayed fifteen lawful feet away from him.

He was throwing curious glances at me, as if something was strange. That's when I realised I was soaking wet, having stood under the rain for hours.

Who cared?

"Can you operate the music-field?" Fridrick asked. "Are you a musician yourself?"

I could have tried to play my favourite 'bang-ting-ting' tune for him, but after such a display of virtuosity I felt shy. "No, I am not a musician, but I would love to become one. Perhaps I could try to enrol for a course at Jex Belaran."

"You wouldn't be disappointed," he assured me in his cool, clear voice. "As far as the music is concerned, I mean. A number of great singers and instrumental performers were taught at Jex Belaran."

I savoured the unreal flavour of the instant. Here I was, discussing music with a Nephilim Hunter in the middle of the night. "A friend of mine used to sing in a choir with a group of Hunters," I threw.

Fridrick frowned, "A friend of yours?"

"Felicia, of the temple of Verzazyel."

"Felicia! I've heard her name several times. Verzazyel's temple is just a few minutes from Jex Belaran." He gave me a look. "For a Son of the Dragon, you have strange friends, Commander."

"Perhaps I am not the most typical Great Warrior."

"Perhaps I am not the most typical Hunter either," he admitted.

"What made you defect?" I asked.

"I did not defect. When I completed my twelve-year training, I decided I did not want to spend the rest of my life being a soldier. Of all the things I had been taught, it was stone making I enjoyed the most. Because it is a solitary art. So I moved to the county of Lasseera and became a stone maker. And what about you? How long did you spend with the Sons of the Dragon?"

"Not even two years. It all came to an abrupt end when they ordered me to go and murder one of the Nephilim – part of the Great Warriors' initiation. The Mother of the Light led me straight to Felicia, who was just too beautiful a soul to be murdered. Believe it or not, instead of killing her I ended up healing her and helping her pass her high priestess initiation – in Verzazyel's cave."

Fridrick gave a short, dry laugh, "I hate to imagine how the Warriors received you when you returned to Mount Lohrzen."

"I didn't bother going back and trying to explain how I found Nephilim people too smart and refined to be killed – something I sincerely believed for a while, after the high priestess bewitched me."

This time his laughter was more relaxed, "Did your friend really become one of Verzazyel's high priestesses? There are barely a handful of them in the kingdom."

"Yes. I believe she has now become the assistant grand master of Verzazyel's temple."

"Impressive! So I have to come all the way to Eisraim to be informed of the latest news from my native county. And by a Son of the Dragon!"

Kartendranath waiting for you. Get ready for the beating of your lives.

"How long since you left Jex Belaran, Fridrick?"

"Five or six years."

"Do you miss it?"

"I miss the music, for sure. Sometimes I miss the people too. And the sharp, awakened atmosphere of consciousness that makes the place unique. Violent, but unforgettable."

"Jex Belaran is something of a legend, isn't it?"

"As is Mount Lohrzen, Commander!"

"In the troubled times that lie ahead, we are going to need every single skill we have learnt in order to carry out the Archive mission, aren't we."

The idea of collaborating with a Great Warrior was too much for Fridrick. He froze. Looking straight in front of him, he refrained from answering.

I waited patiently, astral echoes of his musical feast running through my mind.

Revelation Sky.

"Do you want to have a go at the music-field?" he finally offered, making an act of will to soften his voice.

I hesitated. I could see myself bursting into tears if I tried to establish any high connection, be it from the Point, the Flying Dragons, or anything else. So I decided to wish him a lawfully good night and take leave.

On my way back to Elyani's room, I Point-called Gervin, *"I am better, now. All glory to the teacher! But I feel something cracked above my head."*

"High up in your column of Spirit, three centres of energy have blown up. It happened when the Flying Dragons were pouring their forces into you. Nothing too dramatic. They have given me instructions to fix the problem," the thunderbolt bearer Point-answered.

"What am I supposed to do?"

"Nothing. I will conduct the healing for you. In the coming days, just avoid building too much intensity above your head. You should take advantage of your convalescence to visit the music hall. One of the best places for you to be at the moment."

I arrived home. The rain had stopped. The mists were sparse. I felt a sudden urge to stand on the Blue priestesses' roof and take a look at the high tower of Malchasek.

I decided against it. What good would it do?

Twenty seconds later I was on the roof, contemplating the tower. Hardly five hundred lawful feet away. A bizarre construction, contrasting with the general horizontality of the temple's buildings. The tower's upper rooms had windows, small openings dimly lit by the plass glows of the rooms' *living walls*. One window, however, was lit as if dozens of flames were kept inside the room.

Was it hers?

Point-tuning or probing using any other means would have been against the Law.

Space Matrix access granted. Engage identification search.

How long would it have taken me to reach the tower? One minute perhaps, if I went over the roofs.

I shrugged my shoulders and climbed down into the courtyard.

"From now on, I sleep on the Dragon gate, in the arms of the Mother of the Endless Night!"

The rain started again.

Who cared?

12.10 The sound of the Flying Dragons

At dawn, Gervin voice-channelled to invite me to join him for a meditation. This was to be the first of a long series of practices during which I sat and established eye contact with him, receiving the forces he poured into me. Later on, these sessions were to become my training in the advanced aspects of the power of the Point. But to begin with, all Gervin did was repair my damaged column of Spirit and help restore clarity.

By the time I left his place, I was so exhausted that all I could do was to drag myself back to Elyani's courtyard, collapse on the Dragon gate and fall asleep.

Deep, dreamless sleep, in the arms of the Endless Night.

Alcibyadi woke me up. She surprised me, late in the morning. When she took my hand, I jumped. "Oh my Lord Melchisedek, how could I not feel you entering the protection field?" I hadn't made such a huge mistake since my early days as a Dragon cadet.

Flying Dragons whispering in the heavens.

She spoke to me. I wasn't sure what she was saying, but it felt nice. Warm. She made her voice insistent, until I heard her. She wanted me to go and put dry clothes on. I didn't feel like moving from the gate, but trying to argue with her was not an option, she was in her unstoppable character. When I came back, dry, she projected soft watery Voice frequencies onto me.

She placed a cake in my hand.

"I don't feel like eating."

"This is no food, but powerful magic from the Ancient Days of the Earth! Mother Teyani's recipe. Just what you need at the moment," her tone left no room for discussion.

We shared the cake. She laughed at the strange bubbly reactions it brought up in my energy.

She thought Gervin's idea of making me spend time in the music hall was wonderful. She offered to accompany me there.

"I don't feel like going anywhere."

Space Matrix identification search engaged. Fly Dragon, fly!

She pulled me by the hand.

As we entered the Point-guided corridors, she asked, "Tell me! I want to know how it feels to be a Flying Dragon."

"Yes," I sighed. "So do I."

Her laughter created ripples of joy in all corners of the female wing through the Point-resonance of the field.

Crystalline peace of the guidance field.

Philadelphia. The war will end. My love for you won't.

In the music hall, Karpelion of the Saffron Robe, head music teacher, was in the middle of a lesson with a group of young priests of the Mauve Robe. Alcibyadi sat with me at the back of the amphitheatre.

We listened.

Karpelion's grey beard fell low below his belly button. It moved when he moved but also, strangely, when he didn't. It added something to the music.

Alcibyadi had to leave. I stayed until the end of the lesson, my Point fixed on Karpelion's Point, carefully observing how he operated the music field. And his beard too. I waited for the hall to empty, and walked down to the stage.

The sound of a Flying Dragon who re-enters voidness after journeying beyond the spheres of remoteness.

Standing on the stage, facing the empty amphitheatre.

The music field.

Timidly activating a simple 'ooo' sound.

'Oooo!'

Magical!

Filling the astral space of the hall with long, tentative ooo's. Clapping my hands, utterly amazed. A Dragon dance?

Not yet. I played simple sounds: wind, rain, the beat of wooden sticks. Then more complicated harmonies, doing my best to reproduce the melodies I had heard Karpelion play. Somehow, the imitation didn't sound right.

Who cared? The music field produced magnificent astral sounds.

It brought a semblance of balance inside, tempering the grief with the vertical softness of the fountain.

The Spirit of the Great Ant has invited you to its aeon of strangeness.

Nostrils' alarm! A Nephilim presence was approaching the music hall.

I stopped playing and remained on guard.

The man is making an effort to come towards you.

Wild nostril-wriggling. Time to kill?

Fridrick entered, his hair looking whiter than the day before. Slowly, he walked down the amphitheatre steps. "Want a few tips, Commander?"

Slowly, I unclenched my fists. "I could certainly do with some."

The tall man came onto the stage. He remained a lawful distance away from me. Point-gearing into the field, he instantly filled the space with rich harmonies that sounded like a choir of angels.

Clear horizons, cloudless skies. The magic morning of awakening.

Fridrick let the voices gradually dwindle to a simple 'aaah' whisper. "Try to reproduce these sounds."

I tried my best, but my 'aaah' sounded flat in comparison.

Fly high, Dragon! Space Matrix, waiting for Elyani to fly with you.

"Try to spread your Point-ness into the music field," he suggested.

Easy. Instantly, the 'aaah' sound became more open, and generously vibrant. Fridrick kept showing me how to add depth to the sounds.

A few dozen aaah's later, Fridrick took on a mysterious smile. "Now let me show you that you're already a great musician. See how I hook my Point into this angelic layer? Do the same!"

I tuned into the level of consciousness he was Pointing to.

"Right!" he said, his voice swollen by harmonies from the field. "Now, just let the angels' sound flow through your Point, and connect it to the music field."

Instantly, the amphitheatre's space resounded with a choir of incredibly beautiful voices, heavenly cascades of sounds that submerged the hall with their joy.

Had the Mother of the Light just delivered a new star in front of me, I would not have been more astonished. So much so, I lost the connection.

The space fell silent. "Did *I* make these sounds?" I asked in disbelief.

"Of course!" Fridrick raised his hands, "All you need is a Point!"

I snapped my fingers. "So that's why the Hunters are so good at music!"

"No, Commander," Fridrick's patient voice was tinged with irony, "we don't only transmit angelic choirs! We have our own style of music."

"Forgive my ignorance Fridrick!" I smiled inside. According to Nephilim cliches, the Sons of the Dragon were gross, ruthless beasts devoid of any artistic sensitivity.

"Try another connection," Fridrick suggested.

As I went high up in the column of Spirit, I was instantly hit by a manifold explosion of faraway voices.

The curved hollowness of time.

Seed of a Flying Dragon. Trying to hold onto any of your present views and conceptions would be useless. Everything must be dropped.

14305743895642574325432340987234570234589723450574389564257432543234564578903333456723409872345702345897234509 87...

When I reopened my eyes, Fridrick was unlawfully disconcerted.

How can anyone possibly score 997?

Virginia, I don't want you to die!

"These sounds were..." Fridrick looked for his words, "unusual! Where did you get them from, Commander?"

Philadelphia Six will burn.

I remained blank.

If you don't destroy it, the Rex will destroy us all.

Fridrick waited patiently.

Hiram my brother. Hiram my son.

"Going through a rough time, Commander?"

The rendezvous was missed. Elyani will be badly damaged.

I inhaled a deep breath. "Could be! I guess everyone does, at times."

The man knows. He understands Elyani's endless grief.

"Oh yes!" Fridrick said. "Three years ago, I myself went through hell."

"What happened?"

"My wife died while giving birth to our first child. And the baby boy died with her." Filling the hall's darkness visible with soft harmonies, Fridrick kept talking, "For months, all I wanted was... to die! I left the temple. I went to hide in the mountains of Lasraim." He expanded the sound into a large choir, waterfalls resonating in the background.

Elyani's endless grief. Death on its way to visit her. Soon.

Still blank. I did not know where to look for words.

Fridrick stayed with me a little longer, then he let the music fade gradually. Wanting to leave me in my own space, he started walking away silently.

"Fridrick!" I said.

He turned round.

"Will you give me more music lessons?"

His face opened, "Any time, Commander!"

In the clear fountain, I thought I found a thread to him. "And I need to speak to you about the Renegade Hunters."

"All right."

"We are going to have to find a strategy to defend ourselves against them," I let the fountain flow. "One of my problems is that I have never fought against the Hunters. Perhaps I could practise with you."

"I can't see that happening, Commander," Fridrick closed off. "When I joined the temple of Lasseera, it was on the explicit condition I would never have to reveal any of the secrets that were imparted to me during my training in Jex Belaran."

"I am not asking you to reveal any secrets, Fridrick. I just need to practise against someone who can fight from the Point."

"Sorry!" Fridrick remained firm, "Can't help you there. Loyalty is one of the central values of the Hunters. I will never do anything that could endanger my brethren in Jex Belaran."

"I understand," I said, suddenly questioning the inspiration of my fountain. Here was I, a Great Warrior, asking a Hunter to help me master the art of Point-warfare. Painfully naive.

After Fridrick left, I practised what he had taught me. I spent a few hours exploring the intermediary worlds above darkness visible, letting them resonate with the music field through my Point. It generated amazing sounds, but also created complex geometrical patterns endowed with superior meaning – a cosmological revelation! Several classes of non-physical beings started making infinitely more sense to me, now that I could hear the reflected music of their exalted beingness.

Later in the afternoon, Alcibyadi came back to see me in the music hall.

This time I felt her presence approaching. I tried to connect the space of the hall with angelic sounds that suited the dignity of her energy.

She came down the steps, mesmerised. "Far Underworld!" she walked onto the stage, imitating my voice.

I laughed. It made me lose the thread. The space became silent.

She clapped her hands, "You have advanced a lot!"

"I have just realised that music can be used for cosmological explorations," I announced.

"Like travelling in the spheres?"

"Exactly. Listen!" A volley of staccato low-pitched sounds flared in the space. "This is reflected from the layer just above darkness visible."

"Yes, I recognise this layer!" Alcibyadi marvelled.

After playing the sounds of an octave of intermediary worlds, I offered, "Do you still want to know how it feels to be a Flying Dragon?"

Her face lit up with curiosity.

I tuned into the faraway voices and connected the music-field to them.

"The Spirit of the Great Ant has invited him to celebrate his birth in remoteness, the spreading of his Flying Dragon nature."

"Once full reconnection has taken place, let this be his first long journey through remoteness. Has he started communicating with you?"

"He understands us, but still cannot speak to us. Except in universal language, of course."

"1329675 1350234 22253456543 34502123482035 2342 234?"

...

When I finished, there was a strange glow in Alcibyadi's eyes.

For a long while, we remained silent.

"I have never heard anything like this, Szar," she finally murmured, odd undertones fluttering through her voice, her eyes fixed on the mists that were not in the hall.

"I can't even hear the sounds myself. Once the connection takes place, I go far. I lose touch with the room."

He glides.

12.11 The Renegade Hunters ready to hit Eisraim

The next day, late in the evening, Fridrick and I were on the stage of the music hall. The music lesson he had just finished giving me had left a warm space between us. I took advantage of his relaxed mood to ask, "Will you tell me about the Renegade Hunters?"

"You owe them a lot, Commander," he smiled in his dry, cool fashion. "They have greatly simplified your task."

"How is that?"

"In establishing their own supremacy, they have cleaned up the Northern Lakes. The gangs that roamed those areas no longer exist. They've also cleaned up Perentie and Lasseera. And deserters from the king's army never dare strike in their territory."

"Do the Renegades regard the county of Eisraim as part of their territory?" I worried.

"It forms the southern limit."

I was still groping for simple references. "How many clans of renegades are there?" I asked.

"Three: the Black Hunters, the Foxes, and the Red Renegades. The Red Renegades are by far the biggest clan. Fonken the Red, the leader, has made a pact with the Nephilim giants. In exchange for logistic support, he promised them that if he takes over the other clans, they'll have a percentage of all the loot."

"How many men?"

"The Red Renegades? About seventy."

I nearly fell over. "Seventy Hunters!"

"Yes, but poorly trained. Venom suckers – in Jex Belaran that's how we call those who believe that knowing the basics of venom handling is enough to be entitled to the Hunters' strapped bag. The Foxes are different. Not suckers, much better fighters. Only thirty or forty of them, but far more dangerous. Especially for us, because their headquarters are located in the county of Lasseera (the other clans are all based in the Northern Lakes). Lately there's been rumours of a deal between the Foxes and the Red Renegades. Nothing done yet but if it were to happen, then... the Foxes would feel the *Watchers are behind their asses*. Heard this expression, Commander?"

I shook my head.

"Kind of overconfident, but in a way that works. With *a Watcher behind his ass*, nothing can stop a Hunter. So..." Fridrick's mouth fluttered, his eyes went blank for a second. Then, "...if they strike a deal with the Red suckers, the Foxes will feel confident to extend their operations further south. Eisraim would become quite vulnerable."

"And what about the Black Hunters?"

"There's about twenty-five of them. Led by Murdoch. Now, that son of a Nephilim bitch is a *clever man in the Law*. The Black, they're probably the best trained of the Renegade clans. But in many ways, less dangerous. They follow the Hunters' philosophy. The Foxes and the Rex suckers are wild – Renegade scum out of control. Unpredictable and often illogical with their moves. They use the Hunters' weapons, but no Hunters' wisdom. They kill for no reason. That's totally against Hunter ethics. They could suddenly decide to ransack your temple, or Lasseera. And they're powerful enough to inflict high casualties. Massive damage."

"What about Henrick the prian? Which clan is he part of?"

"None. Works on his own. With only three or four men under him. Incidentally, he's the only defector from Jex Belaran. All other Renegades were trained by Renegades."

"Is he a threat to us?"

"From what I've heard, he's more interested in the counties of the far north than Lasseera or Eisraim. And he went through the real training, *the regular twelve-year Point-pilgrimage as prescribed by the Hunters' Book of the Nephilim Law*. Meaning he abides by Hunter principles. He won't kill, unless absolutely necessary."

"I bet Hunters make an exception to this rule when it comes to the Great Warriors," I grinned.

"No, Commander, that's no exception. Killing Great Warriors *is* part of the Hunters' Law," Fridrick returned the grin. "But not much to fear from the Renegades, from that point of view. They're not interested in protecting Nephilim people. All they want is power. The Sons of the Dragon are the least of their concerns."

"Fridrick, what an unlawful mess!" I pulled my beard. "What are we going to do against these hordes of Hunters?"

Fridrick stayed silent, contemplating the amphitheatre's rows of empty seats.

"Fridrick, if I were to fight against the Renegades, would I stand a chance?"

"No doubt you're a powerful man, Commander. But I don't see how you'd control dozens of Renegades without a fully trained fighting force behind you. Ever thought of asking help from your friends of Mount Lohrzen? If they decided to support a military operation, then a large-scale clean-up could be considered."

I couldn't see that happening. Why would Marek and his men ever want to help eradicate the Renegades? After all, the Renegades were enemies of the Warriors' arch-enemies: Jex Belaran's Hunters.

"What about the real Hunters, those from Jex Belaran? Do you see them as a threat to the Archive project?" I asked.

"Never, Commander! The Hunters' mission is to protect the Nephilim. As long as you're no threat to their people, there's no reason to regard Jex Belaran's Hunters as your enemies."

Point-bringing down the soft humming whisper of winds of space into the music field, I suggested an idea which had been cooking in my mind for a few days, and which I had thoroughly discussed with Gervin. "And what if we made the Hunters of Jex Belaran our allies?"

A spark of interest flared in Fridrick's eyes. "They certainly have the venom to fight the Renegades. But why would they want to?"

"I have the feeling they are not so happy with the proliferation of pseudo-Hunters who violate the sacred principles of their order."

"True. Still, they'd think twice before starting a war against the Renegades. Point-warfare is dirty. Can have devastating consequences."

"My intuition is that Jex Belaran will respond favourably to our offer."

"I guess there's not much to lose in asking for their help," Fridrick deliberated.

"Fridrick, would you be our ambassador?" I asked him. "Could you contact the leaders of Jex Belaran and ask whether they would consider cooperating with us against the Renegades?"

He seemed to like the idea. "I could, Commander! Yes. I could."

Gervin had already given his full backing. "Let this be a message from Szar of the Brown Robe, officially representing the temple of Eisraim, to the grand commander of the Nephilim Hunters in Jex Belaran. Start with the appropriate lawful greetings, then say, 'We, in the temple of Eisraim, have perceived your dissatisfaction with the growing peril presented by the Renegade Hunters, and are offering to make an alliance to eliminate the Renegade scourge before the giants take advantage of it. Ask Felicia, high priestess and assistant grand master of Verzazyel's temple, about the omens.'"

"Is that all?" Fridrick asked.

"The impact of this message could well surprise you, Fridrick."

"Surprise me, Commander!" the Hunter gave an elusive smile.

"Can you Point-call them right now?"

"Commander! Jex Belaran's totally shielded against standard forms of Point resonance."

"Does this mean you will have to travel to Jex Belaran?"

"No. Hunters have secret ways of communicating with each other. I'll do the procedure tomorrow, on my way back to Lasseera." He paused, thoughtful. "It'll probably take a few days before Jex Belaran answers."

12.12 A present from Verzazyel's temple

In the following days, Gervin finalised the repair of my column of Spirit. While this was happening, my instructions were to avoid astral travelling, Underworld travelling, high-intensity connections and Flying Dragon excesses. "You keep yourself out of trouble," Gervin had said. "Don't worry, not for long!" Lawful smile.

I took advantage of this period to get to know the people working in the chapel of the Field Wizards. The more I searched for the traitor, the more friends I found. Master Ferman, in particular. He was the leader of the team of field experts Gervin had gathered in Eisraim – those who worked in direct collaboration with the Masters of Thunder in the Fields of Peace. Ferman, who was in his late fifties, was a quiet, grounded soul. By nature, he didn't speak much. But behind his air of *lawful man of the Law*, he was no blissful sleeper. In the discussions I had with him, I was impressed by his clear Point, his brilliant mind and his phenomenal knowledge of the fields, his father having been Eisraim's chief priest of the windmills of the Law. Since his childhood, Ferman had been involved in the creation and the maintenance of fields, first as a Windmill Keeper, performing rituals under the instruction of his father, then as a stone maker and a Field Wizard. It was difficult to imagine how a man who had been Gervin's close collaborator for thirty-six years could be a traitor to the cause, sold to the Renegade scum.

Twenty-four Field Wizards worked under Ferman. Ferman often referred to them as 'Gervin's men', saying Gervin had carefully recruited them over the years and organised their training. One day, as I asked how Gervin had managed to recruit such efficient people, Ferman gave the astonishing answer: "For most of them, it was simple. Master Gervin got them to reincarnate in Eisraim! Thirty-seven years ago, that is, one year after he became the thunderbolt bearer, four beautiful baby boys were born in the temple from Field Wizard parents. They were Shyama, Ushbudh, Visarg and Balavan. In the following years Meran, Lehr and Orpan were born. And after them, Avan, and Ugr. At each birth Master Gervin told me, 'These are the men we need, Ferman!' At the time I despaired – the task ahead of us seemed overwhelming. 'Master Gervin, what we need are powerful men, not toddlers!' I told him. But he laughed, 'You will see, Ferman, you will see.' And now you can see, his word has been fulfilled."

Difficult to imagine how one of these Field Wizards could have embraced the cause of the Renegade Hunters. Not surprisingly, their loyalty and dedication to the Archive mission was total. They laboured from morning to night, running about the temple from field to field like bees from flower to flower.

I was gradually discovering the complexity of their tasks. At first, I had thought the Field Wizards' function was just to assist Woolly in the making of soft stones. In reality, immense work had to be performed on the temple's fields before their content could be transferred into the Archive. During the transfer, twelve hundred fields were to resonate with the Fields of Peace through the Archive stones. Before this could happen, each field had to be carefully prepared and monitored, and finely attuned to the stones. "A massive enterprise!" Ferman liked to say. "If you knew how many problems we've had to solve in the last thirty-five years! The Point boggles!"

During my meeting with the Archive council, Ran Gereset had dismissed any suggestion that a spying field could be responsible for the information leakage. I was starting to understand why. Gervin's men were top-level Field Wizards, fully conversant with every single type of field to be found in the kingdom. They could undo and redo just about any Point-field in a matter of minutes, and they knew how to push their capabilities to the extreme limit. There was no way in the seven spheres a spying field could have remained undetected by them – not to mention the constant and meticulous scanning operated by the Masters of Thunder who watched Eisraim from the Fields of Peace.

Another reason made it difficult to conceive that any of Gervin's men was the traitor: as part of their training, they had travelled to the Fields of Peace several times. There they had been taught – and thoroughly scanned – by the Masters of Thunder.

The riddle seemed unsolvable. Either the traitor was part of Master Esrevin's team in Lasseera (not all of whose members had visited the Fields of Peace), or the Renegade Hunters had obtained their information through powers completely unknown to me. The next logical step would have been to go and inspect the temple of Lasseera, but Gervin had recommended that I first reinforce my Point by practising with him. And so I spent most of my time playing music, waiting for my column of Spirit to regain its integrity – a necessary step before the full Point-training could be engaged.

One afternoon, as I was in the middle of a music lesson with Karpelion of the Saffron Robe, I received a voice-channel communication from Melchard. "Szar of the Brown Robe, I have here with me a visitor who wants to meet you."

Jinia, how could I let you go?

"Where should I join you, Melchard?"

"We will be in your courtyard in half an hour. Make sure you come alone."

I asked Karpelion to excuse me and took leave, affectionately touching his beard, famous in the temple. According to one of Eisraim's legends, whoever touched Karpelion's beard just after the man *released lawful winds* was assured of receiving a present. Unfortunately, he didn't fart very often. That day, I was lucky.

On my way home, I decided to resist the temptation to stop and cry in one of the stairways.

I just stopped and sat down, doing my best not to cry.

The wound was abysmal.

"Elyani!" I called, as I did each time I halted in that stairway. "It can't be possible! I can't believe you won't be in the courtyard when I return home. I miss you. I miss you. I miss you..."

As I started to cry, I stood up and Dragoned myself through the corridors.

I arrived only shortly before Melchard and his guest.

The sound of Flying Dragons sweeping through the sphere of the Purple Cicada, guided by Space Matrix.

I could have tuned in and tried to guess who the guest was, but I did not feel like tuning in. Nor seeing a guest. Nor anything else.

I was standing on the gate, pulling my Dragon together, when the shrieking alarm-sense-smell of Nephilim spice shook me awake.

Nephilim spice?

Yes, but not a dangerous person. "You'd butcher her in three gateways!" Memories of Marek's voice ran by. Before I had time to sniff the details, arrived Melchard, accompanied by a woman dressed in black, her face hidden by a veil.

Melchard took on his most ceremonial voice, "*Praise the Lord Melchisedek, Szar of the Brown Robe! It gives me great pleasure in the Law to be accompanied by Her High Majesty Pelenor Ozorenan, wife of His High Majesty Filipotonisteraniso Ozorenan, Prince of the County of the North-*

ern Lakes under the Appointment of His Supreme Majesty the King of Atlantis."

Pelenor! I was so taken by surprise that I forgot to return the greeting.

Melchard reminded me of my duty by loudly clearing his throat.

"*All glory to the Lord Melchisedek, Your High Majesty Pelenor Ozorenan, wife of...*" I returned the lawful mouthful.

Melchard declared, "Her High Majesty has come to converse with you about confidential matters, and so, with her permission, I will now leave her in your company."

Pelenor gave her permission with a quick nod, and Melchard lawfully withdrew.

After he had gone, the princess took off her veil.

Seeing her, I was in the princely suite all over again – a dagger in my chest. Breathless, I stood on the Dragon.

"Melchard told me about Elyani," Pelenor said as if she really cared. "I am sincerely sorry."

I couldn't think of an answer. I just gave a lawfully politely absent nod.

"You can guess why I have come," she said.

"I did not expect you so soon, Your Majesty."

The woman has just gone through hell.

"Have I come at the wrong time?" she asked. "Can you not heal me now?" Her voice was not as buoyant and self-assured as when I had met her in Tomoristan.

I tuned high in the column of Spirit. Gervin's instructions were strict: no travelling for the moment. Any jump into astral spheres or Underworlds could permanently damage the centres of energy above my head.

She really loves her husband.

"I need an answer, Szar. I am..." she hesitated.

"...desperate!" The word came not from me but from the clear fountain, with an impulse of Eagle softness that reached straight into her heart.

"Yes, desperate. Completely desperate! After the death of his son, my husband sent me an ultimatum. One year from now, if a child has not been conceived, I am dismissed. I can choose between death or exile."

An eternal vow.

"Will you help?" she pleaded.

Those who love each other, you will not separate.

She looked at me more closely. "What is happening to you, Sir Great Dragon? Since I last saw you, your eyes have become... different."

The eternal vow is already binding.

It broke my heart to tell this woman I couldn't do anything for her at the moment. I clenched my fists and took a long breath. "Your Majesty..."

Flying Dragon requesting access to Space Matrix guidance system for Underworld regions of the spheres of Melchisedek.

"Access granted. Thorough mapping for requested area is available from Space Matrix's Universal Knowledge Bank. Exit via the matrix. Fly, Dragon!"

"Szar?" Pelenor became worried by my silence and my strange looks.

I received a Point-call from Gervin. *"Szar! Do you realise what you have just done? You have successfully contacted your Flying Dragons' Knowledge Bank. Do you understand how you did it?"*

"A complicated story. A vow, which I made to Elyani. In reality I have not made it yet. I will make it in the future. But it's already binding..."

Gervin Point-laughed.

"Gervin, do I have your permission to descend into the Underworlds? It is the only way I can heal Felicia's friend."

"Space Matrix is superiorly powerful. It's the guidance system the Masters of Thunder use for their multidimensional travelling. As long as you follow it, you can go anywhere you want."

"All glory to the teacher!" Then I Point-whimpered, "Gervin, my head is a complete chaos."

"Thunder holds the answer," the master Point-replied.

"Thunder... sounds a long way away, Gervin."

"Your initiation is coming, Szar of the Brown Robe."

I brought myself back, "Yes, Pel... I mean, Your Majesty..."

Princess Pelenor was more and more worried. "What is happening to you, Sir Great Dragon?"

"Your Majesty, I have had to make a few adjustments to my energy in the last days."

"Have I come at the wrong time?" she asked again, her voice stifled with anxiety.

"I think..." I threw some enthusiasm into my voice, "I think you could not have picked a better time, Your Majesty."

Pelenor remained uncertain. "Are you going to heal me?"

Yes, the woman will be healed.

I remained cautious. "Well, I shall do my best. But you must remember that..."

Through the gate, a powerful alignment took place: the She-Dragon of the Deep below, the Universal Knowledge Bank of the Flying Dragons above, and Szar standing in the middle.

I looked straight into her eyes. "Yes, you will be healed."

The Nephilim woman came close and took my hands. "I knew it! I knew you would do it! Felicia knew it too. She promised me."

Forever love, Flying Dragon.

Practicalities had to be sorted out. I explained that the healing could take between two and fourteen days, and I asked if she had come alone.

She raised her hands, "A princess, travelling alone? I wish I could! There are forty-six Crimson guards and attendants waiting for me at the temple's main entrance. But I can use a particular provision in the Law. It says members of royal families can visit a temple and undergo a spiritual retreat, *during which they will abide by the temple's rule*. I will go and speak to the captain of the guards now." Then she inquired, "In Tomoristan, you said the healing was to take place on a gate of the Dragon. Where is the gate?"

I pointed to my feet. "There!"

"I see," she was amused. "You are taking good care of it."

We had to call Melchard back. Lawful protocol obliged the high priest to escort the princess through the temple.

As soon as they had gone, I was gripped by the urge to go and sit on the roof to watch the sunset – and the high tower of Malchasek.

Reason decided against it.

I decided against reason, and I set off up the ladder.

The vow taken from your Flying Dragon's nature. You held onto it.

The first red hues of sunset reflected against the tower's pointed roof. I could not take my eyes away from the upper left window.

What was Elyani doing at that moment?

With all my heart, with all my mind, I am with you, even when I am far away.

"So many voices in my head!" I wished I could discern where they came from: high spheres, Flying Dragons, or my slightly cracked column of Spirit. They could even have been from Elyani.

Virginia, Virginia...

My contemplation was interrupted by a voice channel from Melchard, who had to express his lawful concerns. "Szar, I hope you know exactly what you are doing with Pelenor Ozorenan. If she were to die in your hands, the temple would be in an extremely difficult position. What kind of healing are you about to implement?"

"The princess will be placed in a state of deep hibernation. I will descend and pull forces from the Deep Underworlds in order to reconstitute her gateways."

Melchard wanted to know every single detail of the procedure. "Will we accommodate her in one of the royal suites of my enclave?" he asked.

"When she wakes up from hibernation, she can go to the royal suite. Before that, I need to keep her here, close to the Dragon gate."

The high priest of Eisraim wasn't enthused by the prospect of a member of the Ozorenan family sleeping in the humble bedroom of my courtyard, but I remained Dragon-adamant. "All right!" he finally agreed. Suddenly changing his voice into a warm breeze, he inquired, "You did not receive any news from Elyani, did you?"

With all my heart, with all my mind...

"No, nothing."

"Of course. Are you coping, Szar?"

I didn't answer, letting him conclude the conversation with a few words of encouragement. But as soon as the voice channel was closed, his warm breeze started blowing through my heart, renewed courage pulsing with my blood. I felt much better.

"Thunder-tricks!" I clicked my fingers, sending a thankful thought.

When he and Pelenor returned, they were followed by five Crimson Robe attendants carrying Pelenor's bags.

I came down from the roof, and the endless lawful greetings were unravelled again.

Pelenor had her bags dropped on the lawn, and she waited for Melchard and the Crimson Robes to go before taking the black veil off her face.

"Melchard told me that during my hibernation you would keep me on the Dragon gate. Does this mean I will be sleeping outside on the grass?" Her eyes sparkling with Nephilim spice, she did not seem the least worried – rather, excited like a child.

I shook my head. "Your body will be there, Your Majesty," I pointed to the room adjacent to Elyani's bedroom. "This is where Elyani took care of me during my first descent into the Underworlds."

"That will bring me luck, for sure!" she exclaimed, and she went to inspect the room.

I carried her bags inside and then waited on the lawn while she got changed.

Space Matrix ready. Engage guidance procedure. Fly, Dragon!

When Pelenor came out, she was no longer wearing her royally complicated black dress and veils, but a blue dress like the one Felicia had worn when I first met her. She had untied her long black hair and taken off some of her make up. "Szar of the Brown Robe, now I am no longer Her Majesty Pelenor Ozorenan, but Pelenor of the Turquoise Robe, following the rule of the temple of Eisraim," she announced in a jovial voice. Then she asked, "Do priestesses eat dinner in your temple?"

"Your Majesty..."

"Pelenor of the Turquoise Robe!" she corrected.

"Yes. Hum... priestesses do eat dinner, but as you are to be projected into hibernation in only a few hours, food is out of the question."

"Ah!" she said with resignation. "Szar," she wanted to know, "weren't you standing on the roof when the high priest and I arrived?"

"Watching the sunset, Your... yes, watching the sunset!"

It was not yet completely night. "One must have a wonderful view of the temple from there," she rubbed her hands, walking to the ladder attached to the wall. "Can I see?"

We were sitting on top of the Blue priestesses' roof when Melchard voice-channelled to inquire whether the princess needed anything. Predictably, when he learnt where Pelenor and I were sitting, he was only moderately impressed.

The communication ended, Pelenor burst out laughing. "Am I going to cause you trouble, brother Szar of the Brown Robe?"

"Only if you die, Majesty."

She preferred to keep laughing. Then she asked with curiosity, "Is this where you live, brother Szar?"

I nodded.

"I see. You have pinched the room with the Dragon's gate, haven't you?" Filled with renewed hope, the young Nephilim woman was in high spirits, quite excited to find herself in a totally different – and protocol-free! – environment. She kept asking questions, joking about everything that came to her mind.

I listened to her, answering her questions and trying to laugh with her, my eyes and mind fixed on the upper left window of Malchasek's tower.

Was it Elyani's room?

"Space Matrix Knowledge Bank ready. Waiting for search to be engaged."

And what if I used the Flying Dragons' guidance system to locate her?

"Engage search by resonating with column of Spirit signature."

I couldn't do that! Any active form of probing would have been against the Law.

The window gradually lit up.

"Search successful. Identification confirmed."

I felt a flicker but shrugged my shoulders. What did these voices mean, really? How much could I trust my cracked column of Spirit?

"Come on, Pelenor of the Turquoise Robe. Let us begin!"

We climbed down the ladders and went to the room.

"By the way," Pelenor said, "I brought a present. It comes from Verzazyel's temple in the county of the Snowy Mountains. A certain priestess made it specially for you." She opened one of her bags and handed me a small brown jar of ginger marmalade.

12.13 The night of the Flying Dragons

Pelenor was deeply asleep on the mattress, her aura blasted by two hours of non-stop Voice-projection, her breath nearly stopped, her main gateways snow-white, the space around her saturated with bright sparks of light, the *living walls* shaken by the power.

I was preparing myself to descend into the Underworlds, completely unaware of the catastrophe about to hit.

It was late in the night. I went out into the courtyard. A clear night.

I decided to quickly scale the roof.

In Malchasek's tower, one window was lit up.

Always the same window.

Of course, Elyani knew I stayed up late every night. Had she wanted to send me a signal, she could not have found a better one. Perhaps. Or perhaps, one of the two damn Immaculate was insomniac, or conducted endless rituals at night. How could I know? Tuning into the window would have been against the Law.

But what if the Eagle told me? I closed my eyes and called onto him. No grand connection, just a simple little prayer from the heart.

"O beloved White Eagle,
If it does not harm her,
If it does not harm the Law,
If it is not pure arrogance on my part,
And if you please,
Will you send me a sign?
Just a little sign, please,
To let me know
If this is her window!"

Holding my breath, I reopened my eyes, third-eyeing the landscape with utmost circumspection.

There was no sign.

I bent my head in reverence. "Doesn't matter! I still love you the same, White Eagle." Sensing Alcibyadi's presence crossing my beacon fields, I climbed down the ladders. "It couldn't work, there were far too many ifs in that prayer."

Earlier in the evening, I had asked Alcibyadi to come and monitor Pelenor's energy while I descended into the Underworlds. She arrived in a perky mood, a lily fastened in her hair. "So now, members of royal families travel all the way from the counties of the north to visit you," she laughed. "I'm flattered to have such an important man as my friend."

"I'm afraid it is not Szar who attracted the princess, but the power of the Underworlds."

Teyani's daughter sighed philosophically, "*Fame flees, the Law remains!*"

"Talk about fame! This operation is to remain top-secret. I hope no one in the temple knows about it."

Space Matrix guidance system ready.

Alcibyadi chuckled, "Top-secret, with fifty Crimson Robe guards of the Northern Lakes' royal army camping at the temple gates? *You must be joking in the Law!* The mysterious woman in black staying in Szar's apartment has replaced every other bit of temple gossip. Throughout the day, our friends of Lasseera have been voice-channelling Eisraim frantically to learn more."

"I see. Can't a princess come to Eisraim for a spiritual retreat?"

More chuckles, "A spiritual retreat in your bedroom, Szar?"

"All right, all right." I sighed. "Is this going to create any embarrassment for Master Gervin?"

"If anything, it enhances the prestige of the Brown Robe. When he heard about it, Gervin could not stop laughing."

Remoteness Knowledge Bank engaged. Begin the search.

"I see," I preferred to change the topic. "Tonight is the first time I will descend into the Underworlds using the Flying Dragons' guidance system. Quite likely, it's very safe. But if anything goes wrong for me, you would have to hold Pelenor's energy and keep the hibernation process going."

We went to inspect Pelenor's body of energy. "I have used one of Mount Lohrzen's special techniques: high-powered Voice frequencies that create near-total hibernation," I explained. "See these gateways? As white as snow. When I was working on Felicia, I found that the deeper the hibernation state, the easier it was to remodel gateways." I pointed at three energy centres in the lower abdominal area. "These have to be reconstituted from scratch. I will go down and find diamond and garnet vibrations from the Deep Underworlds, and use them as seeds around which I can crystallise life force and fashion the gateways. And to restart the forces of conception, I will saturate her energy with water of life from the deep rivers."

"Recreating gateways out of nothing!" Alcibyadi was utterly impressed.

"Here, I only need to work on three gateways. With Felicia, I had to reconstitute more than two hundred."

"Voof! With such power, you would even be able to create a living being out of nothing!" she said, holding her belly with her hands.

Vasoukidass knows.

"If I fell pregnant..." she hesitated.

"Suppose!" I imitated Gervin's voice, twinging my beard.

"Suppose! Do you think my baby could have some of this water of life?"

"Dragon's Word!"

Back in the courtyard, I sat down in a meditation position close to the Dragon's gate. Alcibyadi sat by my side. "Do you think you will take me down, one day?"

I laughed. "You should ask Maryani. She is the great master of Underworld travelling! She doesn't even need a Dragon gate to descend."

After a quick, "*Farewell, woman of the Law*," I let myself glide through the gate, and landed in the familiar blue-rock cavern. Wasting no time, I kept gliding down, letting the gate's energy merge with my column of Spirit.

Szar, requesting access to Space Matrix guidance system.

The guidance system's eerie voice immediately replied, "*Space Matrix, access granted. Engage guidance by stating objectives.*"

I let the high end of my column of Spirit handle the communication:

Underworld diamond and garnet needed for reconstitution of gateways in a female human body.

The response was instant, "*Target identified. Fly, Dragon!*"

It sounded too simple to be true. Projected by Space Matrix, I started gliding down the gate's shaft at phenomenal speed.

Far too fast.

12 – The Book of the Flying Dragons

Almost straight away, I received an ominous signal. *"Space Matrix, emergency! A major structural defect has been detected in the travelling vehicle. Urgent repair is needed, or a complete collapse may take place."*

Stop immediately! Let Space Matrix repair the crack.

No! Alcibyadi.

"Alcibyadi," I Point-called, "something is going wrong, and I don't know what! If you don't hear from me soon, call Gervin to the rescue. Remember that Pelenor must not be woken up while her gateways are being formed, or she may become very ill. If she happens to..."

Too late!

There was a crash.

So easy.

Whirling stars. Light dust.

Aeons of strangeness.

Beyond the Abyss of the Deep is the Fault of Eternity.

Look into the abyss.

There, the Mother of the Light is smiling.

Void.

...

Brother Knight, your appointment with destiny!

Philadelphia Six. If you don't destroy it, the Rex will destroy us all.

Hiram, Hiram! What am I going to tell Hiram!

...

Travelling through voidness.

The burning aspiration of glacial extragalactic spaces.

Crossing a thousand fields of stars in a split second.

Stretching time through voidness.

Worlds are born. Worlds die.

Clusters of universes breathe.

Infinity upon infinity.

Aeon after aeon.

To reach

A space of infinite strangeness.

Multidimensional colours, unlike any words.

Sounds, symphonic splendour.

Concatenating smells of immense cognitive import.

The number of qualities increasing exponentially.

Time joking round and round in circles.

The faraway voices coming to me.

"Space Matrix has undone the entire structure of his vehicles. Is he still conscious?"

"The only thread left is his Flying Dragon nature spread through remoteness. He should be able to hear us."

Of course, I can hear you!

"Welcome home, Flying Dragon."

The faraway voices!

The faraway voices I had been hearing for so long.

Am I at last going to know who you are?

A cosmic hush. After what seemed like another aeon, the voice answered, "Your father, I am, Flying Dragon."

Father?

Astonishment as limitless as the yellow bursts of remoteness.

"The Flying Dragon who planted his seed into your Mother, the Dragon of the Deep, when the Earth was young and fresh. Since then, I have been with you from remoteness, with all my heart, with all my mind. But you did not often hear my voice."

And now... am I with you?

"Now you are spread through the spheres of remoteness. But your consciousness is young. Your vastness is not yet aware of itself."

Spread through remoteness? Which sphere of remoteness?

"All of them. This is the essence of your Flying Dragon nature. Let me show you."

The universal breath which runs through remoteness, singing from one edge of the Cosmic Night to the other, as it sang from the beginning, sings now, and ever will dance. I dance, to-and-froing the edges of time, celebrating the glorious birth, an eternally young creation, a world without end, one trillion spheres of remoteness in unison.

That, I am.

And here is the Fault of Eternity, and the Abyss of the Deep!

"Look! At the deepest, the Mother of the Light is smiling."

The spheres of the Wise Spider and its webs of strangeness!

"Listen to the whisper from the Blue Lagoon. A Flying Dragon, waiting for your call. Great joy, there will be."

The mathematical perfection of the Great Ant! "The Great Ant, who has invited you to celebrate your birth in infinity. There you will travel, soon, for a feast in remoteness."

'Soon', in remoteness, means something completely different.

In the distance, a magnificent light.

"Recognise this light?"

The Web of Love! The spheres of Melchisedek.

"Where our beloved White Eagle lives."

The illuminating heartness of the Web of Love, wonder seen from afar in remoteness.

"See what is happening to Szar. He is being repaired by Space Matrix."

Poor Szar, there was not much of him left. His vehicles had been completely undone, his astral body turned upside down through the Point like a glove inside out. Lost in the immensity of remoteness, his Ego seemed but a frail little light.

Lo! The White Eagle is coming to greet us!

12.14 Alcibyadi spread beyond the Great Ant

Hands.
Hands, massaging my body.
A voice.
And another voice. Presence.
A Voice-projection.
Forcibly pulling me back into my body.
It was Gervin. “Teyani!” he called. “I think Szar is back.”
Teyani’s presence drawing close. “Alcibyadi is still completely unconscious. The controllers can’t find her. Isn’t it time for you to intervene?”
“Teyani, whenever possible we must let our young people do these things.”
Eyes opening. Gervin is soaking wet. He is sitting in front of me, Teyani by his side.
“Praise the Lord Melchisedek, Szar!” Such a warm voice. “Welcome back to the kingdom! Thus ends the night of the Flying Dragons.”
Mouth open. I can’t speak.
“Szar, from where you are, I want you to tune into the Flying Dragons’ guidance system and get it to bring Alcibyadi back,” Gervin instructed.
“Space Matrix, search successful. Human entity retrieved, spread beyond the Great Ant’s spheres. Consciousness-condensing process engaged.”
“Very good, son!” Gervin’s hand on my cheek.
Lehrmon’s voice, “Teyani, the controllers have located her!”
“Teyani!” a voice channel. “Teyani, we found your daughter! She has suddenly reappeared at the edge of the spheres of Melchisedek. She is moving incredibly fast.”
“Don’t try to catch her!” Gervin’s voice. Warm.
“B... ba...” I whispered, “back!”
“Try through darkness visible!” Gervin advised.
Easy. “He is coming back!”
“Who is coming back?” Gervin asked.
“Alcibyadi is back!” Lehrmon’s voice, “Alcibyadi is back!”
Gervin laughing. Teyani running.
“The Flying Dragon is coming back!” I whispered prophetically through darkness visible. “I have seen what will happen... a *huge* mess in the Law! We made a plan together... we are going to make a huge, huge mess.”
“What mess in the Law?” Gervin already liked the plan.
“The Flying Dragon is about to return to our spheres. He will send the influence... throughout the kingdom, all voice channels will be interrupted... the stones will become crazy... but not ours. To lure our enemies, we make false stones, connected to the powers of the Flying Dragons. The master plan for the Archive transfer... it’s massive!”

"Glad to see you've been working late in the night, son."

My body. "Jinia!" I still couldn't move it, but I could feel it, sort of. "I must find Jinia. She's one of us." Gervin's hand on my shoulder. "Help, Gervin, I feel weird."

"It's all right, son!" Gervin's reassuring voice, gentle. "Your energy is fine now. All beautiful and shiny."

"Why do I feel so weird, Gervin?"

"Space Matrix has completely undone you and repaired your column of Spirit. No more crack."

"Completely undone? Are you sure they haven't forgotten to re-do me?"

He laughed. "Let me take another look... no, I can't see that any major bit is missing," he teased me. "Perhaps a few gateways here and there, but who needs all of them, anyway?"

Gateways! I suddenly remembered Pelenor. "When can I descend into the Underworlds again, Gervin? I need to operate on the princess."

"Son, each time I see you returning from the Underworlds, the first thing you say is, 'When can I descend again?'" He tapped my shoulder, "Now that the crack has been fixed, you should be able to go anywhere you want, any time! Space Matrix will take you."

I started moving my left hand, slowly clenching and unclenching my fist. "If this is the way Space Matrix takes care of me..." It took a while before I could Dragon myself up.

"Gervin, I feel very, very weird!" I kept saying.

The Master of Thunder kept laughing.

Finally, with his help I managed to reach the bedroom where Pelenor was hibernating. Alcibyadi was lying on the plass floor, her eyes half open, Lehrmon sitting on her left, Teyani on her right.

A pinch in my heart. "Oh, no! What have I done to you this time?"

Alcibyadi smiled. She opened her mouth, but no words came out.

"Do you know where she was?" Lehrmon asked.

"Search successful. Map of remote sphere available in packed super-mind format for Point-analysis."

"Sure!" I said "Beyond the spheres of the Great Ant are gigantic pitch-black spheres of remoteness that are not inhabited by any Flying Dragons. They are part of the Black Night of Remoteness. Difficult areas for travelling. When Alcibyadi followed me, she spread in the Black Night where the spirit of the Dawn of Creation is still vibrant. No wonder she lost her thread of consciousness!"

Gervin raised his hands, "Simple!"

But when I turned towards Pelenor and took a closer look at her body of energy, I had one of the shocks of my life.

"Far Underworld!" I gasped.

"*What is that in the Law?*" Teyani, who had been instructed by Melchard to keep an eye on Pelenor, was unlawfully worried.

"I can't believe my eyes! I must be dreaming," I said.

"Who isn't?" Gervin sighed philosophically, coming closer.

"Alcibyadi!" I called. "Can you be my witness?"

"I think she can hear you, but she still cannot move, nor speak," Lehrmon said. "What's happened?"

"Pelenor's gateways have been reconstituted! Yet I have not done any work on her. Look, there, the three gateways have been crystallised around Underworld gems!" Filled with awe, I turned towards my teacher in Thunder, "Did you do this, Master Gervin?"

Gervin, whose joyful mood remained unabated, lifted both hands. "I am innocent, I swear!"

"Does this mean Pelenor is healed?" Teyani asked.

"Very much so!" I marvelled. "This Space Matrix guidance system is extraordinary. It has repaired her gateways *exactly* as I intended to."

Gervin shook his brown gown, water dripping all over the floor.

"How come we are so wet, Gervin?"

"The answer to this one is quite straightforward. You and I spent most of the night outside in the rain."

I hadn't noticed how wet I was. Clenching my teeth, I pulled a hissing breath with embarrassment. "So the three of you spent the night trying to rescue Alcibyadi and me, is that it?"

Teyani patted my cheek, "My son, Gervin has succeeded in transmitting one of his main qualities to you," she copied the grin that appeared on Gervin's face when he celebrated victory. "We never get bored in your company!"

"This is true!" Alcibyadi managed to whisper, Gervin and Lehrmon laughing their clear fountains off.

The joking continued, Teyani and Gervin discussing the awakening value of surprises, while the space controllers were voice-channelling one after another, asking what the Insane Upperworld had been going on. Lehrmon remained lawfully vague. Amongst it all, Mouridji of the Purple Robe voice-channelled too, just in case we wanted to tell her how our visitor from the north was going. No luck.

Alcibyadi finally managed to get up, and my friends took leave, leaving me Flying-Dragon-spaced out and wet to the bones.

I sat in front of Pelenor's hibernating body and took the lid off the jar of ginger marmalade. Glorious taste! I felt a sudden boost of mental energy. And Felicia's vibration, shining in the marmalade.

"Search successful: human entity located. Engage travelling through intention."

"Oh no, not again!" I spat out a lemon pip, flabbergasted. Space Matrix was ready to zap my astral body through the spheres a-*gain*! "These Flying Dragons never stop!"

Before getting out of my wet clothes, I went to have a quick look at Malchasek's tower. "Just a little sign, if you please..." I set foot on the bottom rung of the ladder.

Last night, my prayer hadn't worked. But with my repaired column of Spirit I no longer had to rely on little prayers full of ifs. Now I could invoke the full power of the Eagle. An oracular blast, piercing its way to Highness – whose window was lit?

On the roofs, a surprise awaited me.

Tears came to my eyes.

"So you heard me, after all!" I whispered.

A long white scarf had been tied to the upper left window of the tower of Malchasek.

12.15 Henrick and Pelenor

It was late in the afternoon when Princess Pelenor woke up. "Henrick! Henrick!" she called.

I ran to her room.

She was in tears, half delirious. She didn't recognise me. "Please, call Henrick!" she wailed in a little girl's voice.

I went and sat close to her.

She was trapped in a dream. "Henrick! Help me, please!"

I took the lost child in my arms. "Peace, my friend in the Law! Peace! Everything is all right. The healing went perfectly well."

She shook with big sobs. "I want Henrick. I want him to protect me."

"Who is Henrick?" I asked, rocking her in my arms.

"My friend Henrick is a great prian. He will help me. If they want to send me into exile, he will take care of me."

"Pelenor... Pelenor... Pelenor..." I used one of Elyani's tricks: caressing someone's aura with soft Voice-projections of their name.

Pelenor clasped her arms around my neck, snuggling against me, "Henrick! I knew you would come. I knew you would not forget me."

"Pelenor..." I kept rocking her in my arms, "Pelenor... Pelenor..."

Her body was soft and tender. "Henrick, I am sorry. I should never have left you. You will never know how much I regretted what I did."

At that moment, Melchard voice-channelled to inquire after the princess' health.

"I monitored her energy throughout the day. Her condition is excellent. She has just woken up."

"Can we transfer her to the royal apartments now?" Melchard suggested.

"No! No!" Pelenor shouted, clinging to my neck. "I want to stay with Henrick!"

Melchard understood his call was untimely. He closed the voice channel.

Pelenor was becoming more and more agitated. Voice-projecting onto gateways on her neck, wrists and ankles, I pulled her out of the nightmare.

Back in her body, she opened her eyes. When she saw she wasn't in Henrick's arms, a deep wave of distress hit her. She closed her eyes again and started crying.

"Peace, Pelenor! Everything is fine. You are healed. Your gateways are all beautiful and shiny." I unclasped her arms from my neck and let her lie down on the mattress, holding her hand.

She kept on sobbing.

I went into the clear fountain, seeking inspiration to soothe her. "Tell me about Henrick," I whispered in her ear.

"He was my friend. I abandoned him."

"Did you love him?" I asked.

"Did I love him! He was my Watcher. I was his Naamah. But I was afraid."

"Afraid of what?"

Her voice became less tense, "When he left. I was afraid when he left."

"When he left what?"

"When he left Jex Belaran," she said.

"Oh, no!" I thought. So this Henrick *was* the damn Renegade Hunter who sold me stolen stones in Tomoristan! I wanted to comfort Pelenor, so I just asked in a neutral voice, "What happened?"

"He and his friend Perseps had a fight, and then Henrick left. I should have followed him, but I was afraid that if he became a Renegade the whole of Jex Belaran would be after him." Pelenor opened her eyes, contemplating the ceiling in silence.

I wiped away her tears with the sleeve of my cape.

"I shouldn't say these things," she whispered.

"Say whatever you like. Tomorrow, you'll tell me what you want me to forget, and I promise I will."

A feeble smile appeared on her face, "Sir Great Dragon knows how to keep secrets."

I gave a Dragon-nod, my hands running on her body, warming up her gateways. "It's not rare to feel sad when you come out of hibernation. It's because your gateways are cold."

"I feel cold," she said.

"Tell me, this Henrick, is he a good friend? Does he know how to warm you up?"

"He is my *only* friend, the only person I can call on when I am really in trouble. The palace of Tomoristan is full of liars plotting behind my back."

"Does your husband know about Henrick?"

"He would kill me if he knew. Or maybe Henrick would kill him." Pelenor started crying again. "It's so sad. There is no one for me in that palace. Filipo is always busy, and there is no one else I can trust. No one."

"Does Henrick come and visit you?"

"Of course. That day in Tomoristan... just before he met you, he was with me. I had arranged your meeting with him."

So *she* had thrown me into the hands of this brigand? I could have screamed the Dragon out of the Underworld.

"Oh really?" I asked, utterly composed.

"I hope it went well for you," she said, holding my hand.

"It was... very revealing, I should say."

Pelenor closed her eyes. "When I was a child, Henrick always helped me when I was in trouble. But later on, when *he* needed me, I didn't help him. I abandoned him."

"So you grew up together?"

"Yes. His father was a Hunter in Jex Belaran. My parents lived in the village close to Verzazyel's temple. They had arranged for us to be married. Henrick was so wonderful to me, he treated me like a queen. Our Getz-relen was such a dream."

"Getz-relen?"

"A custom of the Hunters. After nine years of training, they must undergo a deadly trial. If they succeed in less than nine days, they win a Getz-relen: they can take the girl they want to marry for a three-week excursion to the Snowy Mountains and when they come back, no one is allowed to ask them any questions." Pelenor turned on her side, holding onto my hand. "He was twenty-one, I was nineteen. I will always remember the morning when he came to take me. It was such a dream, Szar! The happiest days of my life."

"And what happened?"

"Oh, that... you're not allowed to ask."

"I mean, what happened *after* the Getz-relen? Why didn't Henrick marry you?"

"Three weeks before the date of our marriage, he clashed with Perseps, a Hunter who later became the head of Jex Belaran. Those two men are stubborn as a Watcher's first-born. Henrick refused to give in, he preferred to leave. But he did not blame me when he saw I was afraid to follow him. He just came secretly one night to my parents' house. He made love to me for the last time, and he left."

I handed Pelenor a drink that Teyani had brought for her. She took a sip. "This is disgusting. Do I really have to drink it?"

I took the cup back. "One sip was probably enough. Tell me what happened after Henrick left."

"I cried. I cried for years. Dreadful years. Never any word from Henrick. It was like being dead. Then one day, Prince Filipo came to visit Jex Belaran. He saw me and... it was like being given another chance. Being loved, being desired – and being rich, being a princess!"

"But then, no baby came," I said, savouring every drop of Teyani's Dragon-warming drink.

"After a year, ugly rumours started running through the palace: was Pelenor capable of conceiving? Everyone was gossiping behind my back. It was awful. Then one day, I received a bunch of orchids just like Henrick used to give me every year for my birthday. And the day after, he found a way to reach my bedroom."

"Did he really?" I laughed, partly because of Teyani's drink. It made Pelenor feel better.

She smiled. "Hunters are smart! They can do extraordinary things. And do you know what happened?"

Teyani's drink had made my mind go bubbly. "He made love to you. And as you did not fall pregnant, he came back and made love to you again. And again."

Still holding my hand, Pelenor frowned, "True. But what has happened to you, Sir Great Dragon? Felicia told me that despite your great abilities, you were... a little naive?"

"So naive, I was!" I let out a long sigh. Then I handed the rest of the drink to her. "Forget about the taste! This is magic."

Trusting my word, Pelenor grabbed the goblet and quickly took a few sips. Through the beverage's power, she let herself resonate with my bubbliness. "You're right! There is something about this drink." Then she dared ask, "Am I really healed?"

From bubbly, I was becoming tipsy. "Your gateways are superb! I don't give you three months before you fall pregnant. You can sense when your body is fertile, can't you?"

"Of course. So it's the end of my nightmare?" she asked, somewhat incredulous.

"Of course! What would you like first: a boy, or a girl?"

"A boy!" she exclaimed with a greedy smile.

"You should speak to Alcibyadi, high priestess of the White Eagle and wise woman in the Law. She might have some tips to give you on how to get a baby boy."

"Yes please!"

"But then," I scratched my head, "who is going to make the baby boy: Filipo, or Henrick?"

She looked Nephilim-straight into my eyes, "I don't know! I love them both."

12.16 Praise the Angels of the Seed!

The next morning, early, Fridrick voice-channelled to announce he was back in Eisraim and wanted to speak to me urgently. I asked Alcibyadi to come and look after Pelenor.

As required by protocol, Melchard came to pay a formal visit to the royal guest. I greeted him in the courtyard and told him the good news: Her Majesty's etheric body showed all signs of prompt recovery, and her mood was excellent. Melchard *lawfully rejoiced* and asked when she would move to the royal apartment.

I went back into the room and asked the princess.

Pelenor had just woken up. "*No way, man of the Law!*" she answered with a loud yawn. "Tell him I'll voice-channel him when I need him."

"Are you hungry?" I asked.

"Not much. I feel a bit vague. Empty."

"Your subtle bodies need a bit of adjusting. We'll fix this later on today."

When I came back to the courtyard, Melchard lowered his voice. "She just wants to be left alone, is that it?"

"Of course! We all know that, don't we?" I replied with a broad smile.

"Of course we do! But if you knew what protocol *really* demands, you would be *horrified in the Law*."

"Melchard of the Brown Robe, am I putting you in a difficult position by keeping a princess in my apartment?"

Melchard gave a measuredly jovial smile. "If it were not for the legend of the Brown Robe, I guess there could be some embarrassment at this stage," he said in his highly polished diplomatic voice. "But it's happened many times in the past that members of royal families came to visit the Masters of Thunder. At the moment, old stories of miracles are circulating through the temple."

I raised my hands toward the gods. "*All glory to the teacher!*" Changing the topic, I asked, "Do you know anything about Nephilim food, Melchard?"

Melchard stroked his beard with great dignity, "*What is that in the Law?*"

"Superior dishes such as fishbone pate, almonds of hell, honey-pickled cucumbers and Watchers' ratatouille. These are just what Pelenor needs at the moment. If you *really* want the county of the Northern Lakes to like you, then supply us with stocks of these."

"I'll do my best!" he promised. The official business over, he relaxed his shoulders and dropped his high priest's voice and face, together with the ceremonial light in his aura.

He held my hands, letting me discover that his eyes were Elyani's eyes.

He held me in his warmth, and for a split-second I found myself in a different world, where sunlight shines from the inside of things, where smiling and dancing are one and the same thing, high priests never have to bother about protocol, and those who love each other are never separated.

In peace.

With devastating simplicity, he said, "Be well!"

Alcibyadi was entering the courtyard.

Melchard held my eyes for one more aeon packed in an instant, and without cosmic notice turned on his heel and left.

"*Praise the Lord Melchisedek, Sir Melchard, High Priest of Eisraim and Grand Commander of the Law for the County of Eisraim under the Appointment of His Supreme Majesty, the King of Atlantis,*" I heard Alcibyadi greet him, far away, in that other world where dancing and smiling are two completely different things.

With lawful measure in every syllable, the high priest gave due answer.

One hundred thousand years later, when Alcibyadi arrived at my end of the courtyard, she found me smiling like a heavenly filosterops.

The sempiternal greetings were short.

"Shining eyes!" she whispered.

I danced her with my eyes, as they do in the sunlight-from-inside world.

"Voof! Flying Dragons?"

"No. Flying Melchard." My attention was caught by the gateways in her belly. "Alcibyadi, what am I seeing?"

She laughed with joy, "Can you see it already?"

"The Dragon I can! The first hues of golden light have appeared in your aura! *Praise the Angels of the Seed!*"

"Yes!" she exclaimed triumphantly. "I am pregnant!"

12.17 Hunters' secrets

The meeting with Fridrick took place in the small room where he stayed when he visited Eisraim. It was in the chapel of the Mysteries of the Nectar God, the largest chapel of Maniya. It was a huge building that backed the chapels of the Wise Witches, the Field Wizards and Baltham. Fridrick didn't want us to meet in the music hall. "Too many fields, over there," he had said. "I want secrecy. Total secrecy."

I found him looking exhausted, but with a shining glow in his eyes. "*Praise the Lord Melchisedek, Commander!* I have great news for you."

I returned the greeting and waited for him to speak. His eyes were blinking strangely, probably due to excitement and fatigue.

"Jex Belaran has responded favourably to your offer," he began. "Perseps, that's the grand commander of Jex Belaran's Hunters, agrees on the principle of an alliance. And he's ready to share highly secret information with you. About the Renegades. He's designed a plan. At least two thirds of the Renegades could be eliminated. In a matter of weeks. But for a start, there's a few things you need to know about Perseps."

"I hear about this Perseps every day!" I thought, wondering if I was going to be told a second time about his fight with Henrick.

"Perseps," Fridrick went on, "he's a very tall man. Some say one of his ancestors was a giant. He himself denies it vigorously. He's not only a powerful Hunter, he's an exceptionally intelligent man. Brilliant strategist. Which is why a few years ago, Joranjeran (he'd been the Hunters' grand commander for more than fifteen years), decided to retire early. He left Perseps in control of Jex Belaran. Even though he's one of the youngest grand commanders the Hunters have ever had, Perseps has already made a reputation for himself. Far-reaching vision. Sophisticated plans. And an implacable will to carry them out. His men call him Kayala-ha. Heard this word, Commander?"

"*Not in the Law.*"

"It's a Nephilim word. It means 'he who never gives up'. Before discussing sensitive information, here are Kayala-ha Perseps' conditions: One, the information is to be kept secret from all, except for the Brown Robes. Two, Perseps doesn't want anyone to contact him, officially or unofficially. Only the Hunters' secret means of communication are to be used. Were you to meet him, Perseps would flatly deny he's ever communicated with you. Or even heard of you. Are you ready to abide by these conditions?"

"I am." This sounded like an initiation oath.

"You're a fortunate man, Szar of the Brown Robe," Fridrick meant what he said. "What I'm about to reveal to you are jealously kept secrets. The Hunters themselves learn this only after years of trials. Initiations." He paused, waiting for a sign of excitement on my face.

Danger, son! Danger!

Point-sealed, I kept the Dragon cool.

He moved on, "The Hunters, as you know, derive their powers from the Watchers. How? Through rituals. Of course. And through *the initiation which carries the spirit of the Hunters' lineage*. But for the rituals and the initiation to be possible, there's to be a seed-connection. A seed-connection. It's a seed of power which acts as *a receiver for the consciousness of the Watchers*. Each of the main Renegade clans has its own seed-connection, which they maintain through soft stones."

"What kind of soft stones?"

"High calibre he-stones. Connected to the Watchers' consciousness. The power that comes out of these stones! It's awesome."

"Does this mean any stone maker could start a Renegade clan?"

"Man of the Law! To manufacture a stone like that, a stone maker needs *a Watcher behind his ass*! And before one of Watchers consent to invest the stone with his powers, rituals must be performed. Extremely long rituals. And difficult. Dead difficult. Horrendously difficult. Why d'you think only three Renegade clans have emerged in the last twenty years?" Fridrick's eyes went blank for a second, then flashed. "Now listen, *there is a phoenix in the pot.* Perseps received intelligence. About the Red Renegades. The seed-connection of these suckers is about to falter. Means their clan's about to cark it in the Law. Their leader, Fonken the Red, he knows it only too well. It's why he's entered into negotiations with the Foxes. To form an alliance."

I saw where he was leading me. “Are there any resemblances between the he-stones which carry the Renegades’ seed-connection and our Archive stones?”

“Dead right, Commander! It’s why Esrevin and Gervin don’t want their stones to be charged with the power of the Archive until the very last moment. As soon as the charge takes place, the stones’ radiation will be picked up throughout the kingdom. So many gangs will be after us,” Fridrick explained.

“So the Renegade clans must be capable of tuning into each other’s seed-connection stones from a distance, and knowing which clan is powerful,” I concluded.

“Dead right! The Red Renegades’ seed-connection is about to turn weak. When it happens, the Foxes and the Black Hunters will know. In a matter of hours. Then they’re dead. Finished.” Fridrick paused, a flutter in his lips. “Now, here’s Perseps’ plan. Suppose the seed-connection of the Foxes was stolen. The Foxes immediately turn their attention to the seed-connections of the other clans. What if, at that very moment, the seed-connection of the Red Renegades was to be artificially boosted? The Foxes would conclude that those suckers have stolen their seed-connection. Swallowed it. What do the Foxes do? They storm the Red Renegades’ headquarters. And a bloodbath ensues.”

Danger, son! Extreme danger!

“But if the Foxes lose their seed-connection, wouldn’t they be rendered powerless?”

“Only after a month. So they’ll have to move dead fast. Perseps’ assessment is, the Foxes will win over the Red suckers. But with heavy casualties. And when the Fox survivors finally catch hold of the Red suckers’ seed-connection, they discover they’ve been fooled. The stone collapses in their hands. They’re finished too – no more Foxes, no more suckers. Now that’s just the big picture. Perseps is meticulous. A man of details. His plans are works of art. But the bottom line is, more than a hundred Renegades disappear. Only one clan left: the twenty-six Black Hunters. But they’re located much further away from us, in the Snowy Mountains. And they abide by Hunters’ ethics, even though they’re Renegades.”

“What about Henrick the prian?” I asked.

“Henrick? As far as I know, not a player in these large-scale games. I don’t think we have to worry much about him.”

“All this sounds wonderful, Fridrick. The only question is, who is going to steal the Foxes’ seed connection?”

Fridrick grinned. “You, Commander!”

I laughed, “Fridrick! Do you mean to say I am going to infiltrate the Foxes’ fortress, steal their most precious stone, and walk out unnoticed by forty Hunters?”

“Not forty. There’ll only be three of them left in the place. Jex Belaran takes care of that.”

I suddenly became interested. "How?"

"The Foxes regularly go on expeditions. Far away. They leave only a dozen men in their headquarters. That's when Perseps strikes. His men create a diversion. They simulate an attack by the Red Renegades."

"Why the Underworld does Perseps need me? Can't he steal the seed-connection stone himself?"

"Your Point-signature isn't registered in the Foxes' Knowledge Bank. This is why Perseps needs you. If any of Perseps' men came near the Foxes' headquarters, their Point-energy would immediately be identified."

"And you want the Foxes to believe that the Red Renegades are to blame, not Jex Belaran," I said. "But do you really think that a Fox Hunter could mistake a Great Warrior for a Red Renegade?"

"After I train you, Commander, I have no doubt they will." No longer blinking, Fridrick had the calm assurance of a man fully in control of his art. "There's another reason why Perseps needs you," Fridrick paused, his piercing gaze fixed on my Point.

To the Point, Brother Knight!

"Once taken out of its altar," Fridrick went on, "the power of the connection-seed stone will become unstable. If one of the Nephilim – especially a Hunter – were to carry it, his consciousness would immediately be locked into the Watchers' mind. The results could be... unpredictable."

That I could easily imagine.

"Who says this stone would not leave *me* dreaming for an aeon in the Watchers' mind?" I questioned.

"There's no Nephilim spice in your blood, Commander."

That hadn't prevented me from being caught in Verzazyel's dreaming web.

"And what's to happen to this seed-connection stone?" I asked.

"You will have to take it to a special place. A sacred Nephilim site. It will be de-activated by Jex Belaran's experts."

Fridrick stopped and looked at me with his fiery Point-intensity, waiting for my answer.

"Fridrick, I need to ponder on all this," I told him. "How long do you intend to stay in Eisraim?"

"Depends on you, Commander. If you decide to go along with Perseps' plan, I'll stay here for as long as it takes. To complete your training. At least a few months."

12.18 Point, venom and triangular seal

When I left Fridrick, I voice-channelled Alcibyadi. "Are you and Pelenor still chatting?"

"In the middle of a fascinating discussion. We are having *a wonderful time in the Law*," Alcibyadi assured me.

"Good! I need to see Gervin urgently. I'll come as soon as I finish."

I ran the Dragon to the enclave of the jewels.

Gervin's aquamarine chamber was full of gigantic arrangements of flowers. "One of your friends sent them to me," he gave a mysterious smile.

"*Who is that in the Law?*"

"Princess Pelenor, of course! After you agreed to heal her, she voice-channelled to thank me. No mention of the healing, of course. She just said, 'Thank you for teaching him.' And yesterday morning, Pelenor's guards brought the flowers."

"How smart of Pelenor to pay *all glory to the teacher!*" Had she wanted to touch me, she could not have found a better way.

"Son, I wish you could have seen that. There were at least fifteen Crimson Robe guards carrying these huge bunches of flowers," Gervin laughed. "As they walked from the temple's main entrance, all the priests and priestesses they met on their way started following them. By the time they arrived here, the procession had gathered nearly a hundred souls. Then in front of everyone, the captain of the guards delivered an official message to me, '*O wise man in the Law,* these flowers *are from you know who in the Law, to thank you in regard to the matters which were lawfully discussed with you.*'

All the priests and priestesses clapped their hands. They had no idea why, but it didn't matter. One by one, they each came to congratulate me, and they personally congratulated the captain of the guards too, who lawfully thanked each and every one of them for their support."

"I see!" I said, thoughtfully twinging my beard. "No wonder everyone in the temple is talking about the Brown Robes."

"Nothing to worry about! If anything, it gives our people a bit of joy and hope, which they badly need in these difficult times." Gervin's high fountain illuminated his smile, "Giving hope is one of the highest missions of the Masters of Thunder."

Lo! There was the White Eagle, coming to greet us.

"You know," Gervin went on, "everyone in the temple is well aware that Elyani, who was chosen by the gods, was about to marry Szar of the Brown Robe. This too gives them hope."

Liquid starlight. I have travelled a hundred aeons. Drink!

"How is that?" I asked, grinding my teeth.

"Her association with the Brown Robe makes them think her chances of success are much greater," Gervin winked at me. "We can discuss this another time. Now, tell me about Fridrick!"

On hearing Perseps' plan, Gervin was direct, "That stone they want you to steal... would be extremely difficult to handle. If it holds a seed-connection to the power of the Watchers, it could take you straight to the abyss – the dark side! Really, the venom intensity associated with that stone must be horrendous."

In that context, I wasn't too sure what venom meant.

Gervin caught my drift. "Venom is the mental energy of gods and angels."

"All gods and angels?" I asked, wondering why Lord Gana's mind should be called 'venomous'.

"All of them!" Gervin explained, "This is the central concept of Point-work: the mental consciousness of gods and angels is so much more intense than that of human beings that it must be kept above the head, using the power of the Point. This remains true whether the angel belongs to the light or to darkness. Angels are beings of a greater magnitude. Their mental consciousness is just too big for human beings. If it is allowed to fall into the head, it burns everything."

Hence the necessity for the Point to operate as a sphincter.

Gervin was in a teaching mood. "If you can contain the super-mind of angels above your head, then it turns into power of the Point. It gives super-fast thinking and high inspiration. It allows you to know the mind of gods and angels, and to fathom their presence. But the very same consciousness, dumped into someone whose Point hasn't been awakened, would render him mad or even kill him. Hence the name venom."

"That which is nectar to some, is venom to others?"

"Exactly. All Point-warfare is based on this principle. Venom is so intense it can kill. The paradox is that holding high venom intensities can be sheer delight, if your Point is strong enough. The mind opens to far-reaching visions and exalted states of consciousness – the consciousness of angels, which is aeons ahead of that of human beings."

I returned to Perseps' plan. "So what would happen to me if I came in possession of the Foxes' seed-connection stone?"

"Your consciousness would be projected into the Watchers' mind."

Not unlike what would have happened to me, had I accompanied Felicia in the crypt of Verzazyel's cave and stayed with her during her initiation.

As Gervin and I were twinging our beards, silently pondering on this difficult situation, an emergency voice-channel reached us. "The central kitchen needs Szar of the Brown Robe! It's unlawfully urgent!"

"*You found him in the Law!*" I answered.

"*Thank the Lord Melchisedek, at last!* Szar, we have been instructed to deliver some dishes to your courtyard, but no one here knows how to prepare them: fishbone pate, almonds of hell, honey-pickled cucumbers and Watchers' ratatouille."

Gervin burst out laughing.

I sighed. "No one knows about Nephilim cuisine in Eisraim?"

"Sorry!" the priest in the central kitchen answered. "We really asked *every single person* we could find in the temple whether they could help us prepare fishbone pate, almonds of hell, honey-pickled cucumbers and

Watchers' ratatouille for Szar of the Brown Robe and his royal guest, and we also voice-channelled Lasseera and the temple of the Western Plains. But this point of the Law isn't known to anyone! If you supply us with the recipes, we'll do our lawful best."

"*No way, man of the Law!*" I answered categorically, as I had received these recipes under the seal of secret. "Just get a few pots ready for me, I'll come and visit you in a moment."

Gervin was still laughing. "Watchers' ratatouille? What is *that?*"

I raised my hands. "Venom to some, but nectar to others!"

"We had better intensify your Point-training right now," Gervin decided, "so you can unleash full power into Pelenor's ratatouille!"

I welcomed the news, clenching my left fist. "So we are finally starting?"

"We are! Now that the Flying Dragons have thoroughly repaired the crack in your column of Spirit, why delay? Let us begin with the triangular seal."

The main method to render the Point impermeable, Eisraim-style.

There was no ritual and no ceremony. Gervin just made me sit in meditation position and tune into the centre of energy that Elyani had finely woven above my head.

She wove your Point. Through the Point, she will be with you, always.

Gervin ignited a sharp triangle of dazzling light, the tip of which coincided exactly with my Point. "This triangle I transmit to you, as I received it from my teacher Orest," he spoke with the gentle reverence that flourished in his voice every time he mentioned his master. "By holding onto the triangle, your Point will be sealed, and you will be capable of withstanding high intensities of venom. Let us see..."

Pressure fell onto my head, not unlike the pounding of a gigantic hammer.

"An angelic frequency," Gervin commented. "Can you feel it?"

Could I feel it! Drowned in deafening high-pitched hissing sounds, blasted by an awesome presence, I had to call on the Dragon to stay vertical. "I think..." The pressure on top of my head quickly became so overwhelming, I felt I was about to be crushed into Dragon puree. "Gervin! I'm not coping!"

The presence faded. The pressure stopped, leaving me trembling.

"Your Point is leaking. Hold fast onto the triangle! Contain the intensity of venom!"

"What kind of angel was that?" I asked, catching my breath.

"The infinite sweetness of Malchasek's choirs."

Infinite sweetness my Dragon! "That was a deadly weapon!" I argued.

"That which is pure love to some..." Gervin pulled a face just like Teyani, making me wonder if she had learnt the art from him after all. "All right, let's try again with something milder."

Another cosmic landslide fell onto my head.

"But hold onto your Point!" Gervin said, holding onto his patience. "Keep it closed! Tight like the tip of the triangle."

I could feel the damn triangle but hadn't a clue how to stop the downpour of energy into my head. "I'm Dragon-trying!" I said, every cell of my body buzzing like the Song of Creation.

"Don't Dragon-try, Point-do it!" Gervin said.

"Gervin, I think I'm getting a headache." Mild words to describe one hundred hammers beating your head like an anvil.

"Of course! You let yourself be flooded by venom. Close the Point-sphincter! Join me in the contemplation of this magnificent angel of Truth."

Whatever I tried, the avalanche continued.

"All right!" Gervin discontinued the presence.

The pressure above my head stopped. The headache didn't.

"I had never realised theurgy was so painful," I took my head in my hands.

"It's the most beautiful of all arts!" Gervin remonstrated. "Now, sit up straight! Let me get the venom out of you."

A mighty ascending flow swept through me, pulling the headache off my head. It was magic! In three seconds all pain disappeared.

Gervin granted no respite. "Hold onto the triangle. Seal the Point!" he ordered, but without calling any angelic presence.

"No! No! No! No! No!" he pulled his beard. This time, a careful examination of his face convinced me that *he* had caught the habit from Teyani, not the other way round.

"I'm afraid this is going to require practice. Now, let me do it for you," he said, blasting the room with a momentous presence while taking control of the tip of my triangle.

Instantly, I found myself dancing with him in the infinity of the sunlight-from-inside world, the sea of Whiteness where Melchard had been waiting for us since the beginning of time.

Lo! The White Eagle, coming to greet us!

Far, far below, there were dancing fields of stars.

12.19 Watchers' ratatouille and temptation from the Watcher

When I left the central kitchen I voice-channelled Alcibyadi again, this time to let her know I was on my way home.

"We are still in the middle of a fascinating conversation," she answered.

Racing through the alleys, I bumped into my old friend, Artold.

"*Praise the Lord Melchisedek, Szar of the Brown Robe! How are you, my friend in the Law?*"

As I returned the greeting, he contemplated the large, covered pot I was carrying. "I see you finally found the dish you needed for your special guest. Is this fishbone pate or almonds of hell?" he asked with a friendly smile.

"Er... well, actually, this one is Watchers' ratatouille, Artold."

He seemed genuinely happy for me. "What a wonderful smell! *And how are your parents, my friend in the Law?*"

I assured him that *I hadn't heard from them for some time* and took leave, hurrying towards the female wing.

In a corridor of the female wing, Mouridji the Prophetess stopped me. "*Praise the Lord Melchisedek, Szar!* How are you, my great man in the Law?"

The small woman closed her eyes. "It's Watchers' ratatouille, isn't it?" she pointed at the dish.

"How prophetic of you, Mouridji of the Purple Robe!"

"And you made it yourself, didn't you?" she said with sincere admiration, lifting the cover and carefully sniffing the contents.

Visibly proud of me, Mouridji put the cover back. "These people of the Brown Robe, they're so *clever in the Law*, aren't they?"

I thanked her for her encouraging comments and started running again.

When I arrived at the courtyard, Pelenor's room was empty.

"Szar!" Alcibyadi called me, "We're on the roof!"

I took two cups, left the ratatouille in the room and joined the two women on the roof. Pelenor was still a bit pale but she was in a joyful mood, having thoroughly enjoyed her seven-hour conversation with Alcibyadi.

While Alcibyadi was taking leave, I carefully inspected Her Majesty's etheric body. The gateways Space Matrix had repaired were holding fast, and the last whitish mists of hibernation had dispersed.

A superb piece of work.

"How are you feeling, Your Majesty?" I inquired when we were alone.

"Quite well! But you're not allowed to call me Your Majesty. The people who call me Your Majesty all lie to me and plot behind my back."

"What does Henrick call you?" I asked.

"He calls me princess," she smiled, "but with him it's different. He started calling me princess when I was eleven years old, you see."

I took a bottle out of one of my cape's large pockets. "Recognise this?"

When she saw the orange liquid, Pelenor burst out laughing, "Where the Watchers' hell did you find a bottle of glorious sunrise?"

"Hunh hunh! I didn't find it, I made it specially for you!"

"Thank you!" she said, holding my hand tight for a second. Before I had time to give her a cup, she had opened the bottle and started drinking. "Glorious!" Having pronounced her verdict she handed me back the bottle. "When she hears about this, Felicia will be so proud of you!"

"How about eating?" I suggested, after taking a sip.

"I'm not very hungry," she said in a little voice.

"And what if we had Watchers' ratatouille?"

She burst out in royal laughter again, “Are you serious?”

“Dragon-serious! It’s all warm. Waiting for us downstairs.”

“Show me!” she said. “I want to eat dinner on the roof!”

When I came back with the pot, Pelenor was dancing on the terrace, her long brown hair floating in the wind. It gave me a shock. With her turquoise dress, her elegant way of moving her arms and the witty glow in her eyes, she looked so much like Felicia that a whole bunch of memories flooded my mind.

I pulled a tablecloth from one of my cape’s pockets, plates and cutlery from another. Remembering the reddish rock of the terrace outside Verzazyel’s cave.

“This is unreal!” Pelenor exclaimed. “Dancing on the roof of the Eisraim temple, praying to the Angels of the Seed... and having Watchers’ ratatouille for dinner with Szar the prian! Who would have believed this a month ago?”

Szar the prian! Now *that* was the Dragon’s last tooth!

“Tell me,” I asked her once she had settled in front of the tablecloth, “I want to know more about Henrick the prian. What sort of man is he?”

She took the cup of glorious sunrise I was handing her. “Why do you always ask me about Henrick?”

“Because I am the only person you can speak to about him.” I pointed my index finger at her, “True?”

“True,” she conceded, and gave in. “He is... a really special man, with a certain... elegant way of doing everything he does. He is soft, but he is strong. So strong! Do you know his friends in Jex Belaran started calling him ‘the prian’ when he was only seventeen?”

“Really? What had he done?” I handed her a plate of ratatouille.

“He had won all the trophies and distinctions of his class. He had even defeated fully trained Hunters in competition. At that stage, Perseps was no match for him. Do you mind if I eat with my hands? At the palace, I can never do this.”

“Of course not!” I grabbed the cutlery and threw it over my shoulder into the Blue priestesses’ courtyard.

Pelenor giggled, “That’s the kind of thing Henrick would do!”

“Did he and Perseps study together?” I asked.

“Yes. They were close friends at the time. They practised kuren-jaya together. Do you know what kuren-jaya is?”

“The Hunters’ style of Point-combat.”

“Oooh!” Pelenor exclaimed in delight, “What did you put in this ratatouille?”

“The Dragon of the Deep.”

She smiled, just like Felicia. “Szar the prian, your Dragon is delicious!”

“How did Henrick and Perseps end up having a fight?” I asked.

“Perseps...” Pelenor remained thoughtful for a moment, stuffing ratatouille into her mouth. “There is something very harsh about Perseps.

Nothing can resist him. He was not as gifted as Henrick, but he practised kuren-jaya with such obstinacy and for so long that in the end, no one could stand in his way. For nearly ten years, he trained from four in the morning till midnight, never taking one day off. Finally, he became the absolute master of kuren-jaya. This is how he came to be called Kayala-ha, he who never gives up." A big chunk of ratatouille fell on Pelenor's blue dress. She giggled.

"What did he and Henrick disagree about?"

"No one knows, they always kept it a secret. Henrick never told me. He just left. And six months later, to everyone's surprise, Joranjeran (who was Jex Belaran's big chief) retired and installed Perseps as the youngest ever grand commander of the Hunters' order."

"How old is this Perseps?"

Using her long sleeve, Pelenor wiped ratatouille off her face. "He and Felicia were born the same year, exactly one lunation apart. They get on together very well, by the way. They grew up together, and you know, it took a while before he became stronger than her – physically, I mean. Once when they were five years old, Felicia bashed him up so badly that he ended up with two black eyes. But then, of course, he quickly grew up to near-giant size, and Felicia had to find new tactics to deal with him." Pelenor chuckled, contemplating another dollop of ratatouille dropping on her dress. "As children, these two formed a dangerous pair. They made their best coup when they were thirteen. They managed to get into the Watchers' secret vaults in the middle of the night, and accidentally activated the powers of the seed-connection stones. The whole town was woken in terror," Pelenor seemed to find this immensely amusing. "The temple's high priestesses decreed that Perseps and Felicia were no longer allowed to spend time together. But nothing could stop them. They met at night. Once they started a fire in the temple kitchen. Worse, they went back into the crypts and created another near-disaster. And then... it was Joranjeran who saved the situation. The high priestesses wanted Felicia expelled from Verzazyel's temple and sent to another county. But Joranjeran, a man of great wisdom and cunning, had another idea. He suggested that Perseps and Felicia be sent on a pretend-Getz-relen. They were hardly fifteen by then. The result was magic. Not exactly what Joranjeran had expected, but still. During their three-week excursion to the Snowy Mountains, Felicia and Perseps fought so much that when they came back, they refused to speak to each other for more than a year. And by then, they had grown up." She stopped, playing with the ratatouille in her plate and drawing strange signs on the roof with her fingers.

"Pelenor," I asked, trying to put the facts together, "there is something I don't understand. If Felicia was so close to Perseps, the Hunters' big chief, then why the Underworld did she go on her pilgrimage to the Red Lands alone? It was an unlawfully dangerous trip. Couldn't Perseps have given her a private escort?"

"No doubt he would have accompanied her himself, had he known. But he didn't know! No one knew. She was trespassing. Her application for a pilgrimage to Verzazyel's cave had been rejected by the temple authorities. Everyone was convinced she didn't stand a chance. They thought she could only kill herself if she attempted to conquer the power in the Watcher's holy crypt. So Felicia lied to everyone. She pretended she had to go with her brothers and visit some remote relatives somewhere in the eastern counties. Six weeks later, when Perseps learnt that she had been found in the county of the Red Lands, he was absolutely furious. Incidentally, Sir Great Dragon, had you murdered Felicia, I hate to imagine what Kayala-ha Perseps would have done to you. By now, the entire order of the Nephilim Hunters would be after you and your temple."

I swallowed high. Talk about a test!

Pelenor filled the cups with glorious sunrise.

"Why didn't Felicia marry Perseps?" I asked.

"It would never have worked. She didn't love him. I mean, he's her brother." Pelenor handed me the cup, "Anyhow, Felicia never really loved anyone before you."

I bit my lip, my eyes fixed on Elyani's window.

Search successful. Engage travelling through intention.

"You know, Felicia has not yet accepted Lord Vrolon's offer to marry her," Pelenor added.

"Is she still crying because of me?"

Pelenor made her voice soft, "Completely devastated." And softer, "Do you sometimes miss her?"

I kept silent, thoughts running through my mind. Now that Elyani had become an Immaculate, would I stay alone for the rest of my life?

"Sir Great Dragon has changed a lot, hasn't he?" Pelenor said. "He is no longer naive like he used to be."

"Could be," I grinned. "Felicia helped a lot."

"If you have changed so much, maybe you would appreciate Felicia differently now. She has... certain qualities that perhaps you did not fully notice when you were with her in the cave," Pelenor passed an accomplice's smile.

"That could well be," I wholeheartedly agreed, remembering how disconcerted I had been during some of my discussions with Felicia.

"Szar, you know that if you wanted her you would only have to say one word."

After having loved Elyani so much, love had a different meaning. "Could I love Felicia?" I wondered, tuning high into the White Eagle and bringing down his Light, using the Point to reinforce the connection.

Pelenor was silenced by the presence.

A cosmic hush followed, a short but safe haven in the mad race of time.

Forever love, Flying Dragon.

When the halo of peace faded, Pelenor asked, "What are you looking at?"

"The top of the tower. See this window with the white scarf?" I told her how I had watched the lonely light in the tower night after night, and prayed to the Eagle for a sign.

Pelenor asked question after question, and she listened from her heart. After a few minutes her eyes were filled with tears. "You love this woman madly, don't you?"

"Madly..." in front of me, the window was quickly disappearing in the mists. "Madly is probably the right word."

"And what if you never see her again?"

I shrugged my shoulders in resignation, "I probably never will see her again. Or I will see her on the day of her ascension ritual, when all the priests and priestesses gather in the main crypt. Perhaps they will allow me to travel in the spheres with her, after she leaves her body. Perhaps they will allow me to claim her body after the ritual."

"Stop! It's too sad." Pelenor wiped her tears with her sleeve. "Is there no hope at all?"

I held onto the silence of the Eagle.

"How come you haven't responded with a brown scarf?" Pelenor questioned.

"My courtyard is too low."

"So what? Can't you put up a flag?" she suggested.

"Deep Dragon!" I snapped my fingers. "A flag, of course!" I exclaimed enthusiastically. "A brown flag she would see each time she looks through her window."

"No! That's not the best way to do it, if you want to give her hope," the Nephilim woman had a carefully composed expression on her face. "Show the flag only when you are in your apartment, and pull it down each time you go out. That way she will always have a reason to look through her window. And she will have much more pleasure when she sees the flag."

I quoted a verse of her Law, "*The Nephilim people are the spice of the Earth*, aren't they?"

"Very true. But wait a minute," she went on, "what about a light that could be lit up on this roof every night?"

"I tried. But the wind blows my torches out."

After a moment of intense cogitation, Pelenor's eyes flashed. "I have a favour to ask, Szar prian! Leave this to me. I will organise the flag and the light."

Pelenor didn't mention Felicia again.

Later on, in the hibernation room, I did some work on her body of energy. As her condition was excellent, she expressed the desire to leave as early as possible the following morning. The sooner she returned to the palace of Tomoristan, the less chance of intrigues against her. The journey to Tomoristan was an easy one: only a few days by boat on the Holy Fontelayana river. I had no major objection to letting her go.

She voice-channelled instructions to her guards, and we agreed that she needed a long night of rest, after which we talked until very late in the night. We even went back onto the roof, just to have a look at Elyani's window. It was lit.

After two hours of sleep, I gave her a last healing session. Then, just before the high priest came to fetch her, she gave me a long hug and a kiss on the cheek. "Remember, if you ever need me, I will always be there for you," she promised. And we agreed that as soon as she became pregnant, she would send me a message – a coded message by which I would immediately understand who the child's father was.

Melchard arrived with dawn, followed by twelve priests. Pelenor had put on her black dress and her veils. Mouthfuls of lawful diplomatic formulae were exchanged, and the procession set off.

I climbed onto the roofs to watch her go.

It was sweet. All the priests and priestesses she met on her way waved at her in friendly fashion, and followed her to the gates. There, the happy little crowd applauded and presented flowers and fruits to the captain of the guards, who felt obliged to give an official farewell speech, thanking each and every one for their support.

12.20 Awesome connections and endless grief

When I next met Gervin, he asked me, "So what do you think of Perseps' plan to steal the seed-connection stone of the Fox Hunters?"

"I don't like it very much, but I don't see what other options are available. These Renegade Hunters are a plague. Unless we find a way of getting rid of them, not only the Archive transfer, but the very survival of our temples are imperilled. We need Perseps. The question is, can his plan succeed? And does he really want an alliance with us, or is he simply manipulating us in order to fulfil his own objectives?"

The Fox Hunters' seed-connection stone is a gateway to the abyss.

"Do you suspect *a spider in the potage*?" Gervin asked.

"From what I understand, Kayala-ha Perseps achieves his goals. At any cost. We'd better not find ourselves in a situation where our interests conflict with his. But at the moment, it seems we both want the same things."

"So we shall accept Perseps' plan," Gervin decided. "Send a message through Fridrick."

"Does this mean I will start training with Fridrick?"

"Give me a few more days to reinforce your triangular seal first," Gervin suggested. "Then you can start with him."

At last I was going to know what kuren-jaya was about.

There followed another session of Point-work with Master Gervin. This time he held the Point for me, taking care of venom leakages.

It was awesome. There didn't seem to be any limit to the magnitude of the angelic connections he invoked. The aquamarine chamber turned into exalted fiery spaces that extended forever in all directions. Infinities held in one point. Touring the Revelation Sky of the gods. To-and-froing the Golden Shield, Highness twinkling in Gervin's smile. I couldn't see a thing, blinded by so much light. Sometimes drowning in seas of ecstatic nectar. Sometimes crushed by the gigantic beingness. Fighting to stay in one piece, my Dragon out of breath running behind Gervin.

Revelation Sky. Kartendranath waiting for you. The beating will be unforgettable.

Gervin laughed. "Three hours is enough for today. Let me clean up your energy." As he spoke he started pulling the venom fallout up through my Point.

"Are you coping, son?" he asked as I was leaving.

"Hum... yes! Of course I am coping!" I said, walking towards the door.

"Son, that's not the door, that's a *living wall*," he smiled.

"Oh yes! Of course." I changed direction and bumped into a large vase.

"Mm..." Gervin frowned. "How about going for a stroll together?"

He took my arm and walked me to the portal of the female wing where he let me go. "A wonderful thing about these Point-guided corridors," he said, "is that you don't really have to be on Earth to find your way."

I set off, Point-sailing with the Lord, my mind spread through the spheres. But waves of grief welled up inside me as they did every time I walked there. The gloomy reality was, Point-trotting the corridors was no longer the inspirational delight it used to be. With Elyani gone, all I could do was let myself be dragged along by the Point as I cried! Alcibyadi and Teyani had said it was good for me, it let the grief out of my system. Perhaps. But the sorrow seemed to have no end.

I sat in my favourite lamentation stairway, holding my head in my hands, and I cried.

A frail silhouette clad in a purple gown came towards me. Mouridji the Prophetess. She sat by my side on the steps. "You're crying because of Elyani, aren't you?"

I nodded, hiding under the hood of my brown cape.

"Well, it's very good that you haven't given up on Elyani. I am proud of you, Szar of the Brown Robe," the old woman said with conviction.

Mouridji always spoke with conviction.

"I wonder why." I loudly blew my nose into my sleeve.

"It makes the world a more beautiful place, for a start," the old woman said. "See, I live in the room nearby and each time you stop on this stairway, I can feel your tears, and it moves me. And then, who knows? Perhaps one day Elyani will need your help."

"They won't even let me see her, Mouridji."

Space Matrix search successful. Engage travelling through intention.

"I know," Mouridji put a compassionate hand on my shoulder. "These two Immaculate priestesses are such damn, noxious, idiotic parrots of the Law, aren't they?"

I chuckled, "Mouridji, these are strong words!"

"What d'you think? No one likes them very much, here. What they did with Holma was not right – simply *not* right! But you are of the Brown Robe, you will not allow the same mistakes to be repeated with Elyani."

"There is nothing I can do!" I cried.

"I understand," Mouridji poured her compassion into me. We kept silent contemplation for a long while, an infinitely delicate purple presence landing in the corridor, mingling with the whitish glows of the *living walls*.

Mouridji, fierce warrior, fighting the battle against the giants by your side. Kartendranath has seen. He likes her.

When the connection faded, we got up. I noticed Mouridji was limping. Signs in her aura showed that her left hip was badly aching. "Are you in pain?" I asked.

"My hip's not very good these days. I used to go to the healing chambers and it made it better. But now that the fields have become as corrupt as the king's palace, the people in the healing chambers can't do much for me." She sighed, "*Old age is a pain in the Law!*"

"Why don't you come and visit me one of these days? Perhaps I could help," I offered. "You know where I live, don't you?"

"Mouridji knows where everyone lives, *young man in the Law*!" she patted my cheek with her wrinkled hand.

12.21 Kuren-jaya, day one

"*Sharpen your Point, man of the Law!*" Fridrick was standing in front of me, ready to launch the first kuren-jaya assault.

"Hey, wait a minute, Fridrick! What am I supposed to do?" I asked.

"Just try to keep your Point together while I'm pouring venom on top of your head."

I swallowed, holding onto my triangular seal. In the last three weeks, Gervin had been doing intensive work on the lower end of my column of Spirit, reinforcing the Point to prepare me for the shock of kuren-jaya.

"Don't worry!" Fridrick smiled. "I'll start very gently. As if this was day one of your combat training in Jex Belaran."

He directed his gaze at me. I didn't avoid it.

For the first time, I was looking straight into the eyes of a Nephilim Hunter. Hawk eyes, piercing black. The power of the spice.

I felt warmth above my head. "What kind of venom is that?"

"Just a wisp of Point-ness. Shall I raise the intensity?"

"*Raise, man of the Law!*"

The large wrinkle which barred his forehead furrowed imperceptibly.

"I can't feel much difference," I told him.

He sent another influence. "What about this?"

Three Flying Dragons entering the remote sphere of the Great Ant.

"Still can't feel anything different," I reported.

"Good Point!" Fridrick declared with satisfaction. "Did Gervin weave it?"

"Hunh hunh! Elyani did."

Fridrick threw another impulse. "What about this?"

A shower of thick, egg-white-like muck fell into my energy. "Absolutely disgusting, Fridrick! What is this venom called?"

"Angel sneeze. It's not very toxic, which is why it's often used for practising."

As I cleaned my energy by pulling the venom up, I asked, "How the Underworld did you manage to pass through my Point? I thought I was holding on fast!"

"I sent an unsettling wave. Just before pouring the venom. It opened your Point without you even noticing it."

The Great Ant, waiting for you. Mathematical poetry. Hiram, o Hiram!

"Let's try again. Could you perhaps unsettle my Point without gunking me this time?"

Fridrick patiently kept throwing impulses at me, until I could sense the waves reaching my Point.

"Mm... subtle!" I exclaimed when I finally perceived the unsettling wave. Hardly a whisper amidst the hissing symphony that ran wildly above my head.

"No, not exactly subtle," he was amused. "As you will soon realise, Commander, there's some much more insidious ways of unsettling the Point of your enemies."

Fridrick kept sending Point-waves at me, taking breaks from time to time so I could clean my energy from the revolting vibrations he Point-disgorged into me.

At the end of the two-hour session, I felt completely sick.

I thanked Fridrick wholeheartedly and let the Dragon walk me to the enclave of the jewels.

When he saw my aura, Gervin laughed in dismay, "Oh no! What has happened to you?"

I let myself collapse between two large vases and picked up a lily. Thanks to the etheric conservation fields, Pelenor's flowers were still fresh like morning dew.

The Black Night of Remoteness, pregnant with the pure energies of the Dawn of Creation.

Gervin came and sat nearby, pouring his loving energy into me.

"I can't understand how it works, but the venom disconnects my consciousness from the Dragon. It makes me lose control of my body. I think I need to throw up."

"That's easy!" Gervin said in a reassuring tone, and he went to get a bucket.

Unfortunately, I could not wait. I started vomiting in one of Pelenor's vases. When Gervin returned, I continued in his bucket.

"*All glory to the teacher!*" he exclaimed when I finished. "Are you feeling better, now?"

"When I go into my Flying Dragon nature and spread through the spheres, I feel fine."

"There are some amazing energies up there."

"The Black Night of Remoteness, in particular... voof!" I whispered.

Gervin waited a moment, holding my energy. Then he invited me to ground myself into my physical body again.

I began to feel my body. "The bucket, please!"

Gervin laughed. He kept his arm around my shoulders, patiently waiting till I finished throwing up. But I couldn't stop vomiting. Thick brownish acrid bile, conjuring images of snake venom. After a while, the Master of Thunder decided, "All right! Let go of your body, go back with the Flying Dragons."

I withdrew my consciousness. The malaise instantly faded. I sat back against the *living wall*.

To-and-froing the edges of time. Darkness brighter than a million suns. He saw the birth of life, liquefied light, when Moon and Earth were one.

"Would you like some water?" Gervin offered.

"Water?" From the spheres, I hesitated. Space Matrix clarified for me:

Water to drink.

"Water to drink, of course! Well, I don't see why. I mean, no thank you. Gervin I think something really important is about to happen in the Great Ant's sphere. Would you like to come with me?"

Space Matrix access granted.

Letting out a long whistle, Gervin voice-channelled Alcibyadi, "White Eagle, Szar could do with one of your visits." He explained what had happened and instructed her, "When I finish giving him a healing, I'll accompany him to the portal of the female wing and launch him in the corridors' field. Make sure you are at the other end to receive him."

12.22 Heralding the return of the Flying Dragon

"How are you, Sir Great Dragon?" Alcibyadi welcomed me to my courtyard.

"Much better, Lady of the Eagle! I cried a quick flood in the corridors. It made all the difference." I realised the lily I had picked up in Gervin's room was still in my hand. I put it in her hand and let myself collapse flat on the Dragon gate.

In the arms of the Mother of the Endless Night.

Alcibyadi untied her long black hair. It fell to her waist, and she placed the lily on the side of her head. "How was the kuren-jaya session?" she asked, sitting by my side.

"I think I'd better keep practising the black dance, just in case. Tell me about your baby boy."

Alcibyadi's smile blossomed. "He is on his way from the Spirit-world. The Angels of the Seed have announced to me that his soul will land in my body in seven weeks. They are pouring so much golden light into me, look..." she directed her presence towards my Point.

"No!" I shouted, sitting up with my fists clenched.

Her bright brown eyes wide open, her head tilted in perplexity, Alcibyadi watched me with her customary devouring intensity, wondering what to expect next.

"I'm sorry!" I delicately put my hands on her shoulders. "For one second, I thought I was back in action. And look at me, I was about to bash you again!"

"You're a dangerous friend," a touch of irony raised the corner of her lips.

"Alcibyadi," I let myself collapse on the gate again, "I don't feel up to it. I'm starting to wonder if..."

"*Hush, man of the Law!*" she interrupted. "Your teacher is one of the most powerful Points of the entire kingdom."

"All right, all right," I shut the whingeing sleeper up. "Will you show me the golden light?" Dropping all defence, I let her take control of my Point.

Her strong, warm presence permeated my energy, and a river of gold started flowing down into me.

The illuminating enthusiasm of the Web of Love.

"Is this how it feels to be pregnant?" I was awe-struck. "But it's magic! Liquid gold, as in the heart of the Dragon. It's like travelling in the Deep – but *really* very deep – Underworlds."

"And it's only the beginning of the pregnancy!" the high priestess rubbed her hands.

"I want to become pregnant too!" I made her laugh. "I'm *sure* Gervin could arrange this. Or maybe Lehrmon could ask Barkhan Seer for me."

The endless grief of the man who drinks the cup of bitter herbs. A great sage, Lehrmon knows how to love madly.

Alcibyadi stopped laughing. "Where is this voice from?" she made a conscious effort not to bite her lip.

"I'm not exactly sure," I sat up straight, taking her hand. "A mixture of Flying Dragon flavours, not all mine. Sometimes it foretells the future.

Sometimes it echoes news from remoteness... strange messages like only Flying Dragon multidimensional words can convey. Sometimes Space Matrix takes over and teases me. When I think of Elyani... that's it. It's doing it again! See?"

Search successful. Engage travelling though intention.

Alcibyadi only caught a glimpse of the signal through my Point. "I didn't get it. Was it Space Matrix?"

I nodded, "Offering to project me into Elyani's bedroom. It does it all the time."

Alcibyadi chuckled. "Have you done it?"

"Of course not!"

"You should check the Law of the Immaculate, Flying Szar-ka. There might not be any provision to prevent them from receiving communications from the spheres of remoteness. Why should an Immaculate not talk to a baby Flying Dragon?"

"I'd be too afraid of messing with her Law."

She didn't insist. "Space Matrix... was that what was guiding you the other night, when I saw you shooting up into the spheres?"

I couldn't remember any of this. "Will you tell me?"

"Just after your accident took place," she began, "I saw you coming out of the Dragon gate and zapping through the mists at incredible speed. I tried to tune into your Point, but the result was not what I had expected. I was instantly ejected out of my body and I found myself travelling behind you. It went so fast, I thought my astral body was going to blow up."

"Caught by Space Matrix!"

"Frightening!" she complained vigorously. "In less than three seconds, we had already reached the edge of the spheres of Melchisedek. We stepped into remoteness, and the pace kept accelerating! It went on and on, until..."

Space Matrix archive viewing engaged.

The explosion.

Alcibyadi, grain of sand in the oceans of remoteness.

Time stops. Infinity takes over.

Space Matrix sends a signal. "Seed of the White Eagle!"

Heard.

From beyond the abyss of the Deep and the Fault of Eternity, an instant response.

A gigantic cloud, unfathomable. On its way. A Flying Dragon matured through many a cosmic cycle.

The White Eagle's lover.

Enveloping Alcibyadi, tiny speck of light, in his ancient presence.

Speaking to her tenderly.

Showing her mysteries of remoteness.

Limitlessness. Lemniscate heart. Elixir of infinity.

"I will return with a present for the Eagle, and a present for Thunder. Be my herald, tell them."

Alcibyadi, Whiteness eternal, sitting on the purple flowers of the lawn, holding my gaze, contemplating Space Matrix's multidimensional archive images.

So much love.

12.23 Kuren-jaya drills

The second training session in kuren-jaya was as much of a disaster as the first one. Gervin had tried to help by Point-boosting my triangular seal and giving me a few Thunder-tips. But nothing worked. I spent two hours being showered, venomised and gunked by Fridrick. This time, the only improvement was that when I returned to Gervin's place, I managed to wait for the bucket before I started throwing up.

Gervin spoke kind words to me, while I vomited and vomited.

Drawing forces from the Underworlds, I finally managed to pull my Dragon together. Early in the afternoon, I knocked at the door of Fridrick's room, ready for another onslaught.

"Listen, Commander," Fridrick said in a gentle voice, "I don't enjoy making you sick."

"Not at all, *my friend in the Law!* I am sincerely grateful for what you are doing for me. And you see, I have been curious about kuren-jaya for so long. Now at last I can appreciate what I missed by not being born in Jex Belaran. Come on, let us start again!"

"I thought of another method. To help you structure your Point," he pursued. "A technique which Jex Belaran's Hunters use intensively." As I hesitated, he gave his dry smile, "Don't worry, I won't plug you into the Watchers' mind."

Fridrick, dead. They killed him.

I followed him to the music hall. There he connected his Point to a space of consciousness around the lower edge of the worlds of the gods, generating a continuous 'uuuh' sound in the hall's darkness visible.

After a few seconds he let go of the sound and turned to me, "Now you do it."

Holding the same connection from the Point, I was unable to produce a continuous note. My 'uuuh' sound wavered up and down the pitch scale, interrupted by a pandemonium of furious shrieks and buzzes.

"Interesting space, isn't it? These impulses that interrupt your sound, they're just like the unsettling waves Hunters throws at an enemy to overrun his Point," Fridrick explained. "When you can hold the continuous sound. Then the leakage is fixed."

Why should an Immaculate not talk to a Flying Dragon?

My uuuh sound kept jumping up and down. “It goes too fast, I can’t even sense the unsettling waves!” I complained

Fridrick practised with me until I could produce a two-second uuuh without any interruption. Then he Point-plugged me into another layer that was even more difficult to render in the form of continuous sounds.

His patience seemed limitless. He stayed with me for hours, carefully observing me and analysing my mistakes, coming up with suggestions that gradually improved my Point-stability. Precise and sharp, he always pre-empted my next move, making me laugh each time he felt despair welling up inside me.

“Do you know what made me decide to enrol in the Lasseera Archive team?” he said at the end of the afternoon, when he saw I couldn’t take any more. “When I first visited their chapel, they were all laughing. A stone on which the team had been working for months had just collapsed. Esrevin of the Brown Robe was the first one to burst out laughing. And all his men followed. It reminded me of Jex Belaran, where people know how to laugh. Once during *the last phase of my twelve-year Point-training*, I made a huge blunder. It nearly blew up the protection field shared by Jex Belaran and the neighbouring temple of Verzazyel. It had to do with the seed-connection stones. The seed-connections stones of Jex Belaran! Massive powers, from the Watchers.

When I realised what I had done, I was terrified. Joranjeran happened to be in the room. He saw the deadly wave coming out of the seed-connection stone. He called on his high powers. To neutralise it. Everyone in the room remained dead silent. Wondering what would happen next. Joranjeran was holding a green drink in his hand. He poured half of it on his head, and he burst out laughing. And when I started laughing with him, he poured the rest of the drink over my head. I had the greatest opening of my entire life.” Fridrick abruptly called a volley of loud low-pitched sounds that thundered like the roaring laughter of a hundred titans.

It was so startling I found myself calling on the Dragon.

With a contained smile, Fridrick filled the hall with more laughter, as if a full amphitheatre was making fun of me.

I laughed with the imaginary crowd and clapped my hands.

Then the astral atmosphere of the hall resounded with a clamour of applause, the jubilation of a crowd.

In the spheres of the Blue Lagoon, the Flying Dragon is waiting for your call. Immaculate thread. Fulfil your vow. Space Matrix will help.

“You can do anything you want!” I marvelled.

“Nearly,” the master musician replied.

“Tell me, Fridrick, this Joranjeran seemed to be a very wise man. Why did he install Perseps as his successor so early?”

“A very wise man indeed,” Fridrick paused, thoughtful. “By the way, he’s still alive. Joranjeran, he’s like Esrevin and Gervin. He’s foreseen times of great unrest and chaos. For the near future. Perhaps that’s why he gave Perseps an early start at leading Jex Belaran. He wants him to be a fully experienced grand commander by the time hell breaks loose in the kingdom. Who knows! Joranjeran took everyone by surprise when he handed the power to Perseps. Many had thought Henrick would be his successor. No explanations were given."

Make him talk. Find the corpse.

"And what about Perseps," I asked. "Can we trust him?"

Fridrick shrugged his shoulders, "I'm sure you'd like Joranjeran a lot, Commander. Perseps... he's not a man of heart like you. There's a certain ruthlessness about him. Made me uncomfortable. Once I was sent on a hunt with him and four other Hunters. Six giants who had been outlawed in the county of the Snowy Mountains had crossed the border. They didn't do anything wrong, just came *to breathe the mists*. And soon after we started the hunt they fled. Out of the county. But that didn't matter to Kayala-ha Perseps. He made us run after their unlawful asses for more than seven weeks. When we caught them, they had nearly reached the Eastern Peninsula. Perseps coldly killed the six of them, one after the other. Point-strangulation with a triangular net is ugly, Commander. Ugly! Right from the beginning of the hunt, he had set his mind on exterminating them. Had they made it to the citadel of the Nephilim giants, it wouldn't have stopped him. Kayala-ha, you see. He would have still found them, and juiced the lawful spirit out of them. For whose benefit? That I am not sure," Fridrick's face closed off. "But I can understand why Joranjeran wanted to install a Kayala-ha man to take care of his people. When hell breaks loose. As long as Perseps rules Jex Belaran, the Snowy Mountains will be a safe haven for Nephilim people. The only thing they could fear is an invasion by the giants. From the east."

"Is that a real danger?" I asked.

"Could become one. In the past, the giants have gone on the rampage. Many times. It's not happened for a long time. But if hell breaks loose, then who knows? The giants of the Eastern Peninsula! They're completely unpredictable." Fridrick recovered his dry smile, "It's because they thrive on Watchers' venom."

"Could they attack us?"

"If they ever decide to, then the Lord Melchisedek have mercy on us!" Fridrick raised his hands. "The giants hold strange powers. Powers inherited from the Watchers. Difficult to match! *Difficult* to match! And they've never waged a war without destroying everything on their way. The six giants I told you about, they were just simple folks. But the army of the Eastern Peninsula, that's different. Elite Point-soldiers, like the Green Guard. Oh, Naamah! Dangerous. You have no idea in the Law. Terrifying."

The giants on my list of potential enemies? That was the last thing I needed.

They will invade Eisraim. They will ransack the temple.

I shivered.

"What?" Fridrick frowned.

"Nothing!" I gazed aside elusively, and I let the conversation die off.

After the Hunter left, I stayed in the hall and kept practising the drills he had taught me.

Later in the evening Alcibyadi popped in for a visit. When I felt her presence entering the hall, I connected my Point to the White Eagle's Light, filling the hall with magnificent celestial harmonies.

"I know this music!" Alcibyadi's eyes doubled in size. "I have heard it many times."

"A strange coincidence!" I tuned into her Point, "Listen! This is the sound that comes with the golden Light of the Angels of the Seed."

A rich fullness of sound warmed the astral space.

She clapped her hands, "Each time I come to listen to you, the sounds are more beautiful. Will you do the sounds of the Flying Dragons for me again?"

I closed my eyes and went high up in the column of Spirit.

A one-week massacre. Tomoristan will fall to the giants. In the month that follows, the counties of the Northern Lakes and Lasseera will be subdued and pillaged – women raped, children slaughtered, the Fontelayana river red with blood. The temples of Laminindra and Lasseera will be ransacked and melted to the ground, not one survivor. Then the giants will march on Eisraim.

When I reopened my eyes, Alcibyadi was holding my hand. "Szar? Are you all right?"

"Mm... Strange spaces... Did I lose touch with the room for long?"

"A few minutes. The sounds you made were... rather frightening."

I called onto the White Eagle's peaceful music, gradually bringing a smile back onto Alcibyadi's face.

The flight of the Eagle at the Edge of Highness.

"How do you manage to do that?" she was puzzled.

I snapped my fingers. "Voof!"

"You know you are not allowed to say this!" she slapped my shoulder.

I let myself fall on the floor as if she had delivered a huge blow, and I filled the astral space of the hall with loud laughter noises.

Alcibyadi took her head in her hands, laughing with the space. As I stayed on the floor, she sat on her heels close to me. "Are you in a joyful mood, Flying Szar-ka?"

"The Dragon, I am! Fridrick has found a new method by which I no longer have to take venom-beatings... at least for a few days. Master Gervin is going to be so bored: no more vomiting in his buckets."

"*Praise the Lord Melchisedek!*" Alcibyadi rejoiced with me. In the lawful chatting that followed, she asked if I had heard that Maryani had just returned to the temple.

"*Lawfully excellent!* I need to speak to her. What about Woolly?"

"Well, well... I believe he and Maryani exchanged a few fiery words when they were in Lasseera."

"Woolly using fiery words? I can hardly believe this. Tell me, what happened?"

"All I know is that Maryani called Woolly *a pig in the Law*, and now she refuses to speak to him. She did not even let him come back to Eisraim with her. Woolly is so desperate that he offered to apologise to her."

The Dragon was nothing short of bewildered, "Woolly, apologise?"

"Yes! But Maryani refused his apology. She said that even if he changed his manners, she was not sure if she would speak to him in their next life."

12.24 A spider in the potage

Gervin was inspecting my energy at the onset of a session of Pointwork. "There is *a spider in the potage*. Something not right somewhere..." he spoke from high in the fountain.

"Did I pick up a wrong energy from the kuren-jaya work?"

"No, I mean something wrong with that plan. Capturing the seed-connection stone of the Fox Hunters..." he held eye contact with the *living wall* of the aquamarine chamber.

"Do you think Perseps is trying to fool us?"

"Mm..." Gervin twinged his beard. "See... this mission is excellent for your spiritual development. And it is one of the best possible preparations for the role you will have to play at the time of the Knights."

If you don't destroy it, the Rex will destroy us all.

I found that astonishing. "Do you mean we are already preparing for the Brother Knights?"

"Of course! We *have* to! During the wars of the Apocalypse, dark forces will unleash such a fury that the very survival of humanity will be at stake – slaughter and devastation such as there has never been since the beginning of the world. You will be there, fighting from the Point, and I will be with you. Learning the Point-secrets of the Nephilim Hunters is one of the many preparations the Masters of Thunder want you to undergo for this task, and so they fully approve of your training with Fridrick. Still, still..." he extended his hand to a bunch of flowers and grabbed a dappled orchid, "there is something that doesn't smell right in this operation against the Fox Hunters."

I wriggled my nostrils but didn't catch it. "Did Master Esrevin have something to say about the traitor?"

"Esrevin, whose sight of Thunder is deep, has spent the last weeks thoroughly scanning his team and hundreds of other people in Lasseera. He has made a few discoveries – a thief in the kitchen, and three old priestesses unlawfully keeping pet filosterops in their bedrooms. But he swears on the lineage that all the men and women who work with him in the Archive project are totally loyal and sincere."

"Then... a spying field?"

"No!" Gervin thundered, categorically.

"Well, well, then... the Renegade Hunters must have gotten their information through some magic weapon unknown to us!" I concluded.

Gervin pulled a face.

This time, there was absolutely no doubt in my mind: he had caught the habit from Teyani, not the other way round.

12.25 The arrival of the secret present

When she arrived in the courtyard, Maryani went and sat straight on top of the Dragon gate, anchoring her energy into the depths of the Earth. Since her return from the Underworlds she had put on a little bit of weight. Her serene beauty was blossoming. Her aura was more golden than ever, powerful vroofing waves constantly emanating from her.

"Have you heard from Elyani?" she inquired.

I shook my head, contemplating the mists.

Maryani rounded her cheeks and blew a soft, whistling sound. A cloud of golden light from her mouth gently wafted towards my heart. When it reached me, I was instantly spirited, filled with her loving intent.

"How do you do that?"

"It's a trick Vasouk taught me. Do you want me to show you how to send clouds like this to Elyani?"

I held my breath for a few seconds. "The Law of the Immaculate is awfully strict. If I started doing things like this, I could create trouble for Elyani."

"I understand," she said, blowing another joyful cloud onto me.

"So you left Woolly at the temple of Lasseera?"

"Yes. I decided I didn't want to speak to him any more. But I asked Gervin's advice first: I did not want personal matters to get in the way of the Archive mission. And do you know what Gervin said?"

"Mm..." I twinged my beard. "Yes! He said it would be excellent for Woolly's spiritual development if you refused to speak to him for a while."

Maryani frowned, "How did you know? Did Gervin tell you?"

"Hunh hunh! There are things I don't need to be told."

"Thunder knows Thunder," she laughed.

"Very much so. Tell me how the Archive stones are going."

"They're blossoming like the roses of Vasouk's gardens. The situation is lawfully fine, all obstacles overcome. Apart from Woolly's bad temper, I mean." She went on, "Normally, stones are left to crystallise in slime buckets for some time, and then taken out and left in the dry air. As long as they're in the slime, they're fragile. Subtle influences can make them dissolve. But dried out, they become quite stable.

A major problem with the Archive stones was that we never knew when the Archive transfer was going to take place, so we had to keep the stones in the slime until the last minute, when they were to be charged for the transfer. The stones stayed in the slime for years, which is why we lost so many of them. But the hermaphroditic stones which Woolly and I have been producing are much smarter. They can be programmed and reprogrammed, even after they have been dried out and stabilised."

"Have you already completed some of them?"

"Nearly!" Maryani said, her face made rounder by her satisfied expression. "Just give me two or three more weeks, and everything will be completed."

"Well, well... Maryani, I hate to tell you this, but there will have to be a change in the plan. I want all the stones to be left unfinished for the moment."

"*What is that in the Law?* Do you realise the amount of effort we have all put into these stones? We worked day and night to be ready in case the signal for the Archive transfer would be given earlier than expected."

"My... we have a few problems. Recently, I have learnt that the Black Hunters, and probably other groups of Nephilim Hunters with them, are regularly kept informed of the progress of our stones. These *bastards in the Law* even know about the Archive! Someone is leaking, and we don't know who. The grim reality is, as soon as the stones are finished we can expect a visit from the Hunters, and it won't be a friendly one."

Maryani let out Gervin's long loud whistle of impending cosmic catastrophe. "That blasts the b... I mean, it's incredible!"

"And it must remain totally secret. The only other person to be informed is Woolly. One of our problems is that the Renegade Hunters regard him as one of the best stone makers in the kingdom. They could try to abduct him."

"What?" Maryani's Dragon turned fierce. "So the Renegades want to start a war against us, is that it? Let me tell you, if they touch Woolly, they will have their war. But why didn't you warn us immediately?"

By the time the Archive transfer takes place, Maryani and Alcibyadi will already have left for the land of Aegypton. The Nagas will protect their way.

"Gervin and Esrevin wanted a few days of total secrecy, to maximise their chances of finding the traitor. In the meantime they personally guaranteed Woolly's safety. Anyhow, as long as you were with him I wasn't worried about him. The Hunters are no match for your powers."

"But what if Woolly went out of the temple alone?"

"Hunh hunh! Esrevin would not let him do that"

"What? But Woolly is wild! When he has something in mind, nothing can stop him, not even me!"

"Not even *you*?"

Maryani caught the smile. "I mean, sometimes not even me. But listen, Szar," she looked straight into my eyes, "I want to go and bring Woolly back to Eisraim myself, and as soon as possible. Agreed?"

"I think I had better agree, hadn't I?"

Maryani smiled with satisfaction and pulled a large, gorgeous yellow stone out of one of her dress pockets.

It was Lilu.

She voice-channelled to Lasseera, "Listen, Woolly," she told him, "I am still not talking to you, but I want you to stay in the temple and wait for me. It's very serious..."

To give them some privacy, I went onto the Blue priestesses' roof and contemplated the mists. So thick one couldn't even see Malchasek's tower.

I waited.

It took at least twenty minutes before Maryani joined me. "It's all arranged," she said with a confident Naga-smile. "He swore on the Last Matter that he would not move his ass from the chapel until I arrived."

"Little Naga, what's happening to your language?"

"I know, I have to be careful," she put on her candid smile.

Out of the Point-blue, she asked, "Will Woolly take part in the Archive transfer?"

From beyond the Fault of Eternity, the Flying Dragon will return.

"Of course! Woolly will be involved in every single stage of it. I want him to be with me on the Plateau of Sorana, when the stones of the two temples are united and the Masters of Thunder perform the transfer of the Archive into the Fields of Peace."

"If Woolly has to carry the Archive stone from Lasseera to the place of the transfer, will you let me accompany him?" Maryani asked.

By then, the five White Eagles will have nearly reached the land of Aegypton.

"Sounds like an excellent idea," I approved.

"I fear great danger, Szar! I want to be with him when it happens."

Lasseera, one large pyre. Esrevin, slaughtered by the giants. Melchard and Namron, killed in the hills. Then the giants will march on the temple of Eisraim.

We received a voice channel from Namron. "Szar, my friend in the Law, a team of sixteen *lawful masons* have arrived at the temple's main entrance. They have brought certain things for you."

"What is that in the Law?" I asked.

"A flagpole, fifty lawful feet long, and also a strange thing. A kind of turret, like the top of a lighthouse. It's very big."

"I'm coming, Namron."

"What is *that*?" Maryani's Dragon flared with curiosity.

"A friend of mine promised to send me a present," I said.

"Oh really? A present carried by sixteen *lawful masons*? Can I see?"

"Of course! Just join me at the temple's main entrance. Now excuse me, I need to run. I'll see you there," I said, stepping onto the neighbouring roof.

"I want to come with you over the roofs!" she said, and started following me.

I stopped, frowning at her.

"Ah, you are not going to start again?" she exclaimed. "I know exactly what I can and cannot do!"

My eyes looking straight into hers, my Dragon vroofing in the depths, Space Matrix geared into her Point, infinity above our heads, I walked slowly towards her.

Maryani, at times you are such an unlawful pain in the neck!

"What?" she said in a small voice, a touch bewildered, unsure of who or what was speaking to her.

I placed my hands on her shoulders and gave her a long and noisy brotherly kiss on the cheek. And I set off, running over the roofs.

"What?" she repeated. Then she started running after me, lifting her dress with both hands. "Wait! Wait for me!" she shouted.

I didn't have to wait, she ran and jumped like a filosterops. In less than three minutes we had reached the archway of the temple's main gate, where Namron lawfully greeted us.

The sixteen *lawful masons*, together with the small crowd that had gathered around them, all looked up and waved at us in a friendly manner.

Carrying the items was no small enterprise. The flagpole was too long to fit in the female wing's corridors. Namron, Maryani and I had to carry it over the roofs. That was the easy part.

Much more involved was the transport of the other item. It was a superb hexagonal turret, more than five feet high. The six sides were made of fine transparent pieces of plass, each approximately two feet wide. The pointed roof was made of copper and so was the floor, in the centre of which was a raised pedestal. On the pedestal, a large oil lamp had been fastened.

The structure was too wide to pass through the stairways of the female wing. So it had to be carried around the temple to a side entrance in the temple's far north, at the end of the female wing. From where it was taken to the courtyard of the Blue Robe. Namron's men helped the *lawful masons*, and so did all the priests who joined the joyful procession. Soon, many more priests and priestesses were attracted by the sound of laughter and handclapping. The small crowd welcomed each newcomer shouting, "Szar of the Brown Robe has received a present! It's for his roof." In turn the newcomers clapped their hands and joined in the excitement, and they came over to congratulate me.

When we arrived at their chapel, the Blue priestesses interrupted their prophecy ritual and came out to help, and they marvelled at the finely crafted work, and they brought out their ladders. Twenty men climbed onto the chapel roof. Using thick ropes, they hoisted the turret, making loud noises to call on the help of the gods. The enthusiastic crowd gave their support, only too happy to do their part by calling on the gods as well.

After great and lawful efforts, the turret finally reached the roof, to a loud ovation from the crowd. Then it took only five hours for the *lawful masons* to fix the turret on the roof. The crowd stayed on the lawn, carefully watching every move.

Finally, the flagpole was attached to the wall of Elyani's former bedroom, from where it reached high above the neighbouring roofs. When everything was completed, one of the *lawful masons* handed me a parcel in which I found a long, brown flag, and ropes to fix the flag to the pole. The first raising of the flag was met with loud and lawful jubilation from the crowd.

Then everyone spent some time lawfully congratulating everyone else. Standing on the Blue priestesses' roof I had to make a short lawful speech to thank the crowd for their support. After this the *lawful masons* left, the Blue priestesses went back to their ritual, and all the other priests and priestesses returned to their lawful occupations.

Left alone on the Blue priestesses' roof, I contemplated the turret.

What are you waiting for?

I went to get some oil from Elyani's room, filled up the lamp and lit a wick. Then I sat facing the direction of Elyani's window, which was still hidden by the mists.

Search successful. Engage travelling through intention.

"Oh, great!" I shouted in exasperation. "And what would happen if I did it?"

Fly Dragon! Fly high.

So easy.

Except, of course, that last time I had travelled with Space Matrix I had found myself spread from one side of the Great Cosmic Night to the other, my astral body haplessly turned inside out and all the rest undone, Gervin holding the Dragon bits together under the rain. Space Matrix wasn't exactly under control, to say the least. What if I mis-aimed at my target and found myself in the wrong room, astral-face to astral-face with one of the damn-obnoxious-idiotic-parrot-of-the-Law Immaculate priestesses?

Kuren-jaya, perhaps?

"Hush, man of the Law!" I told myself off and decided to test the Flying Dragons' guidance system by astral travelling to Maryani.

I tuned into her perky Naga-ravishing presence.

No response from Space Matrix.

I sneered, "If it's lawful you're not interested, is that it?"

I had to invoke the device formally,

Szar requesting access to Space Matrix for guidance towards Maryani.

Instantly,

Search successful. Engage travelling through intention.

It went so fast I didn't even see myself leave my body. My astral body found itself on the deck of a boat on the Holy Fontelayana river.

Maryani was on her way to Lasseera.

"Szar!" she noticed my presence immediately. "How lawfully nice of you to visit. I enjoyed our run on the roofs very much."

"Poor Namron had a bit of a shock when he saw you running with me."

"I don't think so. And how is your turret, *my friend in the Law*?"

"Already installed. I left my body beside it."

"Was it a present from Pelenor Ozorenan?" Maryani asked.

"What?" I was horrified. "Who told you the name of my visitor?"

"No one. It's just a supposition that an old priestess made after reading the aura of one of the guards who camped outside the temple. I heard it from a friend of mine, who was speaking to one of her friends. So she was right."

"Oh, no! No! Maryani... this was a *big* secret," I lamented.

"But it still is! Not everyone knows about it, and they are not even sure. I won't speak. Did the healing go well?"

I took my astral head in my astral hands. "I can't believe this."

"With a healer like you, I bet it all went well!" she boasted with her natural confidence. "If it hadn't gone well, Pelenor would have stayed more than two days. Did you know she is a remote cousin of mine, by the way?"

"That's it, Maryani!" I was *very* upset. "I don't want to hear one more word." I called onto Space Matrix,

For the Flying Dragons' sake, get me out of here!

12.26 Music fields

One evening I was practising my kuren-jaya drills when Ferman of the Field Wizards popped into the music hall. "Sorry to disturb you, Commander," the grey-haired fifty-year-old man said after we exchanged lawful greetings, "I need to check the music field. As you know, it's one of the fields which are to be transferred into the Archive."

I Point-watched his consciousness enter the field, but he moved far too fast for me to be able to follow what he was doing.

"Some beautiful sounds, you were playing," he commented.

I wasn't sure how to take this. I had just spent two hours shocking the space with the most ugly shrieks and buzzes, desperately trying to make my uuuhs last a few more seconds.

To my astonishment, Ferman made the field regurgitate a world of the gods' melody I had played earlier that day. Magnificent harmonies, straight from Revelation Sky.

"But how did you retrieve these sounds?" I asked.

My wonder brought a grin of satisfaction on the Field Wizard's face. "Do you realise that your music will be recorded in the Archive? Same as every single note that has been played with the music field since it was created. Thousands of years of music."

Field Wizards were *lawfully decent men of the Law* with an unlawfully inquisitive mind, a solid sense of humour, lots of stains on their light-grey gowns, and a healthy distaste for Immaculate priestesses. I liked them. But when trying to learn from them, one of my difficulties was that they didn't talk much – apart from the sempiternal watchyafeetforthebottles which they never tired of repeating when a non-initiate came into their chapel, or even to each other, just in case. Seeing Ferman was in such a talkative mood, I leapt at the opportunity.

"Every single note recorded forever!" I forced myself to look as bewildered as I really was. "How can that happen?"

"The principle is simple," Ferman took on the fatherly voice he used with young Wizards. "In normal life, whenever someone speaks or thinks, an imprint is left in the reflecting ethers. But the imprint doesn't last forever. The stuff of the reflecting ethers, even though subtle, isn't refined enough to keep the imprint for more than a certain length of time." He played a few simple notes and went on, "The music field generates its own reflecting ether, an ether of extremely refined quality. In it, the music field has kept all its memories. At the time of the transfer, this will be made to resonate with the Fields of Peace."

"And in the Fields of Peace, what will receive the memories?"

"Particular devices using the reflecting ether of the Fields of Peace, which is of phenomenal quality: incredibly subtle, and incorruptible. Time has no action on it, it keeps things forever." As he spoke, Ferman kept Point-tinkering with the music field. "For an eternal student like me, this Archive is going to be heaven. Do you know we will have access to *all* the damn knowledge of the temple, without restriction? The secrets of every order available to us..." he winked at me, "I can't wait for the disaster!"

When the giants march on Eisraim, the last hope will reside in the field that you and Ferman's Wizards will have created.

Suddenly thirstier for field knowledge, I pressed on, "Can you show me how this music field works?"

At last, you listen to your own voice!

I shivered.

Ferman lawfully politely pretended he hadn't noticed anything. "Sure, my boy!" was all he said. "Just tune in while I do the maintenance work."

From the Point, I watched him de-activate the field and check the power supply. "See how clever it is!" Ferman elucidated, "The power is derived from a large stream, through a particular type of device called a 'self-amplifying field'."

"What is that?"

"A field that draws power from an astral stream. The more power the field receives, the more power it can draw from the stream. Then the power is used to feed the music-field."

"I can't believe how simple it is!" I realised, watching him de-activate and restart the six self-amplifying fields that powered the hall. "But where does the music come from?"

Ferman directed my Point to a supermind space in which myriads of geometrical shapes were dancing.

"Simple," he said, "just connect that space to the power supply, and let a field connect it to the astral space of the hall."

"Is that all?"

"Yes and no. If you want sounds of high quality, then a lot of fine tuning is required."

As he was finishing his maintenance work, the gods inspired him, "You know, my boy," he blew his nose very loudly in the sleeve of his gown, not worrying about the fact that it created an Archive record, "if you wanted, you could create your own fields. That would actually be excellent training for you," he blew his nose again. "Would you like to have your own music field?"

"*Gang gang Gana!* Could I?" I couldn't believe my luck.

"Sure! Want me to show you how?"

Kayala-ha Perseps will give you a poisoned present. Use it to make a state-of-the-art field against the giants.

I promptly grabbed the offer, and we set off for my courtyard. As we walked across the park of lawful congregations, he explained, "I will help you set up the self-amplifying devices and the music field, and after that you can do everything yourself. Undo and redo the field plenty of times, try to make it better. That's the way to learn."

I pondered for a few minutes, then asked, "Could the field do other things than music?"

"Sure, my boy! All you have to do is connect it to other spaces. I'll show you." Passing through a large courtyard of the female wing, Ferman told me, "Once when I was a child, I came here and played a trick on the priestesses. I modified the program of the corridors' guidance system so it systematically brought them here, regardless of the destination they had Point-asked for." He giggled like a child, "I was hiding on the roof, watching their stupefied faces when they arrived in the courtyard. By the time my father arrived to do the repair, there were nearly thirty priestesses sitting on the lawn. My father was *very* upset!"

Arriving at my courtyard, Ferman admired the laurel trees. "I can see the White Eagles have been here," he gave an accomplice's smile. Then he got down to business. He started by tuning into the surrounding astral spaces. "We will take this stream," he quickly decided, directing my perception to the second astral layer above darkness visible.

"Why this one?"

"I've worked with it before. It's quite healthy. It has not suffered too much from the global deterioration."

In a matter of seconds, Ferman had set up the first self-amplifying device. "I'll set up a dozen for you, so you can have fun undoing and redoing them," he said. And less than five minutes later, he announced he had finished. "But the stream is strong, so you'd better watch the power levels carefully. If you boost the self-amplifying devices too much, the entire female wing will hear your music – as well as everything you're thinking!"

"Thanks for the tip!" I gulped, immediately Point-turning down the power.

It only took a few more minutes to connect the astral space of the courtyard to a sound-generating Point-field. "How far do you want the music field to extend?" Ferman asked.

We decided to include the entire territory: not only the courtyard, but also the two bedrooms.

Finally, Ferman walked the periphery of the chosen area, setting up tiny fields, the function of which was to reflect the astral sounds so the neighbours could not hear them. "Check the levels regularly," he warned, "otherwise the Blue priestesses' rituals will be interrupted by strange noises!"

And that was it. The music field was in place. Ferman briefly tested it with a few sounds, then he wished me *plenty of lawful fun* and left to check other fields.

The night had come. I went onto the roof and lit the lamp in the turret. It was still early, and the mists had cleared a little. In the tower of Malchasek, three windows were lit up. I sat and tuned into Elyani's.

Search successful. Engage travelling through intention.

I laughed. "Space Matrix, you really know how to stretch a Point!"

Why should a Flying Dragon not talk to an Immaculate?

"Now the voice is joining in too! Stop it! And what if I took you up on it, and Dragon-did it?"

Search successful. Engage travelling through intention.

I burst out laughing, "But... aren't you going to stop? This is turning into a conspiracy!"

And so what? It is a conspiracy for a good cause.

I was flabbergasted. "But..."

Elyani is desperate to hear from you. Why refuse to speak to her? Use the voice of your Flying Dragon nature.

"But I don't even know how to do that!" I protested.

Nonsense! You know perfectly well how to use this voice – your voice! You have already used it to tell Maryani to shut up.

"True!" I conceded.

I Dragon-stood up, geared my Point into the music field, and called on simple harmonies. The sound of saucepan and spoon resounded in darkness visible: bang-ting-ting, bang-ting-ting, bang-ting-ting...

"So, at the moment, I am talking to myself. Is that it?" I asked.

Your earthly self is conversing with your Flying Dragon nature.

I snapped my fingers and started dancing slowly, remembering the princely suite in Tomoristan – bang-ting-ting, bang-ting-ting...

"Do Flying Dragons know about love?"

Your Flying Dragon nature will spread the White Eagle's Love throughout the spheres of remoteness.

Above my head, an immense vastness.

"Suppose I spoke to Elyani... should I spread the voice through remoteness, or should I direct it to her with the Eagle's softness?"

What a stupid question!

"True!" I admitted, and kept dancing.

The vastness above further expanded. "That's it," loud sigh, "get me drunk!"

Bang-ting-ting, bang-ting-ting... I danced, swept by my Mother's vroofing waves.

Then in a split second, I aligned the Dragon below and the Flying Dragon above. Thunder was my witness.

The kingdom became small, the column of Spirit immense.

The silence of the spheres of remoteness sang above my head.

I spoke to her. "With all my heart, with all my mind, I am with you, even when I am far away. Forever love, White Eagle of the gods."

The fields of stars rejoiced, and the Black Night of Remoteness where the Dawn of Creation eternally rises, blessed my words.

From beyond the Abyss of the Deep and the Fault of Eternity, my father sent his blessing. So did the weird mathematical oneness of the spheres of the Great Ant. And from the spheres of the White Spider, from the Red Clouds, from the Blue Lagoon, from the Purple Cicada, from the Grey Light of Strangeness and from the Great Blue Void, voices combined with voices and echoed my message, again and again.

And I *knew* that Elyani had heard me.

12.27 Fridrick, you are dead!

Weeks passed.

The music field that Ferman had created made a major difference to my training: to practise kuren-jaya drills, I no longer had to wait for the music hall to be free. And I could combine Fridrick's exercises with the movements of the black dance. I still believed that, Point or no Point, it was through the black dance that I would overcome the Hunters in the end.

So I Point-practised and black-danced day and night, pushing my way through the exercises. But despite all my efforts, I remained unable to Point-hold continuous sounds for more than a minute. Kuren-jaya and the black dance shared one feature: each blow was potentially fatal. In a fight against the Hunters, one single leakage was more than enough to end up lying flat on the ground, venomised to the eyeballs, dead beyond recall. Each shriek and each buzz that broke the uuuh was like a death sentence.

The performance had improved to a degree, then it had come to a plateau. Nothing seemed able to get me to break through, not even Gervin's help, nor Fridrick's endless patience. Week after week, the Point's weak point remained.

One afternoon, after nearly twelve hours of continuous practice, I collapsed on the ground and shouted in total frustration, "Dragon's bile and Watchers' venom! I will never make it! Never!" As I let go of the Point, ugly buzzes quickly resounded one after the other. My face on the ground, I hit the lawn with my fists. "Elyani, my white panther... if only you could be here!"

Search successful. Engage travelling through intention.

"You Space Matrix go to Azazel and get lost!" I screamed. "Why don't you hold the Point for me instead of nagging me!"

The result was instant. A beautiful uuuh sound with no buzzing interruptions.

I sat up in amazement, letting my Flying Dragon nature gently hold the Point. The uuuh sound remained continuous.

The keynote of the Great Ant's consciousness is its clarity. Flying Dragons travel from the most remote spheres to come and admire it.

I quickly experimented with the whole range of sound frequencies Fridrick had shown me. Not *one* shriek. Not *one* buzz!

Nothing seemed to be able to unsettle the Point, not even my bewilderment. "How can it be so simple, after having been so impossible?" I was staggered.

Until today, your Point was not ready to connect with the Flying Dragon frequencies at the high end of the column of Spirit.

"So it is that simple!" I kept holding the uuuh sound. I snapped my fingers, "What am I supposed to do next?"

Kill Fridrick!

I burst out laughing and immediately voice-channelled the kuren-jaya man. "Fridrick! I think I am ready for a few more onslaughts. Would you have some time to practise with me?"

"Certainly, Commander. Shall I come and visit you at your place?"

"Please!" I asked. Then I went into Elyani's room and prepared a jug of glorious sunrise for my visitor.

In the last weeks, an odd friendship had gradually been developing between us. It couldn't possibly be real friendship because he was a Hunter (fed on Watcher's venom since his most tender years) and I wore Warriors' clothes under my brown robe (like those disgusting black nightmares). Lawfully, we had *nothing* in common, and *this was the truth*. Still, we spent hours playing music together. And we greatly enjoyed discussing all kinds of topics, from the caverns of Mount Lohrzen in the far south to Jex

Belaran's snowy summit in the far north, with the entire kingdom in the middle. Sometimes we talked from sunset to dawn – like me, Fridrick didn't sleep at night.

He was a sensitive man, still devastated from having lost his wife. He therefore fully understood what Elyani and I were going through. Once, sitting through a night on the roof, sharing memories in the company of Gagar of the Black Robe (a smart cat who often came to visit when Fridrick was around), the Hunter and I even found ourselves crying together, and it had made us laugh so loud that the Blue priestesses politely voice-channelled to ask if everything was *lawfully in order*. From that night onwards, Gagar always sat on Fridrick's lap when we sat on the roof. Cats, I concluded, liked Nephilim spice, especially Wise Witches' cats with sharp black eyes like Gagar's.

That afternoon, when Fridrick arrived in the courtyard, the first thing he did was try my music field.

"Ohh!" he exclaimed, letting a choir of low-pitched angelic voices resound in the space, "you've changed the sound field. Again!"

"Last night, I decided I didn't like its timbre. I made a new one from scratch."

"This one is fantastic! There's living depth in the sounds," Fridrick said with a tone of envy, and he improvised a melody with sharp, vibrant sounds like I had never heard.

"This is amazing, Fridrick! What kind of sound is it?"

"A musical instrument of the future. It works with little hammers. I saw it once when I was exploring one of Jex Belaran's musical Knowledge Banks."

I clapped my hands, following his rhythm. "I wish I could spy on these Knowledge Banks!"

"Careful, Commander!" Fridrick grinned. "Jex Belaran's musical Knowledge Banks are full of the Watchers' music. What if you fell in love with it?"

"The music of the Watchers..." it left me thoughtful. "Now, *that* must be extraordinary."

"Extraordinary is the lawful word! Want me to show you some of it?" he offered.

Stay away from the music of the Watchers!

I swallowed hard, startled by the vigour with which the voice had hammered the order into my consciousness.

To avoid offending Fridrick, I took on a playful voice, "My friend, I already nearly succumbed to one of their daughters. Then I did succumb to their cuisine. If moreover I were to succumb to their music..."

"All right!" he laughed. "I won't try to tempt you. But let me tell you, you don't know what you are missing."

He is right. The music of the Watchers is enthrallingly magnificent.

"I believe you, Fridrick." But no regrets.

To begin the practice, he called an unbroken uuuh sound, which he Point-held for a moment. Then he let me take control of the space, carefully observing my energy.

"Fantastic, Commander!" Without delay, he tried an entire palette of unsettling frequencies, one after the other.

No buzzes. No shrieks. My uuuh sound held.

Fridrick was puzzled. He went on connecting me with more and more difficult spaces, which sent extraordinarily fast-moving unsettling influences.

The uuuh sound stayed unbroken.

Fridrick frowned. "How did you do that? Did you manipulate the music field?"

I shook my head.

Fridrick stood rock-still, his Point-perception totally focussed on me. "Some weird energies are moving through your column of Spirit, Commander."

I kept eye contact with him, ignoring his comment.

He insisted, "Will you tell me what these are?"

Three and only three castes are to know: the Masters of Thunder, the White Eagles, and the Immaculate. Telling anyone else about your Flying Dragon nature would have disastrous consequences.

As I kept silent, the tension built up.

In the weeks prior to this meeting, Fridrick had been giving generously – time, advice, techniques, tricks and secrets. Refusing to answer his question was nothing short of an insult. It not only jeopardised a precious friendship, but also the operation against the Hunters.

The uuuh sound was still going on. I tuned into the clear fountain, seeking inspiration.

Fridrick remained implacable, holding onto the Point and waiting for my answer.

Clicking my fingers, I called onto Gervin's high presence while blasting the astral space of the music field with roaring thunder.

The clamour was shockingly loud. Anyone normal would have jumped. Firmly grounded in his Point-fortress, the Hunter did not budge.

"The Masters of Thunder!" A strange expression appeared on his face. "Are they as powerful as the people of Eisraim like to believe?" he asked.

The continuous uuuh sound still resounding in the background, I gave a nod.

Seemingly satisfied with this explanation he smiled, but did not relax. "Let's see, then... warm up your Point, man of the Law!" he said in a cool voice.

The music field was made silent. I called onto the triangular seal and other protection techniques Gervin had taught me.

Fridrick started with his methods of Point-unsettling, throwing wave after wave at me.

Nothing worked. I remained perfectly sealed.

He called onto more force.

The triangular seal automatically raised the Point-intensity, and the power became awesome. But no venom shower made its way through my Point.

Fridrick didn't speak. He just projected influences at me. Weird vibrations he had never shown me before.

Menacing hissing sounds above my head. The Point held fast.

Right now, Fridrick is unleashing all his power.

I started the slow movements of the black dance.

The hissing Point-intensity further built up.

Now, move towards Fridrick!

Holding onto the power, I started walking slowly towards him.

The Hunter turned pale. The hissing became deafening.

Silent sounds. One hundred Flying Dragons are crossing the spheres of the Great Ant. Remember the rendezvous.

It seemed to take an aeon before I reached him.

In the Blue Lagoon, the Flying Dragon is waiting for the Immaculate priestess. Will you not help?

I was now just in front of Fridrick.

Had it been a real fight, I could have delivered a volley of deadly blows.

Instead, I smiled at him and gently pressed my finger against a vital gateway close to his heart. "Fridrick, you are dead!"

The hissing sounds and the Point-intensity suddenly stopped. Fridrick burst into tears.

"Hey!" I took his arm. "What's happening to you, man of the Law?"

Fridrick was so dizzy he nearly fell down. I helped him sit on the lawn and quickly injected life force into his gateways. And I handed him a cup of glorious sunrise.

Heartened by the beverage, he soon regained his countenance. But he didn't speak to me.

"What was happening?" I finally asked.

He shrugged his shoulders. "I must have pushed the intensity too far."

"And now, are you all right?"

He did not answer for a while. Then he looked straight into my eyes, "Now we can start preparing the attack against the Foxes. I must liaise with Jex Belaran." And he stood up, ready to go.

"Do you want to stay and play the music field before you go?"

He had already turned away. "Lawful thanks, no," he said without turning back, and he left.

– Thus Ends the Book of the Flying Dragons –

13

The Book of the Encounters with Evil

13.1 Looming disaster

Poor Fridrick! According to the Hunters, the Point of Eisraim priests was only good for theurgy (which Renegade Hunters understood as the art of kissing angels' asses). It must have come as a shock that a Point woven for the purpose of theurgy proved more resistant than his Point-fortress built over twelve years of war exercises. Still, the way he had walked out on me was puzzling.

Even more puzzling, why had the voice included the Immaculate on the list of the castes to whom I could disclose my Flying Dragon nature? And anyway, why would those damn obnoxious parrots even want to know?

Speak to Teyani.

I was always ready to speak to Teyani.

In the last days, you will be her only friend.

I turned to a voice channel in darkness visible, "*Praise the Lord Melchisedek Lady Teyani*, wise woman in the Law, great among the sages of Eisraim, restorer of the unique and magnificent order of the White Eagle, teacher of the priestesses who saved my life so many times, and soon-to-be grandmother of one of the mighty founders of the kingdom of the rainbows."

Teyani received me and laughed. "*All glory to the Lord Melchisedek, Szar of the Dragon above and the Dragon below*. Are you in a joyful mood, *my great man in the Law*?"

I voice-channelled a long sigh.

The subject turned straight to Alcibyadi, whose golden light of pregnancy was blossoming by the day. Burning with curiosity, we were anxiously waiting for the baby's soul to land in Alcibyadi's energy. We could hardly wait to read the secrets of its past lives – prophetic reading of babies' souls being one of the favourite activities of Atlantean initiate-grandmothers. Finally I asked Teyani if she had received any news from Elyani.

"None," she answered with concern. "Neither has Melchard."

I picked up a violet flower. An ant was crawling on its petals. "It's been many weeks now. Shouldn't we start worrying?"

Teyani hesitated, "During the past year the Immaculate priestesses alienated the entire temple by releasing bad news about Holma. Perhaps this time they have decided to shroud Elyani's preparations for the ascension ritual in complete secrecy."

"Then we should definitely worry," I decided, tickled by the ant which had found its way to my arm. "Teyani, I must tell you, I often speak to Elyani with my Flying Dragon voice."

"I know! You often speak to me too," she said.

"Sweet Lord Melchisedek!" I swallowed. "Do I?"

Teyani's laughter ran through darkness visible like a fresh stream of joy.

"Hum... Teyani... what sort of things have I told you lately?"

"Don't worry," she took on her motherly voice, "your Flying Dragon nature is very wise. It speaks kind words of encouragement. And by the way, the other day you invited me to travel with you to the remote spheres of the Great Ant. Some kind of birthday celebration for Flying Dragons."

"I see..." I was carefully trying to extract the little ant from my gown without hurting it. "Teyani, I don't understand why Elyani never speaks to me through the Eagle. Does she speak to you?"

"Elyani is not allowed to invoke the White Eagle," Teyani said.

"What?" I exclaimed. "But that is disgusting!"

"*Wait, man of the Law!* Elyani is undergoing a phase of total silence. It is a beautiful practice, leading to phenomenal openings."

"Does it not disturb her silence when my Flying Dragon voice speaks to her?"

"The voices of the Flying Dragons come from beyond the spheres of Melchisedek. They are part of the universal silence of creation," the wise woman said. "Don't stop."

She sensed my distress. "Don't forget that Elyani is preparing herself for one of the most extraordinary rituals of the entire Law. At the moment she might well be full of energy, flying high in Spirit."

No, Teyani, Elyani is going through an ordeal, her energy ravaged by the ritual offering of the elemental forces of nature. Torrents of elemental slime are washing out her life force. Her health is fast deteriorating.

An icy shiver ran from one end of the cosmological ladder to the other.

"Did you hear what you just said?" Teyani asked.

"Yes, I heard," I said, my consternation mounting.

The voice channel remained blank for a while. Then I exploded. "Teyani, there *must* be something we can do. We can't just sit back and let her die!"

Teyani deliberated, "I need to seek advice on the Law of the Immaculate. Meanwhile, wait!" she added in a tone of warning. "Do not attempt anything without speaking to me first."

I answered with the silence of the Dragon.

Teyani's heartness poured through the channel, "I love you, Szar."

Forever love, White Eagle.

The channel closed, I was left annihilated.

"Oh, gods! How can this be? Gods, gods... is *this* what you wanted?"

The gods are wise.

"The gods are wise?" I clenched two angry fists. "Cosmic nonsense!"

I could have screamed the Dragon out of the Underworld. I found myself contemplating the mists, singing,

"*What does a madman do when his house is melting? He dances. He dances.*"

A presence was approaching. The temptation to jump on the roof and run away was great.

The Dragon kept me still.

It was Mouridji the prophetess. She came in and gave a lawful greeting. After the Dragon returned the salute for me, she asked in a small voice, "You said that perhaps you could help me with my hip. It's been getting worse and worse in the last weeks." The old woman looked tired, sad, forlorn. She hesitated, sensing something was wrong, "But if now is not a good time, I can come back another day..."

It took me a few seconds to find my way out of the vagueness. "I think..." I opened a smile, calling on the warmth of the Brown Robe, "I think now is an excellent time, Mouridji!"

I helped her lie down on the lawn and let my hands run on her gateways, exploring her energy. Her pain felt like an ugly etheric false note. "Mouridji, this Dragon-hurts! You should have come much earlier."

"Well, son, for *an old carcass in the Law* like me, walking to your place is no small enterprise. And I don't like to disturb you when you stop in the stairway next to my room."

I bit my lip, ashamed of having forgotten her. "Now, what do I feel here? You have bad stomach pains too, haven't you? And your right knee hurts."

She laughed philosophically, "*The privileges that come with old age!*"

Giving hope. One of the highest missions of the Masters of Thunder.

"Mouridji, you are going to receive the kind of healing a princess would envy," I winked at her, and she knew that I knew that she knew very well Pelenor Ozorenan had been my guest.

She replied with an accomplice's smile.

As I worked on her gateways, Mouridji smiled, "This brown flag you put up, what a beauty! I'm sure it makes Elyani very happy each time she looks through her window."

"Do you think it's all right?" I asked.

"I think it's lawfully wonderful. In the temple, we all think it's lawfully wonderful. I can tell you, from what some people have told me. And if the Immaculate raise objections, well, let's throw them out of the temple!" she was, as usual, unambiguous.

I gave a short sardonic laugh. "And who will do the ascension ritual, wise woman in the Law?"

"You, of course!" Mouridji exclaimed, as if it was plainly obvious.

"Me?" The sardonic laughter rang again.

"Yes, you! If need be, your teacher will help you. This Gervin of the Brown Robe, he is *so clever in the Law*!"

Something flared in the fountain. "Gervin of the Brown Robe performing Elyani's ascension ritual. Now, *that's* an idea, Mouridji!" I thought aloud.

Conjectures ran wild as I was completing the healing.

When I finished, I went and took down the flag, then came back to Mouridji and instructed her to clasp her arms around my neck. Lifting her frail body in my arms, I stood up. "How about flying back home?"

She was flabbergasted. "Do you mean you would carry Mouridji back to her room?"

"Of course I am going to carry Mouridji back to her room!"

The old prophetess giggled, "I hope we meet all my friends on the way!" But as I started walking she had second thoughts. Picking up the ant which had finally found its way to my beard, she said, "But what will Elyani think when she hears about this? Won't she be unhappy with me?"

"Not at all, Mouridji! I think Elyani is going to be *very* grateful to you!"

13.2 Poetry in remoteness

Once more the corridors' guidance system sent me an inspiration. As I was Point-walking back to the courtyard, I decided I would not make a move until the following morning. Some sound thinking was required.

Arriving home, I raised the flag and went straight up on the roof. The dying light of day cast its red glow over the tower of Malchasek, making me feel unsettled. My Dragon became restless. "I can't just sit here and let her die!"

I voice-channelled Gervin, "Help, wise man in the Law! Can I come and talk to you?"

"I was just about to call you! I have some news for you. A thunderous surprise!"

"About Elyani?"

Gervin caught the urgency behind my call. "Come right now! It is not about Elyani."

"Right now!" Twenty seconds to take down the flag and I was on my way running full speed over the roofs.

Three lawful minutes later I was sitting in front of Gervin.

"Let me start with the surprise," he announced triumphantly. "Praise the Great Apollo, the date for your initiation as a Master of Thunder has been decided. It will be the day of the New Moon, ten lunations from today."

When he saw all I could raise was a feeble smile, Gervin let out a long whistle. "I see. We are in big trouble, aren't we?"

"Big trouble!" I reported the facts about Elyani, then without a pause I asked, "Can the Masters of Thunder carry out Elyani's ascension ritual instead of the Immaculate?"

Tuning high in Thunder, Gervin became rock-still, bringing down a charged silence which pushed the *living walls* away, turning the aquamarine chamber into a huge hall vibrant with liquid darkness.

Archive Hall One.

One second later, the aquamarine chamber went back to kingdom normality. "Son," Gervin said in a gentle voice, "I have no idea what this ritual is about. And rituals are like cooking recipes: they are not just lists of instructions that anyone can follow; they are powerful forces transmitted from person to person. The Immaculate are the custodians of the ascension ritual."

I contemplated my left palm, slowly clenching my fist. "Can't we pull the forces from one of our Universal Knowledge Banks? Or can't we find another way to send Elyani to the world of the gods?"

Gervin remained silent, Point-scanning mysterious horizons.

I became impatient and stood up. "I can be anything, I can do anything. Right?" I exclaimed. "Well, I am going to find a way to deliver Elyani to the gods. But for a start, I am going to extract her from the clutches of the Immaculate." Looking straight into Gervin's eyes, I added, "Right now!"

Gervin thundered, "Right now you are going to sit down and do nothing!"

Stunned by the intensity in his voice, I sat down.

"Listen, and listen well!" Gervin continued, throwing force behind each word. "In our lineage there is a well-known principle. When a man is about to receive the initiation as a Master of Thunder, he will be tempted by the Prince of Darkness. Circumstances will concur to make him lose his sanity and deviate from his path. This is *exactly* what's happening to you at the moment! If you yield to your anger and behave like a fool, you will destroy everything!" He shouted, "*Everything!*"

True, I was reacting with anger.

Keeping eye contact with the master, I let the Dragon slowly unclench my fists and teeth. "Letting Elyani die in front of me without reacting," I held fast to the clear fountain, "is this the price I have to pay to become a Master of Thunder?"

"No!" Gervin yelled at me, shocking me with the Voice. "No, we are not going to wait and let Elyani die without doing a thing!" Seeing the unlawfully stupefied expression on my face, he burst out laughing and blasted my heart with his warmth. "But that does not mean we should behave like idiots!"

I swallowed hard.

Gervin pointed his index at me, "Think, my son! Think!"

I drew a long, slow breath, "I thought that asking you and the Masters of Thunder to take care of Elyani's ascension ritual was a good idea."

"And what are we going to tell the Immaculate?" Gervin retorted.

"Can't we just throw them out of the temple?"

"Ha!" Gervin's monosyllabic laughter made the *living walls* tremble. "That would certainly make quite a few people happy. The problem is, it would also poison our relationship with the King of Atlantis. The Immaculate are powerful. If they decide to start plotting against our temple, there is no limit to the amount of intrigue they can foment. And if there is *one* thing we don't need at the moment, it's a diplomatic imbroglio with the King's palace."

Three white roses.

I shrugged scathingly. "Isn't our world going to collapse anyway? Once the fields cease functioning, what difference will it make if we are on bad terms with the King of Atlantis?"

"*No way, man of the Law!*" Gervin was unbending. "There is too much at stake with the Archive. We *cannot* afford to take the risk of facing retaliation from the King's army."

Woe to the young fool if he does not listen to his own voice!

"All right, all right!" I thought. "I'm listening."

Three white roses.

We held a cogitative silence, until I snapped my fingers. "Gervin, I have an idea. It comes straight from the Flying Dragons!"

Gervin twinged his beard, "*What is that in the Law?*"

"What if I found an Immaculate priestess who was ready to conduct Elyani's ritual in collaboration with the Masters of Thunder?"

"Mm...?" Gervin sounded interested.

I snapped my fingers again, "And what if a princess friend of mine convinced the King of Atlantis to call the two Immaculate away from Eisraim, and have them replaced by the other one?"

"Now *that* would make a lot of sense. Tell me more about this Immaculate."

"Her name is Hermina. I met her in the palace of Tomoristan. She is a magnificent soul, Gervin! A great saint who shines with bright-white light and pours love around her like a fountain."

Gervin didn't seem fully convinced. "If she wanted to help us, this would be an excellent plan. But why would she?"

Hermina will help.

"Well..." I hesitated.

Woe to the young fool...

"Gervin, I *know* Hermina will help!" I said with total conviction.

"Oho!" Gervin's smile reflected the warmth of my enthusiasm. Keeping eye contact with me, he paused somewhere in Highness, making the creation hold its breath. It lasted an aeon or two.

"You Flying Dragons will do anything you can to protect the Eagle, won't you?" he finally said, and the creation started breathing again.

My eyes filled with tears.

"Poetry in remoteness. Such a beautiful story, really," he said with sincere admiration. "And one that started long ago. So long ago that when you read what our Archive says about it, you will be astonished."

Edge of Highness. Whiteness eternal. Forever love.

"Gervin, wise man in the Law, please protect me from myself. I don't want to destroy your grand enterprise with my foolishness. If you think I am going astray, I beg you, say so!"

Gervin shook his head. "I can't imagine a better plan than this."

"Do I have your blessing to go to Tomoristan and ask Pelenor Ozorenan for her help?" I asked.

"Take the first boat! But be careful, the period that begins now is the most dangerous of your entire life. The Prince of Darkness knows the time of your initiation as a Master of Thunder is coming. He will seize *any* opportunity to seduce you from your path."

13.3 The princely palace of Tomoristan

Pelenor was shining. "Szar prian! Did you know I was just about to send you *the* message?"

I tucked my head in my shoulders. "Praise the Lord Melchisedek! Yes, I can see it!" I exclaimed, tuning into the hues of golden light in her aura. The conception gateways which Space Matrix had repaired were swollen, replete with life force. The channels running through her breasts were shining-yellow bright.

Bursting with joy, she took my hands. "Your healing succeeded, Szar! I am pregnant!"

I was about to launch a loud scream of exultation but hastily contained myself, glancing right and left. The huge royal lounge, packed with furniture and works of art, wasn't conducive to loud demonstrations of joy. And needless to say, there was field upon field throughout the room.

"It's all right!" Pelenor reassured me, seeing me hesitate. "This room is not completely safe, but it is protocol-free. Szar!" her eyes were lustrous, "I am so happy! I am *so* happy! Three months ago when you came here, my life was a nightmare. Now," she raised her arms, "you have made me a princess again!"

Using a special technique Gervin had taught me, I Point-sent a question into her mind, in a way that no channel of darkness visible could pick up, "The father is Henrick the prian, isn't he?"

She had one second of hesitation, then looked straight into my eyes and gave a nod.

"Princess Pelenor," I applauded, "this will no doubt be a special child, born from such special parents."

Danger, son! Danger! In less than two hours, the bell will toll.

"Thank you," Pelenor answered from deep inside her heart.

I thanked her for the flag and the turret, describing the joyful turmoil her presents had created in the temple. She liked the story, asked a few questions and inquired about Alcibyadi, but concluded, "Szar prian, you haven't come all the way from Eisraim to have a lawful chat with me, have you?"

Tell this woman your visions of the invasion by the giants.

"Pelenor," I told her, "last time I came to your palace I was happier than ever before in my life, and you were desperately in need of my help. Now the wheel of the Law has turned. I am the one who needs your help. Desperately."

She frowned, a lawfully cautious expression on her face. "Szar the prian, in need of Pelenor's help?"

"Elyani's health has been deteriorating fast. With these two Immaculate priestesses in charge of her, there is nothing I can do about it. I need to find Hermina and her attendant Jinia, and I need your help to convince the King of Atlantis to send them to Eisraim, and recall the other two."

"Do you really think Hermina will help you?" Pelenor seemed dubious. "She's never been particularly helpful to me."

One day, God will ask you to destroy a city.

"I am *convinced* Hermina will help. Can I see her?"

"She is no longer in Tomoristan. If I remember well, you and Elyani had to leave the palace in a hurry. After you left, Hermina asked for you. Her attendant was dying. She thought maybe you could heal her."

I bit my lip. "Jinia died? How did that happen?"

"I have no idea. Some illness. After that Hermina left the palace."

Jinia, little Flying Dragon lost in an unfriendly kingdom. How could I let you go? I am sorry, Jinia. I am so sorry.

"Finding Hermina shouldn't be too difficult," Pelenor went on.

Jinia, friend and sister in infinity, I swear on remoteness I will find you, I will take care of you.

"What about getting the King of Atlantis to intervene?" I asked.

"Leave it to me. I will arrange this for you, Sir Great Dragon, but..." Pelenor brought her index to the level of her nose and pointed it at me, painting a mysterious smile on her face, "do you know that you could do it yourself?"

No! Virginia, Virginia, I don't want you to die!

"Me? How would I get a hearing at the King's court?"

Brother Knight, face reality! If you do not destroy Philadelphia Six, the Rex will destroy us all.

Bringing her hands together in a clap, she announced, "Prince Filipotonisteraniso Ozorenan, my dear husband, has decided to bestow a title on you, in appreciation of the outstanding service you have rendered to his county."

"A title? On me?" I burst out laughing, Gervin-fashion. "What title?"

No way! No way! You damn son of a bitch! Realise how many people live in Philadelphia Six?

"Lord of the pink ribbon," she said. "Do you know what it is?"

I raised my hands. "I have no idea!" I answered apologetically.

Bleeding Sun. I can't possibly let that happen! Virginia... No!

"The pink ribbon is enough to get you an audience with the King of Atlantis," Pelenor had an aristocratic glitter in her eyes.

Who's taking the mission?

I let out a long whistle. "Did you help?" I asked.

Hiram, of course. High command wants you and Marek to fly with him.

Pelenor shrugged, "Only a little bit. Filipotonisteraniso wanted to grant you a green ribbon. I convinced him that if he really loved me he had to go at least two grades up, which took you to pink."

Hiram my brother. Hiram my son. How can I possibly do that to you?

"This pink ribbon, what does it look like?" I asked thoughtfully.

Stuff you! Stuff you and stuff your damn mission! Tell Lavash he can go to hell.

"Well..." Pelenor answered, "quite pink, I'd say. You are to attach it to your Brown Robe, on top of your heart."

Fine, Brother Knight! Fine! Wimp out and kill us all, if that's what you want. For God's sake, face reality! The Rex is winning. We're losing the fucking war. The Philadelphias are about to be wiped out. One more battle and there won't be anything left of us.

Pelenor took my hand. "What is happening to you, Szar?" she searched my face. "Sometimes your eyes look strange." There was gentleness in her voice.

Philadelphia Six. A sea of flames.

I shook my head briskly. "Too many visions rushing through my head."

"Are you all right?" she asked.

"Yes, yes," I smiled. "How am I supposed to thank you for the pink ribbon, Princess Pelenor?"

"Thank me?" the Nephilim woman wouldn't hear of it. "Don't even thought-form it! *I* am the one that will thank you, by making sure that Hermina lands in your temple as soon as possible."

Tell Pelenor about the giants!

In the warm space of opening that shone between us, I let the clear fountain speak, "Pelenor, there are other matters I want to discuss with you." I called onto the compassion of my master and went on, "Friend, I see dark clouds coming onto your county. I wish to give you an early warning so you have a chance to protect yourself, and your child. In a few months, or perhaps a few years – no one can know these things with absolute certainty – there will come an ominous night. Dogs and other animals will go mad and wake everyone up. This will be a crucial sign. The people of my temple call it the night of the howling dogs. When this takes place, flee, Pelenor! Flee Tomoristan. Take refuge with your friends of Jex Belaran. Soon after, great unrest will stir the kingdom. Invaders from the east will besiege your city."

"Oh my Lord Melchisedek!" she turned pale with dread. "Are the giants really coming?"

"Who spoke to you about this?"

"My husband has been warned of the danger of invasion, but he and his generals refuse to take the threat seriously."

"Who wants to believe in looming disasters?" I sighed. "For decades my teacher has been trying to warn people the fields are going to collapse, and no one has ever listened to him. I would never venture to prophesy for a court, even with a pink ribbon. If I speak to you now, it is because I care about you."

"I believe you!" she said, tears in her eyes. "Tell me what will happen."

"There will be great disturbances in the fields, which will bring chaos to all the counties in our part of the kingdom. The giants will take advantage of it to go on the rampage. If my vision is correct, it will not be a pretty sight. There won't be much left of Tomoristan after the giants take it. By then, I believe that Jex Belaran will be one of the only safe places in the kingdom. Go and take refuge with Kayala-ha Perseps. The Hunters will protect you."

For years, I had heard Gervin say how much he loathed prophesying catastrophes. Now, I realised why. Pelenor was devastated. I had sapped her joy and wiped the triumphant smile off her face.

A poor way of repaying her friendship.

She cradled her belly with her hands. "Will my child live?" she asked.

"If you fly away early, you will escape the onslaught. I believe you will listen to me, and I believe you and your child will live. This is why I speak to you."

Pelenor wanted me to give more details, but what could I say? All I could foresee was a huge dark cloud sweeping through the kingdom, creating havoc everywhere. "Why don't you go and pay Felicia a short visit in the coming days?" I suggested. "I imagine the Hunters would have received the same information as your husband. They probably know much more about these things than I do."

Pelenor went on asking questions, but there was nothing more I could tell her. I kept the meeting short. As I was about to take leave, I pulled two jars out of one of my gown's large pockets. "Could I ask you to forward this present to Felicia? This one is honey-pickled cucumbers, so... you can easily guess what the other one is."

"Cinnamon sauce!" She lightly touched my face with her fingers, "Should I convey a message when I deliver the present?"

Thank Felicia for the help she has given you with regard to Perseps.

I couldn't possibly say that! The breach of secrecy would have been a blatant betrayal of the agreement made with Perseps.

Woe to the young fool...

"Yes, Pelenor!" I burst out. "Thank Felicia for the help she has given me with regard to Perseps."

13.4 Rendezvous at the edge of the abyss

The mists were so thick I could hardly see fifteen lawful feet in front of me. Nothing unusual for Tomoristan.

I was sitting on the quay, waiting for the boat that was to take me back to Eisraim, when Fridrick Point-called me, *"Commander, I have received a message from Jex Belaran. The seed-connection of the Red Renegades is about to collapse! This means we must strike the Foxes immediately, so they believe they are being attacked by the Red Renegades. There is not a minute to waste. Perseps has already sent his men to create the diversion and empty their headquarters for you. He expects you to be there, ready to steal the seed-connection stone."*

"Right now?" I Point-asked. "I was just about to come back from Tomoristan."

"Don't. Go north. The village that harbours the Foxes' headquarters is called Raelene Vale. It is located in the northern part of the county of the Northern Lakes, close to the Snowy Mountains. I will give you all the details."

"But what about you, Fridrick? Where are you?"

"In Lasseera. I will join you as quickly as I can. Now listen, to reach Raelene Vale, you'll..."

"Hey, Point-wait a minute, Fridrick! You haven't yet told me how I am supposed to throw venom at these people so they believe the mischief comes from the Red Renegades."

"I'll have to teach you how to do this from a distance. For an expert in the Point like you, Commander, that should be no problem." Point-sharp, he picked up my hesitation, "Listen, Commander! Once the Red Renegades' seed-connection goes flat, there is no way in the seven spheres we will get them and the Foxes to slaughter each other, and we'll have all of them on our back. If we do not take our chance now, Perseps' plan is finished. We have asked for an alliance with Jex Belaran, now..."

"All right, Fridrick," I Point-interrupted. "Let me Point-communicate with Gervin first, and I will get back to you immediately."

I stood up. "What does a madman do when his cow is dying? He dances. He dances..."

My chanting roused an old lady sitting close by. She stared at me.

"Nice mists, today, wise mother in the Law!" I smiled at her, lawfully showing my teeth.

She didn't respond. She just turned her head and went back to staring at the mists.

I let it roll off my shoulders and Point-called Gervin.

When he heard what Fridrick had said, he expressed deep concern. "I don't like the sound of this!" he Point-said. "I sense danger. Great danger."

"Do you think I am not yet ready to fight against the Fox Hunters?"

"Mm... no, not that. The real danger lies in that seed-connection stone from which the Foxes derive their power. Once you take possession of it, what are you supposed to do with it?"

"Fridrick will deactivate it through a particular ritual. It sounds like there could be a few spiders in the potage, but what do we do? If we let Perseps down now, why would he ever make an alliance with us again?"

"I know," Gervin Point-agreed. "Yet this stone worries me. The consciousness that comes from it will completely disconnect you from me and the Masters of Thunder."

"Gervin, I believe I should do it, but you are the one who decides."

"I too believe you should do it, but I don't like what is coming. See, son, until now, in every trial you went through I was with you. Even in the bowels of Mount Lohrzen, and in the Red Canyons, when you were healing the Nephilim priestess. You thought I had forgotten you, but you were wrong. I was with you, day after day, night after night. But this time... you will be alone."

"Well then," I hesitated, "perhaps we should delay all this. Maybe I need more preparation."

"There is no time for more preparation. The warp of fields is dying, and so is the kingdom. The time of the Archive transfer is drawing near."

"Alone, do I really stand a chance?" I put it to him.

"We must hope that something greater than all obstacles will be with you. Pray to the Mother of the Light that Truth and Truth alone will prevail."

13.5 Raiding the Foxes' headquarters

It was night. Dressed in the traditional outfit of the Red Renegades, I was sitting in a wood close to Raelene Vale, ready to strike, and wondering how it would feel to kill a man.

Finding the place had been easy. Fridrick had sent me directions through Point-communication. He had also taught me the Red Renegades' style of throwing venom. Not very complicated, really. Whether I would be capable of using the method to kill the Fox Hunters who guarded the precious stone was another matter. According to Perseps' plan, however, that did not matter much. All I had to do was kill the guards, be it just with my bare fists. And then pour red venom into them so as to create suspicion.

Perseps' plan was simple. The Fox Hunters had launched one of their seasonal expeditions into the county of Perentie, east of the Northern Lakes, with more than half their men. Yesterday, so I was told, another nine of them had been called to a mission in the south, so that less than ten men were left in their headquarters – a vast mansion surrounded by warehouses in which the Foxes kept their plunder. Soon a commando of mercenaries sent by Perseps was to set the warehouses in flames, to create a diversion. I had been given the secret code to enter the protection Point-field unnoticed. My instructions were straightforward: let Fridrick Point-guide me to the crypt where the seed-connection stone was kept, catch hold of the stone, and run.

And... kill anyone I met on my way.

The whole plan hinged on one factor: my Point-signature was radically different from that of Jex Belaran's Hunters. And this would be how to convince the Foxes that the Red Renegades had stolen their stone. Had I been trained in Jex Belaran, the Foxes would immediately have detected me by the energy of my Point. Which was why Perseps' Hunters could not have carried out the mission. An outsider was needed, a man who had never participated in fights between rival clans – and yet a man who could kill from the Point.

As soon as the Foxes' stone was in my hands, I was to go south. The stone experts of Jex Belaran had worked out a system whereby its radiation would be eclipsed for twelve days. Meanwhile the radiation of the Red Renegades' seed-connection stone would be artificially boosted, so the Foxes would rush to butcher Fonken the Red and his men.

Twelve days... there lay the hitch! If Fridrick could not deactivate the stone in time, its radiation would become perceptible from afar, and all the Renegade Hunters of the kingdom would be after me: the Foxes, for a start, but also the Red Renegades, desperate to find a new seed-connection stone. The Black Hunters too would be after me, seeing in that damn stone the ideal opportunity to gain absolute supremacy. And so would anyone else in the kingdom who fancied starting a new clan of Renegades.

"What does a madman do when his shed is melting? He dances. He dances." Leaning against a tree, I spent hours slowly clenching and unclenching my left fist, practising the superior art of waiting that Dragon-Master Marek had taught me.

The night was so dark I could not even see my palm. I wondered what Elyani was doing.

Search successful. Engage travelling through intention.

"Space Matrix never gives up, eh?"

If Hermina took over from the other two Immaculate, would she allow me to see Elyani? Maybe not, after all. Anyway, even if she did, the game was likely to be cruel. Elyani's face would remain veiled. The Law of the Immaculate would forbid me to speak to her, or even look into her eyes. And the more help I gave, the sooner Elyani would be ready to take off for the world of the gods.

Elyani's funeral would be mine, though. This I Dragon-knew. Once the ascension ritual was complete, no one could stop me from claiming her body and performing the ritual of the dead for her. *No one!* I sneered, thinking of the Dragon-rage that anyone who dared to stand in my way would have to face.

I had imagined the scene many times. The day of the ascension ritual, all the priests and priestesses of the temple would gather in the central crypt. Then Elyani and the Immaculate would enter and take position in the centre of the vault. The ritual would begin: the chanting of the hymns of the Law, the Voice-projections of long lists of mantras on the Holy Blue Flame, and at least five hours of grand-style ritual. Then everyone but Elyani and the Immaculate would leave the vault, and the ascension would take place.

"What will I be doing then?" I wondered. Probably spreading through remoteness, getting myself drunk on cosmic immensity.

After Elyani had ascended, how would it feel to go back into the empty crypt? Her dead body... would it still be warm?

Behind my back, a nightingale sang, surprising me.

What good will it do you to carry out the funeral?

I shrugged my shoulders. This point was not even for discussion.

Resting on the Dragon of the Deep, I silenced my mind and waited.

At last, Fridrick Point-called. *"Now, Commander! Walk towards the mansion. The warehouses are burning. You should see the flames from a distance."*

I started running through the forest.

A few minutes later, Fridrick Point-called again. *"Can you see the flames?"*

"Not yet! I am still in the forest. But I can smell the smoke," I Point-answered.

"You are about to enter their protection Point-field."

I stopped and Point-tuned in. The protection field was not fundamentally different from the one in Eisraim. Using supermind frequencies, I entered the field and registered myself as Fridrick had instructed me. A few seconds later, I took off again.

"Done?" Fridrick Point-asked.

"So I believe. If they all come after me, we'll know it didn't work."

A hellish vision was waiting for me at the end of the wood. The fire soaked the mists with orange smoke, turning night into day. I kept running in the direction of the house.

"Can you see the mansion?" Fridrick Point-asked.

"Not yet. The mists are too thick," I Point-answered.

Three minutes was all it took to reach the house. The closer I came, the heavier the fumes – but no Foxes! *"Fridrick, I think I made it through the protection field!" I Point-transmitted.*

"Fantastic, my friend! Fantastic!" he Point-replied enthusiastically.

But when I arrived at the mansion, a bad surprise was waiting for me.

"Fridrick," I Point-called, "we have a problem! The house is burning!"

It was a large mansion, at least three storeys. The right half of the building was on fire.

There was no one in sight.

"Go to the door on the left!"

I started running.

"Wait a minute!" I stopped. "This Point-instruction did not come from Fridrick!" I realised. And it certainly did not come from the Flying Dragons either.

"Fridrick! What is happening to you?" I Point-called.

Fridrick didn't answer.

"Damn it! How am I going to find the crypt without Fridrick?"

"The door on the left will lead you to the crypt," the same voice Point-informed me.

There was no time to hesitate. I raced over to the left side of the building. The door of the house was ajar.

I walked in and found myself in an empty hallway where the fire had not yet reached.

I tuned in, Point-searching for the stone of Watcher-ness.

"There!"

It was obvious. An extraordinarily sharp vibration.

My consciousness flared. I entered a space of exalted knowingness.

13.6 A furtive glimpse of the Watchers' mind

The plan of the house was instantly known to me. I opened a door and found a descending stairway. At the bottom, a basement. I followed a long corridor filled with smoke. No one in sight. Left turn... right, left again. Perfect knowingness of where I was going.

In less than a minute I had reached the entrance to the crypt. A guard – one of the Fox Hunters – was lying on the ground, unconscious. From the smoke? Too easy to be true. But no time to hesitate! I rushed through the doorway.

There it was, on a high pedestal.

"The seed-connection stone!" I whispered. The one-inch soft stone had a pale crystalline glow.

I walked towards the pedestal slowly.

Time took on a different meaning. For a start, it slowed down, or rather, my consciousness started operating incredibly fast, visions and thoughts darting through my Point. The thoughts were no normal thoughts, but complex and multidimensional. Comprehending expanded layers of reality, they moved and changed with inconceivable velocity. The concentrated knowingness packed within them was nothing short of awesome.

It was then that I Point-heard the music – the music of the Watchers!

It was perplexing, magnificently enthralling,
A mazelike movement of ever-changing waves
Which enchanted me away from tangible Point-ness
Into eerie, high-pitched realms of improbable virtuality.
By the time I reached the pedestal, only ten lawful feet away,
I had listened to aeons of the Watchers' musical virtual-ness,
I had travelled through times and spaces,
Visited worlds of mathematically infinite dimensions.
I had explored layer after layer of paradoxically laid realities,
Moved to and fro through multifarious exponential scales of intangible wonder
And contemplated myriads of splendidly hyper-real mental constructions.

In short, I had had a furtive glimpse of the Watchers' mind.

My left hand reached for the stone.

A voice sounded a warning, "No, friend, take not this stone! It would burn you. Your hand would have to be cut off."

"Who are you?" I Point-darted.

"Men, in their infinite naiveness, call me a Watcher, but now you understand I am the endless and glorious supermentality of Watcher-ness, which shines bright like the morning star and illumines the spheres. Listen to me, take not the stone. I hold nothing against you, Flying Dragon, and I wish you no harm. So I warn you. Move away and let the fire destroy this stone."

My hand was just about to grab the stone.

"Stop, child! Listen!" the Watcher flung. "You are too young. You do not have what it takes to hold the power of the Watchers. If you venture to harness the stone, you will automatically fall into the hands of another power, which will harm you and tarnish your light."

"If the Hunters can harness power from this stone, why couldn't I?" I Point-asked suspiciously.

"The Hunters were born from my seed. I breast-fed them with my venom. I let them grow in Watcher-ness and carry out my works. But the seed from which you rose was different. This path is not yours. Move away and try me not, or you will fall into the endless pit."

"Why send me into an endless pit, if you hold nothing against me?" I Point-put to him.

"If you fall into the pit, it will not be because I sent you there, but because of your unreadiness to contain my power. Such is the fate of men who try to conquer the power of the Watchers: they fall prey to Ahriman, the Prince of Darkness."

I took my hand back and hesitated, absorbed in the contemplation of the stone. It was a he-stone shaped as an egg, glowing only discreetly.

I tried once more to Point-call Fridrick, but no answer. I tried Gervin. No success. And my Flying Dragon voice was silent, unresponsive.

In the corridor outside the crypt, I heard someone running and shouting.

Prodded by danger, my left hand snatched the stone off the pedestal.

13.7 Orest's teacher in Thunder

The instant my hand closed over the stone, there was an explosion of light. No longer dim, the stone shone with a bright yellow-golden light that illumined the crypt. And... wonder! The hand which held the stone was glowing with the same light.

The atmosphere had completely changed. The Watchers' fast-moving supermental waves had vanished, giving way to a feeling of deep groundedness and solid power.

A man clapped his hands, slowly.

Amazed, I turned round to face him. Had he been in the crypt all along? I hadn't noticed anyone. But it's when I saw what he looked like that I had the real shock.

"*Praise the King of the World, Szar!*" the man hailed me, his voice warm.

Speechless, I looked down at the stone, then back to him in disbelief.

Was I *really* seeing what I was seeing?

"Congratulations! You succeeded," he said. Sensing my astonishment, he asked, "Do you know who I am?"

I shook my head, incredulous.

This simply could not be. It *had* to be an illusion.

The man was clad in the brown gown of the Masters of Thunder. I couldn't see his face, his head was hidden under his hood. But his energy conveyed the unmistakable flavour of the Brown Robe.

I was tempted to run away.

He read my thought, just like Gervin. “No, don’t run away!” he said in his friendly voice. “I am here to help you get out of this place and find your way safely.”

“Who... who are you?” I finally asked.

“My name is Aphelion.”

What a wonderful deep voice, chanting like the rivers of the Underworlds. “Are you one of the...” I started asking, and hesitated.

“Yes, I am one of the Masters of Thunder. The teacher of your teacher’s teacher.

Stupefaction. “Orest’s teacher?”

“Correct, my son.”

“But... what are you doing here?”

“The King sent me to help you, and also to give you some presents. Come on, young man, let us go. We must leave this place.” He walked to the door of the crypt. Outside, the body of the Hunter was still lying on the floor. Aphelion turned towards me. “I know you don’t like killing people, so I neutralised the guard for you. Come on, follow me!”

I looked at the stone, then at him. I still couldn’t see his face.

He turned round and walked out. I followed him. The corridor was full of smoke, but silent. This time it took only a few seconds to reach the door of the house.

As we walked out to the empty yard, I realised most of the building was in flames.

“As long as you are with me you do not have to fear anything, and certainly not fire!” Aphelion laughed. A strange laughter. It made the Dragon shiver. “You know that Cosmic Fire is the central power of the Masters of Thunder, don’t you?”

Bewildered, I followed his high pace through the eerie scenery – crackling, roaring, smoky mists turned orange, spreading the light of the fire far away.

“Where are we going?” I asked.

“We are going to collect your brown gown, of course!” He turned back to me and took off the narrow red scarf around my forehead. “Get rid of this nonsense! You won’t need it.” And he started walking towards the wood again.

I followed, since I needed to recover my gown anyway.

When we reached the place where I had camped for the night, Aphelion stopped and sat down against a tree – the same tree where I had been waiting, remembering Elyani.

“You are worried about Elyani, aren’t you?” he said as I was changing clothes, carefully holding the stone in my hand. “She is still alive,” he added.

Standing very still, I looked at him, a strange shadow in the unreal orange light. “What do you want?”

"I am Aphelion of the Masters of Thunder," he repeated, "and the King has sent me to give you a number of presents, and also to show you that the world is not what people think."

"Who are you?"

"You like truth – a rare quality among men, really – and so I will not tell you lies."

I tried to Point-call Gervin and Fridrick. Still no success.

"Don't waste your time," Aphelion said, "the intensity of the stone is too great. All communications are interrupted. A beautiful stone, isn't it? When you fathom its powers, you will be astounded." He snapped his fingers, just like Gervin, "My first present to you, son! I mean, a present from the King, of course."

Perplexed, I looked at the stone.

"Yes!" Aphelion kept on, "it is yours. Thanks to my help, no one stood in your way when you went to take it, and no one will have the power to take it back from you." Then he stood up and started walking towards the south. "Come on, son, let's go. There is nothing interesting for us in this area."

I walked behind him. "Listen, which King are you talking about?"

"Someone who likes you," Aphelion said, "and someone who is like you, in many ways."

"What?"

"Yes, like you!" Aphelion laughed sarcastically. "Take mediocrity, for instance. You hate mediocrity. So does the King! And you are an extreme person. The King is extreme among the extreme. You admire intelligence and try to cultivate it in yourself. The King's intelligence is phenomenal."

"But what does your King want from me?" I repeated.

"No! No! No! No! No!" he replicated Gervin's expression with startling accuracy. "I am not asking anything from you, just giving you presents. Let me give you another one, by the way. Some information you will appreciate. Do you know that some people have been lying to you about this mission?"

Gervin and I had suspected that all along. But what did this man know, exactly?

"Let me tell you a secret!" Aphelion paced ahead. "At the moment the Black Hunters are trying to fool you. They believe that they can steal the seed-connection stone from you. We will soon meet three of them, who will try to ensnare you in a triangular net. Another Black Hunter, Progos, a stupid giant, is waiting for you further south, with the firm intention of killing you. But there is nothing to fear! With my help, you are going to eliminate the Black Hunters." Turning towards me he added, "That will be good for your Archive, won't it?"

"Eliminate the Black Hunters?" Incredulous, I walked fast behind him.

"The power in your stone will take care of them. And if needed, I will assist you. We will keep walking south, until the Black Hunters find us. And then... the Lord Melchisedek have mercy on them!"

"But how can the Black Hunters know I am in possession of the seed-connection stone?" I questioned.

Aphelion stopped walking and turned towards me, placing his hand on my shoulder. "Deep lies and profound deceit!" he said in a compassionate voice. "This situation is so rotten, you would hate to know exactly what happened, my son."

"Have the Black Hunters been informed by a traitor?" I asked.

"There are traitors everywhere, son. But who is the traitor, and who is the one you can rely on?" he said philosophically. "This is what you need to learn from me." And he started walking again.

I followed him in the night, perplexed as to what question to ask next.

"What about another present?" Aphelion soon proposed.

"Mm... but why do you want to give me so many presents?"

"I told you, son, the King likes you!" he replied. "Now, my next present has to do with your friend Teyani. Tomorrow morning she is going to break her leg. See..."

He conjured a vision of Teyani tumbling down a staircase and screaming with pain. I pulled a face, feeling her suffering in my flesh.

"The corridors' guidance system will be faulty. Some mishap in the fields," Aphelion said. "Would you like us to avoid that?" He snapped his fingers, "How about we send her the flu, so she stays in bed tomorrow?"

"Wait a minute, Aphelion!" I objected. "Teyani is a great seer. Her intuition comes straight from the spheres of Highness. Why should she not know for herself what will happen tomorrow?"

"Precisely, son! Highness is her domain, so what she sees through her intuition is Highness, not staircases. My domain is the physical world. I don't miss staircases. But if you don't believe me, you don't have to send her the flu. You must hurry, though. She will soon wake up. It might actually be too late already."

Deep inside, I *knew* that what he had shown me was really going to happen. Racing behind him, there was a moment of painful hesitation. I finally decided, "Aphelion, yes, I think I would like to help her avoid the accident, if I may."

Aphelion stopped walking and took my left hand, with which I was holding onto the seed-connection stone. He lifted it up to the level of my forehead, "Connect the stone to your third eye," he said. "Yes, like that. Now just send her the flu."

I hesitated some more. Then I tried to focus on the mildest form of flu I could conceive, and sent it to Teyani.

"Listen, son," Aphelion wasn't impressed, "you want to keep her in bed. Can't you push it a bit more?"

I slightly intensified the intent.

Aphelion clapped his hands. "Done! Excellent!" he exclaimed with satisfaction. "I can promise you she won't break her leg tomorrow. I mean, today," he added, as the first light of dawn had already appeared.

"Is it that easy?" I asked.

"Yes!" Aphelion announced in a triumphant voice, and he started walking full speed again. "And remember, the stone is yours. You can use it to do *anything* you want."

I followed, feeling extremely uneasy about this whole situation. Not being able to Point-communicate with Fridrick, how was I going to get rid of the stone? If twelve days from now, Fridrick hadn't deactivated the stone, then the Lord Melchisedek have mercy on me.

"Listen son," Aphelion interrupted my thoughts, "don't worry about the twelve days. As I told you, the stone is now yours. You have all you need to protect yourself and your friends. You will soon see how. Three Black Hunters are after us. They will reach us in less than two hours."

I was horrified. "What? Already? But we've just left the Foxes' headquarters! Does this mean the whole attack was set up by the Black Hunters?"

"Son, as I told you, I will be very straight with you. In particular, I want you to understand that in my company time may not be what it appears to be elsewhere. I will explain all this to you later on. But for the moment, get ready. The Hunters will be here any minute."

"Two hours... any minute..." I wondered what all this meant. Then suddenly, I sensed the characteristic smell. "You are right! I can feel them."

Three Nephilim Hunters, moving towards us. Dead fast.

"Good boy!" Aphelion said. "Shall we wait for them here, or keep walking towards them?"

The warrior inside took over. "Up this hill I sense some powerful energy wells. I suggest we wait for them there."

Aphelion didn't answer, he just kept walking, taking the direction I had indicated. But as we kept going, I noticed, "The Hunters are moving incredibly fast. How can that be?"

"It has to do with time, and some strange things you can do with it, thanks to your stone. I will tell you all about it as soon as we get some time. For now, let us just wait for them here, where the trees are sparse."

13.8 Played by the powers of the King

The Hunter emerged from the mists, hardly sixty lawful feet ahead of us. A tall young man, spice set ablaze in his blue eyes, dressed in black in the fashion of the Hunters of his clan.

"The stone, man of the Law," he threw across in a cool voice. "Just leave it at your feet and walk away, and we won't hurt you."

"Ha! Ha! Ha...!" Aphelion burst out in blood-freezing Voice-laughter. "Look at this young fool!"

The Hunter stayed impassive. "You are caught in a triangular net, men of the Law. There is no escape."

I shivered, remembering Marek's horrific murder by triangular net.

"Imbeci-i-ile!" Aphelion Voice-projected with a vigour that startled both the Hunter and myself. "Don't you know who you are talking to? This man is Szar, the powerful friend of the King of the World. You should be on your knees, imploring him to spare your life."

"I give you one minute to drop the stone and run away," the Hunter hammered.

"Szar, run away? Ha! Ha! Ha!" Aphelion's Voice-laughter rang even louder. "Listen boy, I want you to Point-call your master immediately and tell him that you are standing in front of Szar. I want him to know how you were killed." As the Hunter did not show any reaction, Aphelion Voice-projected at him with blasting intensity, "Now!"

The man trembled. *"Murdoch!" he Point-called. "We have him. But there are two of these Brown Robe priests, not one. And... are you really sure we can overcome them?"*

"Positive!" Murdoch Point-replied.

"Murdoch, you stupid green-beverage sponge!" Aphelion irrupted into their Point-communication. "You have no idea who you are trying to kill. Get out of Szar's way, or there will not be much of your clan left by the next lunation."

To protect himself, Murdoch immediately disconnected the Point-communication. The three Hunters launched their attack.

The venom onslaught was massive. A hundred times stronger than anything I had ever had to withstand from Fridrick. But the seed-connection stone received the venom shock-wave and invited me to reflect it against the Hunters. The three Hunters showed no sign of letting go. They kept building the deadly intensity. There was not one second to waste. "So be it!"

In front of me, the Hunter fell on the ground.

I felt an ugly pinch in my heart. I ran towards the man, knelt down and inspected his gateways with my right hand. "He is dead!" I exclaimed.

Aphelion, his face still hidden in his hood, let out a long sigh. "Well, *of course* he is dead. What do you expect? Do you realise the dose of venom you just threw into him?"

"What about the other two?"

"Well, they're dead too, of course!"

"Can this stone bring them back to life?" I asked, contemplating the yellow-golden light that shone through my fingers.

"Son, what's this nonsense? These men were deadly enemies of yours. For months they have plotted against you and your friends. We are not going to resuscitate them, are we?"

My eyes filled with tears, I bit my lip, passing my hand through the Hunter's blond hair. "Why can't I see your face, Aphelion?"

"You are not yet ready for that, son," he said in a cold, quiet voice. Then he came and sat close to me. "It's the first time you killed a man, eh?"

I nodded, looking down to my left hand. It was glowing, like the stone. An ominous green-gold glow.

"Listen, son, these three men were venom scum," Aphelion was disarmingly gentle. "Truly, by getting rid of them you have saved the lives of a number of people: those which would have been assaulted, robbed, ruined, raped, ripped, you name it! Let me tell you something else. The Black Hunters are planning to attack your temple soon. Worryingly soon, actually. They want your friend Narbenzor-Woolly, the great stone maker. They haven't realised yet that little Maryani is far more skilled than him. And if Narbenzor refuses to cooperate with them, they will crack him open and kill him."

"Why should I believe you?" I asked suspiciously.

Aphelion stood up. "Son, my patience is not without limits. If you do not want to hear the things I came to tell you, I won't try to force you. I will just go my way, and let you solve your problems by yourself." He turned on his heel and started walking towards the south.

"Wait!" I shouted after a few seconds. I hated the thought of Woolly falling into the hands of the Black Hunters.

Aphelion did not stop walking.

I promptly stood up and ran after him, "Wait, Aphelion! I want to know more. Is there something I can do for Woolly?"

Aphelion didn't answer.

"Aphelion, you know how to prevent the attack against Woolly, don't you?"

He sniffed and raised his shoulders, "Of course I do! I have solutions for a number of your problems, young man, for my King is powerful among the powerful."

I had to stride forward to follow his high pace. "Aphelion, you are not going to tell me that you can perform a miracle for Elyani, are you?"

He sneered. "One thing at a time!"

"No way, man of the Law! If there is anything regarding Elyani, I want to know immediately."

Aphelion stopped abruptly. He swung round to me and whistled loudly. "Son, Gervin must have had a really difficult time with an apprentice like you." In a tone that left little space for arguing he added, "For now, if you don't mind, we are going to solve Woolly's problem. Then we can talk about Elyani." And he started walking again. "Now, listen! Murdoch's plan is to get rid of you first, then launch his attack on the temple of Eisraim. Soon, he will send six of his best men against you. If you scare the hell out of Murdoch by getting rid of his Hunters in a spectacular way, he will give up on abducting Woolly."

"Getting rid of them in a spectacular way?" I did not like the sound of this.

"Yes, spectacular," Aphelion said, smooth, tranquil. "See that stone?" He pointed to a rock about a foot long, on the edge of the path. Then he lightly touched my left hand.

Silently, the rock crumbled. All that was left was a heap of pebbles.

"Try it on that other rock!" Aphelion ordered.

Shaken, I stared at the rock.

"Come on! It's easy, using the power of the stone," Aphelion insisted.

"I don't know that I want to do this," I said, looking down to my left fist.

"All right!" Aphelion shrugged and started walking again. "Do as you please. Anyhow, we still have a few minutes before meeting the Hunters."

"What?" I muttered in horror, running after him. "But how can they already be here?"

"The stone you are holding in your hand... its power is so great that it makes time become strange." He paused. "Listen, I warned you. Without a spectacular show of power the Hunters will soon be in Eisraim, and your friends will suffer." He dropped his voice, "They will suffer... badly."

"Aphelion, all this is going too fast for me! Before doing anything, I need to know more about this King."

"Don't worry, we will soon have plenty of time to talk about my King," Aphelion promised. "Smell anything?"

"Oh no!" I exclaimed in dismay. Six Hunters were approaching, fast. "What shall we do with them?"

"Blow their heads off. Not all of them though. Let one run away, so he can tell Murdoch what he saw."

13.9 Eisraim temple, chapel of the Field Wizards

It was late in the night. From outside the door of the chapel, the two Black Hunters tuned into Physsen's Point.

Physsen was dozing, too cosy to notice their presence.

One of the men in black made a sign with his thumb down. The other acquiesced with a nod. Together, they brought down a massive deadly venom shower onto Physsen's Point.

The young man gasped. He fell from his armchair, shattering a large jar on the floor with his head. Dead.

The door was locked. Using small axes, the Hunters swiftly overcame it and rushed into the room.

The chapel was empty. There was only Woolly, working in the cellars.

Following their Points, they ran down the stairs towards him.

The instant he saw them, Woolly activated the Flying Dragon device and closed the access to the crypt of the Archive stones. "What are you doing here?" he shouted.

One of the men pointed his finger at him. "Call for help and you're dead," he yelled. "We know how to hear Point-calls!"

The other one, the tallest – at least two heads taller than Woolly – walked towards him and violently slapped his face.

Woolly fell to the floor.

"Remember me, Narbenzor?"

"What do you want?" Woolly panted, trying to sit up.

The Hunter kicked him, zeroing in on a gateway in his stomach. "It's been a while since our last meeting, hasn't it? It was in the temple of Laminindra, if I recall." He walked towards the blank wall that had been sealed by the Flying Dragon device. "We're taking you for a ride, Narbenzor. But first, you are going to open this doorway. We're taking the stones with us."

Woolly was still gasping on the floor.

"Come on, Narbenzor," the other Hunter coaxed in a friendly voice, "why don't you save yourself a lot of pain, and open the doorway?"

Woolly remained mute.

"Come on, we have nothing against you, Narbenzor, we just need the stones, that's all." Getting no response, he sighed, "All right then," and he poured red venom into Woolly's Point.

Woolly started convulsing and screaming with pain.

Meanwhile the other Hunter went on the rampage, kicking buckets, spilling the precious white slime all over the floor and the baby stones with it. Then, gliding his hand along the shelves, he swept every single bottle and jar, letting them fall off – some on the floor, some onto Woolly.

Among the jars was one which contained Lilu. When it fell on the floor, the precious little stone shattered into pieces.

This sent the wave which alerted Maryani. She was meditating in her room, not far from Teyani's apartment. "Woolly!" she screamed, sending a Point-call. No answer.

The young woman jumped off her bed and started running at high speed, clad only in a light nightgown. *"Teyani!" she Point-called, racing through the corridors. "Woolly is being attacked! Warn everyone in the temple. Call Gervin, Lehrmon, Melchard, Namron... everyone, Teyani! Call everyone! Tell them to rush to Woolly's chapel."*

"Gervin and Lehrmon have gone out of the temple," Teyani Point-answered. "They're on their way to Lasseera. I'll Point-call them anyway, and get all the help I can find."

"Vasouk! Help!" Maryani shouted. Then she accomplished a feat that Mount Lohrzen's Warriors would have greatly admired. While she kept running, she separated her astral body and projected herself down into the Underworlds, zapping straight into King Vasoukidass' royal apartment.

"My, my..." the golden seventy-lawful-feet-long Naga exclaimed in his deep, melodious voice when he saw her. "Isn't that little Maryani? What a happy visitation!"

"Help! Vasouk! Help! They are after my Woolly!"

Vasouk wriggled his nostrils to and fro, rapidly assessing the situation. "Well... darling, why don't you go back up there into your body, that is, your physical body, of course, and let me see what I can do about this most unfortunate situation."

"Quick, Vasouk! Please, quick!" Maryani dashed back into the kingdom.

It did not take her long to reach the chapel. She saw the open door and Physsen on the floor. She jumped over his dead body and raced into the cellar.

The Hunters, who had felt her presence arriving, were standing very still, ready to strike.

Woolly was agonising on the floor, his nose and lips drenched in blood from a few bad kicks, his astral body ravaged by venom.

When they saw half-naked Maryani running down the stairway, the Hunters were slightly disconcerted. One of them Point-called their headquarters, relaying Maryani's Point-signature for identification.

"Berala, you lucky bastard! This one is called Maryani," their friends Point-replied. "We have her listed as a remarkable stone maker. Kidnap her too, she's a bonus from the Watchers."

The Hunter gave a greedy smile, "Maryani! How nice of you to join us!"

The little blonde woman stood in the doorway, perfectly calm, grounded in her Mother the Dragon like a huge mountain of Underworlds.

One of the men walked towards her to catch hold of her.

"Move away!" she Voice-projected with colossal power, filling the air with thick, ancient charms.

The light in the room became eerie, strange hissing sounds resounding throughout. It was as if another world was descending into the cellar, a world in which matter was denser and heavier, odd fragrances wafting in the air.

Stunned, the Hunter stopped, catching his breath, fighting to keep the atoms of his body together.

Maryani's Voice underwent irregular modulations, both high- and low-pitched. "How *dare* you?" she kept Voice-projecting. "How *dare* you?"

Suddenly, the room was filled with the solid golden light of the Naga King, and the awesome intensity of his presence.

"We have a problem," the tall Hunter Point-called his friends. "We have a big problem..." But to protect themselves, the Black Hunters at the other end of the Point-line disconnected the communication.

"My, my..." Vasouk's deep voice resounded loud in the cellar, "what do I see here?"

The Hunters looked around them, wondering what was about to fall on their heads.

Maryani walked towards Woolly, slowly.

At first, the Hunter who stood by Woolly's side remained firm. "We are taking you with us, Maryani."

"Ha! Ha! Ha! Ha! Ha! Ha! Ha!" Vasouk's titanic laugh made every single *living wall* in the building shake.

Maryani kept advancing, slowly.

The Hunter turned pale and stepped back.

When she reached Woolly, Maryani asked coldly, "Who sent you here?"

The tall man in black, his back flat against the Flying Dragon wall, didn't answer.

Maryani screamed with such Voice-intensity that the Hunter, immobilised against the wall, could hardly breathe. "*His name!*"

"Murdoch," he gasped, compelled by the power of the Voice.

"Who is he?" the Voice-projection pinned him to the *living wall.*

"The chief of the Black Hunters," the man's strangled articulation forced its way through the tempest of Maryani's Voice.

Maryani went on in a cool, normal voice, "Listen, Hunter, I want you to go and tell this Murdoch that if he dares attack us again," she paused and drilled her words in, one at a time, "if he dares attack us again..." she resumed full-blast Voice-screaming, "I will find him, and I will kill him. Understood?"

Suffocating, the Hunter barely managed to nod.

"Now get out of here, fast!" she said in her normal human voice.

The man unplastered himself from the *living wall*, gulping for air, and took off so fast that his accomplice tripped on the stairs in his hurry to follow.

Maryani sat on the floor and took Woolly in her arms.

He was unconscious, his face covered in blood.

She started crying, holding him tight against her breast, "Vasouk, please, do something! His life force is nearly gone."

"Well, well... let me see what I can do here," the Naga King answered, taking Woolly into his own space of consciousness.

Soon after, Melchard arrived. Stunned by Vasouk's massive spiritual presence and golden light, he looked around at the scene of utter devastation: bucket-loads of white slime, soft stones and jar debris all over the floor. Maryani, very lightly dressed, holding Woolly in her arms, big tears falling down her face. "Are you all r..." he started asking, but stopped.

Still sobbing, Maryani Point-told him, "The Black Hunters, Melchard, they did it. Have you seen Physsen at the door?"

"Physsen is dead," Melchard Point-confirmed. "But there is more. The Black Hunters have attacked Lasseera at the same time as Eisraim. They did not get the Archive stones, but they have killed at least six people including Oriel, Esrevin's young apprentice in the Brown Robe."

Melchard scratched his head, "But what is happening in this room? The energy is *bigger than the kingdom*!"

Maryani remained silent, gently rocking Woolly in her arms while Vasouk's Light of Lowness was working on him.

It was Vasouk who responded, in his most ceremonial voice, "Praise the Lord Melchisedek, Sir Melchard, High Priest of Eisraim and Grand Commander of the Law for the County of Eisraim under the Appointment of His Supreme Majesty the King of Atlantis."

"All glory to the Lord Melchisedek..." Melchard answered, looking around, wondering whose presence he was supposed to greet.

"My name is Vasoukidass, King of the Nagas," the golden snake went on in his exquisitely polite tone. "Some time ago, Sir Woolly of the Cream Robe kindly extended an invitation to me. I deemed this would be an appropriate time – quite an appropriate time, I should say – to honour the invitation."

At that moment, one of Namron's men, an old soldier, arrived in the cellar. When he saw the mess, felt the presence and heard the Naga's voice, he stopped where he was, his mouth wide open.

"Any casualties?" Melchard asked him.

He nodded. "At least two of our men are dead. And we can't find Namron."

Melchard paused, drawing from Thunder. "Your Majesty, would you be good enough to excuse me?" he said with long-trained diplomatic tact.

"By all means, Sir Melchard of the Brown Robe! By all means."

As Melchard was walking away, Maryani Point-called him, "Have you seen Teyani, Melchard?"

"Not in the last days," Melchard Point-answered.

"Please go and visit her," Maryani Point-requested. "She's terribly ill. I am really worried. It started as a simple flu, but now she is coughing from morning to night and spitting blood. Nothing seems to alleviate her fever."

"I thought it was all finished. Didn't it start three weeks ago?"

"It has been getting worse every day," Maryani Point-answered. "And what about Szar? Have you received any news yet?"

"None. He has completely disappeared."

13.10 The persuasion of the dark side

The mists were so thick that at times I nearly bumped into the trees.

"You don't think I frightened the Hunters enough, do you?" I asked.

Aphelion was walking so fast I almost had to run to keep up with him. "No! I think the way you behaved was pathetic. And useless, moreover."

"They looked pretty frightened to me," I pleaded.

"They fooled you. Couldn't you see that their pledge not to attack your friend Narbenzor was a complete sham?"

I bit my lip, starting to wonder if I had made a big mistake by letting the six Black Hunters escape relatively unscathed.

"You will kill them anyway," Aphelion assured me, "so why not do it immediately?"

"Why should I kill them?" I asked.

"When you see what they have done to your friends, you will realise that you have no other option but to eliminate the Black Hunters."

Anxiety gripped my chest. "What are they going to do to my friends?"

"It is already done!" Aphelion's words fell like a court sentence.

"What?"

"The very same men you allowed to escape have attacked Lasseera and Eisraim. Want to see?"

"Aphelion," I protested, "that does not make any sense. We left them less than an hour ago."

Relentlessly striding on, Aphelion gave no reply.

"Yes, Aphelion," I capitulated, "I prefer to see."

"We had better stop, then," he said, standing very straight, resting his arm against a large cypress tree. "This happened in the temple of Lasseera," he commented, as the image of a large vault appeared in front of my third eye. "Have you ever visited it?"

"Not yet," I answered... "Oh my Lord Melchisedek!" I exclaimed when I saw the images: the walls of two chapels had half melted, causing the roofs to collapse. Four priests had been crushed to death by huge chunks of plass, only their feet and one hand were visible. A priestess lay, her throat pinned to the floor by a razor-sharp plass spike fallen from the ceiling. I recognised two of the Black Hunters I had just met. They were bashing and venomising to death a young man wearing the Brown Robe.

"Who is he?" I asked.

"His name was Oriel. He was a disciple of Esrevin. Now look, this is what happened in Eisraim," he said.

I saw Woolly being kicked in the face and tortured with red venom, Namron lying in the dust with blood all over his face, Physsen's wife screaming with pain when she saw his corpse in the chapel, a little child and a weeping woman close to the dead body of one of Namron's men, and a long funeral procession along the temple's straight path of the Law.

My consternation was beyond words. Appalled, shattered, I stared at the hood which covered Aphelion's face. "All this has happened because of me, hasn't it?"

Aphelion had nothing to answer.

"Did they get Woolly?" I asked.

"Not yet, and that made Murdoch very angry."

"Very angry..." I echoed in a neutral voice, contemplating the shining stone in my left hand.

"Let's go," Aphelion said in a gentle voice.

I nodded, and followed him.

Shocked by the images, I wondered what I was supposed to do next. "Will Murdoch strike again?" I asked.

"Listen son, if you want to prevent further attacks, there is a simple way: threaten Murdoch. Let him send all his men after you, then just get rid of them."

"Murdoch is not stupid," the warrior inside spoke. "By now he must have realised that his men cannot match us. Why should he lose everything by sending all his soldiers to certain death?"

"Leave him no choice!" Aphelion suggested. "Destroy his seed-connection stone, for instance. This way, his only chance of survival will be to catch hold of your stone."

My devastation was slowly being covered by stinging waves of anger. "Destroy his seed-connection stone..." I said coldly, "could I do that?"

"No, not yet. But with the help of my King, I could do it for you. If you wanted."

"And what would your King ask from me in exchange?" I asked suspiciously.

"Nothing!" Aphelion engaged his word. "My King has decided to treat you like his own son. When a father gives to his son, he doesn't expect anything in return."

"Aphelion, can we talk about this King? Who is he?" I asked.

"Son, if you really want to, we can talk now. But if you want my advice, we had better sort out the problem with the Black Hunters first."

I swallowed hard, still striding at high speed to keep up with Aphelion's relentless pace. "And what will happen this time, if I do not follow your advice?"

Aphelion didn't answer.

"I suppose we have to hurry, as usual," I said.

"We had better hurry, yes. Murdoch is not a slow mover."

"Aphelion, I am starting to be exasperated with this time that runs madly! Can't we just return to a normal pace of events? I don't like the feeling of all this."

Aphelion stopped abruptly, turned round, pointed his index at me. "Listen, son," he hammered, "no one put this stone in your hand. *You* took it. It was *your* choice. Now don't blame me for what happens." Then he turned his back on me and took off again.

"All right! All right!" I ran up behind him, "But when we finish with the Hunters, will there be any time to sit and talk?"

"Plenty of time!" he assured me. "Shall I destroy Murdoch's seed-connection stone?"

I contemplated my left hand. "Perhaps you were right, Aphelion... there is no other option, is there?"

Aphelion stopped. "But then, you must be ready to face the Black Hunters. Understand? From the moment their seed-connection is terminated, their last chance of survival will be to dispossess you of your stone."

I nodded agreement.
"Clear?" he insisted.
"Yes, Aphelion."
I couldn't see his face, but I *knew* he was smiling.
He stayed motionless and silent for two or three minutes. Then he raised his left hand and slowly clenched his fist, as if crushing an object. "Remember Szar, Murdoch!" his voice blew like a cold wind in the caverns of sickness. "Remember Szar of the Brown Robe."

13.11 Danagara, the Black Hunters' headquarters

On his return from the temple of Eisraim, Berala went straight to Murdoch's basement office. Without even bothering to send the Point-recognition prompt, the tall man stormed into the room. "Murdoch!" he yelled, his voice cutting through like a knife, "What's this mess? Are you trying to kill us all?"

Despite his small size, Murdoch was well known for his ability to stand like a rock and impress the fiercest warriors. He remained silent, holding onto the power which he drew from the seed-connection, seeking inspiration.

"Do you realise how we lost Jaker and Lops in Lasseera?" Berala went on in his loud voice. "The damn Brown priest just stood in front of them and Voice-vomited hell onto their heads, and they fell like sixteen-year-old virgins venomised before a rape! And do you realise what happened to me, Murdoch? The intensity of light in that crypt was insane. Completely insane! I have never seen anything like it!"

Murdoch remained very calm, letting his man lash out his anger. Then he asked laconically, "What do you think we should do about it?"

"Come back to reality, Murdoch! Do you know what the Brown priest yelled at Progos before letting him run away? *'Remember Thunder, man of the Law!'*" Berala bit each syllable, "Murdoch, the Masters of Thunder exist. They are no legend, and they are too big for us. We have been playing a dangerous game, and now we are burning our fingers. We must immediately make a truce with the Brown Robe."

"A truce with the Brown Robe," Murdoch repeated, his voice neutral.

Loud yells erupted from the seed-connection crypt, which was separated from Murdoch's office by only a thin *living wall*.

Simultaneously, they received an emergency Point-call. "Murdoch, come to the crypt immediately! Immediately!"

"Follow me!" he shouted at Berala, rushing through the doorway that led to the crypt. There, close to the altar on which the precious stone was kept, stood Aphelion's ominous silhouette.

There were two guards in the crypt. "Full intensity!" Murdoch yelled, and together with Berala they attacked Aphelion's Point with all the power they could draw from the seed-connection stone.

Aphelion, untouched by the downpour of venom, raised his left hand in the direction of the stone.

"No, not that!" Berala screamed, throwing himself at Aphelion.

But as the Hunter jumped, Aphelion deviated the venom deluge his way.

Berala collapsed, a soft warm heap on the plass floor. Dead.

Aphelion grabbed the stone. One of the guards tried to jump onto him, but met the same fate. Aghast, the other guard stood his ground, and with Murdoch he watched the precious stone being obliterated in Aphelion's hand.

Aphelion projected a ghastly Voice, "Remember Szar, Murdoch! Remember Szar of the Brown Robe," and he sneered.

13.12 Tricked into using the power of the stone

"No! Please, don't kill me!" Terrified, Progos the giant fell to his knees. "Please, don't kill me! You've won!" he thrust every ounce of strength he had into his plea. "It's all finished, the seed-connection is dead, and they're *all* dead. Murdoch killed himself. And all those you haven't killed left their body last night!"

"Victory!" Standing by my side, Aphelion slowly clapped his hands. "This man is not lying, Szar. We won."

I contemplated the glowing stone in my left hand. "You are going to tell me I would make a big mistake by not killing him, Aphelion, aren't you?"

"Hasn't the villain vowed to murder you?" Aphelion asked.

"No!" Progos yelled, "I thought you were one of the Warriors from Mount Lohrzen, I didn't know about Thunder. I vow I will never do anything against you! I vow on the Watchers!"

I walked towards Progos, leaving Aphelion behind me.

The giant's face was livid, but the prospect of imminent death brought a dignified attitude to his face. He began whispering a prayer to the Watchers.

I went and sat on the mossy ground right in front of him.

"Ah, very good! Very good!" Aphelion exclaimed with satisfaction. "You begin to trust your power, at last!"

I looked straight into the giant's eyes, "Progos, do you know that before your friends attacked me, I had never killed a man?" I slapped his large hand loudly and seized it, holding it Dragon-tight. I projected the Voice, "Do you realise that, Progos?"

At a loss, Progos nodded shakily.

Remembering Thunder, I looked deep into his eyes. With my normal voice I asked him, "Progos, do you have a wife?"

Even more disconcerted, Progos responded with another nod.

"Is she a giantess?"

"Yes."

"What's her name?" I asked.

Big drops of sweat were running on the giant's forehead. "P... Progosina."

Still holding his hand Dragon-tight, I smiled. "I see... your parents married you before you were born, is that it?"

A quick nod.

I let go of his hand. "Go!" I said neutrally.

Not believing his ears, the giant hesitated.

"Go," I repeated. "Go and tell Progosina she saved your life."

Still on his knees, the giant moved back a little, then slowly got to his feet. He remained still for two or three seconds, wondering what I was going to do. He started backing away, then turned and walked.

"Progos!" I called him.

The giant stopped and turned his head, looking down towards me.

I pointed my finger at him. "If I meet you once more, Progos... then Progosina will become a widow."

Looking into my eyes, he let me know he had heard my message.

I watched him go, then went back to Aphelion. "I know you don't approve," I said.

"Who cares, my friend?" Aphelion took a conciliatory tone. "Let us not think about this. Now is the time to savour your victory. Total victory! You have crushed the Black Hunters, put them on their knees and reduced them to nothing! Praise the King of the World!"

"Strange," I thought, "I had a much greater sense of victory when I twinged my beard for the first time." I contemplated the glowing stone, which had remained in my left hand ever since I had raided the Foxes' headquarters. What the hell was I going to do with this thing? Would Aphelion tell me how to get rid of it?

"Let us get out of this forest!" Aphelion suggested, and he started walking again. "Do you like climbing?"

"Yes, very much." Memories of Mount Lohrzen brought the semblance of a smile to my face. "Unfortunately, there are not many mountains where I live. But Aphelion, why do you walk so fast?"

Aphelion burst out in his disturbing laughter, "Szar the Great Warrior surprised at how fast I walk? What a compliment!" He took me by the hand and accelerated his pace. Running to keep up with him, I had to laugh with him.

"How come I have to run, when you are just walking?"

"Use the power of the stone," he said, "and you will be able to follow me."

It sounded innocuous enough. I tried.

"No, not like that!" Aphelion instructed. "Connect your Dragon to the stone."

I did as he said and instantly I could walk as fast as he did. "This is amazing, Aphelion." I thoroughly enjoyed the physical sensation that came with this unusual trotting.

"You like speed, don't you?" Aphelion's laughter was provocative. He stepped up the pace.

To my surprise, the terrain soon became quite steep. "Aphelion," I put to him as we started going up, "how can there be a mountain here? We were in the northern part of the county of the Northern Lakes, and we have been walking southwards all the time."

"Can't you guess?" Aphelion kept laughing.

The Snowy Mountains were towards the north. South of the Northern Lakes, there were no mountains. Apart from the mountain range of Lasraim, of course, but that was far too far away.

More important than geographical considerations was the short-term destiny of the Foxes' seed-connection stone. "Aphelion," I questioned, "I was supposed to find my friend Fridrick and let him take care of the stone. How am I..."

"When you understand who my King is, you will know what to do with the stone," Aphelion shut me up.

The slope was getting steeper and steeper. "Can we talk about this King now?"

"If you want to," Aphelion said. "But shouldn't we try to help Elyani first?"

"Another present of yours?" I asked, wondering if it was wise to let Aphelion interfere with Elyani's energy.

Exasperated by my constant suspicions, Aphelion let go of my hand and stopped so abruptly that I had to call on the Dragon to avoid tumbling forward. "Son," he said in a calm, measured voice, "you don't have to accept my presents. And you don't have to follow me. Now listen, I am going to climb this mountain. *If you want* to go to the top with me, I will tell you about my King. And *if you want*, on the way I will also tell you a few things about Elyani." Pointing a firm finger at me he added, "But decide for yourself what you want to do, and then own your choice!"

Without waiting for an answer, he began to ascend a steep incline.

I looked down to my left hand, glowing with the stone. "What am I going do with this thing?" There was no solution I could see. If I dropped it and walked away, anyone finding it would inherit the powers of the Watchers. And the Renegade plague would start all over again.

So how the Underworld was I going to deactivate it? Fridrick had warned against throwing it into the fire. It could trigger a tremendous release of power with far-reaching, disastrous consequences.

I tried to Point-call Gervin and Fridrick, with no more success than before.

Aphelion was fast disappearing into the mists.

"Wait, Aphelion!" I called, wishing time could slow down a little.

Aphelion didn't stop. I had to run after him at high speed. Only when I caught up with him did he stop. "Have you decided that you want to follow me?" he asked, pointing his index finger at me.

"To the top of this mountain, yes."

"Are you sure?" he insisted.

"Yes, yes."

Aphelion turned round and resumed the rocky climb. I hurried behind him. He was a relentless climber. He never once put a foot wrong, each of his steps calculated with absolute precision. And despite the thick mists, finding good tracks seemed to pose no difficulty for him.

"What is it you wanted to tell me about Elyani?" I asked after we had been advancing for a while.

"I don't know that I can tell you anything after all," he tossed off a shrug.

"Why?" I protested, jumping after him onto a large rock.

"You are too fixed in your convictions. You see the world in a certain way, and you leave no space for other points of view."

Gervin had taught me to abhor narrow-mindedness. I leapt off the rock, "What do you mean, Aphelion?"

"Have you ever considered that reality might not be what it appears to be, and that you might have to reverse some of your opinions completely?"

"My teacher repeats things like this to me all the time!" I said. "He likes to present a theory, getting me to fully appreciate its value. Then, just when I start believing in it, he shows me weak points I had overlooked, and he takes me in another direction."

"Ve-ry good!" Aphelion exclaimed loudly. Then he jumped across a small water stream with an agility which I couldn't help admiring. "Very good!" he repeated as I jumped, trying to imitate the arc of his leap and the beautiful way he had landed.

"What has all this got to do with Elyani?" I asked, pursuing him up a new, steeper track. Trees were becoming sparse, the terrain rockier and rockier.

"Another problem with you is your sentimentalism," Aphelion was direct. "Not wanting to blow off the Hunters' heads was magnanimous of you, but do you realise how much it has cost your friends?"

I bit my lip, remembering the scenes of devastation in Lasseera and Eisraim. He was right, none of this would have happened if I had followed his advice and eliminated the Hunters right from the beginning. An unforgivable mistake, not least because we got rid of them after all.

"I made a mistake, Aphelion, I fully accept that."

The track was now hugging the edge of a cliff. I wished the mists could have subsided a little, remembering with envy the stunning views down into the canyons of the Red Lands.

Aphelion caught my thoughts. "When we reach the place I want to take you to, son," his deep voice held the gravity of the rock, "you won't be disappointed with the view." He didn't say more.

After a while, understanding that he would not speak unless I asked him again, I broached the topic once more, "So what about Elyani?"

"What do you want for Elyani?" he asked.

"Well," I hissed my breath, "a few things... for a start, I would like to know if Hermina the Immaculate will help her."

"An Immaculate priestess?" Aphelion sneered. "All right, if this is what you want! Let this be another present to you." He snapped his fingers. "I give you my word that as soon as you reach the temple of Eisraim, Hermina the Immaculate will arrive. And she will help you."

His words flowed into me like pure nectar from the world of the gods. From the deepest of my heart, I said, "Thank you, Aphelion. Thank you for this."

He shrugged in exasperation, "Son, do you realise that with the power of your stone you could make Elyani a queen?"

"Isn't she going to be a queen if she completes her ascension ritual?" I leapt across a narrow crevasse.

"If!" Aphelion sneered again. "A big if!"

"Could the stone help her succeed?" I asked.

"It certainly could, but then what?" Aphelion spat his contempt. "She will end up no more than a second-class little goddess with no real significance in the cosmic play of the worlds. Why not make her a queen in *this* world?"

"This world will pass, Aphelion. The gods are immortal," I said.

Aphelion stopped and faced me. "I have not passed, Szar!" he took my hand and held it firmly. "Orest and my other disciples died long ago, but I am still here. Come, let me show you certain things."

I still could not see beneath his hood.

13.13 Ahriman, King of this World

The path was no longer steep, but gently winding up towards a large plateau. Arriving at the top, Aphelion made a grand gesture, "Look around you, son. Contemplate the power of the King of the World."

A great miracle began. The mists around us started to disperse. First the full extent of the plateau was revealed: a flat, barren rocky top a few hundred lawful feet wide. Then as the mists kept receding, the mountain below was unveiled. Soon, there was a sky – blue, amazing blue, and clear. A sky never seen by me in the kingdom, only when I had peeped into the worlds of the gods or visited King Vasoukidass' domain.

"Oh my Lord Melchisedek," tears sprang to my eyes, "this is magnificent, Aphelion! So magnificent!" As the mists kept vanishing, I could see more mountaintops, and even green valleys in the distance. Soon, a full mountain range extended before my eyes. I could even discern rivers and lakes, and three villages in the distance. Houses and herds of cattle were nothing more than small dots, making me feel like a gigantic god contemplating his creatures from above. An entire landscape without mists!

A miraculous vision. It made me feel on top of the world. My nostrils wriggling wildly as I drank the unusually sharp, brisk air, I praised the Lord Melchisedek for the beauty of his creation.

"These mountains... what range is this, Aphelion?" I asked.

"The mountains of Lasraim, of course! We are on top of Mount Fulcrum, the highest summit of the range."

Stupefaction shocked the Dragon. It should have taken at least three weeks to walk from the Foxes' headquarters, at the northern extremity of the county of the Northern Lakes, to the mountains of Lasraim. Yet Aphelion and I had been together for less than a day. The breathtaking landscape swept out before me.

Utterly captivated, I sought no explanation.

Aphelion raised his arm, "Now contemplate the Sun!"

Looking up, I beheld the yellow disk suspended high in the sky and brighter than anything mortal eyes could contemplate in the kingdom, where Sun and Moon were never more than vague circles to be guessed at through the mists.

As I gazed at the portentous solar wonder, Aphelion commented, "Do you realise, by the way, that if the stone was not in your hand, gazing at the Sun would burn your eyes and render you blind!"

"*For only the gods can contemplate the glorious Sun face to face,*" I pondered, quoting the verse of the Law.

"Nonsense!" Aphelion countered thunderously, "I am no god, and I can contemplate the Sun whenever I wish."

I looked down to the ground, then turned to him. Dazzled by the light of the Sun, I could not see. I had to call on the Dragon of the Deep to restore my vision. "Who are you, Aphelion?" I asked.

In his deepest and most melodious voice, he said, "I am a man who has been capable of recognising the trends of time, and of discerning who will win the battles of this world. Like you, I was trained by the Masters of Thunder. Like you, I conquered their powers and comprehended their wisdom. Like you, I travelled through the spheres and tamed the awesome forces of the Underworlds. Like you, I won difficult battles, accomplished great feats and miraculous healings..."

"Far Underworld!" I thought. "Did I really do all that?"

"And like you," Aphelion continued, "one day I was visited by Ahriman, the King of the World. Then I saw that his powers were greater than those of any god, greater than any power I had ever come across. And I saw that none but he would be victorious in this world. So I wisely decided to follow him. He gave me more knowledge than I thought could possibly be gained, and made me mightier than I had ever thought I could possibly become. For he is the way, the true path to the ultimate powers of this world. Just look around you, son," Aphelion's hand described a large circle, "all this is his. All other powers will be withdrawn. They will all lose ground and be defeated, one after the other, until he alone rules in this world – *his* world."

Combined with the panoramic view and the elated feeling of being on top of the world, Aphelion's discourse did not lack dimension.

"But who is this King?" I asked.

"Now you can contemplate my face." Aphelion pulled back his hood.

Instead of a face, I saw only darkness. The darkness drew me inside itself, and a monumental figure appeared. The general appearance was that of a man, but a gigantic one. His feet alone extended far higher than the sky. And his body was made of solid, luminescent gold. He wore a helmet which shone a thousand times more than the glorious Sun itself, and his whole bearing was that of a formidable fighter, a triumphant hero on his way to winning battle after battle. He was moving, striding forward at high pace, looking fierce, utterly unstoppable. I saw entire nations at his feet. They followed him. Great was their enthusiasm, loud their clamour. Grand assemblies raised their hands to chant his glory, masses demonstrated their support to him, army after army waged his wars. It seemed every corner of the world was ready to serve him and follow his ways.

Then something unexpected took place. The shining being stopped his titanic march and from his loftiness looked down to me. His eyes, ablaze with fire as in the Furnaces of Doom, delivered a message, 'If you want to be great, follow me!' And he smiled and extended his immense hand towards me.

"Hum... Aphelion, is there really no way I could Point-call Gervin?" I asked.

Aphelion concealed his head under his brown hood again and the vision terminated, leaving me even more blinded than after gazing at the Sun.

Ignoring my question, he encircled me with the richness of his voice, "Son, you should rejoice. Few in the world have the privilege of being personally invited by the King. Understand what it means: the King of the World believes in you! He sees in you a leader. He wants to take you to the summit of the human pyramid, so you may carry out his works and shine his glory. The stone with which you have overcome the Black Hunters is *nothing* compared to the powers he will give you if you decide to serve him. He will give you the knowledge of all things material. He will make you admired and obeyed by *all* men, and *all* women. He will put you in a position where all your desires are satisfied, and no one ever dares go against you." Pausing to let the gravity of his words settle over me, he extended his arm towards me and delivered at near-Voice threshold, "Szar, the King has given you his word. Follow him, and you will become great!"

I swallowed hard. "Aphelion, all this sounds... really wonderful," I said, my eyes fixed on the majestic mountain range. "And your King is, no doubt, mighty and magnificent. As soon as I meet with my teacher, Master Gervin, I will ask him to instruct me thoroughly about all this."

"Szar," Aphelion's words carried a note of warning, "before taking sides with the losers, think twice. Do you realise what will be left of your friends and your temple only one or two years from now?"

I chewed my lip, "You are right Aphelion, probably not much."

"Not much? This I would call an understatement, son. You know that Gervin's days are numbered, don't you?"

Resting on the Dragon to cope with the pinch in my heart, I gave a sinking nod.

"In hardly a year he will be dead. You know this is the truth. Not long after him, Melchard and Esrevin will be slaughtered by hordes of invaders from the east. The giants, Szar... the giants are coming! They will go on the rampage, destroying everything in your temple: relics, statues, buildings, even the gardens and the trees. Incidentally," for a moment, his voice conveyed immense empathy, "one of the first chapels to be desecrated will be Lord Gana's. The giants will rape all the priestesses they find on their way, young and old – when drunk on venom, the giants aren't very discerning in these matters. They will storm through the temple, massacring anything that moves. By then, the Masters of Thunder you met before me will all be dead, Szar. Not one of them will be left, and your lineage will be extinct on Earth." Aphelion's words went sweeping though me like a savage wind of desolation. It made it difficult for me to breathe. I called on Gervin's presence with all my strength. There was no answer.

"Do you realise that a great part of all this destruction and sorrow could be avoided if you came with us?" Aphelion said.

"Do you mean to say you could arrest the fall of Atlantis?" I asked.

"The transition from the kingdom of Atlantis to the kingdom of the rainbows is part of the king's plans, and nothing will stop it. But there is still ample scope as to how it will take place. The stone – the stone that you hold in your hand, Szar – has enough power to keep the giants away from your temple."

I knew what he said was true.

When he saw how deep his words were hitting me, Aphelion softened his voice. "Remember what we discussed before, son, don't be narrow-minded. Reality is not always like you think it is. At the moment, you believe that Gervin's Archive is the greatest enterprise on Earth. Let me tell you, it is not! A man like you deserves better than this, Szar. If you come with me, you will be involved in projects of far greater magnitude."

I shook my head. “I could...” the words choked in my throat, “I could never let Gervin down, Aphelion.”

“Why be so stubborn? Gervin will be dead in less than a year! Reality is not what you think it is, Szar. The problem with you is that you lock yourself in your mental constructions, a sure way of missing life opportunities. Let me give you a simple example.”

I shook my head. I didn’t want to hear.

Aphelion continued anyway, “Do you know that you could have visited Elyani every night if you had wanted?”

“Of course I could have! But by breaking the Law I would have poisoned her relationship with the Immaculate priestesses.”

“Nonsense!” Aphelion thundered. “Another mental construction of yours! If you had been more open-minded and daring, you would have discovered that Space Matrix has a powerful function called ‘disguise’, by which you could have made yourself totally invisible to the Immaculate, although not to Elyani, of course. No one but you and she would have known.”

I felt so sick in my stomach that I could have dropped on my knees, but Aphelion did not stop. “By visiting her, you would have saved her so much anguish, Szar, you have no idea the ordeal she has been going through. So much torture, and for what?” Aphelion stopped his relentless pounding for a moment, to let his words sink to the very bottom. Then he punched in, “Now, all that’s left of her is an agonising wreck. Take my word for it and let me not disgust you with gruesome visions. She is no pretty sight.”

“Aphelion...” I was left gasping.

“Gervin’s knowledge is not absolute, Szar, otherwise...” Aphelion cut across me, “surely he would have told you about the ‘disguise’ function, wouldn’t he? And there are several other things he never told you, some of which he does not know, and some he knows only too well. For instance, if you choose to follow him, one day you will have to destroy an entire city, kill hundreds of thousands of people, your own daughter among them.”

I felt like a small boat capsizing amidst huge waves. “This cannot be true, Aphelion. My master has never encouraged me to kill anyone. He is not...”

Aphelion roared with laughter. “Gervin, not wanting you to kill anyone? What a lot of nonsense! Gervin knows perfectly well that if you follow him, you will have to set this large city on fire, and that *not one soul* in the city will escape. Has he not told you?”

“Aphelion, you are lying. This cannot be true,” I repeated.

“Philadelphia Six will be the name of the city,” he thundered, and in a contemptuous tone, hammered, “Brother Knight!”

The violence in his words took my breath away.

“*Virginia...*” the familiar thought slipped back into my mind, “*Virginia, no! Not that!*” I nearly blacked out.

"You know very well I am telling the truth, Szar!" Aphelion drove on mercilessly. "And let me tell you something else. The Brother Knights will lose the war. If you destroy Philadelphia Six, as Gervin the butcher wants you to, it will be for nothing. The Brother Knights will be on the side of the losers – the eternal losers, those who can never recognise the inevitable trends of time and desperately try to cling onto the past, instead of moving forward and building the future."

I realised I had fallen to my knees. I tried to stand up, but could not find the force. "Aphelion, please..."

Aphelion extended a hand towards me, "You have only one word to say, Szar, and none of this will happen. Elyani's torture will be ended instantly, the giants will not ransack Eisraim, and you will never have to destroy Philadelphia Six. Do not take sides with the losers, Szar. Follow the King! Come with me, and let us win the battles of this world together."

Against my will, my left hand, still holding the stone, raised itself up towards the hand Aphelion extended. "No!" I shouted in agony. "Take the stone back. I don't want it!"

"See this beautiful valley?" Aphelion pointed to a long, narrow pass at the bottom of the mountain. "It is called the Valley of the Necromancer. It holds ancient powers to which my King has given me the key. One word, just one word, and I will take you into the valley, initiate you into the high powers of Ahriman, the King of the World, and let you become a king among men."

Unable to call my hand back, I shuddered. "Take this stone, Aphelion. I don't want it," I repeated.

"Why get rid of a power which is already in your hand? You are using it so well."

I tried to drop the stone, but could not unclench my fist. The Dragon was powerless, I simply *could not* open my hand.

"No! No! No! No! No!" Aphelion warned, "It won't be that easy. You have used the power of the King. You have killed with it. And you have mingled your Dragon with it. You can't just drop the stone and run away now."

I received his words like an arrow in my chest. Pierced to the core, I said for the third time, "Aphelion, take this stone back. I do not want it."

Aphelion understood that I would not accept his offer.

He dropped his hand, and remained ominously silent.

I prayed to the Mother of the Light, preparing myself to bear the brunt of his wrath.

The sky gradually lost its shining blue colour. At the bottom of the mountain, the Valley of the Necromancer was closed over in a veil of mist.

Aphelion stood still, silent.

A formidable blow was imminent.

The mists began to return. I watched them slowly submerge the landscape before me, and then ascend towards us like huge sea monsters ready to engulf us. I remembered the image of Elyani in her courtyard, as I had taken her in my memory before descending into the Underworlds for the first time. Soon, the mists covered the entire plateau, and the air no longer had its brisk quality.

Something completely unexpected took place. Instead of striking the final blow, Aphelion came and sat on the ground close to me and placed his hand on my shoulder.

"Son," he said in the warm voice he had used with me when he had first met me, "I will go to the Valley of the Necromancer now, and I'll wait there for three days. You can change your mind and join me, if you want." Then he gently patted my shoulder, "I want you to remember two things. First, I did not lie to you. All the things I told you were true. Second, my offer remains: you can come to me any time, whether in this life or another. If you ever want my help, just call me. I will come." Still patting my shoulder, he whispered, "We shall meet again, one way... or another."

Then with no other words he stood up and walked away, vanishing into the mists.

I collapsed, my forehead against the rocky ground, sobbing loudly, "Gervin! No! Tell me it is not true! Tell me Philadelphia will never exist."

13.14 More presents

Climbing down the mountain, trying to find my way through the mists, I began feeling a deep urge to take the direction of the Valley of the Necromancer. At first I could not understand why it was so strong. But after a few hours, it became clear: the stone was pulling my Dragon. It was a fight against myself. Every fibre in my body wanted to run to Aphelion's invitation.

Half way down the mountain, a silhouette emerged from the mists. The man was clad in the brown gown of the Masters of Thunder, and he pointed towards the ominous valley.

"No!" I exclaimed in horror when I recognised Gervin's face. The silhouette vanished, but it was soon followed by another. As I kept walking, the hallucinations became more and more frequent and vivid. Again and again I saw Gervin, Teyani, Melchard, Lehrmon, Alcibyadi, all pointing to the Valley of the Necromancer, silently inviting me to join Aphelion. The Dragon pulled, thirsting for Aphelion's presence.

When I arrived at the foot of the mountain, I had to overcome a huge inertia. My body refused to obey when I tried to push it away from the valley. How easy it would have been to run to Aphelion! I felt like a thirsty man tempted with water. I knew the pull came from the stone, but that did not make it any easier to resist. None of my usual sources of inspiration were available: the Flying Dragon voices had been silenced, my Point connection had disappeared, and so had the clear fountain with it. Gervin's presence was nothing more than a memory. I was in complete isolation. I tried my best to keep my gaze averted from the stone, but it did nothing to diminish its power.

Unable to go further, I sat on the ground and prayed the Mother of the Light that my body would not force me to the fatal rendezvous.

Plunged into utter turmoil, it was a while before I realised I could sense-smell Nephilim spice way in the distance. A troop of Nephilim Hunters were on their way.

"Kill them!"

Coming from the stone, the voice was echoed by my Dragon.

"Kill them!"

The Hunters were approaching fast. At least forty of them.

Forty Hunters – a formidable force!

"Kill them! All of them! Use me. Use your power," the stone kept whispering insidiously.

My Dragon's response was fierce: a violent urge to kill, which took me completely by surprise.

"You will enjoy it so much, the superior satisfaction that comes from killing a human being."

By then I could not move the fingers of my left fist. Whatever I tried, it remained clenched. It made me yell in horror, hitting the hand against the mountain rock.

The threatening astral smell indicated the Hunters were fast moving in on me.

"There are forty-nine of them, but it will be easy. Just push my influence against them. Take them one at a time. Let them come close enough first, so you can see them fall into the dust. You will enjoy!"

Had I had a knife, I would have cut my hand off. I scanned the terrain for a sharp stone, but there was none in sight.

The Hunters were nearly upon me.

I fell on my knees again, yelling with all the strength I had left, "No! No! Please!" I cried, "Please, don't force me to kill them!"

"I don't have to force you. You will kill them because you enjoy it!"

"No! No!" I kept sobbing. "Please don't force me to kill them!"

A silhouette emerged from the mists, hardly a hundred lawful feet away.

Only one man.

Very tall.

Blond, curly locks.

Piercing blue eyes.

A leather bag hanging from his shoulder.

When he saw me pitifully on my knees, he looked quite disconcerted. He called out in a perplexed voice, "Are you Szar of the Brown Robe?"

I was so overwhelmed I did not even try to stand up.

"Who are you?" I yelled.

After hesitating one second, he replied, straight, “My name is Perseps, from Jex Belaran. Are you Szar?”

“I am Szar. But why should I believe you are Perseps?”

His eyes fixed on the glow that came from my left hand, Perseps announced, “I brought you three presents, Szar of the Brown Robe. One of them will convince you.”

“Presents? No! No!” I yelled like a madman. “Go away!”

Perseps was taken aback by the violence of my response. “No presents?” he muttered, his Hunter’s gaze fixed on me, seeking inspiration. Then he declared, “Friend, I think I know where your problems are coming from.” And he walked towards me.

“Kill him,” the stone whispered.

“No!” I yelled.

The man stopped. “All right! I stay where I am.”

“If you are Perseps,” I shouted, “then tell me what has happened to Fridrick!”

At that moment, two other men emerged from the mists.

“Meet my friends!” Perseps said. “Waxen...” the younger of the two men raised his right hand, his palm towards me (the sign given to a prian), “and Joranjeran.”

The latter raised his hand in the same way and smiled, slowly nodding his head. “So here is Szar the prian, the man we have been following for six weeks,” his voice was deep and friendly.

“Oh no, please,” I whispered to myself, “not six weeks!”

Elyani, Elyani!

I repeated my question out loud, “Where is Fridrick?”

“Well,” the tall blond man said, “precisely, this was supposed to be the first of my three presents: intelligence.” He waited and watched my reaction, wondering if I was going to yell at him again. Nothing forthcoming, he went on, “There has never been any Fridrick in Jex Belaran.”

“I don’t believe you!” I shouted.

Very calm, the tall blond man nodded understandingly. His two friends had reached him. One stayed by his side, the older one kept walking towards me, smiling in a friendly way. “Szar prian, it seems that someone has been trying to fool you. But we have no idea who that can be. All we can tell you is that Fridrick was never trained in Jex Belaran.”

“What are you doing here, then?” I asked.

“Well, we happen to have a common friend. She sent us to you.” The older man, not as tall as Perseps but still, taller than me, kept walking until he was a four lawful feet away. There, he sat on the ground and started searching in the leather bag hanging from his shoulder. “I am the one who has been carrying the second present – for six weeks, by the way. Ah! Here it is,” he said, and he reached over to present me with an earthen jar. “Ginger marmalade!”

"Oh, no! No!" I exclaimed when I saw it. The jar was identical to the one Pelenor had brought when she visited Eisraim. Without any possible doubt, the marmalade came from Felicia. This man really was Joranjeran.

He looked quite disappointed. "Don't you like ginger marmalade any more?"

"Listen, I'm sorry!" I softened my voice. "It's just that I have difficulty believing..."

Disconcerted, the man remained still, the jar in his hand.

"Yes I do like it, thank you very much," I said, taking the jar from him with my right hand. "But if Fridrick has never been one of your Hunters, why did you communicate through him to make an alliance with me?"

"An alliance? What alliance?" the tall blond man, whom the marmalade had proved to be Perseps, walked towards me.

"What alliance?" Joranjeran repeated in his deep voice.

"Haven't we made an alliance?" I asked, opening my eyes wide.

Perseps sat next to his elder. Both had an expression of uncertainty on their face.

"Listen, am I dreaming or what? You are Kayala-ha Perseps, kuren-jaya champion and grand commander of Jex Belaran. And you are Joranjeran, former grand commander, the man with great wisdom and sense of humour. Right?"

They both smiled with satisfaction and nodded, "Right!"

"And so how come I know these things if..."

"Kill them now!" The impulse from the stone came up with such violence and suddenness that it nearly took me over.

The two Hunters sensed the aborted impulse. They stayed very calm, but I could see they were ready to strike.

Livid, I could barely manage to refrain from trembling.

"Do you want to show me your left hand?" Joranjeran proposed.

"All right."

He came closer and took my clenched fist in his excessively large hands. "What do you intend to do with this stone, Szar?"

"Fridrick was supposed to deactivate it."

The old Hunter smiled like a bear who smells honey, "Do you mean you were going to give it to him?"

"That was the original plan."

"Ha! Ha!" Perseps' explosive laughter was up to Mount Lohrzen's standards. "This Fridrick is a smart fellow!"

What could I answer? The idea that Fridrick could have lied to me was inconceivable. I had practised under his guidance for weeks. He had not only taught me kuren-jaya but also music. He had laughed and joked with me, shared his joys and his sorrows, given me his friendship and his warmth. And apart from the very beginning, he had never tried to conceal his energy from me. So many times he had let my consciousness enter his

Point. How could I possibly miss seeing he had completely fabricated his story? And what about Gervin and Esrevin?

Just by looking at the energy of my hand, Joranjeran understood perfectly well that the stone had gone wildly out of control. "Do you want to give us this stone?" he asked.

"Listen," I said, my voice now cool, "I need to understand better what has happened. If we have never made an alliance, then why are you here?"

"Felicia came to us one evening," Joranjeran explained, "and she said she had received a weird message from you, through Pelenor Ozorenan."

The message thanking her for facilitating the alliance with Perseps... I shivered, thinking what would have happened if I had ignored the Flying Dragon voice.

"Then," Joranjeran continued, "Felicia convinced us to send a few men to go and check that you were all right."

"She was very convincing!" Perseps added with a broad smile.

"We'll spare you the details," Joranjeran said. "So we sent six men after you. On their way south they went to inspect the headquarters of the Foxes which, we thought at the time, had been destroyed by the Red Renegades."

"Nice job you did there!" Perseps interposed.

Joranjeran went on, "When they saw the mess, our men decided to call a large troop to the rescue. Perseps and I deemed the situation extremely serious, and we decided to head the expedition ourselves."

"What mess?" I asked.

"In Raelene Vale, we found twenty-five corpses: twelve Fox Hunters, and thirteen apprentices."

"Not me!" I shook my head. "I didn't kill anyone when I was there."

"Aha?" Joranjeran was perplexed. "This story is becoming more complicated at every turn! And what about all the Black Hunters we found dead in your tracks?"

"Yes, that was me. But how did you locate me?"

"We followed the radiation of your stone. We hated the idea of it falling into the hands of Renegades. Actually, until we met Progos the giant, we didn't know it was you who carried the stone."

"And what happened to those Fox Hunters who survived the raid in Raelene Vale?" I asked.

"The Foxes and the Red Renegades slaughtered each other. I believe there is not much of them left now."

This did not make sense. "Wait a minute!" I said. "How come the Fox Hunters did not try to get their stone back from me? You tracked me and followed the radiation of my stone..." I stopped and corrected myself, "I mean the stone I took in Raelene Vale. Why couldn't the Foxes do the same?"

"Your stone remained silent for at least five weeks, Szar prian. By then, there were no Foxes left."

"Five weeks?" Another major shock.

To my utter horror, I was discovering that more than three months had elapsed since I had raided the Foxes' headquarters in Raelene Vale.

Winds of desolation... "Elyani! What will be left of you by now?"

"Will you give us the stone?" Joranjeran asked again.

Beyond my control, I felt excessively protective of the stone. "What will you do with it?"

Perseps raised his hands, "Deactivate it, of course!"

"Never!"

I opened my mouth but could not speak.

Joranjeran looked deep into me and nodded in understanding.

I grabbed my left fist with my right hand and pushed it towards him. But my fist was so tightly contracted that Joranjeran immediately declared, "If you want to have a chance to get rid of this stone, we will have to act fast, Szar, very fast. To deactivate it, a powerful ritual is needed, which is why such a large number of us came."

"There are forty-nine of you, is that right?"

The old man smiled in appreciation, "Well counted, young man."

"How will you get it out of my hand?" I asked.

"There are two options: either cut your hand, or send you unconscious."

Send me unconscious? There was no way in the seven spheres I was going to let forty-nine Nephilim Hunters perform a ritual on me while I was unconscious.

"Cut my hand off!" I said in a cold voice.

"Szar prian," Perseps patted my left arm as if I were his brother, "this is not a bad hand that you have here. No doubt it could be of use to you in the future. Why not let us send you unconscious for one hour?"

If only I could have taken Gervin's advice! But Gervin was far, and time was short. "Can you tell me why I am unable to Point-communicate with my teacher?" I asked the two men.

"Oh yes, this is very simple," Joranjeran said. "The stone creates an extraordinarily dense field of energy around you. Nothing can reach through. Even we cannot Point-call each other when we are close to you. Why do you need to talk to your teacher, by the way?"

"I trust Master Gervin of the Brown Robe would know exactly what I am supposed to do."

Joranjeran nodded in approval, "I like that." He smiled, winking at Perseps, "In critical times, great prians should always turn towards their teacher."

"Ha! Ha!" Perseps let out another salve of roaring laughter and loudly slapped Joranjeran's shoulder.

"This man has done something for us," Joranjeran said.

"Kill them! Kill them, right now!"

Perseps fully agreed, "The Watchers' balls he's done something for us!" Turning to me, he kept patting my arm, "We thought we were on a deadly war expedition against the Renegades. But each time we arrived somewhere, ready for the battle, all we had to do was perform funeral rites on the corpses you had kindly left behind you."

"So now, we'll do something for you," Joranjeran decided. "If you want, I myself will go and Point-discuss the situation with Master Gervin of the Brown Robe, and together we will decide what to do."

I grinned at the idea of the two old chiefs holding a Point-council.

"That's if you trust me, of course," Joranjeran added.

"Trust you?" I smiled ironically, "After all the remarkable things I've heard about you from Fridrick, how could I not trust you?"

Joranjeran and Perseps laughed loudly. Then Joranjeran began walking away, needing to take some distance before he could use his Point.

Perseps massaged my arm with his large hands. He was worried the painful contraction – and the devouring influence of the stone – might spread to the rest of my body. "So we meet at last, after hearing so much about each other," he said, realising I was better when I talked. For when I let my mind drift, the hallucinations returned, making it hard to hold onto the last remnants of my sanity.

"Of course, I have an advantage, " he said. "The person who told me about you was reliable. It could be that your source was biased."

I smiled, remembering the long red hair, "Whereas of course, Felicia could not possibly have been biased when she spoke about Szar."

"Ha! Ha!" The ground trembled with his laughter. "Do you know, by the way, I would have been *very* upset if Felicia had died in Verzazyel's crypt?"

"Me too!" I said. Then I was shaken by violent shivers.

"Need a blanket?" Perseps offered.

"Kill him now. Do not wait!"

I shook my head, "I am burning hot with fever. I think I need to lie down."

Perseps improvised a pillow for me with his leather bag.

"Perseps," I asked, my voice shaking, "who do you think was behind all this? Who planned the attack against the Foxes?"

"Someone who believed he could fool you and catch hold of the stone. Probably someone with a fair knowledge of the Watchers' lore. Perhaps this man was Fridrick. Perhaps he and Murdoch plotted together. By the way I must warn you, it could well be that Murdoch is still alive."

"I thought he had committed suicide."

"That's what he tried to make everyone believe. But his body has not been found so far."

"I wonder..." I was interrupted by a seizure of violent shivers.

"Kill him. Kill him," the stone kept whispering.

Perseps made me drink and asked, "Can I work on your gateways?"

"Perseps, I am afraid this ugly stone is going to take over and make me kill you. Do you have a knife?"

He slapped a leather pocket attached to his belt. "I do, but..."

"If I start losing my sanity, Perseps, I want you to cut off my hand immediately," I made sure I hammered in my words.

"We'll see. Can I bring my men over?" he asked.

I made no objection.

He called Waxen, "Tell them to come, all of them. And bring the dead wood."

"What's the wood for?"

"We'll need to light large pyres for the deactivation ritual." He kept talking to me, but I hardly heard what he said.

When his men arrived, they were carrying twigs and branches which they piled into six large heaps, hardly ten lawful feet away from me.

I was shaken by compulsive laughter. One year earlier, the idea of an encounter with three Hunters had filled me with dread. Now here I was, surrounded by nearly fifty of them, with their chief holding my hand!

Perseps laughed with me, "You don't have to worry! Do you realise what Felicia would do to us if anything went wrong during the ritual?"

The hallucinations took over again. "Perseps, have you already lit the pyres?"

"No."

"I see flames everywhere, Perseps. A horrible fire, all-consuming."

"The fire of Ahriman, that's what you are seeing," the Hunter said.

"Perseps, what does the Law of the Nephilim teach about Ahriman?"

"This fire that you are seeing... if Ahriman wins, that's all that will be left of this world in the end."

"But who is Ahriman?"

"The Prince of Darkness. His domain is the material world, which is why he is called 'the King of this World'. He knows that if he could isolate the material world from the spiritual kingdoms, then he would rule down here totally unchallenged." Perseps' huge hands were working expertly on my gateways. "In the Law of the Nephilim, there are some well-known verses which say, '*Man of the Law, try not to conquer the power of the Watchers, lest thou burn thyself and fall prey to Ahriman.*'"

The vision of the dreadful fire was taking over. I had to make great efforts to hold onto Perseps' face. "Believe it or not, just before I took the seed-connection stone in my hand," I told him, "a Watcher spoke to me and gave me the same warning. I wish I had heeded the advice."

"Ha! Ha!" Perseps roared. "One should always listen to the Watchers' advice!"

"Is that true, Perseps?"

"Oh, my friend, what a difficult question!" he answered, and we laughed together.

"You were right Perseps," I said after a moment, "my source of information was biased. You're a much nicer person than Fridrick said."

"And you were right too," Perseps joked, "my source of information was biased as well. You are not at all as fantastic as Felicia said." And he kept making me laugh until Joranjeran returned.

By then I had completely lost my physical vision, seeing only Ahriman's fire of hell. Sitting behind me, Joranjeran took my head in his hands. "What an interesting man your teacher is, Szar!"

"Did you speak to him?"

"A fascinating conversation, really. Now listen, there is no time to waste. Your teacher and I have decided we will not cut your hand, but send you unconscious. Gervin said I should explain to you that the ritual will be performed on the stone, not on you, and so nothing will bind you to the power of the Watchers. He also wanted me to tell you that Elyani and Woolly are alive, and a few other things I'll tell you after the ritual. Now we must hurry. I will go and organise my men."

Before I could thank him, he was already gone.

"I wish I could see what's happening!" I told Perseps, who remained by my side.

"Forty-eight mighty Hunters, the best in the kingdom, are holding torches in their hands. They are lighting the pyres and taking position around you, Szar prian."

I laughed again at this massive Nephilim power mobilised to rescue me. "Hey, Perseps, you haven't told me what my third present was."

"Well, the more we spoke, the less I felt like telling you. It was a stone!"

My laughter was choked by violent shivers.

Perseps explained, "When we realised some intrigue was going on, Joranjeran and I decided we would give you a special stone programmed to bypass the protection shield of Jex Belaran. This way we can Point-communicate with each other whenever we need."

"I think I would like to have this stone, Perseps."

"Brave of you to accept another stone from the Watchers!" He became serious, "You'll have to be extremely cautious, though. This stone must never fall into anyone else's hands. Otherwise, Jex Belaran's security could be endangered. So..."

Perseps was interrupted by loud chanting. The Hunters were beginning their ritual.

"Now!" Joranjeran shouted.

And I lost consciousness.

– Thus ends the book of the Encounters with Evil –

14

The Book of the Ascension Ritual

14.1 The prayer of Mareena to Apollo

Having purified herself for an entire day of the gods,
Long-haired Mareena praised the Lord of Lords,
Bathed in the Molten Sea, making herself divinely clear.
She let crystalline breezes raise her body of light
To the summit of the spheres,
This infinite Point-ness where myriads of high worlds
Serve as a foundation for all transient realms,
And where the seeds of all created things are found.
Again she praised the Lord of Lords.
Her divine eyes blinded by the One Solar Light,
She turned towards the solar god
And, surrendering to his golden glory,
She prayed,
"O great and mighty among the gods,
O ancient and magnificent,
O divinely lovable,
O gem of the celestial regions,
O Apollo, shining god,
Please hear the prayer of a humble goddess
Who fervently loves you
And for so long has secretly been in love with you.
Far away and low down,
In a kingdom of insignificance
Lost in grey mists and endless illusions,
A mortal soul is suffering an ordeal
As a result of a celestial wanting.
No doubt the daiva which the gods have cast
Will yield a rich harvest for all mortal beings:

Glorious destinies,
Precious opportunities for transcending human limitations,
Right accomplishments and seeds for the future.
Great is the wisdom of the gods, and far-reaching is their vision.
But, o compassionate divine soul,
Far below us, a human flame is being extinguished.
I know the mortals' time is like all other mortal things –
Insignificant. Cosmic period.
But because I love her and because I love you,
I come to implore your grace.
Let her trial, imposed by wise gods,
Be shortened by the most beautiful of all gods."
Blazing throughout the immensity of spaceless spheres,
Resounding with the unstoppable power of immortality made fluid,
The solar god smiled to Mareena.
Filled with his divinely loving presence,
She knew that he had heard her.

14.2 Harvesting after Ahriman

Ravaged, I was sitting by the temple's main entrance, looking down to my left hand: a pitch-black dent in my aura.

The deactivation ritual had been successful. When I awoke, the evil stone was no longer in my hand. But my hand was left paralysed, its energy no longer glowing like the rest of my aura, but ominously black. For this, the wise Joranjeran had no solution.

The Hunters had escorted me to the Fontelayana river. From there, they went north, while a boat took me south on a quick and easy journey back to Eisraim. Counting the days I had spent travelling to Tomoristan in the first place, I had remained nearly four months away from Eisraim.

The encounter with Aphelion appeared to have lasted less than a day. Yet it had taken a devastating toll. I felt abysmally empty, totally discouraged, my soul bleeding. I stepped through the main gate of the temple. I felt the need to sit on the ground and collect my thoughts while resting in the temple's atmosphere.

A melodious voice called, "*Praise the Lord Melchisedek, Szar of the Brown Robe!*"

Hermina!

Startled and delighted, I silently praised the Lord Melchisedek. The Immaculate had responded! She had come to Eisraim. There was hope for Elyani – a glimmer of sunshine in the ruins of my inner landscape.

Abiding by the rule of Hermina's high caste, I didn't answer but looked above her head and stood up.

Why should a Flying Dragon not talk to an Immaculate priestess?

The voice was back! At last.

The first smile of joy in four months.

Then came the first of the ugly surprises waiting for me.

"Szar, my friend in the Law," Hermina came closer, "I am sorry. Forgive me for arriving so late. When I received your message I tried to come as soon as I could. But the most incredible obstacles blocked me, one after the other, and delayed me for nearly three months."

Three months? Acid venom poured over my heart.

Damn Aphelion had kept his word. "As soon as you reach the temple of Eisraim," he had promised, "Hermina the Immaculate will arrive." At the time I had thanked him wholeheartedly for his help. Now I understood. Another poisoned gift. Three precious months had been wasted for the ominous boon to be fulfilled.

Sensing the profound wave of distress sweeping inside me, Hermina took my hands. But she recoiled as if she had been burnt. After a second of hesitation, she called on a bright light that I saw descending into her column of Spirit.

She took my left hand again. "Friend, I know whom you have met," she poured her loving energy through her voice, "and perhaps this explains the awful circumstances which I found myself locked into during the last weeks."

I had forgotten how beautiful her presence was. Soft, White, vast. The breath of Highness carried by her words brought tears to my eyes.

But what was going to happen with Elyani?

Hermina heard my thoughts. She said she would go and assess the situation with her two Immaculate colleagues, and promised to meet with me after seeing Elyani. Then she lawfully took leave.

As she walked away, my Flying Dragon voice greeted her,

Welcome to Eisraim, Hermina of Highness. Thank you for answering my call.

Hearing the voice, Hermina stopped. She hesitated for a few seconds, wondering where it came from. Then she started walking the straight path of the Law, making me wonder how she found her way in a temple she had never visited before without having to ask directions from anyone.

She draws from a Universal Knowledge Bank in which the priestesses of her caste have recorded the plans of most temples in the kingdom – some kind of Space Matrix for Immaculate priestesses.

Comforted by the voice and its familiar out-of-the-seven-spheres presence, I relaxed. "So you are back, Flying Dragon!" I said aloud, drawing a suspicious glance from an old priest passing by. "Where have you been in the last weeks, can you tell me?"

Where have you *been?* the voice answered.

"All right, all right! I'll never win with you." I began to walk through the enclave of the thirty-three victorious gods, towards Gervin's apartment.

"Now will you please tell me about this 'disguise' function of Space Matrix?"

It engages itself automatically whenever you need it. As I told you many times, Space Matrix is extraordinarily intelligent. If it offers to take you somewhere without you asking, it is quite foolish to refuse.

"All right, I have learnt my lesson!" Then I quickly looked to the right and to the left. "Want to take me somewhere, Space Matrix?"

Space Matrix did not prompt me, but my Flying Dragon voice answered, *Go to Teyani immediately!*

"I need to see Gervin first."

Really, young fool, you haven't learnt any lessons at all!

"All right!" I answered with feigned exasperation, raising my hands, "I will go to Teyani first, then to Gervin."

I turned back and left the enclave of the thirty-three victorious gods. I followed the straight path of the Law towards the entrance of the female wing, comforted by the familiar atmosphere and the luminous auras of the people of Eisraim, the gods smiling at me through their statues. And I rediscovered the precious magic of the female wing's Point-guided corridors, drinking its nectar of clarity.

When I arrived at Teyani's door, I closed my eyes and remained silent for a few seconds, collecting my Spirit before knocking.

True, Aphelion knew what the present held. But the future is not fixed. Nowhere is it written that the Brother Knights will lose the wars against the Rex.

I heard the door open.

I smiled, and opened my eyes. To my surprise it wasn't Teyani who stood in front of me, it was Gervin. His face was grave, he looked tired. He made a step towards me and took me in his arms. With an emotion I had never heard in his voice before, he said, "Praise the Lord Melchisedek, you are back!"

Too empty to know what to answer, I just stood still, letting his warmth come into me.

Gervin held me tight in his arms. "Praise the Lord Melchisedek! Praise the Lord Melchisedek who has brought you back to us." He moved back and looked at me, and for the first time I saw tears on his face.

I bit my lip and started crying with him.

He lightly touched my face, my beard, silently looking into my eyes.

"*All glory to the teacher!*" I finally managed to whisper. "If it wasn't for you, I would never have got myself out of the devil's clutches."

"But if it hadn't been for what you have learnt from me, he would not have come and tempted you as he did." He illumined his tears with the warmth of the Brown Robe, "Really, by giving knowledge, a teacher exposes his disciples to great dangers."

I hugged him. "So good to be with you again! I missed you... so much," I rested my head against his shoulder, crying like a child. "It's been awful,

Gervin, awful! Never seen anything so horrible. Never felt so bad, so empty."

He patted my shoulder. "I know. Before Orest initiated me into Thunder, Aphelion came to visit me too. But now you are back, and even though things won't be easy, there will be some good times for us – this I promise." He took me by the hand. "Come, I know someone who'll be very happy to see you."

He took me through the large empty room where Teyani usually saw her students, then through a short corridor that led to a closed door. Before opening it, he looked deep into me, "Listen, Teyani and I love you a lot. A lot." Then he opened the door, and there came the second ugly surprise.

Teyani was lying on her low bed. Withered and wan, she had lost at least twenty kilos. Her aura stank with the filth of the caverns of sickness. Her face was livid, unlawful black rings circling her eyes. Completely exhausted, she was but a shadow of herself.

"Oh no!" I whispered, realising the hideous truth. "What have I done?"

Teyani greeted me with a feeble smile. "*Praise the Lord...*" she started saying, but a violent cough seized hold of her.

"This is a complete nightmare!" I went to sit at her bedside. As Teyani kept coughing, I turned to Gervin, "Don't tell me this started with the flu?"

Gervin was grave, "It started with the flu, some three months ago."

I could hardly believe what I was discovering. "Couldn't anyone heal you, Teyani?"

Teyani had become quiet again. "*Praise the Lord Melchisedek, my child," she Point-said. "So you have returned to us! Seeing you here is such a joy in the Law. You will never know how much we have prayed for you."*

"I am sorry, Teyani!" I took her feverish hand. "I am so sorry! I never suspected this illness would happen. Not like this!"

"Elyani is alive," she Point-said, "but despite all our efforts we haven't been able to convince the two Immaculate priestesses to let us try to heal her. It has been a difficult period, Szar. As we were expecting your friend Hermina any day, we refrained from openly confronting them. But Hermina never arrived. So, after much hesitation we decided to put pressure on them. So far, they have flatly refused to let us see Elyani."

When I told her that Hermina had just arrived and that we would soon hear from her, a glimmer of hope lit her eyes.

"And what about Alcibyadi?" I trembled. "Did anything happen to her?"

"She's blossoming," Gervin reassured me. He took me aside and led me into another room. "The force you sent into Teyani was horrendously violent," he said, his tone matter-of-fact. "Normally, with an influence of this kind, our procedure is simple: we return it to the sender. In this case, though, we had no idea what was happening to you. We were terribly worried that if we sent the force back to you it would kill you, or at least bring you further confusion at a time when you needed all the clarity you had left, to resist the temptation of the dark side. Even if we had simply lifted the force out of Teyani's body, there was still great risk you might be hit by a shock wave in return. So Teyani decided to keep the influence with her and digest it. But despite all my help, it has proved incredibly resistant."

I was appalled, "I can't believe I did this, Gervin." The scene flashed back to me, "I had no idea! Aphelion was *so* clever..."

Gervin took my left hand and carefully inspected it. He gently Voice-projected a low-pitched sound onto it. The sound made my wrist's aura shine with white-purplish light, but the aura of the hand remained pitch-black. "Teyani might have to wait a few more days," he decided, visibly concerned. "I must try to do something to your hand before we lift the dark influence off her."

"Is it so bad?" I asked. "I thought that if I dived deep into the Underworlds, I could wash out the smear."

"Good!" Gervin approved. "Try it, by all means. But this black energy might prove more tenacious than you think."

At that moment, Hermina voice-channelled, "Szar, please come and meet me immediately in the garden outside the tower of Malchasek."

Gervin sealed my lips with his index finger.

I nodded to reassure him. I knew how to behave with an Immaculate priestess.

"It had to be you!" Gervin was moved. "Who else but you could the White Eagle choose to rescue Elyani?" Then he gently slapped my shoulder. "Fly Dragon! Do not waste a lawful minute."

I gave him another hug. Before leaving I quickly asked, "Has Woolly recovered?"

"Woolly?" the touch of irony in Gervin's smile smelt like a long and complicated story. "Just wait till you see him. There is a big, big surprise waiting for you, Szar!"

"I hope Maryani hasn't turned him into a Naga!"

"You'll see, you'll see..."

"And Fridrick?"

Gervin raised his hands. "Disappeared! He went to try to find you, and never came back."

Not a great surprise, this one.

As I made my way to the tower of Malchasek, I realised I was terrified.

What if Hermina allowed me to see Elyani? Hour after hour I had spent, watching the tower and its upper-left window. The idea I might find myself in her presence made me weak at the knees.

Even worse, what if Hermina did not allow me to help Elyani?

Elyani, I knew, was dying.

No thoughts, just Dragon, I was on my way.

14.3 The world has changed

I found Hermina sitting on a bench outside the tower's main entrance. I immediately directed my gaze above her head. She invited me to sit with her and remained silent for a moment, letting her Light of Highness pour into me.

"Szar, the situation is not good. Elyani is sick, exhausted, and completely discouraged. I have to make a difficult decision: either interrupt the preparation for the ritual, or wait for a miracle to happen."

I felt sick to the stomach. Wait for a miracle! Was that what the two Immaculate had been doing while Holma was dying?

"Szar," she continued, "will you believe me if I tell you that I sincerely care for Elyani and am trying to do the best for her?"

Of course I believed her.

"Szar, if the ascension ritual succeeds Elyani will be reborn with the gods, at the top of the pyramid of the worlds. The gods are not just immortal, Szar, they are *blessed with extraordinary gifts*. Their life is filled with wonders. For as long as this cosmic cycle lasts, Elyani will enjoy their fortune. She will also be able to help a great number of human beings – you, for a start, and many of your friends. So, before attempting anything that could jeopardise the ritual, we must think very carefully. There is a lot to lose, but what exactly is there to gain by interrupting the ritual? You know only too well that the days of the kingdom are numbered. How long before the peaceful life of this temple turns into an unlawful nightmare? How long before *the wonderful harmony of the Law of the castes* turns into complete chaos? How long before epidemics spread, crops fail, angry mobs go on the rampage?" Hermina paused before she spelled out the dilemma with all the gentleness of her High compassion, "What if I interrupted the ritual now, and Elyani died in the disasters that will hit Eisraim in the coming months or years?"

Letting her warmth flow into me, Hermina went on, "Please do not judge my two Immaculate sisters for having hoped and prayed until the last moment that Holma would be saved by a miracle. For they are holy women who in the past have performed several miracles by strictly adhering to *the most ancient and holiest body of the Law*. Tonight they will go. They will leave the temple. They know that everyone here has hated them for Holma's fate, and they know that everyone holds them responsible for Elyani's sickness. But they hold no grudge against Eisraim. They have followed their own truth, regardless of what it has cost them."

She blessed me with the silence of Highness.

Immersed in her Light, it seemed easy to understand the logic of her Immaculate sisters. The priestesses of their order radiated a breath of infinite purity that came straight from the Ancient Days of the Earth, when the world was in perfect harmony: a grand symphony in which all beings and all things celebrated the oneness of the Spirit of God. In such a perfect world, how could a higher grace not intervene when a pure soul like Elyani needed help to complete her high ritual while strictly adhering to the rules of the Law? As the well-known verse said, *The Law supports those who support the Law*. Those great angels who had assisted the Lord Melchisedek at the time of the revelation of the Law on Earth and who had afterwards upheld the Law for men, how could they not come to the rescue of someone who without reservation took shelter in the Law? And so, what greater safety could there be than strictly abiding by the rules and prescriptions of the Law? Surely, it would be safer to *die in the Law* than to go astray from the paths of the Lord Melchisedek.

Did Hermina completely believe this? We all believed that it had been true long ago, during the golden age. But the golden age had passed, and the silver age after it. And now the age of bronze was quickly vanishing, to be replaced by a world of iron in which the High Light of angels no longer governed each and every circumstance of human life. The simple truth was, the great angels of Melchisedek had not intervened when Holma was dying. Why should they intervene now that Elyani was dying?

Hermina!

Intrigued, Hermina lifted her head.

I smiled, amused by the scene. Hermina and I were both sitting in meditation position, facing each other, but looking high above each other's head.

Hermina, the world has changed!

"What a beautiful voice!" she whispered. "It is yours, isn't it?"

Had I nodded, I would have broken the Law of her high caste. So I let my Flying Dragon nature answer, *Yes, Hermina.*

"When I was a child," she said with nostalgia, "a voice like this used to speak to me. It was my friend! It used to tell me extraordinary stories about the remote sphere of the Blue Lagoon and the Black Night of Remoteness."

Can you still hear that voice?

"When I was twelve, it went away. It came to me one night, and it explained to me that it had to go back to its home, far away." As she spoke, I caught a glimpse of the immense sadness the Immaculate little girl had gone through when losing her friend. "After it left, I remember, I was desperate, because I had forgotten to ask its name. I thought that if only I knew its name, I could perhaps find it again, one day."

I could find its name for you, if you wanted.

"Could you really?"

I knew that behind her white veils, a smile had appeared on her face.

Just remember the presence, I said, and I called onto Space Matrix. *Szar, requesting Flying Dragon identification, as Pointed to by human entity.*

Space Matrix immediately responded,

Search successful. Flying Dragon retrieved, presently located in the spheres of the Blue Lagoon. Contemplate the vision of his name in transcendental remoteness.

"What does that mean?" Hermina asked.

Mm... we have a slight problem here. The name of a Flying Dragon is not just made of words. It is a multidimensional representation of its quintessential nature. It can only be contemplated by stepping into the archetypal warp which upholds the cosmic astrality of the spheres of remoteness. Let me see if Space Matrix could translate your friend's name for you.

Unfortunately, Space Matrix's answer was not what Hermina expected: *Simplified translation in universal language is 19307536749320543543 96900534315724950775 6 346236582760 5434645360078753792659821 4876926 0154 3400679 7602987433999785723432534620957434...*

The long series of figures created sharp purple sparks amidst the bright circulations of white light in Hermina's column of Spirit.

Silently, we contemplated the space of ultra-fast-moving shapes.

A few thousand geometrical archetypes later, I repeated, *Hermina, the kingdom has changed!*

The Immaculate priestess lowered her gaze.

Dragon above, Dragon below, I opened my heart to her completely. *Hermina, the time when human beings were to follow the rules of the Law and wait for the angels of Highness to do the rest has passed. Now, contemplative prayers are no longer enough. If we want High powers to help us, we must help them help us.*

In my peripheral vision, I saw her acquiesce with her head. But after a short silence, she said, "The ritual of ascension is such a magnificent and powerful practice, Szar; it is difficult to conceive that it may falter."

Hermina, the fields are collapsing, and all the laws of nature are changing after them. There are hundreds of magnificent rituals which our ancestors used to perform miracles, and which no longer work.

"This is true," she conceded, her voice heavy with the sadness of the world.

Locked, we were, in this cosmic impasse, until something unlawfully extraordinary took place. Hermina said, "So what exactly do you want, Szar of the Brown Robe? Should I surrender Elyani to you and teach you how to conduct the ascension ritual?"

I choked. The Flying Dragon voice didn't. *No, Hermina I am not trying to get rid of you. I can't see who better than you could perform the ritual of ascension. But as the world has changed, so some parts of this long ritual may have to be modified. What I want is simple: to liaise with you and understand what has to be performed, then use every single resource I can find, from the deepest of the Dragon to the high knowledge and powers of the Masters of Thunder, to make it work.*

Hermina remained silent for a while. Then, in a tone that indicated the meeting was finished, she said, "I must ponder on these matters *lawfully carefully*."

14.4 Woolly of the rainbows

When I voice-channelled Woolly, the first thing he said was, "I have a big, big – but I mean really very, very big surprise for you, Szar."

"Bigger than the seven spheres... Woolly, that sounds blasting! Let me guess," I answered, my Dragon consumed with curiosity.

"*No way, man of the Law!*" he shouted through the channel, "I don't want you to guess. I want to see your face when you find out."

"All right, then. When can I see you?"

"Oh... next lawful month, perhaps?"

As I burst out laughing, he ordered, "Stay where you are. I'm coming!"

I sat on the Dragon gate, waiting for him, rediscovering my music field, wondering how long it would take for Hermina to get back to me.

Elyani's fate was being sealed.

With all my heart, with all my mind,

I am with you, even when I am far away.

Whatever Hermina's answer would be, I had decided to start sending music to Elyani. Helped by Space Matrix, I had worked out a system that sent sounds to a particular astral space in the remote sphere of my dear mathematical friend the Great Ant. From there the sounds were reflected into the space of Elyani's bedroom. Technically, this could not be considered a violation of the Law of the Immaculate since it came from far beyond the spheres of Melchisedek.

Practically, it scared the Underworld out of me. Was I ready to speak to Elyani, be it only through the sounds of my music field? Shouldn't I have waited a little? "And what if she does not like my music?"

Frankly, it would be difficult to find a more stupid excuse!

"This is getting to be impossible!" I threw back my head, losing patience with my Flying Dragon voice. "I can't even think in my own head!"

Then I turned to the voice again, "What music do you think we should send her? White Eagle?"

No! Send her music that comes from the deepest of yourself.

"Mm..." I started with the 'bang-ting-ting' tune.

I hope no one in the Great Ant overhears this one.

So what? I didn't mind the idea of perplexed Flying Dragons trying to decipher the meaning of this lawful saucepan-and-spoon melody resounding through extra-galactic spaces. Ha!

Gradually the bang-ting-ting faded, heartness took over.

A gentle flame, White Eagle from inside, dancing through time, little and frail compared to the immensity of remoteness, soft, humble worshipper of the light, profound, one thousand mysteries held in a simple smile, a voice in the creation choir, worlds to come, newborn infinity, the Great Mother's lover.

Wonderful! Exactly what she needs.

I was testing my system, sending astral sounds to the Great Ant and back into my courtyard, when Woolly walked in.

"Woolly! But Woolly...!"

Talk about a surprise!

"But Woolly..." flabbergasted, I forgot to stop the music.

He laughed, satisfied with how blasted I was. "*Praise the Lord Melchisedek, Szar of the Brown Robe*," he said in a distinguished voice.

"Youyouyouyou..." I exploded with joy, broadcasting the Warriors' scream into the Great Ant's sphere, and I ran to him. I Dragon-squeezed him in my arms, and we shouted and danced with joy.

"Your beard is mag*ni*ficent!" I lauded loud.

His newly-grown beard, however, wasn't the prime mover of such exultation, but a consequence. Woolly was no longer Woolly of the Dirty-Cream Robe. He was Woolly of the Brown Robe, apprentice of the Masters of Thunder! We both knew it meant that our destinies were joined far beyond this Atlantean existence, for the commitment to the lineage of Thunder is one that continues from life to life.

"How did it happen?" I smoothed the brand-new brown gown with my hand.

"Oh! It's a complicated story," he sighed.

"Unsurprisingly!" I said, inviting him to sit with me on the lawn.

"Where does this music come from?" he asked, looking around him.

"A music field Ferman and I put together before I left. Do you like it?" I touched a soft-stone pendant he was wearing around his neck and connected it to the field. The space of the courtyard was filled with a complicated melange of high-pitched celestial harmonies and waterfall-like rumbling.

"What a beauty!" he marvelled. "The sounds are so warm."

"Now, speak, man of the Law! I want to hear everything."

He took my hand off the pendant. The music stopped, replaced by the elusive 'ffffoooohhhh' whisper of the Great Ant's Flying Dragon-ness.

"Do you know that the morning before the attack by the Black Hunters, I had decided to reform my language?" Woolly began. "That explains it, doesn't it? The gods must have been shocked."

I didn't hide my amazement, "Reform your language?"

"And a few other things by the same occasion. Fairly major changes, altogether. And then guess what?"

I closed my eyes for a second. "In the hour that followed, Gervin came to you," was what I could see.

"But stop!" Woolly slapped my knee, "I don't want you to guess my story, I want you to listen!"

I raised my hands apologetically, "Sorry!"

"Now," he continued, "I was working on the stones when Gervin suddenly turned up. And do you know what he said?"

I shook my head and remained mute.

"He said, 'Woolly, would you like to become a Master of Thunder?' I had a moment of astonishment and then I answered, 'Or would I rather die a useless and painful death amidst utter chaos in the kingdom, and then be reborn as some filthy, dirt-eating animal in a desolate land forgotten by the gods?' I thought he was joking, but when I saw how seriously he was laughing, I realised he was not. Then you'll never guess what happened!"

"Never!" I promised.

"Gervin said, 'If you want to tread the path of Thunder, you will have to undergo several trials.' And then he told me how you had learnt that the f... I mean the ugly melt-wave that had resulted in my expulsion from the temple of Laminindra had been started by Henrick the Renegade Hunter, not by me. That came as a major shock, to put it mildly. Gervin offered to use his authority to help me clear my name and regain my place in Laminindra, if I wanted. I hesitated a moment and then said I could not see myself going back to that old life and that despite the food, I preferred to stay in Eisraim. And then guess what he said... 'Woolly, you have passed the first test! But the second trial will be no less bitter than the first. If you take on the Brown Robe, you won't be able to accompany Maryani to the land of Aegypton. For, as prophesied long ago by the Sons of Apollo, when the kingdom falls, all the Masters of Thunder and their apprentices will be gathered in the Fields of Peace. There, together with hundreds of other sages, they are to take part in a great ritual aimed at preparing the revelation of our Lord Melchisedek in the kingdom of the rainbows.'"

"What did you answer to that one?" I asked.

"I didn't answer. I just said I needed to think. Gervin left, and I went to speak to Maryani. At the time we were not talking to each other, but we made an exception. At first, she was adamant. She said that if I didn't take up Gervin's offer, she would never – but this time, really not joking – never ever speak to me again. But when I finally said, 'All right, I'll take up his offer!' she burst into tears, and she cried for hours. I had never seen her so upset. Nothing I could say or do seemed to comfort her.

When I returned to the chapel later on, I was so confused! After hours of deliberation, I finally decided I simply could not abandon her, and that I would decline Gervin's invitation. Then I called onto the Great Goddess – the first time I had prayed to anyone since the day of my *nine-year-old's confirmation in the Law*, when I broke my nose (you don't need to know that story). So that night in the chapel, I called with all my heart, 'Mother of the Light, if this is the wrong choice, *please* send me a sign.' Three hours later, the Black Hunters irrupted into the temple."

"Talk about a sign!"

"When I woke up, I couldn't see my body. There was this blasting golden light all around me. I thought that the gods had recalled me from the kingdom. But when I asked, 'Where am I?' this massive voice came to me and said, 'You are in my consciousness, Sir Woolly of the Cream Robe.'

It was the Naga King. When I asked him if I was dead, he answered in his so very polite voice, 'Well, no... not quite, yet, but possibly quite soon, I am afraid.' Then he invited me to rest comfortably in his consciousness and assured me he would give me his full support and guidance towards my next reincarnation."

"King Vasoukidass," Woolly continued, "came back to me after a while with what he called excellent news: I was no longer to die, but only to be paralysed and blind and, he added, quite possibly not even for the rest of my life. You can imagine how delighted I was.

When I regained consciousness, I was in Maryani's room. It didn't take her long to repair my eyes, but it took nearly six weeks before I could move my hands or speak. It was so unfair! She could say anything she wanted, with full impunity. Still, it was not such a bad time, after all."

"What do you mean, not a bad time?" I smiled.

"Yes," he conceded, his voice softened, "it was quite a good time. She was very sweet to me. But it took her a lot of time and effort to get me to walk again."

"And what happened with Gervin?"

"Well, well... I decided I didn't need any more signs. Gervin came to visit me in Maryani's room and I told him I no longer needed to hesitate. I asked him what the next trial was going to be.

He said, 'Find the worst thing in yourself and surrender it to the Lord Melchisedek, then I will give you a brown gown.'

I told him I thought the worst thing about myself was the cynical way I judged other people. I thought I had let go of that just before the Hunters came to get me, by deciding to reform my language.

Gervin assured me there was much worse. He turned to Maryani and said, 'You know what the worst thing is, don't you?' And she answered, 'Of course I do.'

I got impatient. 'Would someone in this room kindly tell me what the worst thing about me is, please?' I asked them."

I took his hand. "Did they tell you?"

In the Blue Lagoon, the Flying Dragon is waiting. Call!

"No!" Woolly laughed, outraged. "Gervin left, and Maryani and I spent the day looking into each other's eyes without saying a thing. Then I completely collapsed. I realised what the worst thing was, and it made me cry from sunset to sunrise."

"And so what was this worst thing?"

"Not complicated, but deep: I hated myself, Szar. I had spent my life hating myself. That's what made me bitter and cynical. And as long as I hated myself, I could never really love anyone. That's what I discovered."

Woolly spoke with simplicity, no longer feeling the need to hide behind words. For the first time, we could just sit together in silence and enjoy each other's presence, eerie 'ffffoooohhhh' whispers from remoteness in the background. A different man, he had become. His face looked softer, his skin shining from Maryani's good treatment. But his nose looked rather more broken than before.

"Didn't Maryani try to heal your nose?" I asked him. "With her powers, she could probably restore it to its original glory."

"No, she doesn't even want to, she says it's karmic. She says if we try to take the karma out of the nose, it will reappear somewhere else, and probably worse. She says she loves me with my nose."

14.5 The vow of the Eagle and the Dragon

Woolly left at sunset. After lighting the large oil lamp in the turret, I tuned into Space Matrix and established the Point-connection that was to reflect my music into Elyani's room via the spheres of the Great Ant.

When everything was ready, Space Matrix prompted me, *Engage flow of sound through intention.*

I started with a timid 'bang-ting-ting' over a soft murmur of the Black Night of Remoteness. I continued with the warm heartness that poured from the Eagle, invoking Space Matrix for inspiration.

Space Matrix revelation. Endless poetic flow. Aeons of accumulated Knowledge. Beyond the mind of the gods.

Elyani's window remained unlit.

Was she so sick she couldn't even light her room? Perhaps she had lost heart during my absence – the brown flag gone, the turret nothing more than a dark silhouette.

Mother of the Light, help!

I kept playing. A duo with the Great Ant.

An hour later night had enveloped the temple. I received a call through darkness visible. "Szar!"

Petrified, I stopped the flow of sound.

The voice was frighteningly feeble.

Elyani! Using my Flying Dragon voice to respect the Law of the Immaculate.

"Szar, Szar..." the call came, bringing the Eagle's softness back into my life, "Szar it is finished. I can speak to you, you can speak to me."

Finished? I asked. *Has the ascension ritual been abandoned?*

"No. But Hermina has decided to change some of the rules."

Change the rules? The idea that an Immaculate priestess could agree to depart from the strict letter of the Law brought an immense feeling of victory. *Praise the Lord Melchisedek! What are the new rules, Elyani?*

"Not completely decided yet. But at least for a period I can see you and be with you, and let you heal me."

When you have wanted something with all your being, all your heart, all your strength, and for so many months, getting it does not always bring an explosion of joy. Sometimes the feeling is that of a powerful momentum that suddenly falls flat, leaving you completely empty.

I cried.

Does this mean I can come to you? I asked, climbing up the ladders to the Blue priestesses' roof.

A silence.

Elyani?

"Yes, we can see each other. Hermina even said I could return to my courtyard if I wanted, but... I am afraid, Szar." A shy voice, "I am sick. Very sick. I have lost a lot of weight and..."

Remember what the Eagle told you when I returned from Mount Lohrzen? Go and see Szar in the night. What if I did the same?

There was no answer. Just the universal silence of creation.

"I want to hear your voice," she said after a moment. "Where are you? Are you standing on the Blue priestesses' roof?"

"No!" I replied through her voice channel, "I have just about reached the tower of Malchasek. I will be at your door in a few seconds. Will you let me in? I have aeons of urgent things to tell you."

"Fly, Dragon!" she replied like Space Matrix. "Fly high!"

From a low roof, I jumped my way down into the small garden outside the tower of Malchasek. Then, slowly, I walked to the doorway.

The large portal was open. It led to an empty staircase.

I stopped, and took a deep breath.

"On the top floor," Elyani voice-channelled, "the first door in the hallway after the steps."

I ran up the staircase and arrived at her door.

Space winds. From one end of remoteness to the other, he travelled.

I opened the door and paused, "My eyes are closed. It's a moonless night in the forest."

"Come, please." Elyani murmured.

I walked in the direction of her voice, searching in front of me with my hands to avoid bumping into trees.

"Here," she said. "On the bed."

In the moonless night I found her low bed and knelt down close to her. My hand naturally moved towards her, then stopped. "Can I touch you?"

Her hand came to meet mine.

The contact sparked a huge heart wave, a flame that extended high up in the spheres. *Rejoice, White Eagle! I shall protect your seed, as my father commanded me.*

What do you say to the person you love when you haven't seen them for an entire lifetime?

Silence. The creation breathes.

Magic of a presence meeting a presence.

With her hands, she turned my head away from her. "Open your eyes," she said.

Dragon! Dragon! How dry and weak her hands were!

In this space of unreality, I found myself looking at the orange glow of my turret from Elyani's window.

"See, from where I am I can see your light," she said. "I placed my bed so I could always see it at night."

Passing her fingers on my face she closed my eyes again, and she turned my head towards her. "But where have you been? I was terrified. No more flag, no light. Even your Flying Dragon voice had become silent."

"Where have I been?" I sighed. "I'll tell you. But... shall I take you home, now?"

She burst into tears. "I can't believe this is happening. I had lost hope, Szar, completely. I thought I'd never see you again. Not in this life."

I took her in my arms. A shock! I could not recognise her body. There was hardly anything left of her. Her flesh had evaporated. Her skin was dry and withered, her life force shrivelled.

I rested on the Dragon, trying to hide how shattered I was.

"I am sorry!" she cried, clasping her arms around my neck. "This ritual has been hell. It's drained the marrow out of my bones. I look old and ugly. An ugly skeleton."

Ripped apart by her pain, "Listen, listen..." I caressed her short hair, no longer curly, "Maryani and I are going to show you what the Dragon of the Deep can do." I held her against me, "Please, my love, we must keep hope. We will find ways."

She couldn't stop sobbing.

"Come," the Dragon had decided, "I'm taking you out of here!"

"Wait! Let me put on my veil. I don't want you to look at me. Not even my eyes. Promise?"

"Promise." I gave her time to wrap herself in the fashion of the Immaculate, hiding all of her head but the eyes.

"Can I open my eyes now?" I asked

"Yes."

I looked up to the ceiling. The plass was grey. Dirty. The *living walls* were sick with elemental filth.

Delicately, I lifted Elyani in my arms. I was horrified by how light she was. "Aphelion," I thought without hatred, "you can rejoice and praise your king. The months you stole from me have taken a devastating toll on her."

Her tears were heavy. I walked, whispering in her ear, trying to comfort her. She cried, pouring out the despair built up inside her over months of solitude.

On our way we met a group of priestesses who stopped and looked at us in complete stupefaction.

I tried to reassure them by displaying a broad smile, worried they might think their ascending goddess was being kidnapped.

"All glory to the Lord Melchisedek, Szar of the Brown Robe!" the priestesses answered in one voice. Had I been levitating along the corridor, the expression on their faces would hardly have been different.

Against my shoulder, the ascending goddess was sobbing.

"It's finished, my love! We're going home, now!" I quickened the pace, not looking forward to meeting anyone else.

But the journey home took an interesting turn. The priestesses we had just met had already voice-channelled all their friends, who in turn called everyone else in the temple. In a matter of seconds, priestesses of all robes rushed out of their rooms and chapels, filling the corridors of the female wing. They did not speak to Elyani, knowing only too well it would have been a violation of the Immaculate Law, but they all hailed me with loud enthusiasm, "*Praise the Lord Melchisedek, Szar of the Brown Robe!*"

Resting on the Dragon of the Deep, I returned the lawful greetings, doing my best to keep a reassuring smile on my face. But as I was walking down an empty stairway I whispered to Elyani, "I'll have to tell you the context, but... during my last journey, I've come to the conclusion that it is plainly impossible to keep a secret in Atlantis."

In the next corridor a few dozen priestesses were gathered. Among them, Mouridji the prophetess. "I am proud of you, son," she declared after lawfully greeting me. "At last, you followed my advice!" She burst into applause, and all the other priestesses followed her.

When we finally arrived at the courtyard, I carefully laid the frail body on the lawn close to Adya's laurel tree. The Moon had not yet risen, the night was completely dark.

I took her in my arms. "What shall we do first: start the healing or call Teyani and Melchard?"

"No," Elyani said, "now is the time to make the vow."

Unforgettable moment.

"This is why you didn't want me to take the vow before... it had to be spoken from my Flying Dragon voice, is that it?"

She lightly touched my face. "The combined vow of a Flying Dragon and a White Eagle, this is what I want."

"You've known about my Flying Dragon nature for a long time, haven't you? How did you find out?"

"Not difficult. Your voice spoke to me."

"So embarrassing!" I whispered. "In the last months I have discovered that my voice has been speaking to quite a few people, but I have no idea what I have been telling them."

"You were explaining to me what it feels like to be a Flying Dragon. And you told me about the wonders of remoteness: the Great Ant – you seem to be particularly fond of the Great Ant – and the Fault of Eternity. The Abyss of the Deep where the Mother of the Light can be seen smiling. And the spheres where your father lives. You said we would go and visit him together."

"Mm..." all this sounded reassuringly well-mannered. "Tell me about the vow."

"I want us to vow that we will not separate those who love each other."

"And what if we have to? Will we never have to fight wars?"

"If we have to, then... we have to!" she said in a little, little voice. "But separations aren't always caused by cosmic necessity. Often they come because of the narrow-mindedness of those who don't care." Tears choked her voice, "If I was taken away from you it was only because of stupid old rules. Truly, I could very well have done the ritual work while staying with you."

"Truly?" Hope flared, "Does this mean that once healed, you will stay with me until the final ritual of ascension?"

"This is in the hands of the Immaculate."

With the help of the Spirit of the Great Ant, clarifying fields of extraordinary magnitude can be generated.

"This vow," she said, "I want it to be as deep as our love for each other, and I want it to be sealed with your Flying Dragon nature. And if ever I succeed and find my way to the world of the gods, I swear I will use my power to help souls who have real heart connections to be reunited. Will you swear, Dragon?"

I will.

Elyani engaged the Word of the Eagle and Voice-projected, "Whenever Truth permits, I shall not separate those who love each other."

Despite her state of exhaustion the power she Voice-projected filled the entire courtyard with white light – a harmonious marriage of softness and strength. The velvety energy made everything vibrate and shine as in the magical Ancient Days of the Earth. The grass started singing a high-pitched melody, and the laurel trees looked infinitely wise.

Elyani, I realised, had learnt a lot from the Immaculate.

From far, the Flying Dragon voice repeated, *Whenever Truth permits, I shall not separate those who love each other.* And its presence came down to meet the white magic Elyani had awakened around us.

In this unreal super-reality we sat beyond time for a while, silently telling each other all the things we had kept inside for so long.

The laurel trees heard, and understood.

"Now," I asked her on our return to the kingdom, "will you let me work on your body?"

She lay down on the grass. "I am all yours, Dragon."

I replied with a long, loud sigh.

"Well... nearly!" she added. "I must remain a virgin, you know."

I burst out laughing, "That still leaves plenty of scope for treating you."

"It is *so good* to hear you laugh!" her voice lifted. "Like coming back to life after the caverns of sickness."

When I let my right hand run on her gateways, my Dragon responded with big vroofing waves of joy. But what I discovered wasn't at all encouraging. Her body of energy was not only exhausted but also caked with elemental filth that clogged her circulations of life force. The resulting vibration was foul.

"A nasty sewage, isn't it?" she commented sadly. "During these months, I haven't had much fun living in my body."

I could hardly believe how compacted the elemental concretions were. "Did all this come from performing the ritual?"

"Unfortunately, yes. Through the fire rituals I was supposed to offer the elementals of nature to the gods. But all I could find to offer was the pollution overflowing from the fields. I tried to turn the exercise into some gigantic clearing of the land. But there was just too much of that muck! It killed me. The weaker I became, the more dirt accumulated inside me."

I started a patient clearing work, bottle-brushing channels and taking elemental slime out of her system.

As I performed the healing I suggested, "Shall we speak to Teyani?"

"But I can't, Szar! I am still an Immaculate."

"So Hermina lets you speak to me, but not to other people. Is that the rule?"

"Yes. So far we haven't broken any Law."

I didn't follow. "How come the Law allows you to speak to me?"

"In the Law of the Immaculate, there is a provision which says that *if an ascending goddess becomes unlawfully ill, a lawful attendant shall be appointed with whom she can talk*. Of course, it is implied that the *lawful attendant* will be a woman, as Immaculate attendants always are. But nowhere is this said explicitly. So Hermina nominated you."

I gulped. "So now, I'm a *lawful Immaculate attendant*!" I forced a high pitch in my voice, "I can't wait to see Gervin's face when he discovers this."

"Hermina said she would let you notify Melchard of your nomination. She hopes no one in the temple will object."

Dragon-fierce, "No one would dare!"

"From what I could hear when you were carrying me through the corridors, there seems to be little risk. What have you done for these people to like you so much?"

"Yes, what have I done?" I sighed. "I think it started when I healed Princess Pelenor, who came to visit. It was a state secret, but of course they all found out. It made them very happy, for some reason. Gervin said it gave the people of the temple a bit of hope. They started believing that perhaps, one day, I could heal you. They all love you a lot, you have no idea. I *know* they have prayed for you."

"How will we thank them?" she wondered.

"By succeeding in the ritual, of course!" I tried to sound encouraging. But the future was not bright. The elemental slime gushing out of the fields was getting more noxious and fetid every week. How in the kingdom could it ever be ritually offered to the gods?

14.6 Flowers for Hermina

The *living walls* were waking up, welcoming the early morning by brightening their glows. Wrapped in her veils, Elyani was dozing in my arms. Frightened by the light of day she hid herself under the bed sheet and snuggled against me. "You don't want to see me, I'm too ugly!"

I gently rocked her against me, "Little Dragon Maryani and I are going to make you *so* Underworld-beautiful. The gods won't be able to resist. They'll abduct you before you even have time to complete the ritual."

"I'll say, 'No way, gods of the Law! Come back at the end of time. I want to stay in his arms an endless little bit more.'" She sighed, "I think I prefer to stay ugly, then. Just keep me in your arms and never look at me!"

"You didn't sleep much."

"With all this garbage in my etheric body, I haven't slept *for many a Moon*. A complete wreck. Unable to get up during the day, unable to sleep at night."

"Just give me a little time. It's already better than yesterday."

"What were you doing to me during the night?" she asked.

"I worked at softening the accretions in your channels. Actually, I cheated. At one stage I put you to sleep for a while so as not to hurt you. That way I could scrape your channels from inside."

"I could feel your Dragon coming inside me. It was as if you were making love to me."

"Sweet Lord Melchisedek!" I trembled.

"Can I tell you a secret?"

"I Dragon-passionately love secrets," I vroofed.

"Ever since the ascension ritual began, I have had a huge desire to have a child with you."

I bit my lip and held her a little tighter in my arms.

"You have no idea how strong it's been. My belly was screaming to be pregnant. At times it turned into an obsession. From morning to night and night to morning, I could think of nothing else but falling pregnant to you. One night, in the beginning, I nearly walked out of my room and came straight to you. Can you imagine the scene?" she shook her head. "Then the Immaculate explained to me that it was not abnormal for an ascending goddess to have feelings of this kind. They said it was because the ritual celebrates fertility in nature. And they said that as I advanced in the rituals I could expect to get big swollen breasts and a dark line below my navel, like a pregnant woman." She pressed my hand against her bony chest, "I didn't do very well, did I?"

"Listen," I caressed her withered breast, "the fields are to be blamed, not you. And I am sure that with the Dragon's help, we can get you to have such *enormous* breasts that..."

"*Praise the Lord Melchisedek, Szar of the Brown Robe!*" Hermina voice-channelled.

Taken by surprise, I sat up swiftly in bed. Elyani chuckled.

All glory to the Lord Melchisedek, Hermina of Highness, and thank you. Thank you for sending her back to me.

"And I thank you for the flowers."

The flowers?

"When I came out of my room this morning, there were glorious offerings of fruits and honey at my door, and the hallway was full of flowers – magnificent bunches. Please convey my gratitude to the high priest, and to the people of the temple."

I certainly will, Hermina. What are your instructions regarding Elyani?

"She needs to regain some strength – and some joy! You are in charge of that. In the coming days, I will do what you have asked: I will explain to you the technicalities of the ascension ritual. There are difficult problems to solve. And I have received some sad news from the temple of Amnia, in the county of the Eastern Shores. Three of my sisters have failed an ascension ritual. As with Holma, the ascending goddess gradually became sick. And after a year she died from exhaustion."

Let us not despair! With the deterioration of the fields many rituals have stopped working. And yet we have found new ways of accomplishing our tasks.

Hermina did not answer. To people of high castes like hers, 'new' meant 'wrong', 'ancient' meant 'right and holy' – since all perfection came from the Law. The idea that modifications might have to be introduced in the ascension ritual sounded dreadful. Hermina changed the topic, exhorting Elyani and I to keep our joy, and she asked me to serve as her spokesperson, passing on her messages to the temple and keeping her informed of what was happening in Eisraim.

The communication ended. I rejoiced, "The flowers are a good sign. They show how much the people of the temple care for you. Now they are going to treat Hermina like a queen."

Elyani was hiding under the sheet, "This ritual is impossible. I'll never make it. I wish I could make all of them happy, but..."

"No! No! No! No! No!" Gervin's voice spoke through me, "It's too early to despair. Do you realise how much knowledge and power are concentrated in Eisraim? Now, we are all behind you," I said, slowly pulling the sheet. And her veil.

The veil dropped first.

"No!" she let out a feeble cry, hanging on to the sheet to hide her face.

"But I want to see your eyes! I missed them so much," I pleaded.

"I'm dead!" she gave up, letting me pull the sheet away.

She kept her eyes tightly closed while I was looking at her. Aphelion's grim words came back to mind, 'not a pretty sight!' Her short hair was thin and sparse. Her skin was dry. So many wrinkles had appeared on her face. She looked twenty years older. Her left eye was red and swollen, and an ugly sore marred the corner of her lip. But most frightening of all was how thin she had become. Never before had I seen a human being look so famished.

I came very close to her and whispered, "Can I kiss you?"

"Do you still love me a bit?" she cried.

"I love you, bigger than the seven spheres. You are my goddess, I would kill for you!"

Fluid infinity. Star elixirs. He travelled.

Elyani opened her eyes, crying like a child.

"Listen, do you realise how much travelling my father had to do so I could fall in love with you? Now I am not going to give up on you that easily. And who cares if you've had a bad flu?" My lips nearly touching hers, I asked again, "Would a kiss break the Law of the ascending goddesses?"

"The Law of the ascending goddesses was written before the kiss was invented," she sobbed. "There are no provisions regarding..."

I moved forward a little and met her lips. Gently. A lawful kiss with only soft vroofing waves in the background, but still... *heaven on the kingdom.*

14.7 Post-mortem of the encounter with Ahriman

Later in the day, when I met with Gervin, he informed me he had projected the Voice of Thunder onto Teyani and expelled the dark influence from her system. Then he carefully examined my paralysed hand. "Did you try to heal it with the powers of the Underworlds?" he asked.

"Last night I descended quite deep. I immersed myself in the rivers of life and it seemed to work wonders, the energy of my left hand instantly cleared. But as soon as I returned into my physical body, it again became black."

"Mm..." Gervin twinged his beard, contemplating the large pitch-black smear that overshadowed the aura of my left hand. "I did warn you... this thing may well prove diabolically resistant."

"But what is it, exactly?" I asked.

"The black substance of Ahriman: a level of physicality which is more or less completely disconnected from Spirit, and over which Ahriman has full control. If Ahriman's influence were to take over our world, this pitch would become the substance out of which all things would be made. Did you notice any difference after I cleared Teyani, by the way?"

"Nothing so far," I answered. "But how come this black energy took over my hand?"

"Aphelion made you use the power of his king. Each time you killed one of the Hunters with his stone, the black energy penetrated deeper into your hand, and its grip on you tightened. This general principle is, the more you use a power, the more it sticks to you. Especially when performing intense actions – actions in which you have to involve your will."

"But I had no idea this would happen! At first, I did not even know I was using the power of this 'King of the World'! I thought the stone was connected to the powers of the Watchers."

Gervin smiled bitterly, "Ahriman and his emissaries are clever, aren't they?"

"Frighteningly clever!"

"Most people are so confused regarding evil," Gervin went on. "They tend to imagine the devil as some kind of revolting beastly figure with hooves and smoking nostrils. Nonsense! The Prince of Darkness wants powerful men and women to follow him, not imbeciles. He knows how to make himself attractive to the strong by taking a formidable appearance. And he is *so* intelligent, *so* clever... look at who he sent to speak to you – a former Master of Thunder! Someone who taught the teacher of your teacher. How could you not listen to him and be impressed by what he had to say?"

"Something remarkably well-done was the speed at which it all unravelled," I reflected. "I realised there was something not quite right about this man whose face remained hidden under his hood. But there was never any time to think." There was always a good reason to rush forward, each move catapulting me into the next one. Before I had time to realise what was happening, he had made me use his stone to kill.

"And see how perfectly he planned his timing," Gervin continued. "If there was *one* period in your life when you could be vulnerable, that was the one – Elyani undergoing this ordeal which, Aphelion led you to believe, you could have ended just by saying yes to him. He also played on the fact that I will have to leave my body in the near future, and that Eisraim could well be invaded and destroyed."

Negating anything that had meaning for me, bringing me to a point of complete despair.

"Still, there is something I don't understand. With all the powers at his disposal, Aphelion could have compelled me to follow him. He could have manipulated my consciousness and turned me into a puppet."

"But then your allegiance would not have come from an act of will," Gervin answered. "Ahriman already has millions of puppets who follow him unconsciously, without the faintest inkling of what they are doing. They will never have the power of someone who deliberately *chooses* to go to the dark side and follow him. Had you willingly made the decision to take sides with him, he would have gained a mighty general, a man of will to fight his battles. Notice by the way that he didn't come to you at the beginning of your path of initiation, when you were a frail apprentice. He waited till you had mastered the Dragon, the Point and the powers of Space Matrix."

"So, really, what Ahriman wanted was my will."

"Yes. And had you given it to him, he would have devoured everything else in you. Ahriman crushes the individuality of those who serve him. Aphelion no longer has a face. Instead, what you saw was Ahriman himself. The Prince of Darkness does not want anyone to have an Ego. His deepest desire is to extinguish the divine flame in human beings and eliminate all spiritual influences from this world. Thus he could rule totally unchallenged."

"What kind of world would that be?"

"A huge burning fire that would engulf everything, leaving only piles of dregs, blackened like the energy of your hand. One way or another, Ahriman will end up king of the dregs," Gervin pronounced.

"Does this mean Ahriman can only win in the end?"

"No! No! No! No! No!" Gervin laughed. "All this is intricately linked to the transition to the Fields of Peace. As you understand, there will come a time in the distant future when humanity will depart from the physical world to inhabit the Fields of Peace – which is why the Fields of Peace are also called the World to Come. The Fields of Peace already exist. You could imagine that one day, humanity will move into them, very much like a family moves into a new home, abandoning their former house. But this analogy is too simplistic. The Fields of Peace exist on a much more refined level of vibration than the physical world. To become capable of living in the Fields of Peace, human beings must raise their level of vibration, that is, change their nature and refine their vehicles of consciousness. When they do so, the physical world around them changes. It becomes more like the Fields of Peace."

"So, the transition into the World to Come will happen by transforming the old house into the new one?"

"Yes and no. To comprehend cosmic mysteries of this kind, we need to cultivate fluid thinking," Gervin's index finger pointed upwards. "In reality, it will be a bit of both: a fraction of the physical world and its inhabitants will be raised to the level of the World to Come, and the rest will be abandoned and remain as dregs. The proportions of what will be transformed and what will be abandoned are not yet fixed. To a great extent, it will depend on human beings themselves. The more transformation work they carry out, the more of themselves and of their world will become part of the World to Come."

Gervin smiled, watching me twinge my beard. "When I say that one way or another, Ahriman will end up king of the dregs, what do I mean?" he continued. "Whatever happens, there will be some rejects, like a husk left behind after the transition to the Fields of Peace. This husk, we will gladly leave to Ahriman. He can then call himself 'King of the World', and rule over the dregs unchallenged. Then he can rightly say, 'I am a jealous god, there is no other god beside me,' for all spiritual influences will have departed from the husk."

"And what will happen to this husk in the end?" I asked.

"At the end of the present cosmic cycle, when the manifested creation returns to the primordial chaos of the cosmic night, the husk will be dissolved."

"But then, what does Ahriman want, exactly?" I asked.

"More dregs!" Gervin answered with a handclap. "The more he can retard and limit the spiritual progress of human beings, the more dregs will be left over for him after the transition to the World to Come. This transition is just about unavoidable, but there is still great scope as to how many human beings will be raised, and how many will be lost. If Ahriman wins too many battles, then a large fraction of humanity could find itself trapped in the dregs and incapable of moving to the World to Come."

"But this Ahriman, where is he? Are there temples that are dedicated to him? Are there orders of priests that follow him?" I asked.

"His influence is global, rather than carried by one specific order. He pushes for chaos and war wherever he can, and he fosters anything that dampens spirituality. His ideal world is one in which human beings would have forsaken God, and anything that isn't strictly material. In the future, he will try to establish false religions that will trap people in twisted beliefs disconnected from spiritual realities. The very existence of the gods will be denied, and people will be prevented from having any spiritual experience of their own. And whoever objects will be burnt at the stake, or handed over to priests who carry out torture on a large scale."

"Religious orders which use torture?" I exclaimed in horror.

"Men will be so blinded by the power of Ahriman that they will sincerely believe it is for the greatest glory of God that they torture other human beings. Remember, Ahriman is diabolically clever. In the kingdom of the rainbows, he will not only promote false religions but also brilliant systems of thought that will succeed in explaining God out of the creation. Entire populations will be convinced that neither gods nor God exist, and that nothing but the material world is real."

"But, Gervin, how could men ever believe that only the material world exists? That's just not possible. All they have to do is close their eyes and look inside themselves, to contemplate darkness visible and other non-physical spheres. Every morning when they wake up and remember their astral travelling, the reality of these spheres is obvious. And even the simplest of men can talk to the souls of the defunct, and hear descriptions of their after-life journey into the higher spheres and their meetings with gods and angels."

"Not so in the future, son. In the kingdom of the rainbows there will be long phases during which most human beings become blind to darkness visible, incapable of leaving their body, ignorant of the art of oracles – and therefore unable to communicate with the gods – and totally oblivious of the Law of our Lord. Then they will be extremely vulnerable to the influence of Ahriman." With the Eagle's compassion Gervin added, "As you yourself discovered, Ahriman strikes his victims when they are the most vulnerable. In the future, there will come a time when great numbers of human beings are so disconnected from spiritual realms that they are only too willing to embrace his vision of a purely material creation. Then he will enrol them in his armies, and push them to fight and eliminate those who wish to reach the Fields of Peace. Some of the worst atrocities of the entire history of humanity will be committed at that time, and the fight will reach its climax in the wars of the Apocalypse. Then the full rage of the Prince of Darkness will be unleashed, and men will not only fight each other on Earth but also in the sky and high in the spheres."

"So the Brother Knights will be fighting against the armies of Ahriman, is that it?" I asked, looking down to my paralysed hand.

Gervin nodded, "The Knights of the Apocalypse. Men and women of exceptional talents, trained over several life-times for these glorious incarnations in which their task will be to defeat the armies of Ahriman."

Despite all my efforts, I couldn't get the Dragon to clench my left fist. "Will I be among the Brother Knights, Gervin?"

"This is up to you," he answered in a neutral voice.

"How could I not follow you?" I smiled.

"No way, man of the Law!" Gervin's eyes flared. "If you lead the Knights, it will be to follow your truth, not to please me!"

The gravity of his words made me ponder.

"One of the things which struck me the most about Aphelion was that he never really lied to me," I noted.

"But at the same time, the picture of reality he drew for you was cleverly distorted. There are no greater lies than twisted truths!"

"So true!" Aphelion had shown me Woolly's face drenched in blood. He hadn't shown me how it was the Black Hunters' attack that had led him to accept Gervin's invitation to join the Brown Robe. "And yet Aphelion was so adamant when he proclaimed the Knights would lose their wars against the King of the World. Was that a true lie or a distorted truth?"

"No one can know the future for sure," Gervin engaged his word. "Human beings have free will, they can modify their destiny. All I can tell you is that the battles of the Apocalypse will be fierce and terrible, and that only by giving their absolute best will human beings have a chance to vanquish Ahriman. From here on, every minute counts. Every little bit of knowledge, clarity and power that you will have gained in this life and the following ones will be with you at the time of the Apocalypse, and will help to tip the balance of the war. The same can be said of all those who will be fighting Aphelion's King."

The burning question had to come, "Gervin, will there really be a place called Philadelphia Six?"

Gervin held eye contact with the aquamarine *living wall* in front of him, engaging his prophetic sight. "This is a very probable future, yes."

The haunting memory ran through my mind,

Brother Knight, face reality! If you do not destroy it, the Rex will destroy us all!

"Is there no way this probable future could be changed?" I asked in a little voice.

"These things I will show you during the final trial before your initiation as a Master of Thunder. Remember what I told you, though. There is no greater trial than contemplating the future. The path of a Master of Thunder is not an easy one. Before you decide to commit yourself to it, you will have to fully understand the long-term implications of your decision."

14.8 Gripped by Ahriman

After Hermina had announced she wanted me to be her spokesperson, I had asked Elyani about the best way of passing on messages to the people of the temple. "If it's not urgent," she had said, "just tell Melchard and Teyani. The information will find its way along the hierarchical pyramid. If it's urgent tell Mouridji, and the news will spread like a fire through dead leaves. And if it is *really* urgent, then voice-channel her and tell her it's a secret."

On my way back to Elyani, I decided to pay the prophetess a visit.

I did not have to knock at her door, she happened to be in the corridor as I was passing. "Praise the Lord Melchisedek, Szar of the Brown Robe!" the old woman greeted me, "And congratulations on your nomination as an Immaculate Attendant."

An interesting start. This was precisely what I had come to tell her.

I returned the greeting and inquired about her hip.

"It's rolling like thunder, son, look!" she said, and she started trotting to and fro like a filosterops. "And my stomach, son... it's heaven! I've been eating like a lawful pig since you healed me, and not one fart in the wrong direction! A prime job you did there, son. I would certainly recommend you to a princess!" she gave her born-accomplice's smile.

"Thank you, wise woman in the Law." The clear fountain inspired me, "Mouridji, I have come to ask your help."

"My help, Szar of the Brown Robe?" Mouridji stood very straight, ready to give her life for the temple.

"Hermina the Immaculate has asked me to convey her messages to the priests and priestesses of Eisraim. I thought that, perhaps, you would be willing to assist me in this task?"

"Me?" she said with complete surprise. "But... do you think I would have the qualities required for such an important task?"

"I have no doubt you do, Mouridji. Hermina would also like to know if there happen to be things the people of the temple wish to tell her..."

"This, I could already tell you a few," Mouridji interrupted. "For a start, they want to know if the two other Immaculate have gone for good."

"They have!" I Dragon-articulated, to Mouridji's great satisfaction.

"Well then," she smiled, "the people of the temple would like to know if there is anything they can do for Hermina. For instance, we have a lovely little garden apartment in which we would be delighted to accommodate her. It is not far from your courtyard, and it is so much cosier than the tower of Malchasek."

Especially knowing the *living walls* of Malchasek were rotting with elemental filth.

"Thank you, Mouridji, I shall pass on the message. From her side, Hermina would like to thank wholeheartedly all the people who brought her flowers and offerings of fruit and honey. And she asked that everyone pray for Elyani. The ascension ritual is going to be extremely difficult."

"Is that all?" Mouridji asked.

"For the moment!" I frowned.

"Trust me," she said in a confident voice, "the temple will know!" Then she took my good hand and asked, "And how is little Elyani? Have you healed her already?"

"Elyani is so sick and exhausted... it might take some time before she recovers. But what worries me the most is what will happen when she resumes the ritual."

"Are you going to conduct this ritual?" Mouridji inquired.

"No, Hermina will. But she is a wise woman, and she will let the Masters of Thunder help Elyani."

Mouridji applauded, "This is exactly what everyone was hoping! They will all praise the gods when they learn this. You know, son," she patted my cheek, "they are all so proud of you for convincing the Immaculate to give Elyani back to the Brown Robe."

I thanked her for her encouraging comments and chatted a little longer before taking leave.

"When you happen to have a minute," Mouridji said as I was going, "my neighbour, Luciana of the Green Robe, has had a hard time with her eyes lately. Sad to say, she's about as blind as the oracle of the King of Atlantis. She's asked me to ask you if you could give her a healing."

Promising I would visit Luciana, I set off, Point-whistling a joyful melody I had heard in the remote sphere of the Wise Spider. When I reached the stairway which for so many weeks had been my lamentation parlour, I tuned into Elyani and voice-channelled, "I love you!"

Hush! The voice channels of darkness visible are not exactly private.

"Sorry!"

Not that anyone would try to spy on me with malicious intent. The temple of Eisraim was the safest place in the world for me. Wherever I walked, I could feel the *living walls* loved me as much as I loved them. But anyone who was travelling through or tuning into darkness visible automatically overheard voice-channel conversations. The sounds wafted in the space, sometimes so loudly that they disturbed the peace of those absorbed in contemplative activities. So, before Elyani could voice-channel her answer, I sent her a Point-message (not so easy to overhear, as they travelled through frequencies that transcended the astral spheres), "*I love you!*"

There was no Point-answer, but I immediately felt a beautiful wave of light rising in my heart. "How the Upperworld did she do that?" I wondered. "*There are so many ways of playing with high energies when one is in love!*" I Point-sighed into her.

In response, another sparkling wave of love with Elyani's flavour of consciousness lit up my heart.

It was at that moment that I felt a dull pain in my left hand for the first time. I looked down at the black shadow, but could discern nothing in particular. As I kept walking, however, the pain gradually intensified. The strange thing was, resting on the Dragon did not stop the pain. It was like a numb pressure, quite bearable. Still, it was a worry! How could it possibly escape the control of the Dragon? When I was being trained at Mount Lohrzen, I had had to deal with hundreds of blows and bruises and bodily damage of all kinds. All I had to do was tune into my Mother the Dragon and all painful sensations were instantly erased.

What the hell was happening in my hand?

14.9 Sweet little Dragon

I found Elyani in bed. This time she did not hide under the sheets. She looked even more exhausted than when I had left her in the morning, and greeted me with a feeble smile.

"I love you, let's start the work!" I said, joining her in the bed and taking her in my arms.

She made herself soft. “I love you. What do you want me to do?”

“Nothing!” I whispered. “Just open to me and fall asleep in my arms while I am working on your body of energy.”

“Sleeping in the arms of the Dragon!” she captured the old magic in her smile and merged into me like a child.

I continued the patient cleaning work in her body of energy, drawing the foul caked substance out of her meridians and insufflating life force into her vital gateways.

She shouted, “Oh, that hurts!”

I softened the healing energy, but she soon started crying with pain. “It’s like being ripped apart,” she said.

I stopped the process and just kept her in my arms, shining my love into her. “These etheric concretions clogging your channels are so badly stuck! I might have to use another method to pull them out. Maybe Maryani will have some ideas.”

I had arranged for the Nagas’ ambassador to come and examine Elyani’s energy and assist me with the wisdom of her bottomless Dragonhood.

“When is she coming?” Elyani asked.

“Soon.” I rocked her against my breast, calling onto the Eagle’s softness. “White Eagle beautiful, soon will be flying again.”

“Will you take me travelling in remoteness?” she asked. “When I was in the tower, your voice often spoke to me about Space Matrix. Sounds miraculous.”

“Space Matrix and I will be greatly honoured to fly with you, White Eagle. But I must warn you about something else. I have made up my mind, I want to take you down into the Underworlds.”

The news was greeted with as much excitement as her near-terminally deteriorated life force permitted. “Can you do that?”

“Don’t know yet. But I will Dragon-try!” I swore. “For now, I just want you to move away from your body a bit, so I can keep on with the work.” And to help her, I Voice-projected a soft blowing sound on the cheap-way-out gateways on her neck.

Her body became all mellow. She fell asleep in my arms. I resumed my scraping and scrubbing enterprise.

From time to time, the dull pain in my hand caught my attention, making me wonder. What healing technique could I try on that?

When Maryani arrived, I woke Elyani up.

I went out into the courtyard and greeted the young woman. Our first meeting since my return from the Ahrimanic nightmare. Like Gervin, she expressed enormous relief to see me back in Eisraim. Then she followed with a fire of questions about how the Underworld I had managed to extricate myself from Ahriman’s clutches. She wanted to know every detail about Aphelion and his tactics.

“Vasouk warned me several times against this Prince of Darkness,” she confided. “He said that because I have been invested with great powers I am very likely to be visited by Ahriman. It is bound to happen, it is just a matter of time. Vasouk said if I were to let myself be tempted by Ahriman and if I chose to follow him, there is nothing the Nagas could do to rescue me. Even worse, they would become my enemies, and they would have to use all their wisdom to destroy me. They *could not* allow Ahriman's armies to take advantage of the powers they have given me. At the time I laughed. I couldn't see myself ever choosing to become Vasouk's enemy. But Vasouk told me off and seriously warned me that the danger was..." she paused briefly, wriggling her nostrils, "'very real indeed and well worth pondering upon,'" she said, imitating Vasouk's slow voice and low pitch.

So well done, I immediately felt warmed by the Naga's humorous wisdom.

Maryani took my left hand. "Vasouk said that because my body has been thoroughly Dragonised, if I were to go to the dark side, my energy would immediately become pitch-black from head to toe," she pulled one of Teyani's most graphic faces.

"From head to toe?" I shivered. "Then perhaps Aphelion's entire body was a shadow, not just his face."

"My, my... what are we going to do with this hand?" Maryani kept speaking like a Naga, this time without even realising it. "Of course, you have tried to heal it with the power of the Deep Underworlds' rivers of life?"

"The Dragon I have!" I said. "I just can't believe it did not work!"

"If you could take your *physical body* – not just your body of energy – down into the Underworlds, then probably the rivers of life would fix your hand. But that, of course, is infinitely more difficult."

"Descending into the Underworlds with my physical body! But who do you think I am? Grand-nephew of the Unborn God, perhaps?"

Immense powers would be required for such a feat.

"Peace, man of the Law! It was just an idea." Then she lovingly poured her gorgeous golden energy into my ugly hand. Absolutely no result. The shadow remained black. The pain stayed the same.

"Elyani is waiting for us," I took her arm. "So you remember the rule, sweet little Dragon? One can't speak to an Immaculate. And one must not look at her, only gaze above her head."

"At this stage, keeping this rule sounds like an excellent idea," Maryani said in an understanding voice. "Imagine, if she had to talk to everyone..."

Elyani, still lying in bed, had covered her face with the white veil. Just as Hermina did, she opened to Maryani and awakened a beautiful white light in her heart. No doubt a secret of the Immaculate.

I lightly touched her shoulder, and stood back.

Maryani gazed at the ceiling, sensing energies. Elyani took her hand.

After a few minutes, Maryani exchanged a glance with me, indicating she had completed her examination. We went to stand outside, the door left open so Elyani could hear.

"It's not too dramatic," the Nagas' ambassador gave her verdict. "I mean, according to normal standards she's dying. But with the power of the Dragon, I don't think it will take you very long to make her energy all healthy and shiny."

"Will you help me?" I asked.

"You don't need me!" she pulled a quick face.

"Of course I need you!" I argued.

She shook her head, "No, you don't!'

"Maryani!" I insisted.

"Listen, you just don't understand!" she raised her voice. "This woman is madly in love with you. You just have to touch her and the room is instantly filled with bright Dragon-sparks. There is not one Naga in the Deep Underworlds that could heal her better than you! Clear?"

"Mm..." I said thoughtfully.

Half-exasperated, half-compassionate, she let out a noisy sigh and went on explaining to me the Dragon-things of life. "Listen, Szar, when a woman loves and desires a man," she spoke slowly and articulately, "and especially when the charge between them is as *strong* as it is between the two of you, then the man just has to *touch* the woman and there is Dragon magic in the air. Do you understand?"

"Mm..." All considered, it did make a lot of sense.

"Any Dragon-thing you do to Elyani will have one hundred vroofing times more power than if I did the same to her," she guaranteed. "The polarity between you is so charged that if you wanted, you could even awaken her Dragon."

Awakening the Dragon! That was exactly what Elyani needed! Not only to go down into the Underworlds, but also to find the strength to cope with the ascension ritual.

"How would I awaken her Dragon?" I asked.

"But it's obvious, Szar! Make love to her, and the power of your Dragon will naturally pass into her!"

I remembered, long ago – not that long ago, really, yet it seemed like aeons – Elyani had come up with a similar suggestion, "Make a child with me, and descending through the Dragon gate will be *no problem in the Law!*"

"But she's an Immaculate, now!" I said in a little voice. "Immaculate priestesses can't do these things."

"Well, well..." Maryani echoed my little voice, "perhaps you could vroof the Dragon into her... in some other kind of similar fashion. Dragon-initiates have several ways of making love without making love, you know."

"Mm..." I said, even more thoughtfully.

Maryani wouldn't say more. She decided I needed to ponder on her enlightening advice. With one of her warm hugs, she lawfully took leave.

When I returned to the room, Elyani, who had been doing her best to contain herself during the lecture of Underworld wisdom, burst out laughing. "Dragon, Dragon, Dragon..." she took off her veil, "what are you going to do to me?"

"Well, well..." I inhaled deeply. "For a start, I am going to put you in a state of deep hibernation for a few days, and clean up your etheric body."

"What?" Elyani protested. "But this has nothing to do with what Maryani was suggesting!"

"I know."

"Are you putting me to sleep because you need some time to think quietly?" she asked with a mischievous smile.

I answered by pulling one of her favourite faces.

"Mm...." she mimicked my voice.

"Just you wait, Lady of the Eagle!" I said vroofingly, touching her nose with my index finger.

"Oooh!" she moaned Dragon-ecstatically under my finger, and she pretended to faint with pleasure.

14.10 What would the world be like without filosterops?

"Who, by the grace of the Lord Melchisedek, is knocking at the door?"

"Szar!"

The door of Teyani's apartment opened, and blossoming Alcibyadi greeted me with tears in her eyes. She was pregnant-beautiful, her aura full of gold, her belly bulging under her loose white dress, and her breasts swollen like those of the Great Goddess.

I had spoken to her a few times in the last days but had not yet had a chance to see her. We just looked into each other's eyes without saying anything. Then she rested her head on my shoulder for a moment. And she took my arm and led me to Teyani's room.

"So when it's not me that you're bashing, it's my mother!" she said as we were walking.

"Don't joke about this!" I whispered in consternation. "I'm so ashamed of what I've done. How is she today?"

"Much, much better."

Teyani was dozing in her bed. When we came in, she lawfully greeted me and smiled with the special joy a mother feels when she has more than one of her children surrounding her.

Following the custom of our temple, I had not brought flowers but a basket of fruit. I put it at her feet and went to sit by her side. Alcibyadi went and sat on the other side of the bed.

Teyani still looked pale and tired, but the appalling greyness I had seen on her face during my last visit had faded, and she was no longer coughing.

She spoke kind words to me. But when I asked if I could assist her recovery in any way, she was adamant, "No, Gervin and Maryani have both clearly said they didn't want you to heal me, or even to be around when they are doing their healing work on me. They fear the nasty influence could be reflected back into you. What is happening with your hand, by the way? Still paralysed?"

"Yes," I looked down to the gloomy shadow. "A nasty grinding pain appeared one or two days ago."

Teyani hated the sound of this news. "That's from me, for sure."

"Teyani, dear wise woman," I took her hands in my good one, "I much prefer to see this influence in my hand than in your chest. I'm *a big boy in the Law*. Lawfully trust me, I will find a way to get rid of this."

"Alcibyadi has decided she will heal you," Teyani smiled.

I looked over to Alcibyadi and frowned.

"I will heal you!" Alcibyadi declared with total assurance.

"Don't you dare touch this as long as you are pregnant!" I became fierce for her baby's sake.

"Just because he saved my life, this man believes he can tell me what I'm supposed to do!" Alcibyadi said to her mother.

Teyani laughed. "Would you by any chance be trying to sway Alcibyadi's mind, Sir Szar of the Brown Robe?" she asked ironically.

"No!" I replied in a firm voice, looking unlawfully straight into Alcibyadi's eyes, "I'm just trying to save the life of a great king of the land of Aegypton."

Alcibyadi smiled with satisfaction, stroking her belly with both hands.

Insisting would have been a complete waste of time. Teyani changed the subject. "We want to hear about Elyani, Szar. What is happening to her at the moment?"

"She's been in a state of light hibernation since yesterday afternoon," I told them. "I have nearly finished clearing all the muck that was in her body of energy. She'll feel much better when I wake her up."

A barrage of questions followed. The two women wanted to know every single thing about the ascending goddess. They praised the Mother of the Light for sending the White Eagle back to her nest. They dreaded what would happen when the practices of the ascension ritual resumed. The task seemed impossible. In a normal fire ritual, a few elementals were picked up and offered to the gods. But the ascending goddess was to open to nature at large and make an offering of it through the fire. It meant drawing a flood of noxious elemental sludge to herself. Even Maryani, with the full power of the Dragon, could not have coped with that. The warp was too sick.

"And it's not getting any better," Alcibyadi said. "Have you heard about the drought in the county of the Western Plains?"

"Still going on?" I asked with surprise.

Aphelion tricked you. Killing the Black Hunters was a major mistake.

"Getting worse and worse!" Alcibyadi said. "None of the extraordinary fire rituals conducted by the assembly of priests have borne results. It appears their stocks of food might run out much sooner than they thought. Then anything could happen, not just famine – riots, pillage... Do you know that even here, in our temple, there have been *major* field mishaps? Two or three months ago the corridors' guidance system collapsed for a few hours."

"This I know only too well," I told them. "It's how Aphelion convinced me to send the flu to Teyani. He showed me a vision of her falling down a flight of steps and breaking her leg. The idea he proposed was to keep her in bed for a day or two."

"A well-known tactic of the devil," Teyani gave a bitter smile, "take a good intention, turn it into a disaster."

"And have you heard about the filosterops?" Alcibyadi went on.

"This morning I was giving Luciana of the Green Robe a healing for her eyes. She asked if I would visit her friend Patrina, whose pet filosterops is very sick."

"All over the kingdom filosterops are falling on the ground and letting themselves die. For no reason. When you approach them they just look at you with their big friendly eyes. They don't even smile any more. No one can heal them. No one even understands why they are dying."

"If it keeps on like this, it won't be long before they completely disappear from the kingdom," Teyani pulled a sad face.

I sighed, wondering what a world without filosterops would be like.

That we may fly together!

14.11 Four of Thunder

Later on that afternoon I woke Elyani up.

When she saw me, her face lit up. She was too weak to speak, so she used the Point, "*I fell asleep in your arms, and I wake up in your arms.*"

"Your body of energy is crystal-clear now. No more accretions in your meridians. Can you hear? It makes a lovely little buzzing etheric sound. The ugly false notes are gone."

"You saved me, Dragon?" she Point-smiled.

"Not yet!" I lightly touched her breast. "Now, I am going to feed you, and feed you, and feed you..." I moved my hand back, as if her breasts were swelling.

To secure a smooth transition out of the hibernation state I let her sleep a few more hours, softly infusing life force into her gateways.

Meanwhile, the grinding pain in my left hand was building up. I was walking the Point-guided corridors on my way to a meeting with the Brown Robes – Master Esrevin was visiting from Lasseera – when I was gripped by such a violent fit of pain that I had to stop and sit down on the floor, letting the Dragon catch my breath.

Kingdom of the dregs: the agony of a world near-terminally disconnected from Spirit.

It took a few minutes before I could stand on my feet again. Lucky I didn't have to be in my body to walk. I withdrew and let the corridors walk me, watching the ominous dent from darkness visible.

When I arrived at his apartment, Gervin was in the middle of a conversation with Master Esrevin of the Brown Robe. I hadn't seen him for years – apart from the meeting with the Archive council in the Fields of Peace, of course.

The sturdy man with prominent cheekbones had aged. He was in his mid-sixties, like Gervin, but looked older than him. He stood up to greet me, grabbing me in his solid arms for a long brotherly hug. "So you survived the meeting with Perihelion!" he said, his voice charged with emotion. "You have made us so happy, son... so happy!"

"Perihelion?"

"Before he chose to follow Ahriman, Aphelion's name was Perihelion," Gervin explained.

Esrevin, whose heart-disciple Oriel had been killed during the Black Hunters' raid on Lasseera, asked question after question, listening to me rather than to my answers, drinking my presence. Like Gervin, Esrevin laughed a lot, laughing being part of the ethic of the Brown Robe (excessive laughing according to lawful standards). But when it came to discussing the encounter with Aphelion, his face turned grim.

"Did you know that before being initiated into Thunder by Orest, Esrevin was visited by Aphelion?" Gervin said.

"When he came to me, he didn't call himself Aphelion but Perihelion – the name which Orest, our teacher, used when referring to him," Esrevin said. "And he showed me such wonders that at one stage, I really asked myself whether I was making the wrong choice by following Orest."

"Tell him!" Gervin urged. "Tell him the kind of things Ahriman got Perihelion to unfold in front of you."

"It was extraordinarily clever," Esrevin began. "At first, Perihelion showed me how I could use the Voice to create levels of reality: small imaginary worlds in which one can live with imaginary people, according to rules that can be established and modified at will. Perihelion made me manifest dream-creations, and he showed me how to make them more and more perfect – so real that I started wondering exactly which was the real world. Then, after getting me to uphold a stunningly beautiful astral universe, Perihelion went on to demonstrate that there was little difference between these imaginary creations and our kingdom. He made me see our world as nothing more than fancy, a complete illusion devoid of any tangible reality, and not especially glorious.

As time went on, he showed me more and more wonders, encouraging me to use his powers to create magnificent works of art in which I myself could then travel and meet some of the people I had conceived through the Voice. At the time, all this seemed most enlightening. Perihelion kept telling me, 'Truly, the kingdom is no more real than your creation. The kingdom is but the dream of its creator.'"

A perfect imitation of Aphelion's low-pitched voice. I shivered.

"Then on the night of the Full Moon," Esrevin went on, "Perihelion showed me the power of Ahriman, making it appear infinitely more real than anything I had contemplated until then... 'At last!' I thought, 'here is something real, something *really* real!' Then I will always remember how Perihelion said in his deep voice, 'Esrevin, will you keep dreaming forever... or will you follow me?'"

"How did you get out of that?" I asked, totally captivated by his story.

Looking at me, Esrevin mimicked the anxiously serious expression on my face, making me laugh. He shrugged his shoulders, "Not a brilliant ending, really! I told him I preferred to keep dreaming rather than follow his reality that lacked heart and Truth. Perihelion insisted for a while, playing on the fact that for years, I had been taught to shed dreams and seek reality. Then the emissary of the Prince of Darkness disappeared as suddenly and mysteriously as he had appeared."

"And what were his last words to you?" I questioned.

"We shall meet again – one way or another."

"Same with me! What does that mean exactly?"

"It means... it means he hopes we'll change our mind and choose to follow him, either in this life or in another one. Otherwise we shall meet again during the wars of the Apocalypse, when Thunder and the alliance of forces of light fight the ultimate battles against Ahriman. Then, no more temptation," Esrevin snapped his fingers and pointed his index at me, "just war!"

Philadelphia Six, a tiny dot in space.
For 13000 years I have known this moment was coming.
Hiram, my brother. Hiram, my son. How could I do that to you?
The Golden Sun is crying tears of blood.
Black Panther to Hiram – Fire!
Hiram to Philadelphia – I love you!
In Archive Hall Five, Barkhan Seer is invoking Thunder.
The entire lineage behind Hiram's Point.
From Erriba to Philadelphia, only an outbreath.
A wall of fire. Thirty-nine targets destroyed in 4.3 seconds.
Hiram to High Command – Breakthrough! The wall is falling.
Lavash to White Eagle – This kid is maruding like a god!
High in Revelation Sky, Kartendranath is laughing.
Marek to Gideon – We shall meet again in the Fields of Peace!
Round clouds of fire. Explosion after explosion.

In the silence of space.
Birds of death, coming from all directions.
White Eagle to High Command – Counteroffensive has begun.
Black Panther to Molten Stars – Confirmed. At least 400 of them.
Marek! Marek! Watch your six!
One more cloud of fire.
Marek, dead.
Lavash to White Eagle – Hold on, Serah! For God's sake, hold on!
Hiram to White Eagle – Locking on Philadelphia Six.
Virginia! Forever love, Flying Dragon!
Suddenly, a sea of flames.

"Szar?" the high priest repeated, touching my shoulder.

"All glory to the Lord Melchisedek, Melchard of the Brown Robe!" I pulled myself out of the Point-vision and stood up to greet Elyani's father.

Strange noises and huge balls of fire in my head, it took a few seconds to adjust back to the aquamarine chamber's *living walls*.

"Do you know that Melchard was never tempted by Perihelion?" Esrevin said.

"Is that true?" I exclaimed with wonder.

Reunion. Virginia in Hiram's arms. Amidst the sea of fire.

"Orest said that Melchard was too pure a soul, and that the devil was too sensible and practical to waste time trying to tempt him," Gervin said.

Melchard made me sit close to him, and he held my left hand. "Where are Lehrmon and Woolly?" he asked.

"They went to visit Lasseera for a few days," Esrevin answered.

"Now tell us about the ascending goddess!" Gervin demanded, and I found myself bombarded with questions. The men, like the women, wanted to hear everything, even the things they already knew.

It took nearly an hour before I ran out of things to say.

Melchard commented, "So you are fulfilling the prophecy."

I twinged my beard, wondering which prophecy that was.

"So many prophecies are being fulfilled at the moment. No one will blame you for losing track of them," Gervin said when he saw me hesitate.

"This one came from Orest," Melchard elucidated. "*When the second last in Thunder saves the last of two ascending goddesses, then the days of Eisraim will be numbered*. Now that Oriel has left his body, only Woolly is younger than you in the Brown Robe."

If one person can bring Oriel back from the dark side, it will be Hiram.

"Tell us your plan with Elyani," Gervin pressed on.

"I think she should be given plenty of time to recover. Plenty of time! The power of the Dragon will strengthen her body. When she gets better, we will gradually resume the practices of the ascension ritual and see what happens."

"Time... time is precisely what we do not have!" Gervin warned. "You must hurry, son. If the fields were to collapse tomorrow, which they could well do, then the ascension ritual would become near-impossible." He paused, and made his voice extremely gentle, "I know it is a cruel thing to ask of you, but if you care for Elyani, then have her sent to the gods as soon as possible."

Cruel was the right word.

With a Dragon-nod, I indicated I had heard the warning.

"After the night of the howling dogs," Esrevin added, "the warp will deteriorate quickly. *All* rituals will get out of control. They will yield erratic results, and cause unexpected catastrophes in nature."

"I was just going to ask you a question about this," I went on. "Why not operate the Archive transfer right now? The Black Hunters and other Renegades have been eliminated, and the stones can be made ready any day. Why take the risk of waiting until the fields further deteriorate and chaos spreads over the land?"

"Look at him! He's already trying to get rid of us!" Melchard joked.

Esrevin burst out laughing.

"I am not the only one who will have left his body by the time of the Archive transfer," Gervin explained. "Not long after me, Melchard and Esrevin will ascend to the Fields of Peace to take part in the ritual of the transfer."

"I don't know that I like this part of the plan very much," I moaned. "Couldn't we change it?"

"No! No! No! No! No!" the three men thundered in one voice.

"What is to be kept in our Archive is not just knowledge," Esrevin repeated what Gervin had told me many times, "but the living seeds of the spiritual traditions which, for hundreds of years, have blossomed in the temples of Eisraim and Lasseera. From the moment the transfer is accomplished, the energy in both temples will fall flat."

"In such conditions, completing Elyani's ascension ritual would be plainly impossible," Gervin said. "And hundreds of priests and priestesses would find themselves disconnected from their gods and angels."

"Not to mention the cataclysmic state of the fields likely to follow the transfer, and which could quickly spread to neighbouring counties," Melchard added.

"All right, men of the Law! Say no more, I am convinced. Elyani must *really* hurry to the gods," I capitulated. "But from your sight of Thunder, can you see what her chances of success are?"

A heavy silence followed.

Gervin closed his eyes, as if he didn't want me to read through him.

I turned to Melchard, who held my gaze compassionately but didn't speak either.

"What we can tell you is that if Elyani were to succeed, it would be a blessing for all those who are to benefit from the Archive in the future," Esrevin said in his Spirit-warming voice. "As you know, we have trained a team of White Eagles to operate the celestial side of the Archive. But these

White Eagles will only be residing in the lower regions of the triangle. If Elyani's ascension were to succeed she would become a permanent denizen of the higher regions of the world of the gods. Excellent for the Archive."

"*Major* consequences would follow," Melchard seconded, "some of which you can easily see for yourself, and others which we cannot reveal to you for the moment, for the gods are jealous of their secrets and do not want any of these matters to be discussed on Earth."

"Another secret!" I thought to myself. "Why am I the only person in Atlantis who can never guess secrets?" I wondered, tuning high in the clear fountain.

Then to my surprise a sudden and massive flash of knowingness thundered down my column of Spirit. "Apollo!" I exclaimed loudly and with the triumphant assurance of someone who *knows* he has seen beyond the veils of superficial appearances. "It has to do with Apollo!"

Coming back to my normal mind, I quickly covered my mouth with my hand, fearing I had irreversibly alienated the gods by divulging one of their secrets.

Kartendranath, laughing. He is waiting for you.

Melchard frowned, while Esrevin was laughing his clear fountain off.

"Have you told him about the brotherhood?" Melchard Point-asked Gervin through a special Point-frequency that was to be used only in situations of great danger.

"Never!" Gervin Point-answered. "And be careful what you Point-say. My apprentice has been over-trained in the Point. He can hear you, for sure!"

To support the statement, I turned to Melchard, "It's true, I've never heard about this brotherhood!"

Esrevin started laughing even louder and Gervin followed him, while Melchard and I were looking at each other in a puzzled kind of way.

I turned to Gervin. "But you haven't told me about Elyani. Does she stand a chance?"

Laughter stopped. The aquamarine chamber became silent, vibrant with the warmth of the Brown Robe.

"If she could succeed it would be a beautiful gift to all of us, both in Eisraim and in Lasseera," Gervin spoke from high in the fountain. "But if she fails, no one will blame her, and no one will blame you either. The ritual of ascension is part of these glorious wonders of the Law which have gradually vanished from the kingdom in the last centuries, because they depended on the high purity of the fields."

This did not sound encouraging at all.

"Fight! Do your best!" Esrevin exhorted. "But understand that this is not part of the trials on your way to Thunder."

"Which is precisely why the lineage of Thunder will give you its full backing!" Gervin immediately added. "Do you realise that the flash of intuition you just had came down straight from the sight of Thunder?"

In any other situation, hearing this would no doubt have made me ecstatic. "Elyani, what am I going to do with you?" I wondered to myself, my eyes filled with tears.

No one seemed to have anything else to add.

Then for no reason, Melchard burst out laughing – huge, thundering laughter that filled the room and made everything resonate with him.

Startled, I turned towards him.

He looked into my eyes, and I had a great awakening.

Far, far above us, I knew that Lord Gana was sitting on the shore of the Molten Sea, and that his mysterious smile held the key.

14.12 The black substance of Ahriman

In the first days Elyani made herself a little child and let the Mother of the Light nurture her through me. Like a babe, she completely surrendered and merged her etheric into mine when I took her in my arms, which greatly facilitated pouring the concentrated life force of the Dragon into her.

Still, the progress was slow. An exhausted etheric body can only take so much life force. In the beginning, all I could do was to hold her in my arms and feed her five meals a day. Using my healing tricks, I had boosted her digestion gateways so as to bless her Immaculate stomach with a ravenous appetite. It worked. Soon, I decided to turn our second bedroom into a fully organised kitchen in which I lovingly prepared complicated dishes for her, experimenting with Nephilim cuisine and other treasures of Atlantean cooking lore that Mouridji helped me gather from the wise people of our temple.

Sweet days, these were! After months of separation, working so hard, Elyani performing fire rituals while I fought to raise my Point to kuren-jaya standards and survive Fridrick's onslaughts, after so much sorrow and despair, we found ourselves reunited, spending our days in each other's arms.

Day by day, Elyani's flesh strengthened. Her mask of despair faded. Her eyes regained their sparkling melange of Point-sharpness and White Eagle softness.

My hand, however, wasn't getting better. The dull pain had become almost constant. In addition, stabbing fits had begun. The Dragon had no control over them. All I could do was temporarily withdraw my perception from that part of my physical body. Three times, Hermina projected her Voice of Highness onto the ominous shadow that had replaced the energy of my left hand, but with no result. The pain and the shadow faded for a few seconds, then returned to their previous state.

"But what exactly is this black energy?" Elyani asked me one night, when the grinding pain was particularly bad.

"Gervin calls it the black substance of Ahriman. After human beings depart from the physical world into the Fields of Peace, piles of dregs will accumulate down here, and this black substance will be found in plenty."

"How can it be so resistant?"

'It's extremely dense. Gervin calls it 'hyper-dense physicality'. And it carries Ahriman's will, which disconnects matter from Spirit. It makes matter refractory to any spiritual influence."

Elyani was in the mood for one of the philosophical discussions we still enjoyed so much. "Is it because you used Aphelion's stone to fight the Black Hunters that the black substance penetrated so deeply into your hand?"

"Exactly! To fight, one needs will. The more will you impact in Ahriman's direction, the more the black substance comes into you, and it sticks. This means the more you are a person of will, the more risk of being contaminated when encountering the emissaries of the Prince of Darkness. Maryani, who is far more powerful than me, would instantly turn black all over if she flirted with Ahrimanic forces."

We went on conjecturing whether Aphelion, whose entire body was overshadowed with Ahrimanic darkness, was afflicted by similar pains.

"Probably not, because he is entirely devoted to Ahriman!" Elyani propounded. "This substance is pulling you to the dark side. If you took sides with Ahriman, the pain would stop."

"But Gervin says that in the long run, it would come back! Ultimately, when Ahriman becomes king of the dregs, his entire kingdom will suffer this pain, like the cry of despair of a world almost terminally disconnected from God."

"Aphelion has chosen a difficult destiny," Elyani said thoughtfully. "In a way, there is some good in the fact that it's by using will that people become actively bound to Ahriman. It means that simple folks who are sleepers and have no will are relatively protected. Passively following Ahriman makes them worse sleepers, but it doesn't tightly bind them to him as it would if they followed him from their awakened free will."

"True." I contemplated my left hand. "But being a sleeper is no real protection either. True, the consequences of being used by Ahriman's powers are nowhere near as heavy as using them actively. But in the distant future, the destiny of those who remain sleepers will be to be swallowed by Ahriman anyway. Entangled in his disconnected world, how will they ever get in touch with their Spirit?"

Hiram, in the hands of the beast. Three times, the Prince of Darkness tried to steal his soul. Three times, he failed.

To lighten our mood Elyani connected my Point to the music field. It released long Flying Dragon whispers in darkness visible.

"That's it," I laughed, "play me!"

"Ffffoooohhhh!" she let out a low-pitched whistle, her lips half-kissing my fingers.

I Point-tuned into the high frequencies of the White Eagle, marrying his glorious solar tones to the galactic whispers. "In the tradition of the White Eagles are there hints on how to behave when approached by Ahriman's envoys?" I asked.

"No. Because our order will soon depart from the material world, Ahriman usually leaves us in peace. Very few of our sisters have had to fight against him."

"And yet you have suffered a great deal from the delay that Ahriman imposed on Hermina," I pointed out.

"If Teyani and I have been hurt by Ahriman it wasn't because of our association with you but because of the role we are to play in the future," Elyani said with the undaunted vigour that ran through her when she talked about the Knights of the Apocalypse.

"My white panther is back!" I held her tight in my arms and kissed the corner of her lips, rejoicing to hear the fierce tone in her voice again. The first time since the stormy days in Tomoristan's princely suite.

"Do you want to know a secret?" the panther whispered.

"A secret? Yes!" I Dragon-shouted with excitement, letting loud and triumphant angelic harmonies resonate in the music field.

"Well..." she said, slightly overwhelmed by the grand sounds, "it is not *that big* a secret!"

"Ah?" I reduced the volume by two thirds.

She laughed and brought her lips close to my ear. "I will not be a white panther, I will be a black one."

I raised the volume again. "A black panther! But that is completely amazing!"

"It will all be your fault. You will be the first to call me a black panther."

I remained thoughtful, picturing the metamorphosis of a White Eagle into a black panther.

Dressed in black, with a large yellow sun on their chest.

"Strange, isn't it, that the Knights should dress in black, when precisely their task will be to fight against Ahriman," I reflected.

Black is the colour of judgement.

Am I being judged?

Every second. This is what Apocalypse means: everything counts. Everything you have learnt, everything you have done, everything you have said, in this life and in every single past life.

"Did you hear that?" Elyani lightly touched my face.

"I don't know."

14.13 The Holy Blue Flame

Every night, I descended deep into the Underworlds. I collected water of life, brought it back and poured it into Elyani's energy. Combined with love, tender care and Nephilim cuisine, it worked wonders. Soon my life was blessed with her frequent laughter again. Her days were no longer spent lying in bed. Instead we sat by the laurel trees in the courtyard or on the roof of the chapel of the Blue Robe, telling each other new and deeper secrets, nearly oblivious of the disintegrating world around us.

One evening after sunset, as I watched her confidently climbing down the ladder, I decided to ask if she felt ready to resume the ritual work.

"Oh, Dragon..." she shuddered, "I wish the world could stop here and now..."

"But isn't this ritual supposed to be one of the most beautiful of all practices?"

"It probably was, long ago," she said in a little voice, "but the slime of the world has become thick. I am *not* looking forward to being gunked from head to toe again."

"But you can't be gunked again!" I tried to warm her up.

"Why?"

"Because I'm here, of course!"

She didn't laugh. She snuggled against me. "Will you stay with me while I do the practices?"

"What an unlawfully good idea!" I snapped my fingers. "If I carefully watch what happens to your energy during the ritual work, I might find a way to deal with the elemental sludge."

Long-haired Mareena.

Convincing Hermina to let me stay with Elyani during the practices was no easy task. Allowing someone from another caste – a man, moreover! – to contemplate the ritualistic secrets of the Immaculate was completely against her Law. At first she didn't answer, she just said she needed some time to think. But the following morning at dawn she voice-channelled to say the gods had inspired her and her sisters in dreams. My request had been approved.

Soon after, she arrived in the courtyard. Wrapped in her white veils, Elyani was sitting on one side, facing the east. I sat in the opposite corner, close to the laurels, my head covered with the hood of my brown gown. After delivering a short greeting which of course remained unanswered, Hermina went to sit by Elyani's side. Together the women started chanting hymns of the Law that were commonly used for the purpose of ritual purification.

I slightly withdrew from my body, letting my consciousness hover above the courtyard, carefully tuning into Elyani's energy, looking for clues.

Nothing particular was happening.

After the first invocations came the phase of purification, in which Hermina Voice-projected mantras and hymns of the Law on Elyani, illuminating body part after body part with white light. As the two warm high-pitched voices chanted the glory of the gods, invoking their help, I wondered which fire they were going to use. In all rituals of a certain status, an essential part consisted of pouring oblation into the fire, sparking a sharp vibration that conveyed an offering of elemental forces to the deity. The fire was lit from twigs, either in a ritual vessel or on a small heap of sand on which sacred symbols were drawn. Hermina hadn't brought any vessel with her, so I concluded the practices of the day would be limited to preliminaries. But at the end of the invocations, Hermina placed her two hands parallel in front of her heart, and she Voice-projected one of the holy names of God. The high-pitched vibration was a shriek at first, then infinitely sweet. Instantly, and to my utter amazement, a Holy Blue Flame appeared in the space between her hands.

Astonished, I quickly pulled myself back into my body to make sure I wasn't being mistaken by some blue astral glow in darkness visible. But this was no illusion. Hermina had *really* lit a Holy Blue Flame – one of the most mysterious of all spiritual principles.

It was about the size of a thumb, and dark blue in colour. But its glow could not be compared to any light, whether physical or subtle. Just contemplating it was enough to be transported into high realms of consciousness. As the Law said, a Holy Blue Flame was a direct manifestation of the presence of God, which is why all those who beheld it were filled with awe and wonder. It was pure Cosmic Fire. The heat it conveyed was spiritual, not physical. When touched, it would not burn the fingers.

Holy Blue Flames were so rare that they were not even found in all temples. They were extremely ancient. According to the legends of the Law, they had first been lit by angels and high spiritual beings who had descended among human beings long, long ago – some at the birth of the kingdom, others even further back in time. In each temple, it was the high priests' function to attend to the Holy Flame and praise its glory, Voice-projecting hymns of the most ancient body of the Law onto it. Great care had to be taken with the Flame, for it was believed that if it came to be extinguished, so too would be the Spirit of the temple.

The fact that a Blue Flame could be lit by a human being came as a complete shock to me. It was contrary to what I had always believed. Even the priests of the Salmon Robe, whose ritualistic lore was immense, had no notion that such a feat was possible. Thus, awe-struck, aghast and abuzz, I contemplated the Flame – a rare privilege which simple priests could normally only enjoy once a year, during the grand celebration of the Law of Melchisedek.

The hymns went on. The two women's Voices, poured into the Holy Blue Flame, were the oblation, sparking tremendous waves in my column of Spirit. It filled me with the exalted presence of the gods, and soon projected me into a state of far-reaching vision in which the kingdom seemed insignificantly small – a thin rung in the infinite ladder of the worlds. I hardly noticed when Hermina left, letting Elyani continue with a long series of hymns that chanted the glories of the gods and invoked their help.

Until that point, everything had gone celestially fine. But as soon as my Immaculate protegée started offering elemental forces to the gods, the situation deteriorated dramatically. Elyani's voice choked, the sharp light of the gods was no longer with her.

The high ritual turned into an ugly mud bath. A flood of dark etheric sludge rushed into her. I could hardly believe my eyes. In a matter of minutes her aura turned grey. All the fine clearing work of the last two weeks was being wrecked.

"Stop!" I shouted, seeing the situation getting worse by the second. "Stop this! It doesn't make any sense!"

Elyani stopped the chanting of the hymns and turned to me. In a little voice, "Shall I extinguish the Flame?"

"What?" I shouted in horror at the idea that a Holy Blue Flame could be stifled.

"It's part of the ritual. At the end of the day, when the recitation of the hymns is over, we extinguish the Flame."

I took off my hood and bent forward slightly, contemplating the Blue wonder with my eyes wide open. "Well, well... that means you have to extinguish it, then," I sighed in consternation. "Is that it?"

"I guess... yes." Elyani could see it broke my heart.

"Well... so be it, then." I closed my eyes and slightly tucked my head in my shoulders, as if expecting a shower of cosmic curses.

Elyani began a last hymn, immediately making me reopen my eyes. No sludge, this time. At the end of the hymn she brought her right hand close to the Holy Blue Flame, took on a sacred gesture and chanted, "Glory to the God who was in the beginning, who is and who shall be!"

And the Flame disappeared.

Turning towards me again, she said in her ritual voice, "All is accomplished."

After a few seconds spent asking myself, "Where am I?" I recovered my thread of normal consciousness and rushed over to Elyani who was unveiling her head. "How are you feeling?" I asked anxiously.

She was in tears. "I will never do it! I will *never* be able to do it!"

After a second of hesitation I took the Immaculate priestess in my arms. "My love..." I searched for words, "it's too early to despair. We haven't yet called on the powers of the Underworlds."

She clasped her arms around my neck, wailing loud, "What do you want to do against the sludge of the entire world? There is *nothing* we can do. It's lost. It's finished. This ritual belongs to the past. Now..." she hid inside my cape and cried big sobs.

I bit my lip, at a loss to find a reply.

I carried her to her bed, which was surrounded by the many bunches of flowers the people of the temple had brought for her. And, patiently, I started cleaning her body of energy again.

"I feel like a rubbish heap," she cried with pain.

"Listen, this is nothing," I tried to sound comforting. "Just give me a bit of time, and everything will be crystal clear again."

"But that's not all! I want to have a baby with you!" she cried.

"Ah! This one is more difficult, knowing that you must remain a virgin," I tried to make her laugh, gently stroking her belly.

Little Elyani was falling apart. "I don't care! I don't want to remain a virgin! I don't want to do that stupid ritual any more! I just want to fall pregnant, and nothing else! Ooooh!" she shouted.

"Beautiful Eagle," I rocked her in my arms, "my belly understands so well how you feel."

"Ooooh!" she cried big tears of despair.

What could I do, but call onto the Light of the White Eagle?

Soft breeze of Highness, descending on us. Adding fullness to our tears.

14.14 Vroof me, Dragon!

I spent the entire day and the entire night cleaning Elyani's body of energy. I also had to operate an elemental clearing of the *living walls* and the courtyard (full of elemental sludge), a healing of our shocked laurel trees, and a repair of my music field. Moreover, all the food that had been kept in the adjacent kitchen had to be discarded, as its energy had turned grey. And by the end of the night nearly all the flowers in the bedroom had withered.

In the early morning when Elyani woke up, she looked at me and her face lit up.

"No ritual today!" I announced immediately, and kissed her forehead.

"Praise the Lord Melchisedek!" she sighed in relief. Then she grabbed me and held me in her frail arms. "What have you done to me, Dragon? I am *starving* in the Law!"

"Hey, hey!" I snapped my fingers. "It's called the gateway of the bottomless pit, and it works like a charm. But I have some sad news for you. I had to throw out all our food, so all I have for your breakfast is what I sneaked from the central kitchen," I said, pointing to a tray covered with cereal cakes and fruits.

"I'll eat anything," she said, hungrily grasping the tray and attacking the cakes.

"I like to see you eat ravenously," I sighed, watching her. "It *definitely* does something to my Dragon."

Elyani giggled. Between two mouthfuls, she asked, "What has happened to all the flowers? Did I eat them during my sleep?"

"I had to throw them out too. Yesterday's ritual, I must say, was a bit of a psychic attack!"

"Mm!" she fully approved, swallowing.

"No need to eat so fast, my love, you have the whole day."

She laughed, and it made her choke. "During the night, Maryani and I spent hours talking about you," I said.

"Sweet little Dragon is like you, she never sleeps?"

"No that's not true! We do sleep – sometimes. Now, we have come to the conclusion that your body of life force should be Dragon-boosted and shielded, so it can resist the onslaughts of elemental sludge."

"Oh, yes," she said, half-joking, half-panther, leaning back against her pillows, closing her eyes and making her body soft. "Dragon-boost me!"

"Elyani!" I sighed.

"Aren't you going to Dragon-boost me?" she opened one eye.

"Hunh hunh! We'll start with the shielding, and we'll look into the Dragon-boosting after dinner. Meanwhile, I will make you sleep again."

"A-*gain*?" she protested.

"But I will wake you up for your lunch!" It *did* something to my Dragon to feed her.

"Do you know what I will be if I ever make it to the world of the gods?" she said. "A celestial cow!" And she pretended to be munching grass in the fashion of ruminants.

"I'll come and worship you." I gave her a light kiss and etherically pinched the 'cheap-way-out' gateways on her neck, sending her back into blissful dreamless sleep.

And I spent another day working on her body of energy. I descended into the Deep Underworlds, collecting water from the rivers of life, and precious gems. I poured the crystalline water into her vital centres and her meridians, making her etheric shimmer like a little Molten Sea. The gems, I incorporated in her gateways – pearly energies in her breast, lapis lazuli in her eyes, a touch of ruby in her lips, plenty of malachite to reinforce her kidney and her hair, and rich gold in her heart. For her liver, bright and generous topaz. And for her skin a delicate mixture of sapphire and diamond.

Maryani helped. From one of her descents she brought back a huge, magnificent onyx, found in a secret cavern under the South-Tartarean sea. The shining black stone was so charged with concentrated vroofing life force that I hesitated to put it in Elyani's body of energy.

"Are you sure we are not going to blast the goddess' breasts with this one?" I asked Maryani.

"You chicken-Dragon!" Maryani laughed at me. And before I could say anything, she set the onyx vibration in Elyani's belly.

So great was the power that Elyani nearly woke up from her hibernation state. For a few seconds, all the gems I had placed in her gateways were set ablaze, and the room's darkness visible shone with beams of all colours.

"Isn't she beautiful!" Maryani exclaimed affectionately.

Long-haired Mareena, looking down to us.

Moved, I bit my lip, remembering the cruel rule of the game: the stronger Elyani became, the quicker I would lose her.

"So goes the daiva!" I mourned.

In the evening when I woke her up, Elyani was glowing. "I feel fantastic!" she exclaimed, stretching her body like a cat.

I looked at her silently, drinking her light.

"And the smell! The smell is out of the seven spheres!" she wriggled her nostrils like a veteran of the Underworlds. "You must have been cooking all day."

"I didn't have time. Mouridji and Luciana came to cook dinner for us."

"It doesn't smell like usual temple food." She leapt out of bed.

"I gave them a few Nephilim tips. They assured me they would keep them a secret." I winked, imitating Mouridji.

"Trust them!" Elyani returned the wink. "But what have you done to me, Dragon? I haven't felt so rested and energetic for months."

While she was dressing and putting a touch of make up on her face, I briefly summarised all that had been done to her body in the last thirty-six hours. At first, it made her laugh. Then she came close to me and made her voice soft, "So you have been working on me all the time."

"We have to move fast, very fast!" I said. "This morning Gervin told me to hurry up again. Apart from news of disasters coming from the four corners of the kingdom, he has received more alarming reports about the deterioration of the fields. The night of the howling dogs is imminent."

"Listen," she said in a courageous voice, "if you want, I am ready to resume the ritual work right now."

"Hunh hunh! I need another night to finalise the work on your body of energy."

"Oh, good! I feel too panther to be an Immaculate," she said with a bright glow in her eyes. "And I am *so* hungry!"

I took her by the hand and walked out in the courtyard. "With what Maryani and I did to you, your stomach should feel like the Abyss of the Deep."

"Yes! This is exactly how it feels!" she sat down on the grass.

As I was feeding her the five-course meal that Mouridji and Luciana had prepared, I explained my strategy. "I'm trying to get your body of life force to resonate with the powers of the Deep Underworlds. This way, I hope it will become so strong and *dense* that nothing can penetrate it, and the sludge will be deflected."

"Why don't you start by killing me?" she said, shovelling large spoonfuls of Shemyaza's puree into her mouth. "That's how the Sons of the Dragon awakened your physical body to their powers, didn't they? They cracked the nut of physicality open by letting you die in a crypt." She paused to refill her mouth with puree, then went on, "Maybe, if you completely separated my body of life force from the physical and cracked it open, I'd become capable of coping with the sludge."

"Maryani and I thought about this," I touched Lohrzen's orichalc plate on my neck. "But when Maryani asked King Vasoukidass, he advised against it. He said that initiations of that kind belong to the past. They have become too dangerous nowadays. After killing you, we probably wouldn't be able to bring you back to life! The Sons of the Dragon manage to make these practices work because of the ancient vibrations they have kept in their mountain. And even so, they lose at least a third of their candidates."

"Well, then... Dragon-boosting must be the *only* solution!" she said with a panther's smile, attacking a huge vegetable loaf of a kind I had never seen before.

"Could be!" I sighed, putting force into a passerby ant.

"Did Maryani tell you how to do it?" she said, returning to the puree.

"Not really."

"Well, I know," she smiled and gazed deep into my eyes. From mid-height, she let her spoon drop into Shemyaza's puree. It made an interesting 'plop' sound. Then she took me by the hand and stood up. "For a start, you need to be joyful. At the moment you are a bit sad. It makes your Dragon shy." Holding my hands, she pivoted slowly, making me turn around her. "Think of the first thing you and I will do when you come to visit me in the world of the gods."

"Mm..." I said, wondering if we would ever get there.

"Bathe in the Molten Sea?" she suggested. "Or watch the sun, perhaps? Contemplating the sun from the world of the gods is a completely different experience, you know? Nothing to do with the teeny dwarfish light we see here in the kingdom." Then she connected my Point to the music field, bringing a Flying Dragon's whisper in darkness visible. "I know! You will take music lessons with god-friends of mine. The world of the gods, it is well known, has the best musicians in the ladder of the worlds! They are said to be jealous of their secrets but with you I am *sure* they will make an exception."

As I was slow to bring a flow of sound into the astral space, Elyani took control of my Point and connected it to the White Eagle, letting his lofty harmonies resonate through the music field.

She played my Point so well I had to laugh.

"And we will fly, Dragon!" she made me turn faster and faster around her. "Fly high in the spheres! When we reach the summit of the seven spheres, you'll say, 'Let's take a quick jump into remoteness!' and I'll say 'Oh?'" Elyani made herself apprehensive and timid, "Do you really think I could?" Then she imitated my protective character's voice, "'But *of course*, Eagle, you can follow me,' you'll say, and before I can answer, Space Matrix will zap us into the deep void of remoteness, so that at last you can tell me a secret that will remain really secret. For if you think that Atlantis is bad for secrets, well, let me tell you, the world of the gods is a hundred times worse!"

She let herself fall on the grass and pulled me towards her in a precisely calculated manoeuvre, so I landed just on the Dragon gate. "Do you think you could kiss me while you are going down through the gate?" she whispered.

I took her in my arms and let the Dragon breeze vroof through the kiss. Then, holding onto her astral body, I let myself glide down through the gate.

Instantly, I found myself in the astral blue cave beneath the courtyard. But Elyani had not passed through. So I came back into my body. "It doesn't work. What shall I do next?"

"Just listen," she whispered with tears in her eyes. "I love you. I fell in love with you the very first day I saw you, and ever since, I have loved you a little more every day. If I ever get to the world of the gods, I want you to come and visit me *every night*. And I want you to promise that the very first night you spend with me, you will make love to me."

I Dragon-kissed her, and a big vroofing wave passed into her.

"Promise me, or I refuse to continue with that cursed ascension ritual!" she cried and laughed at the same time, holding me tightly in her arms.

"I promise!" I laughed and cried with her, "I promise!" And the Dragon sealed my words with a powerful wave that ascended slowly from the base of my body into her heart.

"Oh," she cried, "what are you doing to me? My belly is on fire!"

I rolled onto my back, pulling her delicate body on top of mine, and I let soft, gentle vroofing waves resonate with the onyx vibration in her belly.

"Ohoh!" she laughed, "you make me feel like a volcano. Is this how it feels when you tune into the waves of your Mother the Dragon?"

"Mm!" I nodded, and made the waves a little stronger. "*She is to be known through ecstasy*. The deeper you descend, the stronger the waves."

"O-o-oh!" Elyani softly called out, "I don't want to be an ascending goddess any more, I want to be a descending one!"

Remembering a wall carving I had seen in the temple of the Dragon, I sat up in cross-legged meditation position, my back very straight. Elyani, I pulled onto my lap, her legs around my waist. Holding her body tight against mine, I said, "Somehow, I have the feeling this is the right way to do it."

"When the gods make love, this is their favourite position," Elyani whispered.

"Hey!" suspicious voice, "how do you know that?"

"Long-haired Mareena told me, long ago."

I looked up, as if towards the gods, and contemplated the Moon's silvery shimmer in the mists. Then I looked into Elyani's eyes.

Suddenly grave, we opened to each other.

Time stopped. Started again. Much more slowly. In our mingled warmth, sweet Dragon waves ascended, making Elyani quiver. Playfully, she connected my Point to the music field, and the Dragon waves translated into deep vroofing Underworld sounds. Some resembled the shaking of the Earth, others conjured images of huge ascending waterfalls.

The more Elyani let herself melt, the more blissful the waves, and the deeper I could tune her body into my Mother the Dragon. As always with the Dragon of the Deep, there seemed to be no limit. More pleasure led to more merging, and the more we became one, the easier it was to connect with Dragon immensity. The waves went on and on, sometimes so sweetly that we cried in each other's arms, sometimes so strongly that the sounds in the music field became awesome and fierce.

Then, after hours perhaps, the long-awaited miracle finally took place.

14.15 World of the gods, the blue cascade of Life and Light

In the enchanted landscape of the blue cascade of Life and Light, where the birds of paradise – which are so rare – come to mate, and where the wise gods come to seek inspiration, two of the sons of Apollo approached long-haired Mareena.

She was sitting on the celestial ground, sadly holding her head in her hands, letting herself be warmed by the birds' dazzling sounds.

Alumnus, whose gaze is as bright as the light within the glorious sun, stood in front of her. Peer the magnificent sat by her side and placed his hand on her shoulder. And he spoke to her, "Long-haired Mareena, beautiful soul and great worshipper of our father, Alumnus and I were flying high in the spheres when a bird of paradise came near. Hearing his chant, we knew you were crying."

Mareena caught a wisp of blue Life from the cascade and let it shine through a sad smile.

"Will you tell us, Mareena?" Alumnus said. "Will you tell us the reason for your sorrow? For we love you and would never forgive ourselves if, one day of the gods, an enchanted mirror revealed to us that we had failed to assist you when you needed our help."

"Thank you, friends," said the goddess whose hair held hidden secrets of the Molten Sea, "but, I am afraid, nothing can be done now."

"Are you crying for your friend Elyani?" Peer asked.

"Our daiva has broken her life. Everything was taken away from her: love, health, beauty, all her friends, all that gave meaning to her life. Even the White Eagle no longer shines through her as he used to. A cruel destiny, for an innocent soul who had always worshipped us and had never broken any of our rules."

"Hasn't our father sent a grace to let her be reunited to her Flying Dragon companion?" Alumnus asked.

"Yes, and I praise him for his bounty, and for the skilful wit with which he inspired the High Council of the Immaculate Seven. But Elyani has been so badly tortured by the Prince of Darkness that she will soon die, and our plans will have failed. Despite all my help, despite all my prayers, the ritual is failing. Since the great disconnection, our celestial impulses no longer rule sovereignly over the nature forces of the world of men. Down there, the twilight of the gods is quickly giving way to a dark night of chaos."

"A human life is like an outbreath. Why grieve when it finishes?" Alumnus said. "Let Elyani follow the wheel. Let her be reborn somewhere else and start afresh."

"Our daiva has broken her time track and loosened her karmic bonds to Thunder and the Flying Dragons," Mareena Pointed out. "After she dies she is likely to go astray and wander through useless lives and empty destinies. She will have lost the White Eagle, engulfed like so many other bright human souls in the tenebrous chaos that will follow the fall of the kingdom. And who will have won in the end? The Prince of Darkness."

Peer, who did not like to see the daiva create such inglorious circumstances, tuned into his father's shining bright light. "Let me think," he said.

"Think fast, my beautiful friend, for Elyani's days in the kingdom are numbered."

High above her head, a flock of birds of paradise echoed her sadness.

14.16 Finally, it happened!

Elyani jumped with joy, "I can't believe it has happened!"

"Youyouyouyou..." I screamed with the power of the Dragon, and Elyani followed. And we danced and laughed loudly, thanking the Mother of the Light for her help.

Her eyes wide open, Elyani drank the sight of the cavern. Wriggling her nostrils, she inhaled deeply, "Now I understand why you always do that. It feels so natural when smelling the breeze!"

"This breeze is nothing!" I said, "Wait till we descend deeper." And we walked together in the cavern of blue rock that stood under the courtyard.

"I can't believe how easy it was!" Elyani's wonder filled the cavern. "A few months ago, when you came back from Mount Lohrzen, I was so eager to follow you that I tried to pass through the Dragon gate hundreds of times. There never seemed to be any glimmer of hope, I was always pushed away by the breeze. This time, I didn't even try! I just saw myself gliding down with you, and voof!"

"Many Dragon powers are like this. They are either completely out of reach, or so easy to implement that you wonder why they haven't always been with you."

"So beautiful, so peaceful," Elyani marvelled, contemplating the blue rock.

After a short stroll, I took her by the hand and went back to the Dragon gate. "See, it's a column of energy." I stood in the center of the shaft and held her against me. "Ready?"

She tucked her head in her shoulders and nodded, her face lit up with excitement.

Voof! Down and down, carried by the descending flows of the Dragon gate. I stopped in a large cavern of shining lapis lazuli.

Amazed, Elyani turned her eyes to the distant roof, "The entire temple of Eisraim would fit into this place!"

"This dark lapis is my favourite Underworld gem," I confided, looking at her rather than at the cavern.

Carried by the enchanted feel of the place, Elyani started running. I followed her. Gradually the lapis lazuli was replaced by orichalc, and we finally arrived at a small stream. I knelt down, collected some of the crystalline water, and offered it to her. She fell to her knees and drank a sip from my hand. The exquisite energy made her burst out laughing. "This is... beyond words!"

I poured the rest of the water on her head. "Good for your hair!"

Still laughing, she collected some water and let me drink from her hand. "Thank you. Thank you so much. I feel blessed," she said as I was kissing her hand. "And I can hardly believe my eyes. People in the kingdom have no idea of the incredible treasures that stand below their feet. I wish they could know."

"And it will not get better in the future," I said. "Once Vasouk told Maryani and I that after the end of the kingdom, the Underworlds will become completely sealed to human beings, because the few traditions which are the keepers of Underworld initiations will have disappeared. And so the transmission of forces will be lost."

"Does this mean that no one will be able to go down?"

"Almost no one. According to Vasouk, 'Only a handful of initiates per human generation!' In the distant future, of course, when human beings will have crossed the great waters of regeneration, it will become different. But that will be in such a long time... it may not even be during this cosmic cycle!"

"I want to see more!" Elyani stood up and took me by the hand. We ran towards the next gate of the Dragon, following the shoreline. From there, we kept descending from cavern to cavern, from pink quartz to shining jade and from gleaming silver to pure gold. Further down we reached the paradisiacal gardens where Maryani and I had sat with King Vasouk. We admired the multicoloured birds, filled ourselves with the flowers' incomparable fragrances (a smart bee pointing out the most intoxicating one for us) and tasted a pear – a sheer delight which, Elyani said, would have made the gods themselves jealous. No doubt the Naga king would have agreed with her.

Lying in the grass in a playful embrace, a long blue lizard surprised us. But he promised never to tell anyone – not even his she-blue-lizard, from whom he almost never kept a secret. And because he liked us, he gave Elyani one of his smooth, velvety blue scales that he picked from his left shoulder, promising her that it would bear her luck.

Then I carried Elyani in my arms back to the Dragon gate, not because she was tired but because she enjoyed being carried, her arms clasped around my neck. Smoothly, we reascended and went back into our bodies, which were still locked in the loving embrace.

As soon as she opened her eyes, Elyani whispered, "I want to do it again!"

"Tomorrow night, perhaps?" I suggested, trying to ignore the grinding pain in my left hand.

"No way, man of the Law! I want to do it *now*."

"Mm..." I hesitated. "Are you sure you don't have a headache? The first time I vroofed with the Dragon it left me unconscious for a day. And when I woke up I had the most excruciating headache of my life."

"No, I don't have a headache! And I am so full of energy, I could never sleep now. Please, Dragon, do it again!"

"Vroofing, or descending?"

"I want both!"

And so we glided down through the gate, embracing each other and letting the vroofing waves merge our energies, falling till we reached one of those Deep Underworlds which do not look like caverns but like infinite spaces filled with pure shining golden light. Then and there, for a blessed moment out of time, we became one light.

High above us – or was it below? – the Eagle rejoiced.

14.17 Waves of disaster

The following morning when Hermina arrived for the ritual practice, Elyani was sitting in one corner of the courtyard. My head hidden under the hood of my gown, I was sitting on the other side, close to the laurel trees.

When she saw Elyani's glowing energy, Hermina was delightedly surprised. "My child, I have never seen you so beautiful." She touched Elyani's head and blessed her by chanting a few verses of the Law.

Following the rule, Elyani remained silent.

I withdrew a little further from my body, hoping the Immaculate boss wouldn't ask about my healing methods.

She knows very well!

Hermina sat by Elyani's side, "Today we will do the practice differently. I will stay with you for the offering of the elemental forces, so as to observe carefully what happens to your energy."

Heart-warming words! Hermina was highly intelligent, and her ritual lore was immense. Perhaps she would find a solution. I called onto the gods, "Please, do something for us this morning! Please, show us that you care!"

Heard.

Together, the women began their powerful hymns.

The more they chanted, the worse the pain in my hand. I had to move out of my body, watching the two priestesses from darkness visible. But when Hermina placed her hands parallel in front of her heart to light the Blue Flame, curiosity pulled me back into my body.

Again, she Voice-projected the high-pitched sound and the Holy Blue Flame appeared in the space between her hands. Then, delicately moving her hands, she placed the Flame on the ground in front of Elyani, and the ritual continued.

Stay in your body!

Ignoring the pain, I stayed in my body, gazing at the Flame. The night before, the golden space in which Elyani and I had united our hearts and energies was sublime. But, I had to admit, there was far greater depth in this mysterious Blue Flame. I became so absorbed in its contemplation that I almost lost touch with the kingdom – a mistake that nearly proved fatal to the three of us.

As I was drifting in lofty, expanded spaces of consciousness, the Flying Dragon voice called,

Stop!

The call was accompanied by an emergency signal coming from Space Matrix in packed-thought format,

Extreme danger! Gather all vehicles in one point and remain attuned to the mother connection.

The Warrior's instinct took over. I instantly pulled myself back into my body. Without thinking I yelled with all my strength, "Stop! Stop everything!" not worrying about the fact that by so doing, I was breaking the Law of the Immaculate.

Startled, the two women stopped their chanting and looked at me.

A short silence. With my Warrior's techniques I scanned the space around us.

Then I saw it. "No!" I shouted and jumped up, running towards them.

Breaking the Law a second time, I Point-called the two of them, "*Shield your energy! Now!*"

As I was running across the small courtyard – hardly thirty six lawful feet wide – time seemed to stop. And I saw it again: an ugly wave of elemental slime rushing towards us. It was absolutely enormous, one hundred times higher than the women's auras.

Tuning into Elyani's Point I understood what had happened. Hermina had decided to join in the practice of the elemental offering, instead of just observing Elyani. The combined power of their two Voices had brought an infinitely greater response than they had expected.

A tidal wave of elemental sludge was on its way.

Approaching deadly fast.

Still running, I called onto Space Matrix, "Help! Give me clues!"

In darkness visible and nearby intermediary layers, a major elemental upheaval has been triggered. The wave will not just hit the present location but all adjacent buildings. Seven human entities will be projected out of their physical vehicle, and another seventeen will be hit. Expect major casualties.

"The Blue priestesses!" I immediately thought, and Point-called their chapel, *"Seal yourselves! A torrent of slime is about to hit you!"*

Space Matrix prompted me, *To limit the disaster, forcibly anchor the human entities in deep Underworld layers.*

Elyani, who had united her Point to mine, heard the message. Through the mighty onyx vibration in her belly she tuned into the Dragon gate, plunging her consciousness into the depths of her lower chakras. The result was unexpected. She was projected out of her body and instantly swallowed by the gate, landing in the blue Underworld cavern beneath the courtyard.

The wave was about to hit us.

I stopped where I was, raised my arms and looked down. "Mother!" I yelled, tuning into the Dragon of the Deep. And the Flying Dragon became one with the She-Serpent of Eternal Wisdom.

Time slowed down even further.

Far above, in the sphere of the Great Ant, a vast, majestic Flying Dragon tuned into me, reflecting its infinite clarity into my consciousness.

Deep down, the golden spaces of the Underworld shone through.

Gervin was in the middle of a conversation with Barkhan Seer. He became still and called onto the high power of Thunder.

Teyani too sensed the wave. She Point-called Maryani to the rescue.

Time crossing. Several time lines joined in a moment of eternity.

In the sphere of the Blue Lagoon Hermina's friend is multi-thinking about the past.

Why do I see Mareena each time I dream? Was she the one who decreed the daiva?

Perseps made you a poisoned gift. Use it to stop the Nephilim giants!

Poor blue lizard! It was stronger than him, he had *to tell his she-lizard.*

The Flying Dragon in Great Ant sphere, fascinated with the golden light of my Mother the Dragon. He will come to visit.

Aphelion tricked you, the Black Hunters should never have died. They were to become your most precious allies in the war against the giants.

Lord Gana, playing the molten star in front of the primordial sea.

The Western Plains, ravaged by plagues.

Joranjeran didn't return to Jex Belaran. Together with a small troop, he stayed in the county of Lasseera. You will meet again.

Soon the priestesses of the Dawn of Creation will abandon their body. Not one of them will remain. Who will perform the ritual rites?

Fridrick really loved you.

The five White Eagles will soon depart for the land of Aegypton.

Alcibyadi's sadness, as immense as her love for Lehrmon.

A tiny dot in space. Philadelphia Six, right in front of me. What's Virginia doing at the moment?

Farewell, black panther.

A sea of fire.

There are sorrows which eternity itself cannot heal.

Through the Fault of Eternity, the Mother of the Light is smiling.

14.18 Lohrzen's scream

Elyani and Hermina were lying unconscious on the ground.

Stunned, I walked towards them.

Maryani Point-called, *"Szar, are you alive?"*

Hesitating, *"I can walk."*

"I'll be with you immediately, Szar. I'm running at high speed!"

The courtyard was entirely loaded with thick, grey slimy energy. I found it difficult to breathe. The Holy Blue Flame had not been extinguished.

Resting on the Dragon of the Deep I pulled myself back into my body, and bent over Elyani.

"Oh, no!"

She was alive, but her energy channels were completely filled with grey muck – again! As I laid my hand on her and started clearing the most vital circulations, my eyes were caught by Hermina's body.

"Damn it! She's dying!" I jumped over to her.

Gervin was the first to arrive on the scene.

"Gervin!" I shouted, "Hermina is dying. Not responding to my life force injections. I'm losing her!"

"Take her out of here, quick!" he ordered.

I lifted her in my arms and started running out of the courtyard, while projecting the full power of the Dragon into her. The veil covering her head fell off.

"Sweet Lord Melchisedek!" I exclaimed with amazement. She was much younger than I had imagined. Hardly older than Elyani. Light curly hair falling to her shoulders, her serene face was that of a woman of the north, with a high forehead.

Little Maryani appeared as I was bolting down the corridor. "How is Elyani?" she called, changing direction to run with me.

"All right. But this one is dying," I shouted. "If we lose her, we lose everything!"

We ran to a nearby courtyard that had been spared the tidal wave of slime.

Softly I laid the warm body on the grass. Maryani pulled the grey slime out of her vital channels. I put my hand on her heart, triggering gateways the Great Warriors used in cases of major shock.

Hermina's etheric heart was still beating, but her life fore was rapidly fading.

I swiftly implemented a whole battery of energy manipulations. Nothing worked.

Seeing me powerless, Maryani intervened. She projected a massive dose of Naga-golden energy into the Immaculate's vital gateways.

But with no more result.

Hermina stopped breathing.

"No! No! No!" I lifted up my hands and screamed at the gods, "But what do you want from us? This is *your* daiva! *You* wanted this ritual! Now that you have it, will you tell us what you want?" And from the highest of the clear fountain I called, "Gana! Gana! For the Unborn God's sake, will you let me know what you want me to do?"

"Szar..." Shaken by the violence in my voice, Maryani took my hand. "I don't think there is anything more we can do for her."

Taken by a warrior's rage, I grabbed the orichalc plate on my neck and pulled it violently, breaking the thin leather strip to which it was attached. "Lohrzen! Lohrzen!" I screamed with all the power of the Dragon, "Lohrzen! I call onto your power!"

Using the Voice, I launched the Warriors' scream.

Shriek, sharp, total – the force descended through the Voice.

So intense it was, Maryani started screaming with me.

Letting the Dragon of the Deep resonate through the Voice, I gradually increased the power.

For fifteen seconds of eternity, the Word became Light, and the Light gave life. By the force of Lohrzen's scream, Hermina was being pulled back into her body.

There was a cosmic hush.

Hermina's etheric heart started beating again. In the seconds that followed, her chest lifted up slightly, as if in hesitation. Then it went down, and up again. She was back!

"Youyouyouyou..." Maryani screamed with joy.

Aghast and abuzz, I shook my head slowly, still holding the orichalc plate tight in my hand.

Maryani made herself silent. Hermina had opened her eyes.

For a short, magic moment, we gazed at each other. She didn't look shocked, or even surprised. She just plunged her deep blue eyes into mine.

I smiled, recognising the infinite softness I had often admired in her voice.

Gervin Point-called. *"Elyani is waking up. She looks fine. A fantastic job you have done on her body of energy. It held fast despite the shock. All her major gateways are intact. What about Hermina?"*

"She is alive. Damaged, but alive."

"Hey, you can't look at an Immaculate!" Maryani reminded me, pulling my shoulder.

Still looking straight into Hermina's eyes, I thrust the orichalc plate in my pocket and bent towards her. Then I took her in my arms and half-sat her up, her head against my chest. "Praise the Lord Melchisedek who brought you back to life!" I cried.

"Szar, this is very serious," Maryani insisted. "You must look up, and you can't talk to her!"

I laughed, rocking Hermina in my arms like a little child. "Praise the Lord Melchisedek who brought you back to life!"

Flabbergasted at my total disregard for her lawful reprimands, Maryani watched the scene in disbelief.

"Elyani?" Hermina asked in a small voice.

"She's all right. But..." I brought my head against hers and whispered, "this ritual is *never* going to work, my friend."

"I'm sorry." Hermina started crying. "I am so sorry. There is nothing I can do. It just does not work any more."

Clearly, the fact that the ascension ritual had lost its power was far more distressing to her than the massive shock she had just received.

"Peace, my friend in the Law," I rocked her against me. "Peace."

14.19 The pestilence that came from the windmills of the Law

A few hours later when I returned home, the grey slime had completely disappeared and the courtyard was ablaze with white light. "Sweet Lord Melchisedek, what has happened here?"

Elyani came out to greet me. "Master Gervin operated a clearing," she elucidated. She was a bit pale, but her eyes were sparkling and her energy was shining clean.

I took her in my arms. "You look beautiful. Did Gervin clear you too?"

"Hunh hunh! I did it myself! Since you worked on me, my etheric body has been incredibly responsive."

We stayed in each other's arms, drinking the magic of our togetherness.

"And the Blue priestesses?" Elyani inquired.

"Five of them injured, but no one has died. Maryani is taking care of them."

"What about Hermina?" she asked, making me sit on the Dragon gate and sitting by my side.

"Voof! Hard work! Seven vital gateways were cracked, and the etheric of her right arm and shoulder was turned into puree. She will live, but I don't know that she will ever recover the use of her arm."

"How is her morale?"

"Mm..." I held my temples. "She is a strong woman. Despite the shock, she remained perfectly lucid. Do you want to know a secret, by the way? After I took her back to her garden apartment to heal her gateways, we spent nearly three hours talking. And I don't mean talking from my Flying Dragon voice – just plain conversation."

"Did you really? And what did you discuss?"

"A few things. The ritual, in particular. Trying to find ways to make it work. We discussed each phase and examined every single detail, and I liaised with Gervin at the same time. But..." I shook my head.

Elyani lovingly touched my neck, "What does Gervin think about what happened this morning?"

"He doesn't find it very surprising. The fields have been going downhill frighteningly fast in the last weeks. Floods of elemental slime like this one have been observed in several parts of the kingdom. In the county of the Western Plains a new pestilence has appeared: some kind of flu which has already killed hundreds of people. As if the drought wasn't bad enough! And some new insects are proliferating. They destroy the few patches of vegetation that have escaped the drought. Gervin says all this has come straight out of the elemental slime released from the fields. It's become so bad that for the first time ever, three high priests in the Western Plains have mentioned the possibility of discontinuing the windmills of the Law altogether."

"Deactivate all the fields?" Elyani could hardly believe her ears.

"Extinguish the warp, nothing less! This is how desperate they have become. From nearly all temples in the kingdom we are hearing stories of priests who fall sick and even die after performing rituals, especially the windmills of the Law. And in the counties of the Western Shores the flu is playing havoc with the population. Entire villages are being decimated. A new form of pestilence... no one knows how to control it."

"Does Gervin think they will stop the windmills?"

"Never!" I laughed sadly. "Never, never, never! Anyway, it's probably too late to change anything." I lay on the grass. "And do you know that the filosterops are *really* dying? I failed to heal Patron's little friend. Zonoteros, he was called."

"Zonoteros?" she chuckled at the idea of such a soft and friendly creature bearing the name of the revengeful gods' sixteen-legged bull.

"The filosterops' group-soul is leaving the kingdom. There is nothing anyone can do about it."

She lay by my side and sealed my lips with her index finger. "Hush, man of the Law! Remember you are the one who will teach the Brother Knights to keep their level of joy up."

I let the Dragon smile through me.

"Now for the good news," she went on. "I asked Maryani to arrange a meeting with King Vasouk for us. And he accepted."

I sat up abruptly, "But how did you get the answer? Did Maryani break the Law by talking to you?"

"Oooh!" Elyani burst out laughing. "But how did you find out?"

I raised my hands and addressed the gods, "No wonder you punish us!"

14.20 Tapping from the wisdom of the Nagas

When Elyani and I arrived in the peaceful Underworld garden, Vasouk and Maryani were in the middle of an animated discussion.

"My, my..." the golden Naga turned his huge head towards us, welcoming us with a friendly wriggle, "but isn't that Szar of the Brown Robe, and his friend Lady Elyani, the Immaculate?"

"Praise the Lord Melchisedek, Majesty!" I smiled, already warmed up.

What a voice this snake had! A unique combination of Ego-softness and Underworld force. It made all those who approached him feel like dancing.

"No, she's not an Immaculate when she is out of the kingdom," Maryani corrected Vasouk, "she's a White Eagle!" She went to hug Elyani and took off the veil that covered her face.

I frowned, wondering where that decision had come from.

Maryani matched my gaze, "The Law of the Immaculate has no provision regarding descents into the Underworlds, so that's how we decided it would be," she declared in a tone that left no space for discussion.

"Well, well, then..." I smiled, imitating Vasouk's voice without even realising it.

Vasouk *did* realise though. His scales rippled as he dipped his huge head and brought it up again a little closer to me, his black eyes wide.

"Hum..." I mumbled, terribly embarrassed.

Maryani chuckled and quickly changed the topic, "Elyani, let me introduce King Vasoukidass, Lord of these regions of the Underworlds."

Her face lit up with a smile of wonder, Elyani lawfully saluted the king, mesmerised by the shining golden colour of his seventy-lawful-feet-long body.

The king invited us to sit by his side and, after a few polite exchanges and a quick review of the latest Underworld gossip, I raised the matter that motivated our visit. "Your Majesty, we have come to ask your advice on some grave problems that we are presently encountering in the kingdom."

"Well, yes..." the quiver in Vasouk's nostril showed that he was tapping from his omniscient wisdom, "Maryani exposed the facts – minor facts as well as major ones – and yes, I should say that you have a problem. Have you thought of the possibility of conducting your ascension ritual in the Underworlds?"

I nearly choked at the idea of having to take the eleven hundred priests and priestesses of Eisraim to the Underworlds for the final ceremony.

"But of course!" Maryani pounced on the idea. "After all, strictly speaking, only Elyani and Hermina are needed to perform the ritual."

"Maryani!" I said in consternation, "How would we take Hermina down?"

"Well, well... Szar of the Brown Robe," Vasouk suggested, "since you managed to find a way to bring Lady Elyani down into my kingdom, why not use the same method with Lady Hermina the Immaculate?"

"Er..." I hesitated, twinging my beard, and in the meantime Elyani refrained from laughing while Maryani giggled.

Vasouk moved his head to and fro in slow motion, wriggling his omniscient nostrils. "I see," he said. "Well, perhaps, some other method could be found."

"Once," I conjectured, "I discussed with Lady Teyani the possibility of performing the ritual in darkness visible, or even in the intermediary planes above it. But consulting the Law of the Immaculate, Teyani found that this ascension ritual could only be implemented in the kingdom itself."

"That is also what the Immaculate told me," Elyani confirmed.

"In a way," Vasouk nodded, "I must say, this does not surprise me. And to tell you the pure truth, in the Deep Underworlds the forms of worship are quite different from yours. What you call Highness, we call Lowness, and of course we reach it by descending deep down into the Dragon. A number of your hymns would have to be modified or even, turned upside down, so to speak, which probably would take more time than you have in front of you."

"Well, fine!" Maryani gave a handclap, "Let's make Elyani a descending goddess, not an ascending one!"

Smiling, Elyani exchanged a quick glance with me.

"My... Maryani," Vasouk said in his slow, melodious voice, "if Lady Elyani were to become a happy denizen of the Deep Underworlds, then in the future she could not help her friends as she is planning to. Human beings are too disconnected from our worlds and, quite sadly I must say, this will only get worse and worse. And your Archive friends need her to be with the gods, don't they?"

"True!" Maryani conceded.

"Your majesty," I asked, "if we could find a way for Elyani's energy to cope with the offering of elemental forces, then the final ritual could happen any day. I was hoping that your infinite wisdom of the forces of nature could enlighten us on this point."

"Well, well..." Vasouk undertook some serious nostril-wriggling before continuing, "...the fact is, truly, simply, and bluntly, I am afraid, the forces of nature in your kingdom are out of control. Quite out of control, I would say."

"There *must* be a way to make this ascension ritual work," I insisted. "Your majesty, if *you* had to perform the ritual, how would you do it?"

For a long while, Vasouk looked at me with his large compassionate eyes, slowly rocking his head and pouring his warmth into me. Then he said, "My friends, the rotten situation in your kingdom has developed over centuries and centuries. Despite all my desire to help you, I have no magic solution to restore the balance of forces in your wounded nature. If you wanted me to advise you on how to build a better kingdom over a few thousand years, then I would be delighted to give you my opinions on a number of things – quite important things. But for what you are asking me now..." he paused and sighed. Then instead of finishing his sentence, he sighed again.

Elyani looked down, deeply dejected. I took her hand and held it Dragon-tight.

"Vasouk, can we ask for your help anyway?" Maryani's voice spoke our consternation. "Will you protect Elyani's energy?"

"As much as I can, I will," the Naga king promised.

Understanding that Vasouk would not tell us more, Elyani and I thanked him for his time and his help, and lawfully withdrew.

Maryani walked us to the Dragon gate. "Listen," she said, firing with her buoyant enthusiasm, "I am going to keep asking Vasouk for any possible tips on how to help you. And I will also nag his Naga friends, especially the generals who went to war with him. They're particularly resourceful. And for some ancient reason which you know, they *cannot* refuse to help me."

14.21 The Nephilim giants on their way

When we returned to the courtyard, it was early in the night. Defeated, Elyani sat on the grass, close to what used to be her favourite laurel tree.

"Oh my Lord Melchisedek," I realised, "but all the laurel trees are dead!"

Elyani caressed the already-withering leaves of the tree that had been planted the day of her birth. "You know," she said, "Adya and Melchard performed a ritual on this tree together. Adya knew she was going to die, so she put the light of the White Eagle on the tree for me, so I could come here when I was sad. And it worked. Throughout my childhood, each time I came and sat here the tree comforted me with its loving wisdom."

I took her in my arms. She was but a shadow of herself, "Perhaps it's not just because of the elemental sludge that the tree has died. This ascension ritual has taken me away from the Eagle's light. Until the daiva fell on me the White Spirit was always with me, whatever I did. Now... I don't feel it as strongly as I used to. What will become of me, Szar? Now that the ritual is lost, where am I going to end up?"

"No," I said, Thunder-firm, calling onto my master's enlightened presence, "we are *not* giving up."

"I'm going to die, Szar. I know. I'm going to die very soon. What if I completely lost my thread to the Eagle? Do you know what Gervin has prophesied about the destiny of many high priestesses of our temple?"

Rocking her in my arms, I opened a field of Eagle softness and let her speak her sorrow out.

"*Highly enlightened priestesses,*
Spending your life in contemplative heights,
Resting on the glory of the fields,
Once the warp dies and the kingdom falls,
For thousands of years no temple will be found for you to reincarnate.
Helpless, useless, hopeless, you will become,
Not even capable of remembering this exalted life.
For as long as seven lives in a row, many of you will become mad,
Because nothing hurts more
Than the pain of disconnection from the Light."

"Hey!" I protested, "you're not like this. You're *not* a Blue priestess, you're a panther, a woman of will. Through Teyani, Thunder has trained you for the future."

"There is nothing left of me. I feel so useless. Worthless."

"Worthless?" I shouted outrage. "But everyone wants you! The White Eagle wants you at the Great Gathering. We Flying Dragons want you too. We'll build you a nice little nest somewhere cosy, for instance on the edge of the Fault of Eternity – a splendid view, plenty of space, and never any problems with neighbours. And then Thunder wants you in the Brother Knights – now *that's* a nice little destiny: fighting the wars of the Apocalypse, meeting Ahriman face to face, losing all your friends, and more. And look, even the gods want you! Why do you think they have thrown the daiva? Because they think you're wonderful."

"Gervin's tactics," she murmured. "When someone cries, make them laugh."

"Exactly!" I gave her a big noisy kiss on the cheek. "Now listen, you know very well it's not your fault if this damn ritual doesn't want to work. In these rotten times even the greatest ritualists fail in elementary tasks such as bringing down rain or making crops grow. What's happening to you is not happening to you, it is happening to the kingdom."

In a deep silence, there was opening, and in the opening there was light. Elyani let herself be filled. I felt her relaxing slowly, as she let her energy merge into mine for a blessed moment of oneness.

She confided in a serene voice, "I keep having these ominous visions of giants attacking our temple. During my first weeks in the tower of Malchasek I saw them all the time: huge men coming to ravage our temple. They kill the priests. They destroy the statues. They desecrate the chapels. They melt the buildings down to the ground. The visions had stopped, but in the last days they have reappeared."

"I know, my Flying Dragon nature has shown me the same several times. And Mouridji told me that many people in the temple have received similar prophetic warnings."

The night of the howling dogs is imminent. Soon after, the real chaos will begin.

"One of the most frightening things in these visions is that the temple is nearly empty," Elyani said. "I see the halls, the alleys and the courtyards, and there is not one soul left in them. Did you and Namron make plans to evacuate the temple?"

"No. Maybe everyone will be dead."

Elyani shuddered, "Did you speak to Gervin about this?"

"The wise man in the Law is quite philosophical when it comes to the giants. He says, 'We always speak of the destruction of the kingdom. It will have to be destroyed by *something*. Whether it's the Nephilim giants or something else, does it fundamentally matter in the end?'"

"I find this..." Elyani searched for words, "...only moderately reassuring."

"To say the least!" I laughed in the fashion of my master.

"Could anything be done to protect the temple?"

"To fight the giants, I would need an army!"

Perseps made you a poisoned gift. Use it against the giants.

Images of Perseps came back to mind. He had brought three presents for me: intelligence, ginger marmalade, and a soft stone to reach him through Jex Belaran's protection shield. Using ginger marmalade to fight the giants, *that* would be the Dragon's last tooth!

The marmalade wasn't poisoned. It was made with sincere love.

I let out a long sigh, "Do you know what I feel like doing now?"

"What?"

"Sleep!"

"Ouch! Is it that bad, my love?"

"Perhaps it is, after all."

When things are at their worst, the man of Thunder laughs.

I laughed. Making my Dragon soft against hers, I asked, "Will you hold me in your arms?"

"A Dragon sleeping in my arms? Yes!" she answered enthusiastically. Taking me by the hand, she led me to the room. She undid my clothes, dropped her Immaculate's robe, and took me to her small bed.

"I have one last thing to do for the day," I sat in meditation position. "Come, do it with me. It's going to be sweet."

We sat face to face.

"Working on Hermina this morning, I found a way to connect her to Space Matrix. This woman is such a saint. She can connect with absolutely anything she wants. So we are going to use Space Matrix to reunite her with a Flying Dragon friend of hers."

"Has Hermina travelled through the spheres of remoteness?"

"No, it's the opposite. When she was a child, a Flying Dragon who was visiting our spheres used to come and keep her company when she was sad. I think..." I whispered, "I think little Hermina *drank bitter herbs*."

Being an Immaculate little girl was no easy task, even for a saint.

"And what happened to the Flying Dragon?"

"One day he left. He returned home. This morning Hermina confided to me how devastated she had been when it happened. She cried every night for weeks. You can't imagine how moved she was when I told her that Space Matrix could guide her through remoteness."

Cosmic tears in her eyes, the room filled with her Immaculate light.

The Eagle rejoiced, "So you are fulfilling your vow, Dragon?"

"Perhaps." I called the Immaculate priestess from the Flying Dragon voice.

Hermina?

"Szar!" she Point-answered.

How are you, my remote friend?

"When I stay away from my body, lawfully fine!"

I laughed. *I am afraid this is the case for a number of us.*

"How is Elyani?" she Point-inquired.

Beautiful. Ready to start again tomorrow!

"Sweet Lord Melchisedek!" she Point-sighed.

Are you ready to go, Hermina?

"I am always ready to leave the kingdom!"

I instructed her to tune into the memory of her friend and recall the feeling of his presence, then connected her Point to Space Matrix.

Near-instantly, Space Matrix prompted her, *Search successful. Flying Dragon retrieved. Presently located in the sphere of the Blue Lagoon. Engage travelling through intention.*

In less than a second, Hermina was gone.

Elyani concluded, "So something nice happened today, after all!"

"*Praise the Lord Melchisedek!*" I let myself collapse in the horizontal position.

Lying by my side, Elyani enveloped me. "Tonight, *I* am the Dragon, you sleep in my arms."

14.22 World of the gods, on the shore of the Molten Sea

Lord Gana was sitting on the shore of the Molten Sea, worshipping the primordial chaos with his music.

Light as a breeze, the silhouette of long-haired Mareena appeared in the distance. She walked the empty beach slowly, letting herself be filled with the magnificent harmonies Lord Gana produced from his molten star, the celestial musical instrument.

When she reached Lord Gana she sat on the sand by his side. She touched his feet to show her respect, but quickly, so as not to disturb the flow of his musical inspiration. For a long time of the gods she contemplated the Molten Sea, her feelings carried high by Gana's celestial harmonies.

Gana, still playing the molten star, turned towards her. In a glance, he made her long curly red hair shimmer with his light of bounty, and he said, "So you spoke to the Sons of Apollo about your friend Elyani."

Hearing Gana speak was like drinking nectar. Mareena touched his feet again, "They told me she would be invited to join their brotherhood."

Gana turned towards the Molten Sea again, smiling lovingly. "So all's well that ends well."

"Not really, Lord Gana. The ascension ritual in Eisraim is not going well, to say the least. Despite all the help I sent her, Elyani is failing. All signs are that she will not be reborn among us."

"She can still join the brotherhood, even if she does not gain a celestial birth," Gana said, his eyes fixed on the horizon.

"But we want her here, Gana!" Mareena pleaded sweetly, bringing an amused smile on Gana's face. "The Sons of Apollo think she would be infinitely more useful to the brotherhood if she could become one of us."

"If the Sons of Apollo want her here, then no doubt she will succeed," Gana said, still smiling.

"But Gana, you know it is not as simple as that! Now that the great disconnection has separated the kingdom from us, we can no longer intervene directly as we used to."

The silence of the gods.

Adding a touch of irony to his celestially-famous friendly smile, Gana asked, "Have you come to ask me something, Mareena?"

"I am your eternal servant, Lord Gana. I would never dare suggest any course of action to you," Mareena said, totally surrendered. "I can but implore your divine wisdom, with which you know so well how to inspire not only human beings, but also the gods themselves."

"I see," Gana answered, and he kept playing the molten star.

From the tone of his voice, from the sound of his music, and from some signs in the waves of the primordial ocean, Mareena knew that Gana had already answered her plea. She clapped her hands with joy and again touched his feet. Then she stood up and started dancing, following the god's wonderfully warm harmonies.

Looking straight in front of him, Gana kept smiling.

14.23 Harvesting after Gana

Thunderstruck, I woke up in the middle of the night.

"I know!" I exclaimed triumphantly, sitting up, "I know what to do!" I turned to Elyani, who was not asleep. "Listen, I've had an idea!"

I realised that she did not look well at all. "What's happening to you my love?"

"I couldn't sleep. I feel sick. I'm terribly hot, I think I have some kind of fever. And weird dreams, with my eyes open."

"Dragon overheating, perhaps? Not uncommon when people first come in touch with vroofing waves – serious ones, I mean." I bent over to her, tuning into her feverish energy.

"Tell me your idea!" she said.

"Yes! Yes! Listen," I said enthusiastically, "what if we changed one thing in the ritual? Instead of offering elemental slime, what if we offered elemental forces from the Underworlds!"

"But," Elyani hesitated, "that's not what the gods are expecting. In the ritual, the ascending goddess is supposed to offer the elemental forces of our kingdom."

"Listen, listen... the ascension ritual is very ancient, isn't it?"

"Part of *the most ancient and holiest body of the Law*," she quoted the verse that was so dear to the Immaculate.

"That takes us back to the very beginning of the kingdom, when the elemental forces were still pure – as pure as they were in the Ancient Days of the Earth," I unravelled my plot. "Let me explain something Teyani taught me when she was taking care of me on my return from the temple of the Dragon. It started with a comical situation. Each time I was embarrassed, I would rest on my Mother the Dragon so as not to blush, but then Teyani could hear music inside the Earth. I hated this, but she loved the music. She told me, 'These Underworld forces you are tuning into, in the Ancient Days of the Earth they used to be all over the surface. The Earth was an extraordinary place. The climate was always perfect, and there were magnificent gardens and paradisiacal orchards everywhere. To be fed, all men had to do was collect the fruits nature gave them. So rich and teeming with life force these fruits were, just a bite was enough to *really* feed you – not just your body, but also your soul. The riverbeds were filled with gold sand. And there were precious gems everywhere. You did not even have to dig them up, they were scattered all over the ground.'"

"Just what we saw in the Underworlds," Elyani caught on.

"Exactly! Then Teyani explained how at some stage, before the creation of the kingdom, all these wonders were withdrawn from human beings. The Underworlds were sealed off. Nature started deteriorating, and this was the end of the glory of the Ancient Days of the Earth. But in the Underworlds, this fall of nature never happened. The Underworlds kept the treasures that were lost on the surface."

"And so, in the Underworlds, we should be able to find elemental forces that are similar to those that were on Earth long ago, and that we could offer to the gods. Is that it?" Elyani rubbed her forehead, fighting her post-Dragon headache.

"Exactly! I am *sure* that in the beginning of the kingdom, even though the golden age of the Ancient Days of the Earth had passed, the elemental forces were still quite pure. Anyway, isn't that what the fields were all about, originally? Their purpose was to extend the golden age for as long as possible. And so nowadays, if we wanted to reproduce the ascension ritual as it was in its pure, original form, what better offering could we find than elementals from the Underworlds?" I paused to contain the excruciating pain in my left hand. "Really, why would the gods want offerings of filthy sludge? Surely they will enjoy pure, Underworld-juicy elementals far more."

"But how would I offer elementals from the Underworld?" Elyani asked, still rubbing her forehead.

"I'm *sure* we could establish a connection to the Underworlds, something you could draw from. Especially if the Nagas wanted to help us." I snapped my fingers, "We must try it! Let me talk to Gervin about it."

Wasting no time, I voice-channelled the Master of Thunder and told him of my idea.

Gervin gave it a few seconds of silent concentration, then he said, "Do you realise where this idea comes from?"

"Er... no. I just thought it was a good idea."

"Mm..." he said, and I knew he was twinging his beard.

"Do you not approve of the idea, Gervin?" I asked, starting to wonder if I had called my master too hastily.

"Mm..." Gervin's tone indicated he was tuning high in Thunder. "Szar, I want you to put this into practice right now, and report to me."

"Elyani is sick. As soon she is a bit better, we'll start."

"Right now!" Gervin repeated, in his unstoppable warrior's voice. "Call the Immaculate and try your method immediately. And get back to me as soon as the ritual offering begins."

"Yes, Gervin!"

"I will hear from you soon," he concluded.

"*All glory to the teacher!*"

After the communication, Elyani looked deep into my eyes. "Voof! I have not often heard Gervin speak like this."

"It's his Apocalyptic warrior side," I smiled affectionately. "Now, how am I going to find Hermina? By now, she must be spread in remoteness like three grains of salt in a cauldron of soup. I wonder if..."

A voice-channel call from Teyani interrupted me.

"Szar?"

"Yours in the Dragon, Teyani!"

"Szar, is Elyani close to you at the moment?"

"I am taking her in my arms, right now."

"My dear friends in the Law, I have some important things to tell you. Today, you and Elyani are going to have to be very strong." She paused, and in an infinitely sweet voice, she said, "You know how much I love you. Well, I want you to remember that the Eagle loves you a hundred times more."

I swallowed hard. Elyani's eyes filled with tears.

"Now I want you to close your eyes and tune high in the clear fountain with me," Teyani said.

We followed her into the heights of the column of Spirit, and the presence of the Eagle met us. For a brief moment all our worries disappeared: Elyani's grief, the pain in my hand, the collapsing fields and their monstrous vomit, the Nephilim giants on their way, and the rest. There was but the all-encompassing High Light and Love of the Eagle.

By the time our awareness was brought back to the room, Teyani had closed the channel.

"Beautiful light," I whispered, transported by the Eagle's enlightenment.

Find Hermina. Waste no time.

I called her. Predictably, there was no answer. So I invoked Space Matrix, for whom finding a grain of soul in the ocean of remoteness was no Dragon of a problem.

Search successful. Human entity retrieved, spread in the sphere of the Blue Lagoon. Consciousness-condensing process engaged.

Elyani and I listened in awe. But a few seconds later, Space Matrix sent another message, *Human entity is resisting the consciousness-condensing process.*

"Please, Space Matrix, try a little harder!" I prayed.

The entity is endowed with a higher degree of free-will. Forcing her would be against the code of ethics programmed in Space Matrix.

"Is there no way to send her a message?" Elyani asked.

It was the Flying Dragon voice that answered, *Of course there is. You don't even need the voice of a Flying Dragon. From your Point, simply tune into Space Matrix's Universal Knowledge Bank. A connection will immediately be established.*

"Come with me, follow my Point," I invited Elyani.

Tuning into Space Matrix was always a phenomenal experience, with not only the sharp awakening power of Point frequencies of consciousness, but also the out-of-the-seven-spheres vastness of the Flying Dragons' multidimensional enlightenment. The feeling was one of awesomely ancient knowingness and wisdom. Space Matrix had first been established aeons before the birth of the human hierarchy. Ever since, it had been re-established at the dawn of each cosmic cycle.

Beyond words and beyond human concepts, the communication took place. It was instant and eternal at the same time – beyond space and time, and yet embedded in the archetypal web of remote astral spaces. And it had heart, but not like the little heart of human beings; rather, the endless heartness of cosmic consciousness as flavoured by the enlightened void of galactic immensities.

Space Matrix announced,

Consciousness-condensing process successfully completed. Human entity has reintegrated the spheres of Melchisedek.

14.24 The spark which gave Life

I found Hermina in tears, lying on the floor of her garden apartment, her head uncovered. I went and sat by her side, directing my gaze to the ceiling. Instinctively, my hand moved towards her gateways.

I stopped myself, remembering the Law of her caste.

I grabbed a pillow, placed it under her head, took her hand and called onto the Eagle's Light for her. "Listen," I pleaded, "can't we use the rule that says that when an Immaculate priestess is very sick, an attendant can be appointed and talk to her if needed? I want to be your attendant."

Hermina became stone-still, engaging in a Point-communication.

"No," she said after a few seconds. "The high council of the Immaculate won't allow it." With extreme gentleness she pushed my hand away.

Can I at least talk to you with my voice of remoteness?

"Yes," her voice choked with grief, "please talk to me, Flying Dragon. And I can talk to you. But the Immaculate council will not allow you or anyone else to heal me."

Hermina's pain was heavy on my chest. Her vital gateways were still half-cracked, the right side of her body of energy turned into puree, her right arm paralysed.

I wished the Immaculate council could go to Azazel and get lost!

"Hush, man of the Law!" she said with her unique softness. "Do not judge that which you do not know."

Did I get you into trouble by talking to you yesterday?

"These things are not what you think, friend," she smiled. "The Immaculate never judge anyone, and they never punish anyone. If we stick to our strict rules it is not because we are narrow-minded but because Highness is what matters to us – not our life down here."

There must be something I can do to help you.

"The spheres of the Blue Lagoon are magnificent, Szar. Immensely magnificent. And the Flying Dragon... When I was a child, I had never realised how enlightened he was. May the Lord Melchisedek bless you for what you have given me."

To her, the journey didn't last a night. More like a few months.

She let her High Light shine into me. "Now tell me more about this idea you mentioned when calling me back."

Using the Flying Dragon voice, I endeavoured to explain why I thought that elemental forces from the Underworlds could be offered instead of the kingdom's elementals.

"A major departure from the ritual procedure," Hermina concluded in a thoughtful voice. "I must ask the Immaculate council about this. But..." she paused one second, "if I could connect your Point to them and let them read you, there might be more chance of them accepting."

Let my soul be read by a council of Immaculate witches? Never in seven cosmic cycles!

Say yes!

Horrified, I immediately Point-called Gervin and explained the situation. To my unlawful astonishment, he immediately Point-replied, *"Do it!"*

"But Gervin, if I open my Point to them, they will know all about our Archive."

"These women are among the greatest saints in the kingdom. You can trust them as you trust Thunder. They will respect our secrets."

Difficult to Point-swallow, but, "All glory to the teacher!"

Slightly tucking my head in my shoulders, I opened my Point to Hermina and let her connect me to the Immaculate council.

What was going to happen?

Nothing!

A split-second later, Hermina announced, "My Immaculate sisters have accepted your suggestion."

"Already?" How could that be? I hadn't perceived a thing, not even from the Point. Meaning I had completely missed the action.

Mysterious caste, these Immaculate.

Hermina said, "Let's go!" and to my amazement she stood up.

Where do you find the force to stand up, Hermina?

"Not from my body, that is for sure!" Limping, she slowly walked to her bed to collect her white veil.

Are you all right?

"My soul shines. Who cares about my body?" She covered her head.

No doubt Marek the Great Warrior would have been impressed by this woman. Humbled, I followed her along the temple corridors. Thank the Lord Melchisedek, she had moved to the garden apartment Mouridji and her acolytes had prepared for her. It was much closer to Elyani's courtyard than the tower of Malchasek. Still, it took a while to get there.

It left me plenty of time to wonder why the Immaculate council had accepted my plan so readily.

Who said they accepted it readily? In Highness, aeons of deliberation and inspired consultation with gods and angels can take place in less than a human second. A high being has helped.

A high being? Which high being?

Do not try to find out for the moment. Tomorrow you will meet him. Only then will you realise how much you owe him.

Did this mean my idea could work? Suddenly filled with hope, I tuned in high in the clear fountain.

The gods are more unpredictable than you think. No one can know in advance if they will accept the offering. If they do, the ritual succeeds. If they don't, Elyani finds herself in an extremely difficult position – having left her body, dead to the physical world, but unable to ascend to the world of the gods. In her present state of emotional exhaustion, anything could happen.

It was nearly dawn. When we arrived in the courtyard, Elyani was sitting on the Dragon gate. Hermina went over to her and let herself collapse on the ground. She lay flat on the grass, trying to recover some strength.

Her distress was heavy.

Elyani and I tuned high into the Eagle's Light for her. It was easy. After the meditation with Teyani, the Eagle's presence hadn't left the courtyard.

"Thank you," Hermina said after a few minutes. She sat up and instructed Elyani to begin the hymns of the ritual.

Elyani chanted. Hermina remained silent.

When the time for lighting up the Blue Flame had come, Hermina said, "Today, my child, you will have to take on the gesture of the Flame. I cannot move my right arm."

Elyani placed her hands parallel in front of her, creating a field of energy linked to her heart. Hermina Voice-projected the shriek mantra that instantly manifested the mysterious Holy Blue Flame.

Projecting her Voice into the Flame, Elyani continued the ritual.

Meanwhile, I Point-liaised with Maryani. She was only moderately enthused by my plan. *"Do you really think it could work?" she Point-questioned. "No doubt this offering will be more enticing than the foul sludge which rots the kingdom's nature. Last night, during a meeting I held with fifteen of Vasouk's most enlightened friends, the same suggestion came up. But Lord Sarpaling, a Naga who has spent several hundred years living with the gods, said he had never seen them accept an offering of this kind."*

"Maryani, somehow I believe in this idea."

"Of course you realise that until the end of the ritual we have no way of knowing if the gods are satisfied. I discussed this point with both the Nagas and with Teyani. At the conclusion of the final practice, if the gods show

interest they manifest their presence in the form of a huge light hovering above the audience. But even this is no guarantee they will take Elyani."

"Do you have any other solution, Maryani?"

"Well... no."

"Well, then, let us try this method for the moment," I Point-concluded, and I went on explaining the details of my plan.

When the phase of ritual offering was about to begin, Elyani stopped the recitation of the hymns.

I went to sit by her side. "Go ahead with the hymns of the elemental offering. But instead of opening to the forces of nature around us, open to the Dragon-waves that Maryani and I will be sending you."

"Shall I tune into the Dragon gate and try to draw energies from beneath the Earth?"

"No, the Dragon breeze would make you sick. Maryani and I will filter the breeze and then direct it to your lower chakras. So your task is straightforward: tune into the vroofing waves that come up from the lower part of your body and offer them to the gods."

After a few seconds of prayer, Elyani resumed the chants.

I connected my energy to Maryani. The Nagas' ambassador had taken position in the Dragon gate, far beneath us. She established an ascending flow of exquisite golden waves, which I relayed to Elyani's lower chakras.

The quality of Elyani's Voice immediately changed: a certain buoyancy and joyfulness started flowing through her. Colourful waves of energy poured out of her mouth, feeding the Holy Blue Flame.

Maryani gradually increased the intensity of the waves. The power in Elyani's Voice rose correspondingly. Sensing her exultation, I had to pull the alarm bell.

"She is Dragon-overheating already!" I Point-called Maryani.

"Shall I decrease the intensity?" Maryani asked.

"No!" Gervin Point-intervened. "Raise the intensity."

"We are going to burn her out," I Point-warned. "At the end of the practice she will collapse in a heap on the floor."

"Maryani, call Vasoukidass to the rescue!" Gervin ordered.

Instantly, the unmistakable golden flavour of the Naga king appeared in Elyani's aura.

Maryani further increased the intensity.

"How many more hymns to go before the end of the elemental offering? I Point-asked Elyani.

"Seven," she Point-answered as she kept on chanting.

My Dragon was flooded with so much golden light that I had to make great efforts to remain present to the kingdom.

Elyani's Voice was becoming more and more charged, vroofing with Underworld power. I could feel the tremendous elation and the dancing ecstasy in her, and I did not like it. Disastrous consequences could follow.

Dragon bliss is powerful medicine. One must get accustomed to it gradually, otherwise it can kill.

"Raise the intensity!" Gervin Point-instructed.

Elyani's Voice became a huge fire that poured into the Holy Flame. And to my amazement, the Blue Flame started growing in size. Soon it was four lawful feet high, and still growing.

"The Dragon-overheating is reaching unreasonable proportions," I Point-warned again. "I think we should make a break."

"Keep going!" Gervin said.

I Point-asked Elyani, "How many more hymns to go?"

"Four!" she Point-answered. "But I feel fantastic! Fantastic!"

"Increase the power!" Gervin Point-directed Maryani.

The Holy Flame was nearly seven lawful feet high. A torrent of light was pouring out of Elyani's mouth, charged with the irresistible magic of the Ancient Days of the Earth, when youthful volcanoes celebrated the thunderous might of Cosmic Fire, and omnipresent veins of ruby-red lava echoed the burning glory of the Web of Love, fresh titanic powers trampling on black earth and spreading their enthusiasm in the six directions of space, nature itching with adolescent urges, her swollen fertile womb delivering torrents of new and extravagant creatures. Holding onto the core of Dragonness so as not to crumble under the extravaganza of life, the ignited fury, the tidal wave of Voice, it was like being back in the death crypt of Mount Lohrzen.

"Gervin," I Point-implored my master, "I don't know that even the Great Warriors of Mount Lohrzen could take this kind of intensity."

"What does Vasoukidass say?" Gervin Point-asked.

"About the same," Maryani Point-replied after consulting with the Naga king.

"We keep on!" Gervin ordered.

The Holy Blue Flame kept growing in width, licking our auras, ready to consume us, creating strange flares in the Dragon, infinity made light, humming Song of Creation and forerunner echoes of the trumpets of the last day, when all is accomplished and all matter is dissolved.

"How many more hymns?"

"Two."

"Mother of the Light, have mercy on us!"

Elyani's aura, a flame twenty lawful feet high, a temple of light, solid gold with motley sparks, harmonies of all colours, I love you, bluer than the Blue Lagoon, I tread the razor's edge of time and timelessness, when you and I were children in infinity, gushing purple fire, speed up, Kartendranath looking down from the cascade of Life and Light, two birds of paradise are mating, I remember the end of time, speed up, Fridrick is dead, the Hunters will be back, Lord Proston will say yes, Virginia, 997, Hiram king of No Limits, Vivyani no lònger in the caverns of sickness, speed up, Gana's helmet Philadelphia Six a sea of fire the gods are wise Kartendranath has prepared the triaxe Revelation Sky...

"Gervin, I'm losing the thread! Help!"

"Hold onto Thunder!"

A loud scream, "Stop!"

Elyani immediately discontinued the chanting.

Standing up by the force of God, Hermina shouted again, "Stop!" With a low-pitched Voice projection, she made the Blue Flame vanish.

Maryani stopped the ascending flow of golden lava. The size of Elyani's aura instantly diminished by three quarters, bringing it to its near-normal dimension. But she was still ablaze with Underworld gold, Ancient World's magic, gushing purple fire, motley sparks, the Blue Lagoon and the Wise Spider, scalene fighters setting everything ablaze on their way, and the White Enlightenment of the Eagle's flight at the Edge of Highness.

In the eerie silence Elyani stood up, entranced.

I stood up with her, not daring to touch her, trying to hold the energy for her, but where is that Dragon, Mount Lohrzen under my feet, I feel vast.

She turned and started walking slowly, her spiritual presence spread throughout the entire temple, the Great Ant watching from a distance.

Hermina and I followed her with our eyes, holding our breath.

Slowly, Elyani reached her laurel tree. She brought her hands close to its leaves. After an aeon packed in a second she applied both hands to the branches, and the tree was sparked with a gigantic flame of energy. Massive, the flame reached higher than the terrace on top of the bedrooms.

Lo! The Ancient Days were back, awesome and beautiful, like one hundred Nagas diving into the ocean of ultimate matter.

The flame had Life, and Life came to the tree.

And in the Life, a magnificent sound was heard, a Voice that came straight from transcendental Highness and whispered all the secrets of the creation, starting with the Great Dawn that already knew everything long before anyone started wondering about it, as it sang before the beginning and ever will sing, song without end...

Abruptly, the flame disappeared. Everything became still.

The kingdom was back. Its mists. Temple noises in the distance.

Elyani fell on her knees.

I rushed over to her and took her in my arms.

Hermina is giving her life for Elyani and you.

Startled, I turned to the Immaculate. She was standing motionless, contemplating the Dragon gate. Before I could tune into her, Gervin called, this time through darkness visible. "The ascension ritual must take place tomorrow morning," he stated in his calm, Apocalyptic voice.

"What? But Gervin, we have just started this new method. We have no idea if it will work. Shouldn't we wait till the gods send us a sign telling us they like our offering?"

Hermina, who had already Point-consulted her sisters, answered Gervin, "The council of the Immaculate has agreed. Tomorrow morning."

14.25 The last night with Elyani

After a frantic day during which everyone in the temple was running in all directions to prepare the central crypt for the final practice of the ascension ritual, I returned to the courtyard.

The feeling inside me was utter desolation. This came as no surprise. I had known right from the beginning that as soon as a solution was found I would lose Elyani. But Gervin's sudden decision had shocked my Dragon. At first, the verdict had left me in a space of unreality. Was Elyani *really* going to leave the kingdom tomorrow? But as the hours passed, and especially as I went into the crypt and took part in the rehearsal of the hymns that a number of male priests were to chant at the opening of the ritual, the bleak reality imposed itself on my mind: in less than a day, Elyani would be dead. And there was no guarantee she would be reborn among the gods. As both Gervin and Teyani had repeated often enough, "The minds of the gods, human being can never know!" We had *no way* to intuit whether the immortals would accept our unusual ritual offering.

I found the ascending goddess sitting on her knees on the Dragon gate. She was still enveloped in the infinitely sweet Eagle presence Teyani had put on us early that day. The courtyard looked surprisingly normal, considering the enlightened madness of our rehearsal.

I went and sat in front of the woman. For a long while we looked into each other's eyes silently.

The laurel tree caught my attention. An etheric glow had reappeared in its leaves. "Praise the Lord Melchisedek! It is alive!"

"The flame of Life brought it back to us."

"I can't believe you coped with so much power!" Throughout the day, I had Point-liaised with her to make sure she did not have any Dragon-overheating symptoms. But thanks to the Nagas' protection, she did not have even the slightest fever or headache.

"The only after-effect was the usual one... this burning desire which could make me do anything to have a child with you."

"Well, well..." I took her in my arms, "Vasouk, inspire me!"

"What shall we do about this problem?" she finished my sentence in the slow, low-pitched voice of the Naga king.

"Precisely, nothing!" I changed the topic. "Was Hermina satisfied with the ritual this morning?"

"Yes. If she had to interrupt it, it was because the Holy Blue Flame was about to engulf me. This must only happen at the time of the final practice."

"Is this how it will happen?" I asked. "You will be offered to the gods through the Blue Flame?"

"*The flame carries offerings to the gods,*" Elyani quoted the well-known verse that applied to all fire ceremonies. But in this case it took on a completely different meaning. It was no common fire that was to be used for this ritual, but the mysterious Blue Flame. "Tomorrow, after the offering of Underworld elementals, I myself will be the final offering," she said.

"Entering the Blue Flame!" I made my voice enthusiastic, resting deep on the Dragon to contain my tears. "It is bound to work! How could the gods resist such a beautiful offering?"

After a long embrace, Elyani asked, "Did Gervin tell you why he wanted the ritual to happen tomorrow?"

"Catastrophic news reaches the temple every day," I smiled optimistically. "In all counties, buildings are going mad. They grow unlawful bumps in all the wrong places. And that new pestilence which started in the Western Shores is spreading alarmingly fast. It's killing thousands of people, nothing seems to be able to contain it. And in the Western Plains, after all these months of drought, famine looms. People are desperate. There have been riots. The king has had to send three battalions to restore order. It's happening all over the kingdom, the sludge vomited by the fields is worse than ever."

"This ominous night of the howling dogs... it could even happen tonight, really," Elyani said in a soft voice.

I shivered. Now, *that* would have been the Dragon's last tooth!

I tried to find some reassuring words, "My love, it could have been last night, or the night before, or any night of the last months, really."

But this was not reassuring at all. She gave me a look.

The night of the howling dogs will be preceded by a phase of paradoxical clarity. Good for you, bad for the Nephilim Hunters. The sunset of the Law.

"Good!" She took me by the hand, "I want to go and watch the sunset with you." And we went to sit on the Blue priestesses' roof.

Silently, we watched the mists become red and gradually darken, sitting in the Eagle's space of infinite sweetness, drinking each other's presence like precious nectar. Then we went back into the courtyard and started discussing strategy.

"Tomorrow," I said, "Maryani will take position under the crypt. She says she doesn't need a Dragon gate to create the ascending flow of Underworld elementals. This afternoon we rehearsed together. I stood in the crypt and received the Dragon waves she was sending up. It worked very smoothly. And so, as far as you are concerned, the situation should be exactly the same as this morning, except that I will not be sitting by your side. I will be in the audience with Gervin, Lehrmon and Woolly."

"I think you should be with me on the stage!"

"So does Mouridji," I reported. "When she learned I would not be sitting by your side, she was outraged. But wise Hermina insisted it should be so. It must have to do with the Holy Blue Flame. Suppose it grew so big that it engulfed me too! I might be vaporised in Highness."

"Or perhaps the gods would take the two of us!" she said.

I sighed, wondering what it would be like to spend a night together in the world of the gods. She wondered that too, but we didn't mention it.

I made her lie on the grass and let my hand run on her body, reinforcing her gateways, pouring life force into her, and holding her by the same occasion.

Working on her for the last time.

Dragon, Dragon, let me not burst into tears and collapse!

I dreaded doing anything that could upset her energy and jeopardise her chances in the great trial.

When I finished, I started again. And at the end of the second round, we both decided that a third round was needed. And a fourth one, because nothing in the Law said we shouldn't.

I asked if she wanted some dinner.

"I must fast," she said. "Do you know that in the pure form of the ritual, the ascending goddess is supposed to spend ten days fasting in total silence before undertaking the final ascension practice?"

"Should I leave you alone, then?"

"Oh, no!" she grabbed me into her arms. "Hermina said that in our case it would not make any difference. The silence is to empty the ascending goddess of all imprints. But she said that since I will be receiving vroofing waves from you during the ritual anyway, I might as well be with you tonight."

"What else did she say?"

"Ascending goddesses are supposed to be ecstatically happy, and so I must not cry. That's another reason why Hermina wanted us to be together tonight. She said I would cry less."

"Hermina is an angel." I prayed the Dragon to bring a little joy to the ascending goddess' face.

"I made something for you," she said, and she disappeared into the room. When she came back she was carrying a large cup. "Dragon's milk," she announced.

I remembered the day of my first descent into the Underworlds.

"Do you still have the image with you?" she asked.

"Till the end of time! You were sitting here, in front of me. First you said the Dragon's milk would save my life. Then you told me to contemplate the courtyard and fix its image in my memory. But I couldn't take my eyes off you."

She sat close to me and handed me the cup. "Today, preparing this drink, I have understood that Dragon's milk is not at all what I thought it was."

"Tell me!" I said, automatically sense-smelling the beverage.

She smiled affectionately, and I knew she was remembering the story of Sniffing Dragon. "The secret is that the ingredients are nothing!" she raised her hands. "They are there only to help you permeate the beverage with the vroofing power of the Dragon."

I took a sip. It immediately triggered a fresh, bubbly little ascending wave in my energy. "Dragon-delicious!"

"If *you* made some Dragon's milk," she said, "you could put so much power in it that whoever drank it would roll on the floor, laughing their Point off, having visions that go as far as remoteness..."

"...but as I came back from my first descent too late to be worthy of receiving the secret recipe, that will never happen," I said in a poor-me voice, sighing exaggeratedly.

"Oooh! No, don't speak like this! I will give you the recipe if you want."

"Would you?" I was even more moved than anxious.

"I love you!" she exclaimed. As I saw she was going to cry I immediately made myself playful and begged her, "Tell me, I can't wait! I have wanted to know this secret for so long!"

Bringing her lips close to my ear, she started whispering the recipe.

"What?" I soon exclaimed, and with genuine stupefaction. "I can't believe this! You must be joking in the Law."

"Not at all. This is the pure truth," she said. "And it's not all..."

As she continued, I laughed and applauded in amazement.

"Far Underworld!" the revelation left me stunned. "No wonder the secret was so well kept! You were right, it probably saved my life!"

"This time, that is it. You know everything about the White Eagles," Elyani grinned. Then she became grave, speaking straight from the clear fountain. "Let me tell you another secret. Do you know that in the future you will be a White Eagle?"

Curious, I looked into her eyes for enlightenment.

"It is true," she said, "Teyani and I saw it several times. The Eagle's presence will be with you, and you will be dressed in white. You will carry out his works, and help his presence reach those who need him."

I closed my eyes, imagining myself clad in a white robe. "Is that to happen in this life?"

"No, much later."

"But I thought the Knights of the Apocalypse wore black?" I said, taking another draught of Dragon's milk.

"Mm..." she closed her eyes and tuned into her prophetic sight, "with the Knights, of course you will be wearing black. But even then, his White presence will be with you. And you will be riding a white eagle."

I closed my eyes, trying to picture myself riding a white eagle. "Will that be the bird that flies so fast and spits fire?"

"Yes. The fastest of all birds."

There's nothing faster than a Scalene 333.

"Can you see it?" I asked.

"Right in front of my eye," she answered in her panther's voice.

Get her to speak about the Knights. Make her strong, call onto the Panther in her.

"While you're there, I want to know more about No Limits," I asked. "Ever since you first mentioned it, that place has been a Point-puzzle to me. Once you said there will be herds of elephantos, another time you said it will hardly be bigger than our courtyard. How am I to make lawful sense of that?"

"When I see it, it's obvious. It is when I try to explain that it's difficult. But now that you've become a great expert in the Point, I could show you the images. Point-tune into me. Can you see these people who are riding horses? That takes place in No Limits."

I saw a dozen men and women wearing strange hats and riding horses full-speed. Using ropes, they were trying to capture cows. "So there are cows and horses. Is No Limits some kind of farming enterprise?" I asked, wondering who could possibly want to farm elephantos.

"No, no. It's a place where everything is possible. Look!"

I saw three men swimming under water together with a large grey fish. "But these ones are naked!" I exclaimed with surprise. "Are they native savages of some sort?"

"No, they are your best friends."

"My friends, these naked savages?" To cope with the disconcerting vision, I finished the Dragon's milk in one go.

"Everything is possible in that place. That's why they call it No Limits. Look!"

I saw a man jumping off the edge of a cliff. He fell for a few seconds, then he started flapping his arms as if they were wings and he went up again. "I see. This is happening in the field of stars!" I said, watching the man's astral travelling.

"It's in the field of stars, but it has nothing to do with astral travelling. Look, this is the white eagle you'll be riding."

For the first time, I saw it clearly. A strange flat triangular object. It moved in the field of stars, very slowly. It looked rather ugly to me. "But this isn't a bird!" I said, disappointed. "And it's not even white!" It was nothing like the wonderful picture of a white eagle carrying me through the spheres, as I had imagined until then.

Gideon to Hiram – Has my DAU gone completely off its brain or did you really *shoot 11 Omega-99's with nothing but sting missiles? Confirm.*

"You are flying back to No Limits," Elyani told me. "With another Knight. A very special Knight."

Hiram my brother. Hiram my son. O, Hiram!

"But I thought the bird flew much faster than that!" I complained to Elyani.

"Hunh! It seems slow, but it flies extraordinarily fast – the fastest the Knights can get. You're extremely proud of it."

I wondered why. The next image was that of a gigantic hall in which many similar 'birds' were lined up in a long row. The hall was full of people. They were giving a huge ovation to a young man who was coming out of one of the flat triangular things. He was very small. And ugly.

Hiram! Hiram! Hiram! Hiram...!

"This place is massive!" I exclaimed, finding it hard to believe how small the people were compared to the birds. "Is this No Limits?"

"No. On the way to it."

The next image was that of a stunning woman with black hair, dressed in a weird black outfit. As soon as I saw her eyes, I took Elyani's hand. "That's you, I know."

"True. Do you like her?" she said in a playful voice.

"She is magnificent!" I was fascinated by the magnetic power that radiated from the woman. "Now I understand why she's called a black panther. She looks fierce."

"The Knights are pretty fierce, my love. You would probably never be interested in her if she was too soft."

"She is looking at me, isn't she?" I drank the woman's image. "What's she telling me?"

Ready?

Ready.

So the time has come to say...

"...farewell." Elyani abruptly stopped the vision and looked deep into me. "You have no idea how much this woman will love you, Szar."

I contemplated her face. "Amazing how different the Panther looked, and yet how much she was you."

"Take me in your arms."

"Forever love, White Eagle!"

14.26 The verdict

Three hours before dawn, I arrived at the aquamarine chamber. The door was open. When I walked in I found Gervin in the company of Woolly and Lehrmon. The three men welcomed me with long hugs and loaded eye-contact, praising the Great Apollo. When they asked how I was, all I could answer was, "No thoughts, just Dragon. Ready to fight for her."

Dragon-focus, flooded with the Eagle's presence.

"Good," Gervin nodded gravely, contemplating my clear fountain. "And the ascending goddess?"

"Strong. There was so much light, Gervin – so much light! The Eagle has enveloped us in his wings. It was... beyond words. I stayed with her until Hermina arrived. But Hermina worries me. She's extremely tired, and weak."

"You know of the message she conveyed to Mouridji, don't you?" Lehrmon asked.

"What message?"

"During the night, Lady Hermina went to visit Mouridji in darkness visible. She asked her to thank the people of the temple on her behalf for all the offerings, the love and the support they have given her. She said the temple of Eisraim was the most sincere spiritual congregation she had ever visited. And she said that when she dies, she wants to be entombed in our crypts."

The dead bodies of Immaculate priestesses were not cremated like those of ordinary priests and priestesses but buried, so their saintly vibrations could be preserved. Their tombs, like the tombs of great sages, became places of inspiration and prayer. By deciding to leave us her body Hermina was no doubt making a high gift to the temple.

I hated the news. "Did she say she was going to die?"

"No, not exactly. But she said that if she died, she wanted you to perform her funeral rites," Lehrmon said. "Didn't she tell you?"

I bit my lip and shook my head silently. Conducting the funeral rites of a saint was an extremely high privilege. By choosing me Hermina knew she would honour my teacher, and the Brown Robe with him.

To hell with honour! Had I not called Hermina to Eisraim, none of this would have happened to her.

The Dragon rebelled, "We can't just let her die like this!" I turned to Gervin. "There *must* be something we can do."

Gervin shook his head. "Hermina knows what she is doing," he said in his softest voice. "Besides, many are those who will be departing in the coming months. Sad as it may sound, there are some more stupid ways to die than at the conclusion of an ascension ritual."

The thunderbolt bearer took my arm and the four of us walked towards the central crypt. Melchard, being the high priest of Eisraim, was to arrive separately. We met long processions of priests and priestesses on their way to the ritual. The members of each order gathered together, forming groups easily recognisable by the colour of their robe.

In the central crypt each group took position in a precisely determined way, as prescribed by the Law of the castes. According to the Law of Melchisedek, any gathering was to reflect the perfect harmony of the system of the castes, in which the place of every individual was fixed. A thousand people were coming. We had to wait more than four hours for the underground hall to be filled.

Such a gathering normally happened only once a year, during the celebration of the Law of Melchisedek. But on this special occasion the mood was not just solemn, it was grave.

How many more times would the entire temple family gather?

Everyone – or nearly everyone – had started to realise that the days of Eisraim were numbered. By the time the next celebration of the Law was due, what would be happening in the temple?

Would there still be a temple?

Rather than panic, the realisation that the end was approaching had created a profound wave of awakening. The Spirit in the temple was stronger than ever. Many priests and priestesses had started asking themselves questions that would otherwise never have come to their minds. They could see no solution to the looming catastrophe, but by putting all their heart in calling for help from their gods and angels they created a highly charged spiritual atmosphere. The presence of the one thousand was awesome and magnificent.

Their solemness reverberated in the chanting of the hymns. Having taken their places, one thousand men and women joined their voices and their vibrant aspiration, filling the crypt with the light of devotion.

The priests of the Grey Robe went on the central stage and chanted hymns of the most ancient and holiest body of the Law, entrancing the audience with the powerful magic of their Voice. Several groups of priests and priestesses followed them, displaying the facets of the Law which their orders were specialised in, treating the audience with enthralling Voice-projections.

Then came the twenty-two Attendants of the Spheres of the Law. These were highly experienced priests from different robes, with unique Voice powers. They slowly walked towards four large spheres that stood on pedestals, one in each corner of the central stage. The pedestals were approximately six-feet high, and the diameter of the spheres three feet, so that the spheres towered above the priests.

I had always thought these spheres of the Law were made of orichalc but that morning, carefully observing them, I started wondering whether they were physical or whether, like the Flying Dragon device that sealed the entrance to the crypt of the Archive stones, they were purely made of subtle energies – not physical.

The spheres, like the Blue Flame, were part of 'the wonders of the Law', ancient mysteries imbued with the holiest presence of the Lord Melchisedek. But for this presence to be revealed, the spheres had to be set in motion. This was the task of the Attendants of the Spheres. Two of them stood in the centre of the stage, connecting with the Highest God, while the others took position close to the spheres. When the central connectors gave the signal that the Lord Melchisedek had responded to their call, the priests started Voice-projecting mesmerising low-pitched sounds onto the spheres.

A deep wave of energy shook the audience.

Instantly, the wonder began. On the four corners of the central stage the spheres started revolving slowly, making a low-pitched hissing sound.

The priests raised the Voice-intensity, making the spheres of the Law spin faster and faster.

After a phase of gradual build-up, the spinning of the spheres became so fast that their movement could no longer be discerned. Their colour changed. From orichalc, they took on the same deep blue as the Holy Flame. This was accompanied by a change in the spiritual atmosphere of the hall. A massive presence made itself felt – this unique grand force known as 'the presence of the Law' which, long ago, the Lord Melchisedek had manifested on Earth as the foundation stone of the kingdom.

So intense was the presence that I started blissing out of physical reality, like many others in the crowd.

Gervin Point-shook me, "This is no time to travel through the spheres, son! Soon, your part will begin."

Now that the spheres of the Law were spinning, the time had come for the carriers of the Holy Blue Flame to make their entrance.

Led by Melchard, who on this special occasion was not wearing his brown robe but a shining crimson gown, six high priests entered the hall, slowly carrying a large wooden piece of artwork on which rested a flat chalice. In the chalice shone the Holy Blue Flame which, thousands of years ago, high angels had given to the first of the high priests of Eisraim, and which had ever since been kept, nurtured with Voice and transmitted from generation to generation.

When the majestic procession ended, the Flame was ritually installed on the centre of the stage, and the Crimson high priests began a fire ritual addressed directly to the Lord Melchisedek.

As the awe-struck audience worshipped the mysterious Flame, I could but wonder again. Had I *really* seen Hermina light similar Blue Flames with a fifteen-second Voice-shriek?

Hard to believe.

I wished these people could have known. But the fact that Holy Blue Flames could be lit by human beings, and not only by gods and angels, was arch-secret. Judging by the amazed glow in the eyes of those assembled here, that secret was well kept.

In the middle of the fire ritual to Melchisedek, the priestesses of the Dawn of Creation made their entry. Again wonder ran high in the audience, as everyone tried to catch a glimpse of the endless void that stood beneath their veils.

"How come there are only six of them?" I whispered to Gervin.

"The others are very sick," Gervin whispered back. Pre-empting my next question, he added, "They don't want to be healed."

So be it, Lords of Destiny!

The ritual to Melchisedek continued for nearly an hour. When the last hymn was completed, Gervin took my hand.

A pregnant silence.

Two frail silhouettes made their entry into the hall.

Gervin held my hand tighter.

Slowly, the two women in white walked to the stage.

Ripped apart. A desperate impulse came up inside me. Rebelling, "No! We can't just let this happen!"

Maryani Point-called, "I have taken position in the Underworlds with King Vasoukidass, who has gathered one hundred Nagas around us. His best generals are all here, together with high ritualists and experts in various lores. The mood is high. We have the power in hand, we are ready to use it. Are you ready?"

"Hermina and Elyani have just entered the hall," I Point-answered. "It will take at least one or two hours before the offering of elemental forces begins."

"We'll start sending you the ascending flow anyway, to make sure that everything happens according to plan."

When the two Immaculate arrived on the stage, the high priests moved back. Chanting a special hymn, Melchard relinquished the Flame, temporarily entrusting Hermina with the function of high custodian of the Law.

Hermina and Elyani began their chants.

I started receiving friendly golden waves from Maryani and her Naga friends. But they were ridiculously weak compared to what they were when we had rehearsed.

"Are you holding back because it is not yet the offering practice?" I Point-asked.

"Holding back? You must be joking in the Law! What we are sending up at the moment is massive," Maryani Point-answered.

"Then we have a problem. I am hardly receiving anything."

"It must have to do with the large number of people assembled in the hall," Gervin Point-intervened.

"The Nagas agree with you, Master Gervin," Maryani Point-said.

"Have you reached your maximum intensity?" I Point-asked.

"Maximum intensity?" Maryani Point-laughed at me. "Wait, man of the Law! We are going to show you something..."

"No! No! No! No! No!" Gervin was Point-adamant. "Maryani, don't increase the power too quickly. Be extremely gradual, otherwise you will trigger a catastrophe."

Slowly, the golden Underworld waves increased in strength. But it soon reached a point where other people in the audience started resonating with the waves. Some started feeling unusually hot. Others were wondering why their lower chakras were vibrating unlawfully intensely.

"Maryani," I Point-warned, "this is never going to work! By the time we reach the elemental offering, they will all be Dragon-overheating, and then the Lord Melchisedek knows what can happen. We must find a way to establish a more specific resonance between you and me."

"Lord Amar has just had a fantastic idea," Maryani Point-replied. "We're going to ask the seven architects who are sitting with us to quickly establish a golden shaft under you. Like a Dragon gate, but a Naga-made one."

"Creating a Dragon gate!" I Point-marvelled.

"It's happening, right now!".

Breaking the Law, I could not take my eyes off Elyani. Together with Hermina she was still chanting the preliminary hymns of the ascension ritual.

So many memories rushing through my mind. I had to switch onto no-thoughts-just-Dragon fighting mode.

After a few minutes, I felt a big flush of hot, ascending golden energy.

"How is our golden shaft?" Maryani Point-asked.

"Wonderful. I can feel it, just under me! Woolly seems to be responding too," I Point-commented.

"I wonder why!" Maryani Point-chuckled.

The energy increased, making my Dragon shine with golden light. By my side, Woolly started shaking, then after a few seconds became still again. He and I exchanged an accomplice's wink.

"It seems to be working like a charm," I Point-said. "And the people around us are no longer responding to your waves."

"I wish you could have seen how the Naga architects pierced that shaft!" Maryani Point-raved. "It was superb."

"What will we do to thank them for so much help?" I Point-wondered.

"No, they are thanking you for inviting them to take part in such an exciting exercise," she Point-insisted. "Down here, it's a celebration."

The hymns continued. I thanked the Mother of the Light for having created the Nagas. But after a moment I was taken by doubts.

I Point-called the Naga party, "The energy is reaching me perfectly well, but who says I'll be able to transmit it to Elyani? She is at least a hundred lawful feet away from me, and there are hundreds of people in between."

After a moment of deliberation, the Nagas sent their answer through Maryani. *"Vasouk suggests that you try the method on Woolly. Send him close to the stage, and resonate with his Dragon."*

Woolly, who was Point-listening, pulled a face. *"Moving away from those of my caste? That would be a major departure from the Law."*

"Do you mean you've never broken the Law before?" Maryani Point-lashed at him.

"Not in the middle of a celebration of the Law!" he Point-threw back. "If one thousand people become outraged, the room will turn into a complete mess."

"True!" Maryani Point-conceded.

"I don't care!" I said. "I'm not taking any risks."

Gervin gave his immediate support, "You have my blessing. Thunder is on your side."

Slowly and with a dignified, ceremonial attitude, I started walking towards a red ritual banner, which was held by two poles on the edge of the central alley. I couldn't just stay there and do nothing, so I made up something lawful. I reverently bent my head for a few seconds.

All the priests around were looking at me, their eyes wide open, wondering what in the kingdom I was doing.

To give myself a lawful countenance, I grabbed the poles and pompously held the banner in front of them.

The priests who, needless to say, had never taken part in an ascension ritual before, thought this was part of the ceremony. Law-abiding as they were, they bent their heads reverently, copying what I had just done.

Stifling a grin, I held the banner in front of me and imitated the majestic attitude of the Crimson high priests, slowly marching along the alley that led to the central stage.

It worked. Believing this was part of the ritual, all the priests and priestesses reverently bent their head as I passed them.

When I reached the edge of the stage, I became still and Point-called Woolly, *"Now! Send me the energy."*

"How do I do that?" he Point-asked.

"Let Maryani show you."

Meanwhile, all the Crimson high priests were reverently bowing their heads in front of my banner.

"Sounds like we have disaster on our hands," I Point-called after a few seconds. "I am not receiving anything!"

"Yes, this smells like disaster. But maybe you should be the sender, and Woolly the receiver," Maryani suggested.

As slowly and pompously as I had come, I returned to my original position, making everyone bend their heads on my way. I left the banner on the edge of the alley and went back to stand on the golden shaft.

Then I whispered to Woolly, "Just do what I have just done!"

"How will I know if I am receiving the energy?" he asked anxiously.

"Man of the Law, it's going to blow your ass!" Maryani Point-reassured him.

Gervin grinned to refrain from laughing, Woolly took on a superb face and like a king, paraded towards the banner.

Painful suspense. Was Woolly going to receive the golden waves?

If not, the situation would turn into the nightmare of all nightmares.

For at least twenty seconds Woolly reverently bent his head in front of the banner. Then he took it in his hands, and slowly walked the alley towards the central stage.

It seemed to last for an entire aeon. While everyone in the audience was bending their head, I prayed for help from the Flying Dragons, holding deep onto the golden shaft.

Revelation Sky. The Sons of Apollo are watching.

As soon as Woolly of the Brown Robe arrived at the stage, I started blasting his Dragon with Underworld forces. Thank the Mother of the Light, his aura instantly flared with golden light. I gradually increased the power, making his aura double in size, to the complete amazement of the assembly.

"Stop," he Point-called after a few seconds, "or I am going to pass out!"

"Working fine!" Maryani confirmed.

I discontinued the projection. Woolly turned round, showing the banner to the crowd, and he started marching back along the alley.

Immensely relieved, and totally unaware of the colossal misjudgment I was making, I sighed and relaxed.

It took another half-hour before Elyani arrived at the hymns which preceded the elemental offering. As we had agreed on before, she Point-called me to briefly check that everything on my side was in order. *"Ready?"*

Unaware of the approaching catastrophe, I Point-replied, *"Ready! And you?"*

"Ready!"

Because all eyes were on her, and all Points tuned into her Point, she couldn't possibly say more.

Resting on the She-Serpent of Eternal Wisdom, I kept my tears for later.

After a few interminable minutes, Elyani finally began the hymns of the elemental offering. Drawing energies from the golden shaft, I tuned into her belly and lovingly resonated with her. But despite what I was sending, I could not see any modification in her aura.

Was it because of the distance?

I gradually increased the power.

Elyani sent an emergency Point-call, *"What's happening? Where are these elemental forces from the Underworlds? Are you sending?"*

"The Dragon I am!"

"I'm not receiving anything!"

I immediately Point-instructed Maryani to raise the intensity. A massive bubble of golden energy rushed up through the shaft.

"And now?" I Point-called Elyani.

"Nothing."

The intensity was further increased. My aura became so hot with the gold of the Nagas that all the priests around looked at me in surprise. Resting on the powers of the depths, I threw a huge connection onto Elyani.

"And now?"

"Still nothing."

Alarm!

If no Underworld forces were offered in the Flame, the power of the hymns would soon start attracting the elemental sludge of the fields instead. Mantras, when Voice-projected by master-ritualists such as the Immaculate, were unstoppable living forces. These particular hymns were designed to send elemental forces to the gods. If we did not supply sufficient offerings, the hymns themselves would draw from our elemental surroundings.

And then...

A nightmare vision flashed before me: Elyani, Hermina and the whole assembly hit by another tidal wave of slime. One thousand people lying dead on the floor.

Hermina immediately perceived the gravity of the situation. She sent an emergency Point-call, *"Szar, either you do something at once or I have to interrupt the ritual. I can't take the risk of creating a carnage."*

"Can we take a break and start again?"

"Impossible! According to the Law if we stop, then the ritual must be cancelled. And it is all finished!" Hermina Point-said.

"Don't stop now, Hermina! Give me a chance!" Then I instantly Point-called my master, "Gervin, I am going to have to make a huge mess. Do I have your blessing?"

"Thunder is behind you," Gervin Point-assured me.

To the complete amazement of everyone in the hall, I started running full speed towards the stage.

"Maryani!" I Point-called, "I need another golden shaft, quick!"

"Another shaft?" she didn't hide her stupefaction. "Where?"

"*Right under the stage, where Elyani is sitting. It's dead urgent, Maryani!*"

As I reached the stage, one of the Crimson high priests tried to stop me, "*Man of the Law, you cannot...*"

Fortunately for that man, Melchard intervened, promptly pulling him out of my way.

Under the stupefied eyes of the audience I jumped onto the stage and landed close to Elyani. Following Hermina's instructions, she hadn't stopped the chanting.

Tuning into the depths of the Earth, I vroofed the Dragon into the ascending goddess.

But it was already too late! Attracted by the power of the hymns, a grey haze of slimy elementals swamped the hall. On its own, it wasn't deadly. But much more noxious waves were bound to follow.

I sent a panic Point-call to Gervin and Melchard. "I need the room vacated immediately. Call on Namron and his men."

"I will take care of that!" Gervin Point-replied without a trace of hesitation. "You take care of Elyani."

"Maryani!" I Point-called for help, "I am going to need a lot *of power, and very soon! Where are you at with the shaft?"*

"Nearly halfway already," she answered.

From a distance, I tried to draw energies from the golden shaft that the Nagas had established earlier.

No success.

Was it because the room had turned into complete chaos? People were running in all directions, rushing towards the doors, shouting in unlawful panic.

On the stage, the chanting was going on.

It was painfully obvious – unless something substantial was immediately poured into the Flame, the hungry hymns were going to destroy us all. So I Point-instructed Elyani, *"Tune into my Dragon. Offer it to the Flame!"*

The result was instantaneous, but not what I expected. Before I could even try to resist the phenomenal momentum of the hymns, I was projected into a space of dazzling light.

No more noise, no more chaos!
The silence breathed infinity. Peace beyond words.
And in their light-blue sky of eternal wonders
I saw them, glorious, lofty, splendid and serene,
Shining through their domains of infinite Point-ness,
Towering with ease over the seven spheres.
There they were, standing in front of me – the gods.
They looked at me and smiled,
And in a glimpse I understood that a god's smile,
Even when elusive, is no ordinary smile,
But a secretly-pregnant and mysterious seal
Which can overturn fate, and change many a human destiny.
Cosmically puzzled at the strange karmic twist
Which had made me land in their world,
I gathered my consciousness and Point-spoke to them,
"O Immortals, I praise your light and your wisdom!
Awe-struck, and abuzz with your celestial harmonies,
I bow before you, and your wondrous nature, your glorious origin.
But, I am afraid, some tragic misunderstanding has taken place –
A deplorable mistake, a ritual imbroglio
For which I must take full responsibility and blame.
I am not the one which your celestial daiva has named.
The pure soul which you expected is still in the kingdom.
And I, despite all my respect for you
And all my admiration for your world,
Have urgent works to do in the kingdom."
They smiled.
"Gervin!" I Point-called. "Please do something! Quick!"

When I recovered my senses, I was lying on the floor close to Elyani, who was still singing the hymns of the elemental offering.

"Are you all right?" Elyani Point-asked.

"Mm?" I Point-wondered. Wasting no time, I asked, "How many more hymns to go?"

"Six!"

I sat up and looked at the eerie scenery. The Holy Blue Flame was still hardly larger than a thumb. In the corners of the stage, the four spheres of the Law spun majestically. Out there a noisy crowd was evacuating the hall in panic.

Hermina! What is happening with the ritual?

"I need more elementals to feed the Flame," the Immaculate Point-answered. "If you cannot raise the power, then the hymns will soon attract sludge from the fields."

Plunging my Dragon into the depth of the Underworlds, I tried to resonate with more force. But for some inexplicable reason, there was only a faint response.

"Maryani! Where are you at with the new golden shaft?" I Point-called

"Nearly finished. You should be able to draw from it already."

"I don't understand what's happening. I can't feel anything."

I kept probing the depths, seeking the golden shaft.

"That's it, the shaft is finished!" Maryani Point-trumpeted. "And it's huge. The seven Naga architects are standing just under the stage."

"Listen! I don't have your powers but still, it is plainly impossible that my Dragon could miss seven Nagas standing just under me. There must *be something very wrong somewhere. Are they sure that their shaft is at the right place?"*

"Szar, of course they are sure! These are great architects of the Underworlds. They Dragon-know their business!"

I looked around me, searching for a clue.

"How many more hymns?"

"Four!" Elyani Point-answered.

"Szar," Hermina called, "the next hymn is a much more powerful one. The danger is extreme."

The room was only half-empty. Woolly, however, had kept his position on the other golden shaft. I briefly tuned into him, but could not feel any Dragon intensity.

"Maryani, what's happened to the Dragon shaft under Woolly?"

"Still there. Flowing nicely," she Point-assured me.

"I can't feel it!"

"Must be because of all the people standing between him and you."

But there was no one left between Woolly and the stage.

That's what gave me the solution.

I jumped off the stage. Instantly, I could again feel the mighty ascending flow of golden energies under Woolly's Dragon.

"Szar!" Elyani Point-called, "Come back immediately! I have nothing left to put in the Flame, it's going to create a disaster!"

I jumped back close to her, so she could tap from my Dragon.

Gervin, who had stayed connected to my Point all along, had also understood. *"The spheres of the Law! There must be something wrong with them! They disconnect the stage from the Underworlds."*

"What shall we do, Gervin?"

"Tell Hermina to stop them immediately," Gervin Point-ordered. "I am lost in the crowd. I'm too far. It would take at least three minutes before I could reach you."

"Stop the spheres? Impossible!" Hermina Point-objected. "This must take place according to the lawful procedure. It lasts nearly one hour. Otherwise a disaster in the Law could ensue."

"Hermina!" Gervin Point-thundered, "You take care of stopping the spheres, and I'll take care of the disaster in the Law."

Letting Elyani continue the ritual by herself, Hermina stood up and walked towards one of the spheres, Voice-projecting a low-pitched sound onto it.

Immediately, the spinning started slowing down. The Blue-Flame colour of the sphere started fading.

There followed a massive explosion. No longer disconnected from the Underworlds, the stage received an enormous bubble of golden energy from below, sent by the seven Naga architects who had been pushing with all their strength, fighting the strange field of energy created by the spheres of the Law.

The hymns, starving for energy, immediately projected the Underworld bubble into the Holy Blue Flame.

The Flame flared instantaneously, reaching the high ceiling of the crypt.

"No!" I yelled with all my strength as I found myself engulfed in it. "Take her, don't take me!"

– Thus ends the Book of the Ascension Ritual –

15
The Book of the World of the Gods

15.1 Born from the Molten Sea

Light.
Light unthinkable. Bright like the morning of the creation.
I lowered my gaze, unable to hold the sky's intensity.
Too much beauty hurts.
I plunged my hand into the sand.
Warmth and fortitude. Sound eternal.
Every grain of sand shining like gold, and crafted like a work of art.

"How could the gods do this to us? If they didn't want Elyani, why did they send us an oracle in the first place? And after all this sorrow and all this hard work, they could at least have left us together in the kingdom." Separating us by making *me* ascend while leaving *her* in the kingdom... That, truly, verily, and very verily, was nothing short of the Dragon's last tooth.[1]

On both sides, the empty beach extended to the horizon. An incredible panorama, never seen in the kingdom, where the mists always limited visibility. Subtle musical harmonies floated in the air, caressing my being like a light breeze.

Had the situation not been so appalling, I would have been uplifted. Ecstatic! In this place, just breathing was enough to feel on top of the world.

In front of me, the Molten Sea.

I sought comfort in her infinite silveriness. Deep like the Great Dragon herself. For she *is* the Great Dragon! The Molten Sea, on top of the spheres, is what the sea of prime matter is in the Deepest Underworlds: the beginning of manifestation, the creative source out of which all things in

---

[1] According to the conventions used in *Atlantean Secrets*, this entire book should be written in italics. However, to make reading easier, the text was kept in normal script.

our spheres were made. From Golden Shield above to Golden Shield below, not one thing in the spheres had its being without her. In her is Life, that divine quality from which the gods drew their nectar of immortality. And the Life is the light of the gods, the sovereign principle that beings of darkness could not overtake.

Dragon-spirited by the sea of unlimited potential, I stood up. I paid my respects to the Molten Mother and I started walking along the beach, determined to find the quickest way back to the kingdom.

It was then I saw a shining white cape lying on the sand.

Elyani's astral travelling gown!

My Point instantly began a search for the White Eagle.

No one in sight, but I Point-sensed her presence in the sea. As I turned towards the waves, the music became louder. Glorious sounds!

One minute earlier I thought I was contemplating the Molten Sea. Now I was rediscovering her.

More than beauty – perfection.

Perfection shakes the depths of your being.

A compelling feeling of oneness. One with the astounding essence of Life in the waves. One with every grain of sand. One with Revelation Sky's infinity. One with the One God behind all this.

But why did it hurt so much?

Infinite nostalgia versus infinite unity. The sorrows of the kingdom like an abyss under my feet.

Past a certain degree, there is something devastating about beauty.

Such a fine line between opening and being ripped open.

I saw her.

At first I could only discern her head.

She was floating on the ocean. The gentle motion of the waves was bringing her to the shore. The celestial harmonies became louder still, forcing tears to my eyes.

Slowly, she drifted, as if carried by the sounds.

Sounds, waves, unfathomable depth.

One, the infinitely creative essence of the Molten Sea.

Two, Elyani's essence of Eagle-ness.

Three, Flying Dragon nature sparked in a fragile flame of human Ego.

One, two, three, turned into one.

An all-comprehending oneness made sound.

Oneness eternal. Impregnable joy. As it was in the beginning.

No, I couldn't hold it. Too much joy can blow a man apart. And what if all this was but dreaming in the mind of the gods?

Hold onto the Point!

Instantly, Gervin's power ignited above my head. And lo! From the one breath, a creative infinity of numbers were born.

The Molten Sea, I discovered from the Point, was a sea of numbers. Mathematical wonders! Dancing archetypes, generating each other. Two from One, three from two, hop to forty, swing to infinity. Each and every archetype linked to each and every one by formulae of creative powers. Total, liquid synchronicity. Timeless speed, the universe is in place. From the dance of the numbers, the world of the gods has emerged. And from the gods, the rest of the creation.

So many ways of looking at the Molten Sea.

As she neared the shore, Elyani's naked body gradually emerged from the water.

I was shocked by her beauty. She looked nothing like the frail, exhausted priestess I had left in the kingdom. She was resplendent. Her curly brown hair was vibrant with the power of the Molten waves, her white skin luminous, a perfection of curves leading from the oval of her face to her neck and shoulders, her belly-button shining like a diamond, her hips wide, her flesh strong, her chest generously open, and her breasts... her breasts were those of a goddess!

Most striking of all was the shining glow in her eyes. Never had I seen her gaze so bright. Ignited power rendered soft by the loving magic of the wave. Being looked at by her was like being touched, caressed, held in her arms.

Serene, she came close to me.

Speechless, I contemplated her.

With the soft fire in her eyes, she lightly touched my chest.

"Szar!"

"Elyani! Have I..." my voice choked. "Have I been the witness of your birth?"

Her face lit up with a celestial smile. "Praised be the high gods for letting you watch."

Uncertain, I took her in my arms.

"Again I had lost you, and again I found you!" her voice, clear like the sky. Revelation Sky, the radiance of a galaxy of angels.

I started kissing her. Hesitantly, "Does this mean... we won?"

"Total victory! Now kiss me again, it makes them very happy."

"Happy? Who?" I frowned, wrapping her in her travelling cape.

"The gods who came here to watch my birth."

I could see only an endless empty beach. "Can they hear us too?" I tried to remember all the things I had said earlier, when I was blaming them for my misfortunes.

"Who cares if they can hear us, since anyway they can know our minds entirely just by glancing at us," she said.

Totally unreassuring! I preferred to laugh. In front of the gods, I gave Elyani a long kiss nurtured with the infinite tenderness of the Molten Sea's merging power.

"Let us go," Elyani whispered in my ear. "They have seen enough of us." Taking my hand, she started walking along the beach.

Was it real?

It had all happened in less than a second.

15.2 Building Elyani's house

Light.

Light!

"Stunning light!" I marvelled, as we were walking on the fine golden sand. "And the sky..."

The sky! Alive. Awake. Bluer than blue, and filled with presence.

A revelation.

"Let us find a place we like and build a house," Elyani said.

I stopped and contemplated her shining eyes. "My love, I cannot stay. I must return to the kingdom. Gervin is waiting for me."

"I Point-spoke to him at the end of the ascension ritual, when the gods came to take me. He gave you twelve hours," she said in a reassuring voice.

"Is that all?" I had often heard that in the world of the gods time passed much more quickly than in the kingdom. "I am probably very late already."

"No, you are not. The gods can take some licence with the time of human beings. Just leave it to me, I will stretch these twelve hours. You will *not* be late." She took my hand and started running. "See those dunes in the distance?"

I ran with her. "Close to the palm trees?" Before I realised what was happening, we had already reached the dunes.

Astounded, I pulled my beard – a solid, Dragon-bushy beard, far more vibrant than the one I had left in the kingdom.

Elyani kept running. "To these trees!" she pointed to the edge of a forest. It seemed to be miles away.

Instantly, we were there. Miraculously transported. Under the branches of gigantic banyan-looking trees. "Figs of life," Elyani said. "Extremely old and wise."

"How does this work? How did we get here so quickly?"

A flock of shining-white birds landed on a nearby branch.

"To reach a place, all you have to do is look at it!" she inspirited me with her words. "Very different from the kingdom, where the eyes can only see and not much else. Here, by using your eyes you can do many different things!"

One of the birds established eye contact with me.

"Little bird, you are amazingly beautiful!" I didn't hide my admiration, deeply moved by the friendly way the bird looked at me.

It was like being in front of a person, not a bird.

"See," Elyani said, "he is talking to you with his eyes."

My Point was enchanted by the exquisite combination of lightness and warmth that came from the bird. "What is it saying?"

"He says he likes the light of the White Eagle, which he can see behind your heart."

"Truly? Tell him I am very flattered."

"No need to tell him that, he can see for himself," Elyani was amused. She pulled me by the hand, "Come, let's find a place for our house."

"Our house?" I laughed and followed her. The bird left his branch and followed, hovering above us.

"Here, it's perfectly safe to have a bird above your head," Elyani said with a mischievous smile.

"Safe?"

"Heavenly birds make no droppings."

"What about the gods?" I couldn't help asking, running by her side amidst the figs of life.

"Hunh hunh! There are no toilets in the world of the gods. And you don't have to eat through your mouth." She stopped in front of a big bush full of dark-red berries. "Want to try?" she asked in a velvety voice, touching my eyes with a soft gaze.

"How could I say no?" I sighed, tipsy with so much charm.

"Just use your eyes!"

I looked at the berries with the intent of tasting them and was instantly filled with a wave of exquisitely sweet vibration. "This..." I searched for a word that could describe the perfection of the taste, "this is..."

"Divine!" Elyani snapped her fingers. "These are called Aphrodite's berries. They are no ordinary food, even to the gods."

The white bird landed on a branch just above Elyani's head. He also turned his eyes towards one of the berries. But this time the berry disappeared, consumed by his gaze.

Wonder! "How did he do that?"

"It's a normal way to eat," Elyani turned towards the bush and consumed a berry with her eyes.

I tried again, strengthening my gaze. But the taste became so intense I had to stop.

"Mm..." Elyani gave a goddess' smile, charged with the mysteries of the sea of dancing numbers, "Perhaps you are wise not to eat too many of these. They sometimes do strange things to the mind of the gods."

"Hee! Hee! Hee..!" the bird burst into high-pitched sounds which uncannily resembled laughter. Elyani laughed with him and in a few quick glances, the two of them consumed a whole bunch of berries.

Elyani took my hand and was running again, letting out a thunderous "Youyouyouyou..." Not just louder but also infinitely more musical than brother Floster at his best.

Soon we reached a long straight path in the forest. Elyani pointed to the horizon, "The gods have a saying, *you can go as far as you can see*. See?"

Using our eyes, we projected ourselves forward. Incredibly fast. Wherever we looked, we instantly landed, immediately looked ahead, and projected ourselves again. It gave an extraordinary feeling of power. Space was being conquered through travelling. From time to time I glanced at the sky.

The bird was following.

Finally, Elyani had us land in a fragrant patch of lemon-scented grass. Sunk into the grass, her arms spreading wide, "Voof! These berries have made me feel dizzy."

I contemplated the perfection of her face and closed my eyes, wishing I could capture the magic of the instant. Forever.

Space Matrix, archive recording engaged.

"Oh, look! A pine forest!" Elyani exclaimed.

By the time I opened my eyes she had already gone. I stood up and walked to the path, looking for my Eagle.

An eerie experience. At first I just looked in the distance, searching for the pine trees. But the further I tried to see, the more my vision expanded. I started discerning a wealth of fine details, as if my consciousness was being projected into the things I wanted to see. Then there was a sudden, dramatic enhancement. From narrowly focussed, the vision became all-encompassing, taking in the entire three hundred and sixty degrees of the horizon. I could see and be in all places at the same time: the shore of the Molten Sea where gods were praying, meditating and playing music; forests, plains, rivers, cascades, all of astonishing beauty, and even a faraway city – a stupendous city of light, celestial wonderment made architectural.

Amaravati.

The globalisation of perception created a glorious explosion in my Point, as when tuning into the Universal Knowledge Banks of the Flying Dragons.

Elyani? My eyes showed her to me. She was walking on a small winding path in a nearby pine forest.

Instantly I was walking by her side.

The trees! Nothing like the pine trees of the kingdom. They were gigantic. Their needles were vibrant threads of light. Even more striking was the spirit of the forest. Joined in a choir that sang high in the spheres, the trees were ardently calling for the presence of God.

"I have always wanted to live in a pine forest," Elyani let herself be filled with the forest's high spirit.

A noetic flash dawned on me, "Now I understand what is so special about pine forests – I mean, in the kingdom. They catch some of the spirit of the celestial forests. Look at these trees! Their aspiration... they are calling for Cosmic Fire with so much strength that the Lord Melchisedek can only respond and resonate with them!"

If I could call God with such mighty fiery aspiration, no doubt I would be a great warrior of the Spirit.

Inspired, I continued my praise, "I bow to you, trees! Seeing you, I better understand who my master is." Turning towards Elyani, "Gervin is so much like these pine trees, isn't he?"

She pushed her lips forwards and gave a grave nod, Thunder-fashion. "We must tune into the trees and ask their permission to build our house among them."

We closed our eyes a few seconds, invoking the spirit of the forest.

The response was immediate. Carried by the scent of the pines, precious oil of light came to us and filled us, boosting the shining of our eyes. A wave of fiery aspiration reached our Points. The forest was inviting us to join in and call God.

We started walking silently in the forest, Point-guided by the spirit of the pines. With a touch of sadness, I noticed the white bird was no longer with us.

We had already reached a small clearing. "Here!" Elyani decided. The forest Point-spoke through her, "This is where the pines want us." She gave a handclap, "Now let us build this house!"

I looked around, wondering what construction materials we were going to use.

"I haven't yet decided what I want the outside of the house to look like, so let us start with the inside," Elyani said.

I frowned, somewhat disconcerted by this free-style building technique.

"Ah, don't worry!" she said. "If we don't like it, we'll change it."

Had we been in the kingdom, I would have been seriously concerned.

Elyani took me to the centre of the clearing. "We need a bedroom, for a start. What could it look like?" she asked playfully.

"What are our options?"

"Extravagant, completely extravagant, and totally out of the seven spheres," she answered straightforwardly.

"Why not the princely suite that we had in the palace of Tomoristan?" I joked.

"Yes!" she approved enthusiastically, and she glanced around her.

To my astonishment, we were already standing in a perfect replica of the grand bedroom in Peļenor's palace.

"Just like that?" I exclaimed in disbelief, contemplating the eighty-lawful-feet-long multi-cornered bedroom and its carpet of grass, its unlawfully immense four-poster bed, its armchairs shaped like hands, and its excessive collection of works of art.

"Yes, just like that!" Elyani snapped her fingers. "In the world of the gods, this is the way we do it."

15.3 The tactful mirror

I sat on one of the hand-armchairs, resting my elbow on its thumb. "But how do you know how to do all these things?" I asked Elyani.

Still dressed in her White Eagle's travelling cape, she came to sit in front of me. On the other hand.

"This is one of the beauties of being born in the world of the gods," she explained. "You don't have to be a helpless child for many years. When you need to know something, you don't have to wait till someone teaches you. The knowingness of the things of this world comes to you automatically. It is part of your nature."

"You mean, it is part of the nature of the gods."

"This knowingness is with you too, to a certain extent. For as long as you are here, you too are in a god's body," she said.

I looked down to my left hand. It was neither paralysed nor marred by a dark shadow. "So what difference is there between my body and your body?" I asked.

"You have a visitor's body. It has several of the powers that come with a god's body, but not all of them. And its essence of immortality is not as permanent as that of the gods."

"Which means?"

"As long as you stay in this world, you cannot grow old. But you couldn't stay here forever. After some time, visitors fall back into the kingdom, or into some other sphere."

"Twelve hours!" I grinned.

"Some visitors stay here for entire years of the gods!" she said.

I sighed, wondering how long I would be staying during my next visit. "What about you? Can you really stay here forever?"

"Not quite forever. At the end of a cosmic cycle the world of the gods is dissolved, together with all the spheres under the Golden Shield. Then the gods die."

"But that's in a Far Upperworld of a long time!"

"Is it, really? Time passes so quickly amongst the beauties of our world," she sighed. "That is the problem – the gods of this world have everything, but they know that one day they will die."

"Still, there is so much time in front of you. Spending an entire aeon in such a glorious world must build something immense in your consciousness. After only a few hours I already feel completely different – so clear!"

"Which reminds me of a warning that must always be extended to visitors when they first arrive here. You must keep in mind that what you are seeing around you isn't the exact appearance of the world of the gods. Your perception is still distorted by all the limitations you have brought with you from the kingdom. It takes some time before you can see things as they really are here."

"So what I see is not really what I see?" It made me feel insecure. I forced a smile on my face, "Exciting, in a way! It means there is much more to discover." How would the pine forest appear to me if my perception was freed from earthly bondage?

I stood up and took in the room again, "Maybe it wasn't such a good idea to try to reproduce a human bedroom, after all. I'm sure the gods would see this as an attempt to cling to human limitations. I wonder what a real god's bedroom looks like."

Especially knowing the gods never sleep.

The goddess was smiling.

I came close to her and lightly touched her face, "And what would *you* look like if I could see you with the vision of the gods..."

As my fingers passed over her lips, she blew softly, making my hand shine with golden light.

"And what do *I* look like, by the way? Is there a mirror in this room?"

"There are a few, but you must be careful."

"Careful?"

Was there something frighteningly ugly about my visitor's body?

"In the world of the gods, mirrors are very different. The mirrors of the kingdom are so dumb! All they can do is reflect your image, without any wit or tact," she said with that sophisticated touch which had been with her since she inherited her goddess' body.

"Mm..." I twinged my visitor's beard. "In a world where everything revolves around sight, I guess it comes as no surprise that mirrors should be special."

"Very special," she said, pulling a light face, "some more than others, of course."

I sat on my hand-chair again. "Tell me more. How should one behave in front of celestial mirrors? What can they do?"

"At the very least, a good mirror will help you improve the way you look. It will make suggestions about how you should dress."

I found the concept immensely amusing. "Do you mean to say it will show you how you look in different dresses?"

"Yes, but not just that. By looking at yourself in the mirror you will immediately know which dress is appropriate for any particular circumstance. And the mirror will also come up with designs for new dresses, and for make-up."

"Do the gods wear make-up?" I asked with surprise.

"Szar-ka!" Elyani raised her hands. "But of course! Make-up in the kingdom is but a pale and rather foul-smelling imitation of the make-up we have here! Our make-up is made of light, precious oils and life essences."

I was becoming more and more curious about what I was going to discover in the mirror.

"There are many other things mirrors can show you," Elyani went on. "They can tell you many secrets. Some mirrors are disgustingly gossipy. Only interested in repeating what other gods say about you. But well-behaved mirrors are not like that. They show you deeper aspects of yourself, and visions about the future, or sometimes the past. And sometimes, especially if they have a sense of humour, they trick you. They show you bizarre reflections of yourself, or comical situations that could happen to you that day. But they know they have to be tactful. It is not rare for gods to get angry at their mirrors and break them. Hence the saying of the gods, *don't make me break the mirror*, meaning 'don't push me too far.'"

"Is this why in the kingdom a broken mirror is considered a bad omen?"

"Lawfully exactly! It suggests that a god is angry and does not like the course things are taking."

"The world of the gods is a complicated place," I started to realise.

"You have no i-dea!" Elyani laughed.

"I think I don't need to look at myself in a mirror," I decided.

"Oh, but I want you to, Thunder-man! I want you to see how beautiful you are." She took me by the hand and led me to a large mirror close to the four-poster bed.

When I saw myself, I was stunned. My face was not just glowing, its features were so finely cut I could hardly recognise myself.

"Is this me, or is the mirror being polite?" I asked.

"It is you, my love, just as I see you."

"I can't believe how different I look! Is this what happens to all visitors?" I questioned.

To my surprise, the image changed. The mirror started showing me other visitors, male and female.

"See," Elyani said, "you are more beautiful."

"This mirror is being tactful!" I Point-intuited. I took on a firm voice, "Mirror, I want the truth!"

Suddenly, much more beautiful visitors appeared.

"Thank you, mirror!" I laughed. "Now, would you kindly show me something I could wear. Something decent, so I don't shame Elyani when we meet other gods."

The next image was glorious. Instead of my rough brown gown, I was wearing a finely designed, extraordinarily complicated costume of white light.

"This will go well with the Light of the Eagle," Elyani approved.

"I'll take it!" I snapped my fingers. Using the power of my eyes, I instantly changed my brown gown into the costume shown by the mirror.

Elyani was still wearing the simple astral travelling gown I had put on her at the beach. She gently pushed me away. "Let me see if I can surprise you with something *really* beautiful."

I went to one of the balconies to take a look at the forest.

"Elyani!" I called. "Come and see, quick! Something... something incredible has happened."

15.4 The hyper-real world of fire

Elyani walked to the window.

The clearing was at least five times larger than when we had arrived. And a stream of crystalline water flowed in front of us. Flowers had appeared – extravagantly beautiful flowers as in Vasouk's Underworlds. There were also bushes, full of Aphrodite's berries.

"The forest has pushed back its trees for us," Elyani said. She closed here eyes and sent her love to the pines' Spirit.

She now wore a shining lapis-lazuli dress, the colour of my Mother's most inspiring caves.

"You are... stunning!" I told her with my eyes.

"I am yours, man of Thunder," her eyes replied.

I had difficulty coming to terms with this sudden transformation of the landscape. Our room was on ground level, so I jumped over the balcony and went to inspect the water. As I was walking, I shrugged my shoulders, remembering that to reach the river all I had to do was look at it. I kept walking, anyway. "Elyani, all this is starting to make me wonder how real this world is. It all changes too easily. Is this not some kind of illusion that deceives us?"

Elyani transported herself to the stream. "There is always a certain degree of illusion, whichever world you may be in. But there is far less illusion here than in the kingdom," she said, dipping her bare feet in the water.

"But in the kingdom, things are much more fixed. They don't change all the time," I said.

"Of course they change all the time – but much more slowly. Everything in the kingdom is agonisingly slow, and human life is terribly short. So people don't have time to realise that mountains move, continents change shape, new animals appear while others disappear. In fact, the very appearance of human beings is dramatically altered from epoch to epoch."

"But isn't there some kind of denseness in the kingdom, a solid groundedness which makes things more tangible, and which seems to be lacking here?" I argued.

"This earthly denseness, the gods would call inertia. A lack of fire, a lack of light. Matter in the kingdom is opaque and dull. It has Spirit inside itself, but it is out of touch with it. Whereas in the world of the gods, matter is infinitely more in touch with its fire," Elyani moved her fingers quickly, sparking a bright halo around her hand. "Look around you, Szar. These trees, this grass, this sky... do they look unreal?"

"No," I conceded.

Actually, they looked a thousand times more real than anything I had contemplated in the kingdom.

"Super-fast, super-dense, super-charged!" I realised.

"Super-charged with fire, this is exactly what it is. In the world of the gods, the fire element is infinitely stronger than it is in the world of human beings. The Law of the gods says, 'Our world is a world of fire. Our matter is fire, our mind is fire.' This is why our bodies shine, and so do the trees, the rivers, and every single thing you can see in our plane."

"But how come it is so easy to move from one place to another, or to create a house?" I questioned, watching shining-red butterflies hovering above Elyani's hair.

"Precisely because in this world, matter is teeming with fire element. The fire in matter resonates with our fiery consciousness, and swiftly responds to its impulses."

My philosophical character was being engaged, "And you would say exactly the opposite of the kingdom. Down there, matter lacks fire element, and so do people's minds. Which is why everything is so slow, and everyone is so asleep," I sighed, watching one of the red butterflies land on Elyani's breast.

I could see the difference myself. Having been here barely an hour, I already felt more awake, more lucid and sharper than I had ever felt in the kingdom. So what would someone feel like after spending a hundred years in a *real* god's body, not just a visitor's one?

The Point boggled.

Elyani gently blew on the butterfly on her chest, intensifying its shining redness.

Another butterfly, enjoying her breath, came close to her lips, flying against the friendly air stream.

"Seen from here," I said thoughtfully, "it appears that human beings have some serious handicaps to overcome."

"To say the least!" Speaking against the butterfly, she went on, "But if human beings could reveal the fire that is hidden in their matter, then they would overcome all the limitations that make their world a caricature of the world of the gods."

Raising the level of fire in matter... the Naga king couldn't have agreed more. I had also heard Gervin broach the theme several times. It was one of the central themes in the higher aspects of Thunder initiation. "Really..." I smiled at the red butterfly flirting with Elyani's lips, "this is why the Nagas are so irresistibly powerful: they live in Underworld regions, where matter is far denser than in the physical world. And yet they have conquered the fire. They have found the keys to open matter. They have lifted the veils which cover the fire."

Leaving Elyani, the butterflies flew towards me. "Do you think that the Nagas are more powerful than the gods?" I asked.

The butterflies turned back and flew away, as if disgusted by my question.

"The Nagas are great, and wise, and I will be eternally indebted to them for the help they gave us," Elyani began. "But do not judge the gods shallow, Szar. Here, on top of the worlds, there is a certain high spirit found nowhere else. The gods are the creators, the spark that sets all other spheres into movement. Whatever you can think of, they can do. And usually they have already done it, plenty of times. If they had not, you would not even be able to think about it."

Using my eyes, I transported myself close to her. "The number of things a god accomplishes in a day must be Point-blowing. Not to talk about *what* they do, of course."

Memories of the forests of the kingdom came back to mind. Compared to the celestial pines' fiery spirit, they were but insubstantial shadows – nothing more than illusions of forests. Fire masked by thick fogs.

The scale of reality was being turned upside down. I started wondering how I could even have thought that the fire of the gods was the illusion, when so obviously it was exactly the opposite.

Elyani caught my thought. "It sometimes happens to visitors from the kingdom. At first, when they see the perfection of this world, they wonder if they are dreaming."

These petty human limitations that visitors bring with them!

"It makes them believe the world of the gods is too beautiful to be true," I smiled, ready to give Elyani a very serious godly kiss.

But Elyani turned round. "Mareena!" She ran towards a young goddess who was walking into our clearing.

"Elyani!" the goddess smiled with her eyes.

Was this Mareena?

When I had met her a few years earlier, after a travelling accident that had left me stranded in one of the worlds of the triangle, I had only seen her as a beautiful woman with long red curls, dressed in an emerald dress. Now I discovered an incandescent shape, divinely fascinating, charged with the might of Revelation Sky. Had I needed some confirmation of what Elyani and I had just discussed, I could not have received a better one. Mareena was pure fire. The awesome power that radiated from her was definitely no illusion!

Her youthful appearance was particularly puzzling to me. She definitely looked younger than Elyani and I. Yet she was the ascending goddess who had completed her ritual in Eisraim more than four hundred years ago.

In those happy kingdom-days when those chosen by the gods always succeeded.

In a glance, Elyani told me all the things Mareena had done for her. It came as a complete surprise. I thought that after throwing the daiva the gods had abandoned us. They had not. During the difficult months that had just passed, Mareena had been constantly sending forces and inspiration to Elyani. She had approached several powerful gods and convinced them to intervene in our favour.

So the gods cared?

Long-haired Mareena saluted me in a glance. In the same fashion I returned the salute. She and Elyani went on talking with their eyes.

Watching them interact was fascinating. They remained still, just looking into each other's eyes. I could sense a swift and vast flow of information to-and-froing between them. But despite all the training that Master Gervin had given and which, according to kingdom standards, made me a Point-expert, I was unable to follow their exchange.

Too fast for me.

I bit my visitor's lip, suddenly feeling the heavy weight of my human handicap.

The beautiful Elyani heard my thoughts and ran towards me, "Szar! We have a surprise for you!"

"A surprise?" I eye-replied with mixed feelings. 'Gods' and 'surprise', what a dangerous association.

"Mareena has arranged for you to have a music lesson with someone you have wanted to meet for a long time."

"Who could that be?" I said, forgetting that all I had to do to get the answer was to Point-tune into Elyani.

"Lord Gana!" she rushed into my arms.

"Lord Gana?" Astonished, I turned towards Mareena. But the goddess had disappeared. "Has she already gone?"

"She had some urgent matters to attend to. The gods are always so busy!"

15.5 Looking down to the kingdom

As we went back into the house, I asked Elyani how I was supposed to behave when meeting my hero-god, Lord Gana.

"Don't forget to touch his feet when you meet him," she said. "The feet symbolise creative power. This is especially true of the gods, whose cosmic function is to create. Touching the feet of a god means making yourself receptive to what the god has to give. Often, this turns into far more than just a symbolic mark of respect. A flow of energy passes from the god into you, conveying profound inspiration or even powers of consciousness."

I remained silent, wondering what would happen when I touched Lord Gana's feet. "What else?"

"Lord Gana is a lovely god to deal with – a real angel. He will take care of you. Just show what you have always felt for him."

"Is he really one of the gods who were born from the Molten Sea at the dawn of this cosmic cycle?"

She nodded, "Part of the second creation – the beings whose cosmic role was to replace the asuras."

"Incredibly old intelligences!" I said, enthused with curiosity.

"Don't expect him to look like an old man," Elyani smiled.

"Same as Mareena!" I shared my amazement with Elyani. "She has been here for hundreds of years, and yet..."

"*The gods are always sixteen*," Elyani quoted the Law of Melchisedek.

I had never realised how literally this was to be taken.

Thinking about time made me remember I only had twelve hours to spend with the gods. "Any idea what is happening to our friends in the kingdom at the moment?"

"I must show you exactly what happens when the gods look down to the kingdom." Elyani took me by the hand and walked to the four-poster bed. "We can use a mirror, or use sight. Which do you prefer?"

The Brown Robe spoke through me, "Sight, of course!"

Elyani transported herself onto the bed, landing in meditation position. I sat in front of her. For a few seconds she plunged her gaze into my eyes, awakening a wave of ignited enthusiasm in my heart.

Fire, fire... so much fire!

Dance for a million years. Or two.

She kept pouring force into me through her eyes, feeding me with liquid sky – nectar. In a split second, the touch of sadness evaporated. I burst out laughing, utterly elated. "What are you doing to me, goddess?"

"Take my fire. Take my love!"

"What if I exploded with joy?" I said, contemplating her goddess' bust, rendered even more glorious by the shining lapis-lazuli dress.

"I think your visitor's body will be solid enough," she said seriously, as if exploding with joy was definitely within the realm of possibilities.

Gods!

She looked down, as if through the bed. Adding a touch of Vasouk-ness to her voice, "Well, well... what is happening in that good old kingdom?"

Looking down with her, I saw a magnificent carpet of luminous white wool. "What is *that*? It looks huge!"

"The kingdom of the mists seen from above. The gods have a saying, 'Clouds were designed to be looked at from above.' Aren't the mists much more beautiful when seen from above?"

"Are these the thick mists of the kingdom? But human beings have no idea how magnificent they are!"

"That is one of the problems with human beings," she remarked. "They are so much in the middle of things that they end up seeing nothing at all. Now... who shall we try to see first?"

"Gervin, perhaps?"

"*All glory to the teacher!*"

The next image showed Gervin, seen from above. He was having a conversation with Teyani, in her empty white room. They were both sitting on the floor. Unusually, Teyani's back was propped against the living wall. She looked tired and slightly dejected. Gervin was cheering her up.

"Let me show you something the gods can do!" Elyani plunged her hand into a heap of white flower petals that had mysteriously appeared on the bed. Then she threw the petals as if through some kind of window.

Immediately, Teyani's room was flooded with white light. Gervin and Teyani smiled with wonder, and they looked up towards us.

"Can they see us? " I asked.

"No, but they can feel our presence through the light."

"This is blasting!" I exclaimed. "Can I do it too?"

"As much as you like! But don't forget to send your love with the petals."

Using both hands, I quickly threw the entire pile of petals on my beloved friends in the kingdom. "Can I have more p...?"

Three large heaps of petals had already appeared on the bed.

Joyful like a three-year-old who believes the creation is all his, I shovelled down the piles of petals with my hands.

In Teyani's room the white light flared. Gervin burst out laughing. Deeply moved, Teyani started shedding tears.

"Magic fun!" I laughed with Gervin, throwing more petals.

Elyani held her hand flat, as if on top of Teyani's head.

Raising the fire in Teyani.

Teyani's eyes became brighter. Her natural confidence reappeared on her face.

"Let's not send too much at a time." Elyani warned, "The light of the gods is powerful. Too much of it can start great fires in the hearts of men. Even the wisest of them."

Then she went to Melchard, whom we could also see from above. He was sitting on his bed, sad and tired.

This time, Elyani didn't throw petals. Softly, lovingly, she blew upon him.

Melchard's face immediately lit up. He looked skywards and smiled with the same wonder, tears in his eyes. And he started speaking, but I could not hear his words.

"What is he saying?"

"He has regrets. He wishes he could have taken better care of me when I was a little child," Elyani said in a serene voice. "His life hasn't been what he would have liked it to be. He had to play the role of the high priest of Eisraim and abide by a strict protocol that isolated him from those he loved. He wishes he could just have been a priest of the Brown Robe, sharing the fun of Gervin's life, being with Teyani when she brought up Alcibyadi, Lehrmon and me. And I think he would have liked to be your friend."

Twenty-five years of solitude. The price to pay to ensure enlightened leadership over Eisraim – indispensable for the success of the Archive project. Still...

"What could we do for him?"

"Soon, he will ascend to the Fields of Peace. Then he will reap the reward for all his work," she said. "Meanwhile I will flood his dreams with visions of the worlds of the gods."

Elyani stopped the soft breeze and looked into my eyes. "Now, your turn!" Extending her hand, she offered the kingdom to my vision.

Using the power of my eyes, I opened a window to Alcibyadi. She too was resting on her bed, holding her pregnant belly with her hands.

"This is wonderful," I exclaimed, throwing piles of white petals on her head. "As soon as we look at them, their faces light up with joy."

"One of the many privileges that come from being at the summit of the worlds," Elyani paid her respect to the One God.

Carried by the celestial momentum I proposed, "Let's do the same for the entire temple! Let's flood them all with light!"

"Hunh hunh! That we cannot do."

"Would it require too much power?"

"No, power is not the problem. It is much more complicated than that. It has to do with destiny. Whenever we interact with someone, we interfere with his destiny. There are strict rules governing what the gods can and cannot do with the destiny of human beings. With individuals, the rules are relatively lax. But when it comes to large groups, we must be extremely careful. There are high gods and angels who send impulses to the people of the Earth, directing their long-term evolution. These Lords of Destiny know exactly what they are doing, and they do not allow others to interfere with their work."

"Mm... So, really, you will not be able to do much to defend the temple of Eisraim against the giants," I said with disappointment.

"No, not much," she shook her head. "I will be able to bring down love and light – inner support to a number of souls. It will make a great difference to them in these trying times. But as to saving the temple, there is nothing I can do. The fate of Atlantis has been sealed. It must fall and end, so another kingdom may begin. Going against this transition would be violating the will of the high Angels of Destiny."

With a low-pitched whistling sound, I blew a loving breath onto Alcibyadi and her baby.

"She knows it is you. She can feel your presence," Elyani assured me.

Alcibyadi basked in the light, sending me her love in return.

Gods, I had never realised she loved me so much!

Elyani's words had left me pondering. "How does it happen, exactly, when the gods interfere with individual destinies?"

"Choose someone!" Elyani said in a playful voice.

I thought of Felicia, but then questioned the appropriateness of that choice.

"Yes! Let's help Felicia," Elyani said enthusiastically. "Open a window onto her!"

Sitting on top of the worlds, all this was so easy! In the twinkling of a god's eye, we were looking down to Felicia. She was sitting in meditation position with her eyes closed, facing an altar.

"Is this Felicia?" Elyani exclaimed when she saw the face of the red-haired woman. "But she is beautiful! Ten times more beautiful than I was. And she is intelligent. And she *really* loved you!" Elyani made herself White-Eagle tender. "Sir Great Dragon, I am deeply moved to think that you preferred little Elyani to such a special woman."

"Please don't be jealous of her," I asked in a little voice, wondering what could happen to a woman who incurred the anger of a goddess.

She shook her head slowly, "I can only empathise with her. I know only too well what it costs to lose the man you love."

So there *were* benefits in letting an ascending goddess experience the full scope of human misery.

I started thinking, "Perhaps the gods were wise, after all."

Elyani looked down to Felicia again, "What can we do for this high priestess?"

"When the gods interfere with a human destiny, what do they do?"

"Look!" Elyani said, "This is her line of destiny."

In a high archetypal space, I saw a curved line of light that described complicated meanders.

"Same as her time track?" I asked.

"Yes, but on a higher level. The archetype of her time track."

Pointing to an area where the line took a radically different direction, Elyani said, "This is when she met you." Then Elyani pointed at another area, further along the line, "Now, she is here. See how the line is fragile and uncertain? Not much is happening in her life at the moment." Showing another area further along, "Look at these ugly knots. Tragic events that will cause her great sorrow. Quite soon." Elyani paused, tuning into the high knowingness of the gods. Then she said, "Look, now I am curving her line of destiny, so it misses the knots."

I was surprised, and slightly disturbed, at this simple and quick surgery of Felicia's destiny. "But do we have the right to interfere with her future?"

"Oh!" Elyani's subtle smile reflected the mysteries of her godly nature, "This is a question on which different gods hold quite different opinions. Some like to foster human free will. Others think the destinies of human beings are so straight and boring that any intervention of the gods can only be a blessing. And in a number of cases, they are not wrong." Elyani opened another window, which showed an elderly man working in a market stall.

"Nice beard," I commented.

"Yes, but there is not much else to rejoice about. Look at his line of destiny! Faint, desperately straight, completely uneventful. From his teens this sleeper has repeated the same routine every day: lawful morning chanting, eating, going to work, eating, going to sleep. Any little twist that we could impress on his line would prove a major factor of awakening for him. But then of course, it may shake him badly by the same occasion. See the dilemma?"

I nodded, wondering what to wish for this man. "And so... what do gods do in such situations?"

"Usually nothing. The gods have better things to do than spend their days worrying about human destinies," she said, closing the man's window. "In the past, though, the situation was different. Humanity was only made of sleepers. Without any interventions from the gods, absolutely nothing would ever have happened in the kingdom. So the gods were in charge of shuffling the lines around, arranging twists and meetings of destiny."

"I don't like the sound of the twists, but the meetings sound interesting."

"Let me show you," she said, Point-scanning high archetypal spaces. She opened two windows: one showed a tall blond man, the other a pretty brunette with large black eyes, both in their late twenties. "Look at these two lines of destiny. They resonate beautifully with one another, but they never cross. It's because he lives in the Western Shores, and she lives in the Southern Plains. Now look... I curve the man's line, so it touches hers for a few days."

"Will they end up together?" I wondered whether I should be delighted or concerned for them.

"Well... they will meet. After this, I leave it up to them," the wise goddess said.

She went on explaining, "In the past, the high Angels of Destiny entrusted the gods with the function of stirring and enlivening human time tracks. In those days – a golden age on Earth – whatever happened to men and women came straight from the gods. Then came the great disconnection."

"Did the gods give up on human beings?"

"No, but the Lords of Destiny decided the time had come for human beings to develop free will and rule their lives themselves. It had to happen. They couldn't remain puppets of the gods forever. So, gradually, the gods stopped intervening in human affairs. Of course, that does not exclude the occasional twist, for instance to give a little help to an individual who has prayed to you. But when it comes to the global course of human events, the gods no longer pull the ropes as they used to."

Elyani softly blew a warm celestial breeze onto Felicia's head.

Felicia smiled, blissing on the breeze and wondering where it came from.

Before closing the window, the goddess promised, "I'll keep an eye on her. But from what I can see, her friends in Jex Belaran are taking good care of her."

"Thank you," I said from deep inside my heart. Looking down again, "What about Hermina?"

"Hunh hunh! You must look up, my love. Hermina is no longer in the kingdom, but in Highness."

"Is she dead?" I asked, taken by a mixture of sadness and guilt.

Elyani nodded, "Grieve not, man of Thunder. Where she is now, the Light and the bliss are greater even than in our world. Just as we tower over the worlds, so the angels of Highness tower over the highest gods."

"All this is Point-boggling!" I exclaimed. The time had come for me to shed this silly human habit of feeling sad when friends die – especially when by dying they ascend to glorious levels of existence. I directed a thankful concentration, love to our friend in Highness.

"How far down can these windows be opened?" I asked Elyani. "Could one of them show us the Nagas?"

"Of course!" she immediately opened a window onto Vasouk's palace.

In the main function hall, a large reception was being conducted. The Nagas were celebrating the successful part they had played in the ascension ritual. There were hundreds of guests, mainly Nagas. The mood was high and merry. King Vasoukidass was awarding special Underworld distinctions to the seven Naga architects who had so swiftly built the golden shafts under the central crypt of Eisraim.

Standing close to the king was Lady Maryani of the White Eagle, and by her side...

Sir Woolly of the Brown Robe!

When we saw him, Elyani and I stood on the bed and jumped with joy, clapping our hands and letting out our loudest 'Youyouyouyou...' ever.

"These restrictions which limit the gods' interventions in the affairs of the kingdom, do they also apply to the Underworlds?" I asked.

"No, not really," the goddess answered.

"Shall we flower-petal them out, then?"

"Out and throughout!"

Using our eyes, we creatively poured a torrential rain of golden flowers onto Vasouk's function hall.

Unlike in the kingdom, the result was not just an illumination. The actual flower petals made their way onto the Nagas' heads, decorating them as if with garlands, and covering the floor.

At first the assembly of Nagas was perplexed by this golden shower. But as soon as they realised where it came from, they all started shouting with joy, beating the floor with their tails – the Naga way of applauding. They all congratulated each other, and they praised King Vasouk who, well, well... actually, was rather quite delighted at this no doubt unusual, yet highly dignified treat given to his guests.

"What excellent timing!" I said, "Just when Vasouk was awarding the Naga architects with their high distinctions."

"See, you are already talking like a god!" Elyani said, the corner of her lips raised with a touch of irony. "The gods always think that the timing of their intervention is perfect, even if they arrive when everyone is dead."

The petals kept raining.

15.6 Patagendradass' myth of the wound

"I feel so high!" I exclaimed, jumping off the bed and walking towards the balcony. "Do the gods always feel like this?"

"Just about," Elyani followed me. "If anything, the feeling of enthusiasm builds up with time. The more you resonate with fire, the more enthused you become. With the high gods, enthusiasm takes cosmic proportions."

"Compared to us here," I said, "the people in the kingdom look so defeated. Mind you, they have plenty of good reasons for that. It's so difficult to do *anything* down there."

"And by the time any work of substance has been completed, they're nearly dead already!" she sighed.

As I sighed with her, my eyes were caught by the splendour of the forest. "The pine trees are so much more beautiful than when I arrived!"

Of course I was the one who had changed, not them.

My vision sharper, I could see how perfectly chiselled every single pine needle was. My heart warmer, I could better hear the trees calling God in unison. My kidney purer, their aspiration appeared like a gigantic flame.

Clean strength, pure passion.

"Look, your white bird has come to visit."

There he was, casually pacing up and down the grass close to the water stream, as if patiently waiting for me.

I started walking towards the bird in slow, velvety fashion, so as not to frighten him. "Another human limitation!" I told myself.

Drawing from the knowingness of my visitor's body, it was clear that in the world of the gods animals aren't frightened of anyone. No one hunts them.

So I ran towards the bird.

When he saw me, the bird joyfully flapped his wings.

I sat on the grass in front of him. "*Praise the Lord Melchisedek, bird.* My name is Szar of the Brown Robe. *How are you, my friend in the Law*?"

The bird responded with a shy look.

"But of course, you are welcome here!" I answered with my eyes. "Such a magnificent bird! Elyani and I are honoured."

The bird's friendly round black eyes shone with a mysterious glow.

"Patagendradass!" I replied, "What an interesting name."

Elyani had transported herself by my side. "In the language of the gods, it means, 'he who is a great devotee of Patagendra, the bird god'," she translated.

"Mm... *And how are your parents, my friend in the Law*?"

The bird suddenly zapped high in the sky.

I turned to my goddess, "Did I say something wrong?"

"Not at all! Patagendradass just wants you to go and discuss his ancestors with him. Look, he is waiting for you," she pointed at the bird who was hovering high above us.

"Do you mean to say..."

It sounded so incredible, I could hardly utter the words. Resting on the fire, I tried to push all human limitations and conditioning out of my mind. "Of course, we can fly, can't we?"

"Of course!" the goddess took my hand. "Can I come?"

Too much air. I found it difficult to breathe.

"Is this really true?" I asked. "Are we really going to..." But my voice choked, and I burst into tears.

Elyani took me in her arms. "My love, my love... what is happening to you?"

"Don't know." I contemplated the celestial nature around us. "All this is so... so beautiful. These trees, the bird, the water... and the sky!"

The sky was the most magnificent of all.

Revelation Sky, the keeper of all secrets.

"All this is so divine. So perfect. When I realise it has always been here, and I didn't even know it existed..."

I cried.

Revelation Sky, why did I have to live so far away from you?

Patagendradass gently landed on my shoulder and helped Elyani unfold a warm presence of light around me.

A friendly bird lightly touching my neck with its feathers. Elyani, beautiful like a goddess... It made me burst into sobs, as if all the pain of the human world was falling on me. "We are so lost, down there. The kingdom is so grey, so hopeless. We have been abandoned by God."

Elyani held me in her arms. I shed tears on her breast, "We have been abandoned by God, this is what it is. We have been abandoned by God."

"The kingdom hasn't always been like it is now," the White Eagle whispered. "And the life of human beings will not always remain grey."

"It feels like it has been grey for so long!" I kept crying.

"True, it feels like this," she kept whispering in my ear. "But in reality it will take such a short cosmic time before human beings reach the Fields of Peace. Hardly worth crying."

Easy to say at the top of the pyramid of the worlds!

"This short cosmic time is dragging on and on..." I sobbed.

We remained silent for a while. I just opened to the spirit Elyani was pouring into me.

In the world of the gods, sorrows are nothing like they are on Earth. They don't stick, for a start. And even more than on Earth they are opportunities for great outpourings of Light – this Light of Highness which, even though available everywhere and at all times, is so much easier to behold when dwelling in the fire of the gods.

My spirit was being refilled. “Are the Fields of Peace as beautiful as the world of the gods?” I asked.

Elyani could hear through my voice that the grief was fading. Taking on a playful voice, she shouted in outrage, “As beautiful as the world of the gods?” She burst out laughing. Patagendradass, still on my shoulder, accompanied her with an evocative volley of high-pitched laughing sounds. So close to my ear that I jumped in surprise.

Holding on to my shirt, he stayed on my shoulder.

“Come on, Patagendradass, let us show him!” Elyani decided.

Before I could realise what was happening, I found myself high in the air, overlooking the pine forest. Unhampered by mists, the landscape extended forever on all sides. Sublime visual feast! There were hills and valleys, meadows, rivers, waterfalls, forests, and the Molten Sea in the distance. Not only were all these infinitely more perfect and beautifully chiselled than their equivalents on Earth, but an intoxicating fragrance of life breathed through them – a superior unity which upheld these wonders and bound them together in a great symphony. Nature was one, and in this oneness all sang together: birds, crickets, waterfalls, but also trees of variegated wisdom, herbs of miraculous properties, strange animals of light as could no longer be seen in the kingdom.

Patagendradass was flying around me protectively. He kept asking with his eyes, “Are you all right, now?”

“Celestially fine. Renewed by fire!” I turned to Elyani, who was floating in the air close to me. “Is it because of my human conditioning that I see nature in a way that parallels nature on Earth?”

“No, this is how it is: nature on Earth is a replica of this nature.”

“But how come this nature is so much more beautiful and perfect?”

“The same applies to just about all things on Earth, I am afraid. They are but imperfect replicas of their celestial prototypes.”

I remembered how King Vasouk had once taught Maryani and I that matter on Earth had lost touch with the forces of primordial chaos – which was why the Molten Sea could not be seen in the kingdom. On Earth, the noble chaos of prime matter had turned into an elemental mess, only capable of vaguely reflecting the archetypal perfection of celestial things.

Patagendradass had been carefully listening to our words and thoughts. In a voice that resembled a chanting wind, he declared, “If everything is so beautiful here, it is because the gods woke up early. He who wakes in the first hour inherits heaven.”

“How not to fall in love with a world where birds are wise?” I laughed, affectionately contemplating my shining white friend.

Concerned I might not take Patagendradass seriously enough, Elyani intervened. “In the world of the gods, birds and other creatures are highly inspired. Through them, celestial nature speaks her wisdom. And some animals are the representatives of extraordinarily ancient spirits, whose wisdom is a topic of wonder to the gods themselves.”

I asked my bird friend, "Are you a topic of wonder to the gods themselves, Patagendradass?"

With a modest smile in his eyes, the bird answered, "The wonder of the gods is no wonder to the wise; for the gods are wise, and the wise wonder a lot."

"Mm..." I Point-meditated on his words. "And who made you so wise, my wonderful?"

"Patagendra, my bird god, received his knowledge from Amabaranina the ancient cloud of wisdom. Most ancient Amabaranina was, is and will be. When the gods were children, his glory stood high and beyond the spheres already."

Patagendradass' words carried vibrations that were strangely reminiscent of those of the Flying Dragons. "Where does this Amabaranina live?" I asked.

"After enlightening the spheres for many a cosmic cycle, he departed from the creation, and now dwells in Highness," Patagendradass declared.

I sighed thoughtfully, filled with the wonder that Patagendradass communicated through his words when he spoke of the ancient cloud of wisdom.

"Friend," the bird went on, "if you want to become a god, wake up early. Just meditate on this truth for a whole cosmic cycle, and a high god you will become."

"Patagendradass, I need some explanation," I said, noticing that a friendly wind was making us drift slowly towards a nearby range of mountains.

"It is as simple as flying!" the bird smiled with his eyes. "At the beginning of this cosmic cycle, after the great night, the gods woke early. Thus out of the primordial cosmic maelstrom in which all substances were souped together, they took the best matter – the one which was teeming with fire. Out of it they built the best of all worlds for themselves, on top of all the other spheres. And as time passed the substance of their world kept improving. For the grosser materials were decanted and fell down from their sphere, while the most refined matter from other spheres kept ascending to them, naturally and effortlessly."

"Mm..." I snapped my fingers, looking down to gigantic waterfalls under us. "So is this why matter in the world of human beings is so... let us say, average? We woke up too late. We could only take what was left."

"Thus it was, and thus it will be in each cosmic cycle. Those who wake up late inherit the dregs." When he saw me frowning, Patagendradass immediately added, "Not to say that your kingdom is made of dregs, of course! For you human beings woke up only half an aeon after the gods, at a time when reasonably good material was still available in plenty."

Sweet and sour smile, "Thank you, Patagendradass, I understand exactly what you mean." Remembering one of the creation myths told in the Law of Melchisedek, I became perplexed. "But I thought that at the beginning of this cosmic cycle, human beings and gods all lived together in the same light."

"This is true," Patagendradass said. "I remember very well, for I was there too. In those days, human beings were sound asleep. Great difficulties we had with them, really. For even though they were asleep, there was so much light around them that they believed themselves awake. The light, of course, was not their own light, but the light of the gods. But this they could not see. They just slept blissfully in the warmth of the gods. And as they believed themselves awake, they never made any attempt to stop sleeping.

So human beings slept, and slept, and slept! Their slumber was becoming heavy on the gods. For the gods never sleep; they hate things that lack light, speed and sharpness. As time went on, the sleep of human beings started dimming the light of the gods, slowing down their pace. A separation became unavoidable. For everyone's benefit, really! If human beings had been allowed to bask in the light of the gods forever, they would have continued sleeping until the end of this cosmic cycle. And for sure, the Great Night that is to engulf all things at the end of the cosmic cycle would not have helped them wake up!"

Looking down, I saw the first spurs of the mountain range. As we were coming closer to lofty summits, we projected ourselves higher up in the air. Faced with the immensity of the landscape, the mind boggled: thousands of snowy mountain peaks, making the highest mountain ranges in the kingdom look like sand hills.

Holding tightly to Elyani's hand, I tapped from Patagendradass' fountain, "Once separated from the gods, did some human beings awaken?"

"Only very few of them," Patagendradass replied. "Truly, my friend, this separation was a sad moment. Even though they kept sleeping, human beings felt completely abandoned. Until then, they had always enjoyed the comfort of the light of the gods, and the warmth of the gods' presence. Suddenly they found themselves falling down into darkness, and cold."

As Patagendradass was speaking, images and feelings Point-flowed into my consciousness.

An immense distress.

A bottomless pit.

Nothing can possibly hurt more than feeling abandoned by God.

I understood, "This total despair, it was similar to what I was feeling earlier, wasn't it?"

"Very true, friend. Ever since that separation took place, all human beings carry a wound in their heart. We, the celestial, saw human beings fall down from our world. But they, of course, saw the opposite. They saw our light ascending away from them, as if we were leaving their world.

We were their light, their joy, their love, their warmth, and their link to the Divine – their connection to God. All at once, everything was taken away from them. Their sadness was beyond words. It was their first sorrow, and it was abysmal. In their heart, it has branded a wound that has never healed and often makes them feel like an abandoned child.

But time passed and human beings forgot what caused their wound. The destiny of human beings is to forget! Now they still feel the pain and the emptiness, but do not understand where it comes from. And so they wander in their world, trying to fill the emptiness in hundreds of ways that never really bring them satisfaction. More than anything else, they seek love. This is because, as long as they were merged in our light, they were nurtured by the love of God, which permeates the fire of the world of the gods and shines in all things celestial. But the love they can get from their parents, their husband, their wife or their children never really fulfils them, no more than all the other substitutes with which they try to soothe the wound. The wound came from being separated from the Light of God. It will only be healed by being reunited with the Light of God."

Contemplating the snowy summits from above, the three of us pondered on these words of wisdom.

"I want you to see what snow is like in the world of the gods," Elyani said, playful. She instantly projected the two of us on top of a mountain.

When my bare feet landed in the snow, I was amazed. Instead of being bitten by cold, I felt an extraordinarily brisk, sharp clarity.

Pure like a hundred thousand years of silence.

Combined with the stunning panoramic views of the gigantic mountain range, the acuteness of awakening created a Point-elation of celestial proportions.

"I feel as clean and clear as the Great Ant!" I exclaimed. "If there is one place to make you feel on top of the world, this is the one!"

In the distance I discerned a colossal mountain. It reached so high in the sky of the gods that, despite the far-reaching vision of my visitor's body, I could not see its top.

"Mount Meru," Elyani elucidated. Patagendradass had landed close to us and was joyfully flapping his wings against the snow. She asked him, "Patagendradass, did you say that at the end of the last great cosmic night, the gods were the first to wake up?"

"Heaven, no!" Patagendradass promptly exclaimed. "The gods *did* wake in the first hour, but the asuras had woken long before them."

"The asuras?" I asked.

"The elder brethren of the gods," Elyani answered. "They were the first gods, but something went very wrong with them. They had to be replaced by a second creation of gods."

"What went 'very wrong'?"

"Awesome was the power of the asuras," Patagendradass replied in a noetic flow. "But they became proud, imbued with themselves. So much so that they refused to recognise their power was none other than God's power. Rather than see their light as the Light of God, they declared themselves the light of the worlds. Rather than praise God and surrender to his infinite Oneness, they wanted the whole creation to worship them. Rather than serve God and carry out his works, they wanted to rule from their own egotistic will. Throughout the creation, great calamities resulted. And so the Lord Melchisedek withdrew their mandate, and replaced them with the gods."

"And what happened to the asuras after this cosmic dismissal?"

"Some vanished into nothingness. Others waged long wars against the gods," Patagendradass said. "Actually, I believe, one of the asuras landed in your world."

"Ahriman," Elyani explained. "After being defeated by the gods, Ahriman was expelled into the physical kingdom."

"Do you mean to say, the gods got rid of Ahriman by sending him to our kingdom?" Intoxicated with the elated feeling of highness, I burst out laughing. "Thank you, gods! How very nice of you! We human beings do appreciate this kind attention."

Carried by the same elation, my two friends laughed with me. But Elyani cautioned, "Let us take him out of here quick, lest other gods hear him and take offence!"

The wise Patagendradass nodded his agreement.

15.7 The cosmic dance

Back at our house, I kept being shaken by uncontrollable fits of laughter. I sat on the grass. A large sunflower turned towards me with curiosity.

Waving at the sunflower, I told my friends, "This story about Ahriman... Dragon-hilarious! Tell me, do the gods intend to send many others like him to us human beings?"

"It has been predicted, I believe, that in the future another great asura will make his presence felt in the material plane," Patagendradass answered.

The news made me laugh so loudly I had to lie down on the grass.

"These nectar breezes from Mount Meru..." Patagendradass said.

Elyani sat on the grass close to me, resting my head on her lap. She caressed my hair, "This is what the nectar of immortality does to you – not just to visitors, also to the gods."

"Nectar of immortality?" I sat up like a Dragon-in-the-box. "But I thought nectar was a fluid, not a breeze?"

"A fluid, yes. A Spirit-fluid. But so much of it flows onto Mount Meru that fine vapours are carried to the surrounding mountains by the winds."

I lay down again. "Makes me feel so high! Not just intoxicated, hhhi-i-i-igh!" I vociferated. "My Point towering over the ladder of the worlds. As if I could do *anything*. Anything, anything, anything... I could even fight against Ahriman." Carried away, I sat up and shouted, "Where is this Ahriman? Bring him to me! I'm going to beat the Dragon out of his brains. I'll send him down into the Furnaces of Doom!" I made myself float a few centimetres above ground level and exploded in roaring laughter.

"Nectar, nectar..." Patagendradass sighed.

"I love it, Patagendradass. I *love* it! Do you drink it too?" I asked.

"Everyone in this world drinks the nectar."

"No wonder they are never sick! Can I have some more?" I asked.

"Later, perhaps," Elyani said. "The nectar is like the vroofing of your Mother the Dragon. Get accustomed to it gradually..."

"...or you might explode into infinity!" I let myself collapse on her lap again and contemplated the sky.

Revelation Sky, extending above us forever.

So alive!

A million times more vibrant than the last time I had looked at it.

Fly, Dragon!

"What would happen if instead of hovering above neighbouring regions, I made myself an arrow and flew straight up?" I asked.

"Friends, I must go," Patagendradass said. "Thank you for these lovely moments in your company."

Had I said something ungodly? Promethean arrogance, perhaps.

"Thank you, Patagendradass! Please come back," Elyani invited our new friend.

"Come back!" I echoed with my eyes.

"I will," he promised, "I will." Then he slowly took off and friendlily hovered above us for a few seconds, after which he zapped high in the sky and disappeared.

Nectar-boosted, I stood up and started dancing. "I could *really* do anything."

"Such as what?" she suggested in a goddess' velvety voice, standing up in front of me.

"Speed up, for a start!" Still dancing, I playfully projected myself to her right side, then behind her, then to her left, then in front of her. I kept moving from one position to the other, increasing the speed up to the point where it seemed I was standing in four places at the same time.

"See," she nodded, "you can draw from the knowingness of the gods!"

Remembering statues of dancing gods with several pairs of arms, I further increased my speed, projecting my arms up and down, making short stops in six stations.

"A god with six pairs of arms!" Elyani laughed and danced with me.

"Music!" I shouted. With my eyes I manifested a music field similar to the one I had made in Eisraim. "Probably grossly human-limited, but we have to start somewhere." I filled the clearing with a swift, joyful melody.

The pine forest accompanied the tune with a soft humming.

I tried a more daring dance. Accelerating the pace, I projected myself in sixty-four different places in the clearing, moving from one to the other as fast as the Point allowed me to.

Dancing with me, Elyani multiplied her arms and legs. She followed my movements in such a way that wherever I stood, I could look straight into her eyes.

The living sky enjoyed the dance. It took over the music field and replaced the simple melody with a grand playful symphony, giving a completely new depth to the sixty-four-stations dance.

And lo! my Mother the Dragon was with us. She danced through Elyani and me, as if to please the sky of the gods. The sky, on his side, watched all the more carefully, making his symphony tender.

In each of the sixty-four stations my Mother inspired me to move in a special, distinct way, conveying the cosmic meaning of one of the sixty-four orients of time. It made perfect sense to the sky.

Inspired, Elyani changed her style. Through fast projections, she too made herself sixty-four. Wherever I stood she stood in front of me, mirroring my movements. In the centre, she started moving so fast that her arms became countless and looked at times like long veils, at others like the wings of the White Eagle.

Revelation Sky and my Mother the Dragon, fascinated with each other's infinity.

From each station, the sky told her through my eyes, "I love you."

From the centre, my Mother responded, "I love you" in all sixty-four directions.

Aeons of cosmic dance played in a second.

Then I abandoned all stations, stopped all movements. I simply stood a few lawful feet away from her.

The music field became silent.

Elyani became one, still, her gaze fused with mine.

The sky held his breath.

I walked towards her and played our old melody,

'Bang-ting-ting, bang-ting-ting...'

Despite the exquisite quality of the tones and the celestial scenery, it still sounded like saucepan and spoon.

A goddess' smile, remembering how much we had desired each other.

I stopped, hesitant.

She opened her arms.

Three more steps, and I was in her arms.

The sky gave the kiss.

The Dragon of the Deep received it.

It lasted a long, long time. Far more than seconds.

Then I took her hand, and slowly walked with her towards the house.

Would a god have transported her, rather than walk?

No. From the knowingness of the sky, I knew. In this precious moment, a god would have walked. Slowly.

When we reached the bed, I undid her lapis-lazuli dress with my eyes.

With her eyes, she made my white costume fall onto the grass carpet.

Politely, and because it understood this was the first time, the mirror reflected nothing.

In wonder with each other, we lay on the bed.

Then we made love. Simply. And probably not how the gods would have done it.

We made love as we had wanted to for so long.

The sky, whose wisdom I was just starting to understand, joined with the Deep Dragon. Together they blessed us.

15.8 Making love in the world of the gods, part 2

As soon as we finished, I wanted to do it again.

Fatigue, like sleep, is unknown in the world of the gods.

"Tell me, how do the gods do it?"

She looked into my eyes.

The chasm of ecstasy was instant, total. Point-Point-blowing.

The fixture of a thousand volcanoes condensed in an atom, a firequake shaking the ladder of the worlds, bliss imploding the entire Molten Sea into one drop.

It left me blasted and panting, "Oh... Oh... Oh my God! How did we do that?" I said. The room had disappeared, replaced by pure gold. The light was so dense I couldn't even feel – far less even see! – my visitor's body.

"So is this the way they do it?"

"There are all sorts of ways," she whispered, restoring some normality to our reality. Back under the blankets of the princely room's four-poster bed, she snuggled against me.

I burst out laughing, grabbing her celestial body in my visitor's hands, ready to make love to her again, kingdom-fashion. But I was taken by ethical concerns, "Wouldn't the gods regard this way as... hum... old-fashioned, perhaps, or even... animal-like?"

"And so what?" the enamoured goddess slowly rubbed herself against my visitor's body. "Do you know that when they make love, the gods sometimes turn themselves into animals?"

"Do they?" I exclaimed, suddenly feeling more confident. "But these must not be like the animals on Earth. They must be refined, celestial animals of the world of the gods. Aren't they?"

"Well, well... sometimes, yes. But not always!" she said. "What animal would you be?"

"Mm... a huge, hot dragon with green scales. Mm... no! Red scales, and long, long flames coming out of my nostrils. I like dragons. And you?"

"I was going to say a bird of paradise – those which are so rare. But with a huge dragon, it would *never* work!"

Again we made love. I played her body like a celestial musical instrument.

The bed turned into waves, the blankets into the sky.

There was music throughout the spheres, and far away beyond them.

The thought came to my mind, "Can you *really* be a bird of paradise?"

Instantly, she transported us into another room.

Was it a room, or a faraway place?

There was a gigantic cascade of blue Life and Light,
And two birds, with rainbow feathers and onyx eyes.
Through the knowingness of the cascade, I discovered
That birds of paradise mate in a strange fashion.
Fascinated, they stand in front of each other,
Their onyx eyes locked in a passionate embrace,
And they sing the myth of creation – but starting from the end.
When, having reached the Beginning, they finish,
They become silent, of course.
The cascade stops. Time holds his breath.
"Hush!" says the universe.
Slowly, the birds move towards one another;
This can take an aeon, or sometimes much more, depending on the birds.
Finally, they touch each other.
Then they merge instantly, and become one forever –
And this is why the birds of paradise are so rare!
Far, far below, Maryani heard the silence, and she understood.

15.9 Lord Gana, the revelation

Never before had I heard such music. It created an eerie space that enlightened the entire beach.

Walking on the golden sand, the Molten Sea to my right.

In front of me, Lord Gana.

He was sitting cross-legged on the sand, facing the Molten Sea, his eyes fixed on the horizon. He wore a golden helmet shaped like a circular urn that shone and illuminated all the directions of space. He had long golden hair and, I noticed, he did not wear a beard.

Fascinated, I contemplated the special quality of golden light that radiated from him.

"I know this light! I recognise its flavour!"

It was so familiar. Thousands of times in the kingdom it had descended on me. It had inspired me, warmed my spirits, enthused my Ego. In all difficult moments it had supported me. Gradually, it had become so much part of me that I hardly noticed it any more.

Now I realised this light had been coming from Lord Gana all along.

I owed him everything!

My eyes filled with tears.

Patagendradass, who had kindly escorted me here, discreetly flew away.

I kept walking towards the god, letting my Ego shine with his light.

He held his hands parallel in front of him, as in the gesture of the flame. Between his hands, there floated an extraordinary musical instrument made of light, like a star. One foot long, it was comprised of thousands of thin light rays of all colours. The beams radiated from a central core of blazing white light, hardly the size of an Aphrodite's berry.

He played the instrument with slight movements of his hands, but also with his heart. The multicoloured star stood just in front of his chest, the light of his heart mingled with it.

When I arrived at his side, I stood motionless for a while, contemplating him.

With a gentle Point-impulse, he invited me to sit with him.

I sat cross-legged on his right, facing him. And I bent forwards and lightly touched his feet.

Out of nowhere, a golden helmet appeared on my head. Similar to his, it was shaped like an elongated bowl. It shone with his special golden light.

And the revelation commenced.

Profound, multi-faceted vision.

An I am, multidimensional and eternal.

The Golden Shield above my head, my feet grounded in the Deepest Underworlds' Sea of Lightning.

Fields of stars in my hair, the deep seas are my kidney.

To my heart, the Fields of Peace, Gervin waiting for me.

There are a million rungs in the ladder of my worlds.

Above, Revelation Sky's secrets flashing like lighting, a thunderbolt carpet laid by the One God.

Revelation Sky, unfathomable wisdom.

In the concentrated Point-ness of the sky's unlimited expanse, ancient mysteries, the knowingness of all existing things, and keys for all futures. Point-ness isn't enough. Only through Point-ness-ness shall you know him.

Through the golden helmet, the column of Spirit and Revelation Sky are one. Truth and Fire, Lord Gana's edge, partaking of his omniscient vision.

I saw the birth of the gods. They woke up in the Molten Sea, the waves took them to the shore. They created their own world.

I saw them drink the nectar, conquer its power – the divinely mad, exalted, unstoppable power with which they fought their titanic enemies the asuras.

I saw wars in heaven. They lasted for aeons, causing unspeakable ravage in the spheres. I saw mind-boggling challenges, battles of cosmic proportions, engagements that lasted for centuries, abysmal evil threats that only the power of the Highest God could overcome.

By the power of cunning, Spirit, and indomitable boldness, the gods won. They drove the asuras away from their world, castrated their arrogance, extinguished their ancient powers, threw most of them into oblivion, cast the others down the ladder of the worlds.

I saw the triumphant gods raising their hands towards the unlimited sky, drunk with the victory which gave them complete mastery over all the spheres.

The creation was theirs, and so was eternity. Shining glory, bright as Highness. An endless sunrise unfolded in front of them.

Then I saw them add wonder to wonder in their own world: forests of wisdom, gardens of paradoxes, cities of light, dwellings with windows ajar on all dimensions. Their relentless creative fire was unleashed throughout the spheres. From the power of their mind, world after world was conceived. With their genius they illumined all creatures. Over their creation, they ruled sovereign and unchallenged.

Seeing how the gods had created, seeing the celestial source of their inspiration, I understood myriads of secrets. I saw the ropes that pull the forces of nature in each world, and the intelligences by which they can be controlled. I saw the blueprint of each layer, and its archetypal modus operandi. And together with the grand perfection of the cosmic warp, I saw the celestial sense of humour with which paradoxes had artistically been laid in each and every sphere.

From the helmet, in a global flash, the highest secret of knowledge was revealed. Simple, absolute, final...

The key to omniscience is to become Revelation Sky.

Revelation Sky, who forever lies over the Molten Sea like a lover on his lover.

The music stopped. There was a cosmic silence.

His eyes fixed on the horizon, Lord Gana directed his hands towards me. He placed his fabulous musical instrument of light between my hands.

"A molten star," he Point-revealed. "Easy to play. Just let the Molten Sea shine through you."

Oh gods, so much love!

Surrendering to my Mother the Molten Dragon, I let her take over my hands, my heart.

The beach was filled with glorious musical harmonies again. I smiled in complete amazement, hardly believing that such celestial perfection of sounds could be flowing through me.

"This molten star is for you. It is my present," the god Point-said.

Stunned and humbled, I wondered how I could express my gratitude.

"Play for me!"

Blessed, I let the Molten Sea play through me. She became alive in my heart, my hands, and the very fabric of my being. Through the music, Revelation Sky was one with her.

Fullness, completion, infinity.

Then with a Point-nod, the god indicated the meeting was ending.

I stood up, wondering how ever to thank him.

His smile tranquil, his eyes fixed on the horizon, he gently sent the answer into my Point,

"Be glorious!"

15.10 Calling onto the power of the nectar

Rather than transporting myself home directly, I decided to go for a long walk of a minute or two in the gigantic forests bordering the shores of the Molten Sea.

Preciously holding the molten star in front of my heart, I bolted towards the forest of wise figs, still wearing the golden helmet that Lord Gana had placed on my head.

I looked for Patagendradass and birds of his feather.

They were far away. Through the sight of the helmet, I saw them. On the other side of Mount Meru, flying fast over gardens full of wonders like those around Vasoukidass' palace. The birds were heading south-west, towards a blazing city of fire.

Tejovati.

Resuming my stroll I followed a winding path in the forest, using the 'project-as-far-as-you-can-see' method. The path described many curves, I went through a super-fast succession of small jumps. Space conquered through travelling. Thoroughly intoxicating.

But it soon appeared that I was being followed.

Someone was behind me on the path, copying my jumps and projecting himself on my trail.

My first reaction was to accelerate. But whoever was behind me had no difficulty matching my pace.

After a few seconds, I stopped and let the god reveal himself.

He projected himself and stood in front of me, barring my way.

"At last a god with a beard!" I thought, politely smiling at him and wondering whether I should touch his feet.

A strange figure! Clad in a shining silvery armour which left his head, arms and legs uncovered. His youthful face was fierce. His whole countenance was that of a warrior, his black eyes incandescent with the power of the nectar. Hanging on the side of his armour was a complicated weapon, an axe with three diamond heads, radiant.

Looking me in the eyes, he said sarcastically, "So here is the Great Warrior, the black dance master who has challenged the kuren-jaya experts!"

The fire in his voice sounded explosively aggressive. Wondering what he wanted, I replied in a humble voice, "The feats of men, I am afraid, do not rank high compared to those of the gods. My name is Szar, my Lord. What can I do for you?"

"I know your name!" he replied with irony. He walked two steps forward and touched my shoulder with his index finger. "Would you like to fight against a god, Szar?"

It had to be a joke. "How could a man even think of fighting against a god?" I said with a meek smile.

The god pulled a contemptuous face, "That, a Great Warrior?" He took his finger away from me.

"My Lord," I said, "the things I have seen in your glorious world have made me feel like worshipping the gods, not fighting them! And..."

"A coward, that's what he is!" The god raised his hands and looked up, as if addressing someone who stood high in the sky, "Why should this *visitor* ever be my brother?" he said, emphasising the word 'visitor' with disgust.

Clearly, I hadn't said the right thing.

"But why would such a powerful warrior as yourself want to fight against a mere mortal?" I asked, wondering what I could do to please him.

He didn't care to answer my question. He just said, "If you refuse to fight against me, then I will take your molten star, *Great Warrior!*"

Before I could do anything, he had already grabbed the musical instrument and started walking away along the path.

"Hey!" I shouted in shock. But the warrior's instinct immediately took over. I erased the emotion, made myself Dragon-calm. Following the god, I took on a conciliatory tone, "Friend, this molten star is extremely precious to me. Could I perhaps try to please you in some other way?"

Looking straight in front of him, the god kept walking. "If you want to be a dirt, then stay in the dirt – *visitor*!" he spat in contempt. With the back of his hand, he carelessly slapped me in the face.

The blow hit me with such violence that my feet lifted off the ground. I fell on the path, flat on my back.

He stopped and turned round to look at me, and burst out laughing, "Ha! Ha! Ha! Ha! Ha!"

Dizzy as I was, I wondered why I was not feeling any pain. And... which strange line of initiatory connections had led this god to take on the unmistakable laughter of Mount Lohrzen's Warriors?

He turned round and started walking away again.

Pulling myself together, I stood up and ran after him. "Please, friend! This molten star means too much to me, you cannot..."

"I am *not* your friend. Go away!" he kept walking.

"But Lord Gana gave it to me! Perhaps we could call him and ask..."

"*Go a-way, visitor!*" the god shouted in anger, as if nagged by some noxious insect.

I stopped, wondering what to do.

I couldn't possibly fight against a god!

Feeling helpless, I watched my molten star being taken away. The feeling of unfairness was overwhelming.

I ran behind him again. "Listen! *Please*, don't take the molten star!"

"Go away! You don't need this beautiful thing. You don't belong here," he said. As I came close to him he lifted his arm, as if to slap me again.

This time the warrior's reflexes took over. I stood very still, my fists in front of me, ready to start the black dance.

The god turned round to face me.

"Aahah!" he looked into my eyes with renewed interest. He pushed the molten star aside, letting it float in the air a few lawful feet away from us. "Shall we fight, then?"

I unclenched my fists and slowly shook my head.

He frowned with anger, ready to lash out at me again.

"Help, Lord Gana, please, help!" I Point-called. "What am I supposed to do now?"

Point-immediate answer, "Fight him!"

More than illogical, this sounded absurd. But Lord Gana's orders weren't for discussion.

Launching the Warriors' fiercest scream, I rushed onto the god and hammered a volley of blows onto vital gateways in the neck area, his chest and abdomen being protected by the armour.

Waste of time! My blows didn't do anything to him. With one kick, he sent me back into the dirt.

Quickly standing up, I launched a second assault, which ended up the same way – my face in the dirt.

"I'm afraid you are going to lose your molten star!" the god sneered.

"Lord Gana!" I Point-called, "do you *really* want me to fight this god?"

"Fight him!" Gana Point-repeated.

"All right then!" I shouted. Jumping to my feet, I called onto the power of the nectar.

The warrior god watched with a satisfied grin.

I rushed against him, yelling in fury.

Time changed flavour. It both stopped and sped up at the same time.

Spirit-fluid, precious nectar, trickling down through the top of my head.
Not a breeze, this time. The real thing.
Sweet, sweet, it is so sweet. Elyani, I love you more!
And more.
The blazing substance coming into my blood.
BURNING FIRE!
Upside down volcano gushing its fire into me.
Unbearable. Everything is going to explode. Hold it! Hold it!

Agony.
Death.
The Great Abyss, where the Mother of the Light is smiling.
7712459326403406718467329406945746832958716503563474583465714383247465934587634592638306045037684501195643814992...
The nectar is a god!
Two Flying Dragons are on their way from the spheres of the Blue Lagoon.
Jinia, how could I let you go?
Ablaze, my soul; I contemplate the glory of the nectar god.
Stone, cavern, darkness, there is no death.
The sky of the gods, eternally lit with the Fire of the nectar god.
Truth and Fire, Fire and Truth,
I am walking on the edge,
Mother of the Light, protect my way!
The nectar is God.
There is no death.
Nectar or no nectar, Philadelphia Six will burn.
Rolling on the ground with the warrior god, furiously hitting each other.
Ablaze, my soul; I contemplate the glory of the nectar god.
Divinely enraged.
Bashing his head with fire.
The fire in the Furnaces of Doom? None else but the nectar god.
Venom into my eyes. Who needs eyes?
An explosion of lava in his knees.
If only I could crack his armour.
Vials of wrath. A master-blow into his nose. This time he is hurt – really *hurt.*
A screaming god is like rolling thunder.
His fury unleashed.
But why did they have to kill Fridrick? And who did it?
Let the god bash me, and let me catch his axe by surprise.
Go on, bash me... bash me!
This world is my world.
I belong here.
Bash me! Go on!
The sky of the gods is with me. Always. FOREVER WITH ME!
Got you, celestial bastard! I have your axe in my hand!
Raising the axe, ready to strike.

"Stop!"

In the cloud of dust I stood still, holding the axe high, delaying the blow.

Holding his breath, the bearded god looked at me, wondering what I was going to do.

"Stop!" Lord Gana Point-repeated. "If you hit him with this weapon, you are going to damage him."

"But... don't you want me to?" I Point-asked. "Isn't it what this exercise is all about?"

"No!" Lord Gana replied. "Had he wanted, your adversary could have killed you right from the beginning of the fight."

I dropped the axe. It fell on the ground silently.

The warrior god gave one of these celestial smiles that hold more secrets than a human mind can comprehend in an entire life.

An interminable silence, at least two seconds.

Then he took a step towards me.

I raised my fists, ready to start again.

He stopped where he was. "Peace!" he promptly said to avoid another engagement. "The molten star is yours, friend!"

Now I was his friend?

Still so many things I didn't understand about the world of the gods.

"How are your eyes?" he inquired.

I looked at him in disbelief. Then I looked down to the axe. But I wasn't seeing with my eyes, I was seeing through the helmet's vision.

Through my eyes, I saw only clouds. I had been badly burnt.

"I'll survive," I said, resting on the fire to try to correct the blurriness which clouded my vision. "These visitors' bodies are much more resistant than I thought. How is your nose?" I asked him.

"That was *very* well done!" he said, visibly amused. "Can I show you something?" He waited for my nod to come close to me. Then he lightly passed his fingers in front of my eyes.

The blurry vision instantly disappeared. But the sudden drop in action had left me trembling.

"My name is Kartendranath," he said, and he gently slapped my shoulder.

I bit my lip, trying to hide the trembling. Using my warrior's tricks, I had globally disconnected all bodily perceptions. After such an onslaught, however, I hated to imagine how many broken parts I would discover when engaging in a thorough examination of the visitor's body.

With another celestial smile, Kartendranath plunged into my consciousness. I felt his presence swiftly sweeping through me, repairing my energy.

The trembling let go of me. It was replaced by a feeling of superior well-being. My body had been completely renewed.

Fresh like a newborn. Strong like a gigantic fig tree of life.

Clearly, the god enjoyed seeing me so perplexed by his behaviour. He took on a teasing voice, "Do you know why this visitor's body is so resistant, by the way?"

I shook my head, Point-suspecting he was about to deliver another blow.

"Simple! It's because *I* made it."

Speechless, I looked at him in awe.

The youthful-looking god burst out laughing. Saying no more words, he just turned and walked away.

"But..."
Was I supposed to thank him for my body?
Had I not received so many blows, I would have found the whole situation divinely funny. But gods... what a beating!
I noticed he had left his weapon on the ground. "Kartendranath!" I called. "You forgot your axe!"
The god turned round, "No. The triaxe, I brought for you. A present. For you and your friends with the yellow disk."
The Knights?
My repaired visitor's eyes opened wide with astonishment.
"No need to thank me. But use it carefully!" Kartendranath raised his index finger in warning. "It's a very dangerous weapon." And he burst out laughing in the thundering fashion of the Warriors, "Ha! Ha! Ha! Ha! Ha!"
Then he turned around and quickly disappeared.

15.11 Awakening

Through the helmet, my mind and Revelation Sky were one.
Looking up, "Revelation Sky, I belong to you. For ever and ever."
I belonged!
For the first time, I belonged somewhere.
It was heaven.
Enough of the walk! "Farewell figs of wisdom, I will return."
In a split second, I was hovering three hundred lawful feet above Elyani's house.
Feeling extraordinarily high on nectar.
Two gods had visited the house. Through the helmet I could see the imprint they had left. Powerful gods, shining the energy of Apollo.
Elyani transported herself close to the water stream. She was no longer wearing her lapis-lazuli dress but a much more complicated one. It changed colour depending on how it was looked at. From high up in the air, sky-blue with a few touches of wind. As I gently came down towards her, the dress became White Eagle and shone with joy.
Elyani contemplated me, her face lit with a lover's smile. "A supermind-helmet, a molten star and a triaxe... you look like you have been living in this world for an entire aeon."
It was about how I felt. "So much has happened since I left!"
"A lot has happened here too. I have made staggering discoveries."
In a world of fire, curiosity can be an all-consuming force. "Tell me! Stagger me!"
"Man of Thunder, hang on to your helmet!"
Rather, the helmet was hanging onto me.

When Lord Gana had first put it on my head, I had thought it was some kind of hat. Celestial aesthetics, or perhaps etiquette. Soon I had realised it was not just made of one sheath of energy, but of many concentric layers. Within the elongated bowl there were thousands of foils, each revolving within the other. As I was sitting by Lord Gana's side, all the layers started spinning extraordinarily fast, their energy combining with my Point and other centers above my head.

Awake, I felt! Nectar flowing into my Point. Life transcendental.

Vertical thunder is the knowing of Revelation Sky.

Awakening.

Awakening! Finally, I understood what Gervin meant.

Through the helmet it became clear, the awakened one can see forever.

"Sit down!" the goddess playfully pushed me.

A massive impact. It threw me flat on the grass. The visitor's body could take it.

She laughed, falling on her knees by my side. The sunflower turned towards her, reflecting a million years of joy.

"This is what the gods told me: the daiva..." she began, "the daiva that brought us here was part of the master plan of the Sons of Apollo. They are the ones who sent the oracle that nominated me as the ascending goddess."

So *they* were responsible for the oracle?

"Showing their excellent taste!" I preferred to joke.

"But it was not just because of me! They wanted me here because of Teyani, Barkhan Seer, you, Gervin and... Szar, this story is not at all what we thought it was. Nothing to do with fulfilling ancient Atlantean customs. You and I have been recruited to take part in an extraordinary adventure – a training which is to span thousands of years."

The helmet sat me up. "A training for what?"

"The Knights, among other things! The Sons of Apollo want to train us, so in turn we may take part in the training of the Knights of the Apocalypse. The ascension ritual was a trial, to see if we had the dimension to take part in the adventure."

This ugly mess, only to test us? That I found difficult to take.

Bitter memories were flooding my mind. That daiva which had left me a powerless pawn in the celestials' game. Holma left agonising, care of the Immaculate. Beautiful Elyani taken away from me, condemned to an ordeal, tortured with the elemental muck of the kingdom and turned into a miserable wreck. Months of agony, love trampled, love destroyed. Hermina having to sacrifice her life...

Why did it have to be so sordid? Where was the meaning?

Except of course that Hermina was now with her angel in Highness, and Elyani had been reborn a goddess.

And Lord Gana's helmet was sitting on my head.

"Do we know what has happened to Holma?" I asked.

"Gone for the Great Journey. She will follow the wheel of reincarnations, like everyone else in the kingdom."

"The gods didn't like her, perhaps?"

"Szar, the gods had nothing to do with Holma failing her ritual! Throughout the kingdom, ascending goddesses have been failing rituals. Not the fault of the gods if Atlantean fields have become rotten."

"But why should the gods care about the Knights?"

Why should the gods care about human beings at all?

"Szar, Szar, open your heart! The gods *do* care. What the Sons of Apollo have planned is a giving of gigantic magnitude. But it is aimed at awakening human beings, not relieving them from their tasks."

997, all records beaten. Hiram, triaxe champion, is king of No Limits.

Awakening.

"Szar, I have seen the future," Elyani manifested a white rose and placed it in my hand. "There will be many battles to fight. For the light. For your friends of the white rose. The gods want to make us strong, so we have something to give."

Giving is the privilege of the strong.

"My friends of the white rose..." through the helmet I caught a glimpse of them.

Philadelphia... the war will pass, my love for you won't.

It became luminous.

Loving the Philadelphias with all the might of Revelation Sky.

I saw the Philadelphias, cities in space. On the edge of the abyss. About to be taken over by Ahriman's armies. Only a miracle could save them.

The legend of the Knights.

I fingered the radiant triaxe attached to my belt.

"The Sons of Apollo told me Kartendranath wanted to invest you with the triaxe, but only if he found you worthy of it," Elyani declared.

Gods, did he *really* have to beat me up like that?

"Being trained by the gods must be... interesting," I pondered. "So what am I supposed to do with this triaxe?"

"It's a supermind weapon. For the Knights."

The helmet was showing me a gigantic battle. In space. Birds of death and birds of life. In all directions, huge balls of fire.

Target 3, destroyed. Target 4, destroyed. Target 5, destroyed... Serah! Serah, they're retreating!

The turning point in the third battle of Mercury.

Target 8, destroyed. Target 9, destroyed... Clouds of fire and Eagle's wings, unleashing the power of the triaxe.

Time crossing.

Carrying Elyani the Immaculate back from the tower of Malchasek. Her body withered. Light like a handful of Eagle feathers. A moonless night.

Flying a Scalene 333, Mercury in sight. Target 11, destroyed. Target 12, destroyed...

Victory. Victory igniting my heart like an irresistible Flame, the Eagle on the Edge of Highness.

Point-smashing enemy fighter after enemy fighter with the triaxe. Target 14, destroyed. Target 15, destroyed...

The sky on fire, like a bleeding sun.

Mothership 7 to Molten Stars – 29 holes in their defence line. You've done it! They're finished! Retreating all over the place.

Lavash to White Eagle – not a retreat, a debacle!

In the central crypt of Eisraim, running full speed towards the stage, Elyani and Hermina about to attract a deluge of sludge. "*Maryani! I need another golden shaft, quick!*" From Revelation Sky, Kartendranath is watching.

Philadelphia 34 in flames. Philadelphia 55, a small cloud of space debris. Philadelphia 6, captured by the Rex. All other stations intact. After six months of fighting, the Rex's generals are on their knees. The Knights have prevailed.

The Philadelphian spirit has been kept alive.

Feeling totally wild, unstoppable. Target 17, destroyed. Target 18, destroyed... Solar flares behind me.. Above my head, Kartendranath is dancing the triaxe war dance.

A dancing god is a universe in motion. Still like the morning of creation.

The vision stopped. Everything became quiet.

I lay down on the grass and looked above me, contemplating infinity.

Revelation Sky, endless peace.

Getting more magnificent by the hour.

Alive. Total. Eternal.

I took Elyani's hand, "Now you are where you belong."

"I am," she said, very much a black panther. "Whatever it took to bring me here was the expression of the highest wisdom. Here is where I must be. Here is where I can be *alive*."

Belonging. The magic word.

It rang perfectly true. "Elyani belongs here!"

Revelation Sky had always known that.

"Today..." I hesitated.

As I was about to say it, it sounded so enormous. Impossible.

Yet it was the truth, I knew with the omniscient certitude of the helmet.

Courageously, I resumed, "Today I have made a discovery. I do not belong to the kingdom. And I do not belong here either. Up there!" I pointed straight up, "This is where I belong."

Revelation Sky. I am yours, for ever and ever.

Strange it took such a beating for me to realise.

I felt like a little child. "Do you think it's possible?" I timidly asked the goddess. "Are there people who live in this sky?"

"There are myriads of worlds in Revelation Sky."

An infinity of worlds, packed at the tip of the triangle.

"Why don't I see them?"

But you do see them!

Knowingness of Thunder.

An explosion of vision.

The helmet and Revelation Sky, eternally one.

I jumped to my feet. Vertically one with the sky's infinity.

Connected infinity. A web of meaning was being revealed, starting from the Golden Shield above and linking all the spheres.

Seen from Revelation Sky it all made perfect sense.

Every single thing.

Fate hadn't been decreed by the gods' daiva. It was the interconnectedness of all things which, in its infinite wisdom, had inspired the gods.

Every single thing which had happened to us made sense, every second of our story. So did every second of the story of billions of other souls.

In God's dance, every step has meaning.

But only when seen from Revelation Sky!

For the first time since I had arrived in this world of fire, I detected a touch of sadness in Elyani.

"You *do* belong to Revelation Sky," she said, contemplating eternity in my eyes. "God knows how many worlds there will be between you and me in the end!"

"No, it won't be like this!" I took her hand and slowly danced with her. "Remember the words of the Eagle after Alcibyadi asked if destiny would separate us."

Setting the perfection of her body in slow motion, she recited the oracle, "It will and it will not. Then it will not and it will, but not how you may think it would, for in the end it won't.'"

"The truth, word for word!" I Point-marvelled. "It will and it will not: in the beginning we were separated, and yet my Flying Dragon nature was with you. And if I hadn't been so fearful, Space Matrix would have taken me to your room every night! Now the second part of the story begins, when 'it will not and it will'. You are the goddess in the world of fire. I will be the worm crawling in the kingdom's dirt. But this is no real separation. Now I know how to love you, wherever you are. A few layers of mist won't prevent me from feeling your presence. I will be with you, one thousand times more than when you and I were together."

Anyhow, I had always known how to do that.

Simply the continuation of the pact of love my father the Flying Dragon had made with the White Eagle:

Edge of Highness. Whiteness eternal. Forever love.

With all my mind, with all my heart, I am with you, even when I am far away.

With the movements of her arms, Elyani created an enveloping mist. Caressingly, "And in the end?"

The gold of the first morning, "In the end we are one, everywhere, all the time! But the end started long ago! It is already done."

A breath from Highness, infinity below my feet, infinity above my head, I was no longer sure whether I was the Flying Dragon or the White Eagle.

Now I understood why the Mother of the Light had always wanted me to meet Elyani: so I could discover that love has a thousand meanings.

They thread the creation into eternity.

Elyani made herself vast. A goddess' trick. She was standing in front of me, dancing, and at the same time she was the forest and the river, the sunflower and every blade of grass in the world of the gods.

"Is this how the people of the kingdom will perceive you?"

"No," she said, bringing down a vision onto me. Clad in a long white dress that left her arms uncovered, she was holding a torch in her right hand, her right arm raised. The torch shone with thousands of rays of light, inspiration for mind and heart, fiery enthusiasm. "This is the vision the people of the kingdom should connect with if they want me to reach them. By sourcing the rays of light, they will be led to the mysteries of the gods," the goddess hinted. "And another way of reaching me is through the pine forest. Calling on me when meditating on pine trees, tuning into their essence, will lead them to my abode."

The ardent aspiration of millions of pine trees calling in unison for God.

Elyani made herself vast again. She was the forest of gigantic figs of life and the Molten Sea's endless shores, golden-yellow like ripe corn. She was Amaravati, the wondrous capital of the gods, and Tejovati, the fiery city. She was the snow that covered the mountain range around Mount Meru, and the rivers that ran from the mountains to the sea.

In her horizontal vastness, she gave herself to me.

I became the sky, lying on top of her.

So many ways of making love in the world of the gods.

Contemplating her, I finally understood what is so special about a god's smile. It reflects the mysteries of Revelation Sky.

Smiling infinity... this is what being a god is all about!

Before merging into her, my last words were,

"The gods are wise!"

15.12 The departure of the Flying Dragon

Elyani was wearing a dress of silveriness. It matched the waves of the Molten Sea perfectly.

I was holding the molten star between my hands, playing for her.

We were walking on the sand.

The beach was so different from what I had seen when I had first arrived. Every grain of sand was a fiery world of its own, mysterious, profound. Every wave carried a new impulse of creation. The breeze whispered ancient myths and secret lores. The air breathed with the knowing of all things.

"Here!" Elyani decided.

I couldn't have agreed more. It was a spot where, six hundred years-of-the-gods ago, the Sons of Apollo had held council. The space was still vibrant with their luminous deliberations and the verticality of their judgement.

We sat down on the sand, facing the Molten Sea.

The Molten Sea, who became Elyani each time I made love to her.

I let the molten star float by my side.

"I will take good care of it," Elyani promised. "I have already created a room in our house specially for it."

Bringing the count to seventy-four. Each time I went out, Elyani added a few rooms to her house. Still, the dwelling had a long way to go before it reached the standards of this world. A god's house has thousands of rooms at the least, many of them worlds of their own.

I turned to my goddess, "So what is going to happen to you, now?"

"The Sons of Apollo are going to teach me the things of this world. There is still so much that my mind cannot comprehend. I am still operating too much like a human being, I must change category."

"Human conditioning and limitations," I gave a god's smile.

Human beings have been the slaves of gravity for so long. It takes major adjustments before they can behold the reality of the gods.

Lifting the corner of her divine lips, "When they were at our place, the Sons of Apollo caught me blinking twice."

"Blinking!" I slammed my visitor's forehead, feigning outrage, "How could you possibly blink?"

The gods *never* blink! In their world, whenever you see someone blink, you know for sure he hasn't been here for long.

"The Sons of Apollo have special processes to erase the limitations imprinted by life in the kingdom," Elyani went on. "Incidentally, they said it was one of the reasons you had to go. Had we stayed here together, it would have been much more difficult for us to let go of our human conditioning."

Lord Gana had told me more or less the same thing. He had said that after leaving this world I was to go and visit my father, and he had insisted I should go without Elyani. Same reason – if we had crossed the Abyss of the Deep together, we would have carried too much of our human nature with us. It would have prevented the complete immersion required for a full reconnection with my Flying Dragon nature.

We remained silent, eyes fixed on the horizon. Without blinking.

Kartendranath's bizarre words kept running through my mind, "Why should this *visitor* ever be my brother?"

There was cosmic meaning behind these words, I *knew*.

"Kartendranath isn't planning to incarnate as a human being and become one of the Brother Knights, is he?" I asked Elyani.

"I don't think so. The Lord Melchisedek has decided that the fight against Ahriman should be carried out by the members of the human hierarchy. The gods will assist the Masters of Thunder and the Archive people in teaching the Knights, but they will not fight in their place."

So why did Kartendranath suggest that we could be brothers, then?

From the knowingness of the helmet, it was evidently related to the arch-secret brotherhood which Gervin had never told me about, and which Melchard had once Point-mentioned in front of me by mistake.

"Hush, man of Thunder!" Elyani caught my train of thoughts. "These things are very secret."

She knew. She knew all about it.

"Too secret for me?" I practised smiling, well aware I would soon be back in the fetters of a human body.

"The Sons of Apollo do not want this topic to be discussed in the kingdom at all. And so they have decided to wait until you come back before telling you about it."

"This sounds like a Dragon of a secret!" I sanctioned with a handclap. "I love it already."

A white arrow of light was darting towards us.

Patagendradass!

"Patagendradass, how nice of you to come and say farewell." I extended my arms in front of me and joined my hands in the shape of a cup. "Please, bird of high wisdom, let me touch your feet."

Patagendradass landed on my palms. He was holding a twig of acacia in his beak.

"A twig of acacia, symbol of the immortality of the soul!" Elyani breathed softly onto him. "How kind of you, wise bird."

"So you are returning to the kingdom, friend?" Patagendradass said with his eyes.

"Not immediately. I shall first go and visit my father, who lives in the spheres of remoteness, beyond the Abyss of the Deep and the Fault of Eternity. Lord Gana has commanded that before returning to my master, I go and immerse myself in the wisdom of the Flying Dragons."

"Great is the wisdom of the Flying Dragons," Patagendradass said with the wonder of the wise. "How long will you stay away from the spheres of Melchisedek?"

"An aeon, or two perhaps. But this does not matter. The spheres of my fathers are so far from ours that one can travel there and return in less than one second of the kingdom's time. Sometimes, it even happens that one returns earlier than one left."

"We played on this to stretch our twelve hours a little further," Elyani told the bird.

"Clever!" Patagendradass rejoiced. Then he looked deep into me, "Friend, I have come to tell you that I have looked into your future, in search of prophetic advice that could be of help to you. And I have seen the crucial work that you and your friends are to accomplish in the kingdom." After a pause, the wise bird went on, "There are great obstacles waiting for you."

That I knew only too well.

"So many things could go wrong," I nodded. "Do you have any clues to give me, Patagendradass?"

"Yes my friend. One piece of advice, coming straight from the high prophetic wisdom of the bird-god."

I listened from the power of the helmet.

Patagendradass' eyes flashed, "A giant made you a poisoned gift. Use it against the giants!"

"I know who this giant is," I told him. "His name is Perseps. And the present was a stone, presently in the pocket of my brown gown in the kingdom."

From the knowingness of the helmet, it became clear the stone contained many secrets about the Nephilim and their fields.

"But of course!" I exclaimed, enthused with Patagendradass' superior sense of wonder. "I see exactly what to do! Thank you, my friend. Thank you!"

Patagendradass made himself a flame of aspiration, letting my gratitude reverberate onto his god.

So wise.

From the sound of the waves, I knew that the time had come.

Holding Elyani's eyes, a wave of sorrow pinched my heart. "There is so much beauty in this world."

"You can come and visit my house any time!"

I took her in my arms, packing an eternity into one second.

Then I lay on the sand.

Elyani sat on my left side, and she took my hand.

Patagendradass dropped the twig of acacia onto my heart. Then he went to stand on my right palm.

I looked up straight above me, eyes fixed on Revelation Sky.

"I will return!" I pledged.

I called onto Space Matrix, "*Szar, requesting access to long-distance guidance,*" and I tuned into the energy of my father.

Space Matrix instantly responded, "*Flying Dragon retrieved. Engage travelling through intention.*"

Elyani lightly caressed my face, closing my eyes, "Fly, Dragon! Fly high!"

– Thus ends the Book of the World of the Gods –